Nov 2019

Spooked.

Diana M.W. Rosengard

Thanks for your support & friendship!

Spooky reading

Diana Rosengard

This is a work of fiction. All names, characters, businesses, events, locales, and incidents are either the products of the author's imagination or used in a fictitious manner. Any resemblance to actual persons, living or dead, business establishments, locales, or actual events is purely coincidental.

Published by Horseshoes & Hand Grenades Publishing, LLC
135 S. 3rd St. Saint Helens, OR 97051
www.hhgpublishing.com

Cover Illustration Copyright © 2018 by Horseshoes & Hand Grenades Publishing, LLC
Cover design by Horseshoes & Hand Grenades Publishing, LLC
Book design and production by Horseshoes & Hand Grenades Publishing, LLC

Printed in the United States of America
Publisher's Cataloging-in-Publication data
Rosengard, Diana M.W.
Spooked. / Diana M.W. Rosengard
ISBN 978-1-7329152-0-6
1. The main category of the book –Fiction –Other category. 2. Another subject category – Supernatural. 3. More categories – I. Rosengard, Diana M.W. II. Spooked.

Second Edition
11 10 9 8 7 6 5 4 3 2

This book is for Luvine Martin Wiener,
who loved a good ghost story.

Prologue

Now.

There are a lot of things you might expect to think before you die. Here are the thoughts that came, unbidden and unexpected, in the moments I lay dying:

I can't believe I trusted this psychopath.
Taco bar isn't much of a last meal.
Now I'll never know what happens next on Riverdale.
Wait—are these underwear clean?
Get off me, GET OFF ME, GETOFFME!

Not exactly the epitaphs you hope will adorn your headstone.

Lying here, I can see that when I started down this road, I really thought I was headed, okay, not for a happy ending exactly, but at least a marginally satisfying one. Vengeance isn't sweet, but it does have a way of meeting a deep need, feeding some animal instinct still lingering beneath our civil niceties. Since I'm not all that nice, I was willing to settle for a gratifying, if still somewhat bitter, resolution.

Turns out, you don't even get that when it all comes crashing down. All the dreamers and saints and philosopher kings got it wrong. There's no tunnel of light or choir of angels or wise old man waiting in a train station. There's not even a boring orientation ceremony with free fro-yo and limp balloons.

And for the record? I did not have some last-minute epiphany where I loved every instant of my stupid, boring, useless life. It sucked, even retrospectively.

Yet here I am, my entire life boiled down to wave upon wave of inane crap that won't matter at all in a precious few moments.

When the terror comes, it is potent enough to have its own weight. Real and heavy, I can feel it pressing down on every part of me.

And then there is suddenly nothing.

Nothing but silence.

1.

Then.

I needed to get out of bed.

I'd already missed so much class I was pretty sure the entire semester would be a wash. Student Support Services, the network of kindly middle-aged female administrators that functioned as faux parents for the academically challenged and emotionally distant at Astoria College, had told me so. Repeatedly.

First in emails, gently inquiring after my "health," their polite way of asking me if I was as crazy as everyone was saying. Then, as I missed more classes, slightly more forcefully, but always with a gentle patina of other people making decisions that were supposedly in my best interests. These efforts culminated in a 'tough love' meeting forced on me by my school assigned therapist, Dr. Yates, and Mrs. Fogerty, the Director of Student Support Services. It was an uncomfortable meeting for so many reasons, especially with everyone tiptoeing around the reason I had gone off the deep end in the first place.

Mrs. Fogerty couldn't seem to decide if she wanted to wring her hands or hug me. She kept half-standing from her desk, then sitting abruptly back down. The overall effect reminded me of a broken wind-up toy. Every time she jumped out of the seat, I heard "Pop! Goes the Weasel!" in my head.

Dr. Yates worked the opposite end of the intervention spectrum. She stood in front of me, hands clasped and lips pursed, gazing solemnly with unblinking eyes. She looked like a statue of some cold but eternally patient saint, frozen in time while she waited for me to seek forgiveness for my sins.

"Callie, this is serious," Dr. Yates frowned grimly. I wondered if it was possible to obtain 'grim' lines, like frown lines or smile lines. If so, Dr. Yates was in trouble. "You are not only in danger of failing every class for the semester, but your GPA will take such a dive that there may be no way of saving your grants and scholarships." Mrs. Fogerty, her wispy brown curls tinged with a halo of encroaching grey, was slightly warmer. "Ms. McCayter, it's not that we don't understand and sympathize with what you are going through. Obviously, you and Elizabeth were very close…" She stumbled over the words. "I can't imagine how hard this has been for you."

I glanced up at Mrs. Fogerty. Seeing the pity in her eyes, I immediately looked down again. No matter what happened, I would not break in front of them. I'd already had one public freak out this week, which was all I was budgeting myself. After yelling at a girl I'd never seen before in the cafeteria who tried to tell me how much Izzy meant to her, I'd locked myself in my room with a week's worth of frozen bean burritos in my fridge and refused to open the door for anyone.

That was the reason we were having this very-special-episode of Callie's Mental Breakdown. It turned out that when you wouldn't come out of your room voluntarily, sometimes they compelled you. I'd only left my room to avoid immediate suspension, but that didn't mean I had to speak.

Also, I'd run out of burritos.

When I didn't respond, Mrs. Fogerty continued. "The time has come to make some decisions. You've barely left your room, much less been to class, in almost three weeks. Midterms have come and gone. You won't let us provide you with a medical withdrawal. You don't seem to be able to catch up at this point. You're tying our hands. We want to help you, but you have to tell us how."

I stared mutely at my hands, chipping away the last remnants of my nail polish, trying to remember when I'd last painted my nails. Had Izzy painted them? Had it been that long? Was that possible? Could I still have chips of bright sparkly turquoise paint on my nails when my best friend had been dead almost a month?

How could the glittering flecks still be here when Izzy wasn't?

I knew they were waiting for me to speak. All I had to do was open my mouth and say the right things. I could tell them how hard it was and how I missed her every day and how I needed their help to get through the unbearable pain. Then they would nod solemnly and make sympathetic noises and there would be a big group hug.

I've never been very good at giving people what they wanted.

Eventually, my silence won out. Neither cajoling nor threats were going to make a dent in my mask, perfected over the course of nineteen years. All their words of wisdom and worry meant nothing. My expression barely registered that I'd heard them. With a heavy sigh, they released me with a request that I think carefully about what I wanted.

I'd stumbled back to my room, trying hard not to notice the stares and whispers following me across the tiny campus. The meeting had taken so much out of me. It was all I could do to avoid breaking down in public. I'd made it through their joke of a memorial service tear-free, and not one person had seen me cry since the night Izzy died. I was kind of proud of that. Maybe everyone thought I was unhinged, but I wouldn't allow anyone to think of me as weak.

As soon as the door was locked behind me, I collapsed onto my bed and quickly drifted into the half-sleep that ruled my days and nights. I couldn't remember the last time I'd slept thoroughly, the last time I hadn't woken up crying because I knew, even before I turned over, the other side of the room would be empty.

I had to get up. I had to figure out what to do, if I wanted to stay, where I could possibly go if I didn't. I didn't want to stay at Astoria College without Izzy, but I didn't have a home to go to. Astoria was my home now, like Izzy, along with her sisters and parents, had been my family. Izzy was gone, but there wasn't anywhere else to go.

Which means you have to get up.

"And I will," I mumbled to myself as I fumbled with the snooze button, resetting the alarm by touch. "In fifteen minutes.

2.

When I got to the door of the classroom, I almost chickened out. "No guts, no…" I muttered to myself. Then I shoved the door open and scanned the room for an empty seat. Spotting one nearby, I collapsed into it. Dr. Cliff barely broke his lecturing stride as I got out my notebook, trying to ignore the eyes boring into my back. I felt Dr. Cliff glancing at me as he wandered from side to side in front of the class.

Astoria was a small college of fewer than two thousand students. Our high school had been bigger. It was safe to say that when Izzy died, particularly given the circumstances, I became a campus celebrity by default. Izzy was "that dead girl" and I was her "crazy roommate." Luckily, Dr. Cliff tended to lecture faster than a person could write, so keeping my notes straight took the lion's share of my attention.

When class ended, I grabbed my things and shoved them in my bag. I was suddenly sure that if someone said a single word to me I would either hyperventilate or punch them, whichever suited the occasion. Maybe both. I didn't realize Dr. Cliff was standing next to me until I felt his hand on my shoulder. I whipped my head up, my expression hardening into a look Izzy teasingly referred to as my "fight face."

Dr. Cliff yanked his hand back like I'd shocked him. "I'm sorry, Callie. I didn't mean to startle you." He rubbed the hand that had been on my shoulder in an unconscious way. "I'm glad to see you in class. We still have a few weeks until finals, so it's possible we might salvage your grade *if* you're willing to work at it. Come see me during office hours next week and we can talk about making up your missed assignments."

"I'll do that, Dr. Cliff." I ducked my head, uncomfortable under his searching gaze.

"Tuesday between one and three."

"Yes, sir."

I slipped out of the empty classroom, grateful for the reprieve. As I exited Halsey Hall and headed away from the Academic Quad, I was greeted by a typical winter day on the Oregon Coast. The skies were a silvery haze; the clouds a flat, smooth ceiling. It gave every short winter day a sense of timelessness as you passed from morning to noon to early evening without the light ever changing, the sky glowing with a whiteness more like moonlight than sunshine. On certain days, when the fog rolled in toward the town over the ocean, it looked as though the world was enclosed in a snow globe of grey glass. The misty drizzle hanging in the air gave an added sense that the globe had been recently shaken, and the people inside were waiting for everything around them to settle again.

From the Astoria College campus, which was arranged as a set of buildings tumbling down from three quarters up Coxcomb Hill toward the Columbia River estuary, you could see all the way out to the place where the broad river met the Pacific, two forces breaking against one another, forming and reforming frothy white lines between the dark waters and the slate blue of the skies.

In other words, it was a perfect day in Astoria, a place so different from home it still surprised me every time I looked out my window at the vast enormous fir trees. When it came time to apply for college, Izzy and I had applied to a handful of small liberal arts schools scattered around the country. Both of us were tired of the Houston heat and humidity and wanted more adventure than staying nearby offered. We'd thought about splitting up, but in the end, most of our applications were to the same places, and we were thrilled when Astoria College, a small but prestigious school near the top of both of our respective lists, admitted us both.

For me, college meant a new beginning. Houston held enough bad memories for me to last a lifetime, so my college criteria included a school that would provide a huge physical buffer. I'd looked at schools in the Pacific Northwest because being close to Portland and Seattle meant I could see any band I wanted for a decent price, and access to shows was a necessity. I told people I'd chosen Astoria College because it had a well-respected academic program that would help me get into graduate school, but the truth was I wanted a fresh start where no one knew me. Except for Izzy, of course.

Izzy chose Astoria for different reasons. She told people she liked it because of the strong arts and communications program and its ties to some young and upcoming fashion designers in the Pacific Northwest she admired. In reality, I suspected Izzy liked Astoria in part because it meant an easy transition into a small campus community where she would continue to be universally worshipped for the effortlessly cool, trendsetting, natural leader she was. Izzy was a Queen Bee to be sure, but unlike so many of the other girls we'd grown up with, she was never cruel or grasping about it. She just had that sparkle that made people notice her, and where the spotlight shone harsh on others, it made Izzy shine.

Sure, Izzy could have gone somewhere like Parsons or the Savannah College of Art and Design, but Izzy was never someone who quite did what everyone else was doing and, frankly, she liked being the center of attention. While marching to the beat of my own drummer had always resulted in marginal acceptance at best, Izzy made it work for her. In the social pecking order of the universe, I was the girl in the corner everyone thought ate paste, and Izzy? Izzy was Beyoncé. And as she pointed out as we'd shopped for decorations for our room, "You have no sense of style, Callie. Trust me—sticking together means never having to look back on your college photos in horror and shame."

I pulled my ratty Astoria College hoodie closer at the memory, trying not to think of what Izzy would say about my current appearance. I hardly ever needed a real coat in Astoria's light misting rain, and the hoodie made it easier to hide my face, reducing me to another unidentifiable figure moving across the wide lawns and winding paths.

As I trekked across campus, I let my mind drift and kept my eyes on my feet, trying not to trip or attract too much attention to myself. I let play my music at random, barely noticing as one song slide into the next. It was another sign of how much had changed post-Izzy. Once upon a time, I could kill an entire day carefully curating themed playlists and posting them online or devote a week to reading every word in the latest issue of *Mojo*. Now music was an act of self-defense. Between the hoodie, the loud music, and sunglasses that were completely unnecessary nine months a year in Oregon, I could make the sojourn across campus and back without having to speak to another living soul. That suited me fine.

Steeling myself, I headed toward the Student Center, avoiding the small puddles of rainwater colored with loose dirt from the cobblestone campus walks. I had some time to kill before my mandatory check-in with Dr. Yates, and I knew putting in an appearance in the cafeteria was something that fell into the "normal" category. Even if I didn't feel normal, I figured doing a decent impression of it was the minimum threshold for staying.

I walked into the dining hall, handing my swipe card to the attendant. After reviewing my options, I moved listlessly through the grilled cheese and tomato soup line, which seemed the least threatening option among the enthusiastic attempts by college catering at various exotic foods. I tried to ignore the people around me, but I could feel them sneaking looks at me. With my earbuds blaring, it was easy to pretend they weren't there, that I couldn't feel their furtive glances.

I plopped down at an empty table in the corner and began nibbling at my sandwich. I was surprised by my appetite; I couldn't remember the last time I felt hungry. I took it as a sign at least part of me was functional. It felt strangely comforting, so I got up to grab an apple.

When I returned to the table, someone was sitting in the empty chair across from mine. I would have recognized the back of his neatly trimmed blonde head anywhere. Colin Turner's clean-shaven face and preppy clothes stood out on our otherwise "come as you are" campus, and even from the back his neatly pressed jeans, tucked shirt, and matching brown leather belt and shoes made him unmistakable. I walked around the table and slid into my chair, propping my foot up in the seat next to me. "Colin."

"Callie—" he quickly swallowed and wiped at his mouth with a napkin "—I can't remember that last time I saw you. I was starting to think you never left your cave." His friendly eyes crinkled as he smiled to show he meant no offense.

"Yeah, that seems to be the theme of the day."

When I didn't smile, he cleared his throat nervously. "Is it okay if I sit here? I saw you were alone and thought you might like some company. I can move…"

I hated the look on Colin's face. He was handsome in a way that made you expect to see him on a baseball card, clean cut and as All-American as apple pie, but he lacked the overblown confidence you saw in the kind of boy who had been a high school hot shot. Instead he had an air of hesitance about him, like someone a little too fined-tuned toward rejection to have ever been truly popular. At the moment, I couldn't decide if his hesitation was part of his natural nervousness, or because he was worried I might fly off the handle.

"No, no," I said wearily. "It's fine—great actually. You're the first person who's spoken to me today. How are you?" I asked, hoping to deflect the conversation to any topic that didn't involve me and my feelings.

He looked down at his food. "It's been hard." I didn't need to see his sad eyes to know what he was thinking.

Colin dated Izzy briefly our first year. Izzy was a big believer in not getting tied down. She was never mean about it, and she scrupulously told the guys she dated that she wasn't interested in a serious relationship. Every guy she dated seemed enthusiastic about the arrangement, but quickly grew irritated that Izzy wasn't available when they wanted her to be, usually because she had a date with someone else. About that time, Izzy would break it off. She stayed friends with most of them, but held them at a distance in case they got the wrong idea again. I couldn't remember anyone who held it against her, but she left a trail of broken hearts in her wake.

Most of her suitors lost interest once they realized Izzy wasn't looking for a serious relationship and her reticence wasn't a game intended to make them chase her. Colin, however, had what Izzy considered an annoying knack for deflecting her attempts to put him off. Personally, I found his optimism toward his prospects with Izzy charming, if a little pathetic. He seemed convinced Izzy would come around if he worked hard to win her over. He was never pushy, just…persistent.

Had it been me, I might have been persuaded. Not Izzy. His refusal to give up brought out the cranky in her. She didn't understand why he couldn't get the hint. From the way he wouldn't make eye contact with me now, he was probably the only other person on campus who could understand what I'd lost, who was suffering with me.

"I still can't believe she's gone." He pushed his food around his plate. "I keep thinking I see her." His words were soft and sad. "I'll be walking across campus and I'll see someone from behind. For a split second, I think, 'It's Izzy!' Then I look back and it's not her, it's obviously not her." He turned his face away, staring studiously out the window. "But I keep seeing her. At least, I keep thinking I do." He paused. "How are you doing?"

"I am a shining example of perfect mental health." Colin fidgeted in his chair, confirming my suspicions that the rumor mill was working overtime on me. "Why?" I asked with mock innocence. "What have you heard?"

"Nothing." His Adam's apple bobbed in his throat.

"Has anyone ever told you you're a terrible liar?"

He paused, smoothing the sleeve of his spotless hoodie. "I'm not asking you what other people think. I don't care what they say. I'm asking you."

He leaned forward, so willing to hear whatever I had to say without judgment, I was talking before I could stop myself. "How do you think I am?"

"I think you're a mess." His gentle tone took some of the sting out of his words.

"Geez. Don't try to spare my feelings."

"No, I mean…" He seemed to be weighing his next words. "You've lost a lot of weight. You look like you haven't slept."

I pretended to be engrossed in my apple. "I guess I haven't been eating or sleeping much."

"Are you…" He took a deep breath, the words coming out in a rush. "Are you leaving AC?"

"And give you a shot at my lauded position as History department curve killer?" I said, mustering a half-smile. Colin was a sophomore and a history major like me. We had a couple of classes together.

"I noticed you haven't been in class."

"I'm staying." I forced myself to sound more sure than I felt. "If they'll let me, I'm definitely staying."

"If you need my notes…"

"Thanks. I'm more worried about my papers than my exams." I groaned at the sheer amount of work in front of me. "I think I have three due in the next two weeks."

"I'm sure they'll give you an extension if you ask. I think everyone in the department would be happy to see you, you know, out in the world." He cast his eyes down at his plate. "I'm happy to see you," he added with an embarrassed smile.

"Thanks." It was kind of nice to be missed. Now it was my turn to be awkward. "Look, um, I know that Izzy wasn't always the nicest to you—"

"She was." I squinted skeptically at him. He returned my gaze, exuding a determined confidence that seemed like a challenge. "Izzy just didn't know what she wanted. I would have waited."

"I know." The oath and affirmation hung there between us, an unexpected pact. Here was someone else who loved Izzy, who missed her, who was still waiting for her to come back. I liked Colin better for it.

I dropped the half-eaten apple to the tray and stretched my arms wide, working at the knots of tension between my shoulders. "I guess I should get my stuff from my room. I'm headed to the library to study."

As I stood up and, tray in hand, turned to leave, a familiar laugh cackled above the general din of the cafeteria, drawing my attention. I froze, staring at a table near the entrance of the cafeteria.

Crowded around it were the three of the first-year girls who had been with Izzy the night she died, the ones who should have been there when Izzy made her way back to campus. Looking at them, laughing and carrying on, you'd have never known they'd broken the sacred party oath that you never leave a woman behind and abandoned my best friend to her ugly fate.

In that moment, I was hit by a wave of black fury, swaying on my feet as it crested over me, burying all other impulses. If I had been a star, I would have imploded, sucking every person in the cafeteria into the dark nothingness I felt inside.

Suddenly, I hated everyone around me. I hated how fake they were. It was the exact same thing that had happened when my mom had died of cancer when I was eight, and then when I'd moved in with the Millers during my sophomore year of high school to get away from the horrors of living with my dad.

People were always the same. They tiptoed around you, acting like they cared, when deep down, they didn't. Sure, they were always full of sympathy and sadness when you were standing in front of them, but the second your back was turned, they went right on living their lives, smiling and laughing as though the world was the same as ever, like nothing had changed. Somehow they were able to ignore the giant hole in their lives, slip back into their mundane obsessions like who slept with whom last weekend and whether there will be a pop quiz in class on Monday.

I wasn't built like that. When the world as I knew it came to a sudden and abrupt end, I wasn't good at pretending it hadn't. It was of the few traits that I shared with my father. When my mother died, he'd become something dark and ugly. Standing in the cafeteria, watching three of the girls who had abandoned my best friend, I suddenly understood him a little better than I'd ever have imagined possible.

I didn't realize I was shaking until Colin appeared in front of me, pulling the rattling tray from my hands. I turned back toward the table, grabbing the back of a chair as I took one deep breath, then another, trying to calm myself down.

Setting down the tray, Colin leaned back against the table next to me, arms crossed as he observed the oblivious girls. "If looks could kill, those firsties would be piles of dust right now," he said bumping my shoulder with his. I cut him an angry glance, but he wasn't looking at me. His eyes stayed on the girls. "I hate them, too, you know."

I choked out a hoarse laugh. "You're too nice to hate anyone."

Colin turned his head so that his lips were so close to my ear I could feel his breath on my neck. "If you think that," he said in a voice so low I could barely make out the words, "then you really have the wrong impression of me."

I cocked my head a little, checking to see if he was serious. His eyes were icy, the friendliness gone like someone had switched off a light. "Maybe I do." I felt a flutter of admiration. I could see I wasn't the only one who had been changed by Izzy's death. It made me feel a sense of kinship toward him I'd never have believed possible.

Over his shoulder, I caught sight of the clock on the wall. I was late for my appointment with Dr. Yates. "Crap! Gotta go." I reached for the tray.

"I can take it," he offered, placing his hand on my arm to stop me. I glanced down at his hand, and he withdrew it quickly.

"I got it." I grabbed it tightly. I appreciated the sentiment, but I was capable of carrying my own tray across the room, even if it felt like everyone was watching me do it.

I was halfway across the cafeteria when he caught up with me. "What are you doing this weekend?" Colin smiled, already back to the sweet, eager boy who had pursued my best friend. Maybe I was wrong about his skills of deception; Colin was much better at faking it than I was.

"Cleaning my room, reading, mountains of laundry. Why?"

Oh, nothing." He coughed and a slight blush pinked his neck. "A bunch of us were going to a movie on Saturday. I was wondering if you wanted to come."

I narrowed my eyes at him. Surely he didn't mean as a date? He seemed to read my meaning and became even more embarrassed, the red hue spreading into his cheeks. "As a friend, of course."

I thought about his phantom Izzy sightings, about the tears in his eyes, and smiled as relief swept through me. "What movie?"

"We haven't decided yet."

I looked at his hopeful expression. "Maybe. Let me know what you decide to see."

"Great." Colin beamed at me. I headed toward the exit, stopping to scrape my plate into the compost bucket before depositing it in the return bin.

"Hey, Callie?" I heard him call out. "It was really good to see you." The wide grin he gave me was so genuine I couldn't help return it. With a small wave, I shoved my earbuds back in my ears and slide my sunglasses into place. I was careful to keep my eyes on the floor and my attention away from the table full of traitors as I stalked past them out the door of the cafeteria.

3.

When I reached the Counseling Center, Ms. Bloom, the receptionist, greeted me as she always did, with a smile of knowing pity that made my skin itch.

"I'm here to meet with Dr. Yates," I mumbled, not bothering to remove my sunglasses. I watched as her bright pink lips moved, but I couldn't make out the words over the music. Tired of waiting for her to catch on, I gestured pointedly at my ear. I felt a tiny thrill of triumph when a look of frustration flashed across Ms. Bloom's face, but then it was gone again, the perpetual smile permanently affixed.

"She'll be right with you," she said loudly and slowly, as though the music made me both deaf and dumb.

I collapsed into the worn vinyl chair to wait. Walking across campus was exhausting. I longed for my dark room and tiny bed. I grabbed a magazine from a pile strewn across a nearby table. I flipped through the pages without seeing them, trying to look busy and to keep from chewing on my fingers. Izzy had made me stop biting my nails on the grounds that constantly having my hand in my mouth was "full of germs and gross" and "no, seriously, Callie, it's super gross."

I couldn't imagine what she'd think of the state of my nails now, which I'd bit so far down to the quick that I'd begun chewing on the skin around them. I'd always been kind of restless, but I felt acutely aware of my fidgeting now. Everyone on campus was always staring at me, obviously waiting for me to freak out. So I tried to act normal, which inevitably resulted in my default over-caffeinated, knee-bouncing, foot-tapping jittery state morphing into a jerky, awkward, obviously self-conscious mess. Even my own body was alien to me.

Okay, seriously, when is Dr. Yates going to come out so we could get this over with? They're going to kick me out if I leave. They're going to kick me out if I leave, I reminded myself over and over, gritting my teeth.

Dr. Yates opened her door and motioned for me to enter. I shoved myself out of the chair and pulled the earbuds from my ears as I walked into the office. *Time to get this torturous show on the road.*

Dr. Yates perched on the edge of her straight-backed wing chair. In her matching cardigan and pale pink shell, Ms. Yates always seemed more suited for a cameo in a 1950s-screwball comedy than relating to the trials and tribulations of a modern college student. Her hair was as a pale corn silk which I'd only ever seen in a twist or neat bun pulled away from her face.

"How have you been?" Her pencil hovered over her legal pad.

I took off my sunglasses and crammed them into my pocket. "Since when—our meeting yesterday?"

"No," she exhaled a small, delicate sigh. "I was thinking more generally. We haven't had a real session in…," she flipped through the pad, "…almost three weeks. What have you been up to?"

"Finger painting, mime theatre, making a thousand origami cranes for peace. You know, the usual."

"Sarcasm isn't going to get you anywhere." She pursed her lips. "You're hurting. That's obvious to anyone who looks at you.

But I can't help you if you won't let me."

"I don't need your help."

"I think you do." She scribbled something on the pad. "And I'm not the only one. We have serious concerns about your safety."

"More like you're afraid of getting sued," I muttered.

"Do you really think that?"

"Nope." I smiled savagely. "I don't have any family, remember? My mom is dead. My dad is who-knows-where. And now Izzy's dead, too. There's no one left to sue you."

"What about the Millers?"

I swallowed. "What about them?"

"Have you spoken to them since they were here to get Izzy's things?"

"No." I studiously traced patterns on the carpet as I recalled my encounter with Dr. Yates the Monday after Izzy died. She had been one of the oh-so-helpful administrators to descend on my room, attempting to fix me. Dr. Yates had the particularly poor taste to suggest we begin boxing up Izzy's things together. She said it would be a kind thing to do for Izzy's parents and might also help me "begin to come to grips" with my loss.

I had a vague memory of screaming at her to stop touching Izzy's stuff and get out of my room, loud animalistic moans that continued long after she'd stepped into the hallway and I'd slammed the door in her face, clutching a pillow to my mouth to muffle the sound. Eventually someone else did it, but I never knew who. I'd been out of the room, I couldn't even remember where now, and when I'd come back, everything was gone. Izzy's side of the room was blank, wiped clean of every sign she'd ever been there.

The only thing of Izzy's that was left behind was me.

The whole incident was wrapped in a reddish haze, but I could still see my face, tea-streaked and blotchy, as I'd leaned against the door, my forehead pressed against the long mirror mounted on it, struggling to breathe. It was the face of someone I barely recognized, a wounded emptiness in my eyes that I'd only seen in the eyes of my father. Even now, the memory startled and terrified me. If I was honest with myself, it was part of the reason I was still trying to cling to some semblance of my life at AC. I felt like staying here was the only thing standing between my survival and my turning into the one person I'd never wanted to be.

Dr. Yates waited for me to say something more, a benign expression intended to convey gentle helpfulness on her lips. Watching her survey me was like looking at that strange, sad girl in the mirror. It was something that was and wasn't happening to me, something I hated but also couldn't control. If I were someone better adjusted, or maybe just less stubborn, it might have made me talk. Instead, the weight of her gaze grew heavier with each twitch of the clock's hands, until I could barely suppress the anger coursing through me.

"How are you going to help me, Dr. Yates? Are you going to talk to me about my feelings?" I snorted in derision. "You want to hear about how much I loved Izzy and her family? How they were the only ones who loved me? How they blame me for her death? Hell, how I blame myself?"

"I think you know this isn't your fault."

"How it is not my fault?"

"Accidents happen." She made a wide gesture with her hand, as if motioning to the broadness of the universe.

"Why does everyone say that?" Despite my best efforts, I was starting to lose my cool. "Things don't just happen. People make them happen."

"You want someone to blame."

"There are people to blame!" I slapped my hand on the arm of my chair. "People make choices. People make decisions. And then other people pay for them."

"Izzy paid for them."

I gritted my teeth. "Yes."

"And when you say people…" she flipped though her notepad again, as if she couldn't remember their names. "You mean the girls who were supposed to be with Izzy."

"Among others."

"Gloria Capreni, Lauren Young, Shannen Pomerantz, and Bethany Schaeffer."

Just hearing their names set me seething. "Yes."

Dr. Yates sat the notepad aside. "These girls are just like you, Callie. They—"

"No, they are not."

"—are your hallmates, your classmates. They are hurting from this loss, just as you are. They were Izzy's friends, too."

The image of Gloria, Lauren and Shannen together in the cafeteria flashed through my mind, smiling and laughing. "No, they are not."

She leaned forward. "Don't you think you're being a bit unfair to them?"

I actually laughed, just once, a hard sound exploding from my chest. "I really don't."

"Really?" She tilted her head to the side, a gesture of scrutiny. "Try to imagine it from their perspective. Like you, they feel a sense of responsibility for Izzy's death. But what could they do, really? They weren't driving the car that hit her. Neither were you." She clasped her hands in her lap, and the gesture had the absurd effect of looking as though she'd clasped them in prayer. "What could any of you have done?"

"I could have saved her!" I gripped the arms of my chair, my fingers digging so hard they ached with the effort.

"No. You couldn't."

I practically leapt to my feet. "Yes! I could have." I shifted my weight and eyed the door. If I didn't get out of the office immediately, I was going to lose it. From the slightly pleased look masked as deep concern on Dr. Yates's face, that was exactly what she wanted. She'd been trying to push my buttons this whole time.

"How?" she pressed. "What could you have possibly done?"

I wanted to stop talking to spite her, but instead words poured out, a river of emotion running over my carefully constructed banks of self-control. "If I had been there, this wouldn't have happened. She asked me to go to that stupid party with her, but I said no. Like I always said no. If I had been there, she wouldn't have gotten drunk and been wandering up the hill by herself when that asshole hit her. I would have kept her out of the road. I would have kept her safe. I would have…"

My hands shook uncontrollably. I wheezed in and out, my chest constricted as though I'd been running up hill for miles. It was a familiar, terrifying sensation, one that took me back to some of the scariest moments of my life. I hated it, that feeling of feeling too much, of losing control, or being unable to stop my body from reliving past pain like it was fresh and current.

Dr. Yates was saying something, but it was like she was talking to me underwater, the words garbled across the space between us. I grabbed at the arm of my chair as the world twisted, and then righted itself. Dr. Yates stood up, reaching towards me.

Before I was consciously aware of what was happening, I bolted from the office. I barely registered the look of shock on Ms. Bloom's face or Dr. Yates telling her to call Campus Security as I wrenched open the outer door and sprinted away from the Counseling Center. I kept running, not seeing the people I knocked into. I had to get away from them, all of them. My legs ached and my chest burned, but I kept going.

4.

When I finally stopped running, I was in the middle of Clatsop State Forest, a large wooded area with mapped hiking trails and park facilities. The forest runs for several miles from the back of campus and up into the mountains of the Pacific Coast Range, surrounding the school on the eastern side with a persistent curtain of greenery. Without meaning to, I'd left the cobblestone campus path along one of the back parking lots and continued where it extended past the campus' edge. I didn't quite remember how I'd gotten there. I'd kept moving until my body decided to stop.

In late November, it was already near dark. The dim light filtered down through the canopy of trees, throwing shifting constellations of shadow across the gravel hiking path. Behind me I could hear the faint sounds of the campus–the occasional calling out of one student to another, cars pulling in or out of the lot–but the trees made it all seem farther away than it was.

Spotting a bench a few feet ahead, I collapsed onto it. I don't know how long I sat, head resting against the wooden back, eyes closed. It could have been five minutes, but it seemed like forever. I hurt all over. My head felt stuffy and full but the rest of me felt empty, like I had cried out my insides.

As my muscles stiffened, I heard the rustle of obvious footsteps and a rhythmic clattering of metal on metal. Whoever was approaching didn't want to surprise me, which meant it could only be one person: Jayden Houghten.

Jay was generally regarded as one of the nicest guys to ever put on a Campus Security uniform and harass under-aged drinkers or provide late night escorts from the library to the commuter parking lot. After a four-year tour in the Marines, Jay found his way to higher education at AC, landing a job as a security officer and then taking advantage of the tuition reimbursement that came along with it. At twenty-three, Jay was older than the super seniors. By day, he was a sophomore studying physics with the goal of becoming a mechanical engineer. By night, he worked for Campus Security to cover "the costs of attending this a fine, prestigious institution," as he liked to put it. Georgia born and bred, Jay's southern charm was out of place in the cool Pacific Northwest, but he was known to get more cooperation out of surly students with a flash of his dimpled grin and an "aww shucks, ma'am" than the steeliest officer's glare.

Jay didn't normally go on shift this early, but there was no mistaking the sound of keys bouncing against his uniform duty belt or his solid shuffle, kicking up leaves for my benefit. Since Izzy died, Jay had shown the good sense to announce his presence whenever he came near me, allowing me the opportunity to turn him away. That was more space than most of the people who were so very concerned for my well-being usually granted me, and it warmed me to him as a result.

"Hi, Jay." I opened my eyes as he sat down on the bench next to me. "How'd you find me?"

"It's not a huge campus."

I turned to look at him and found him staring at me. His deep brown eyes always sparkled with a kind of hidden knowledge that made me feel young and inexperienced, like I didn't know if he was laughing with me or at me. Even now, after everything, he still looked at me like that. I swallowed, focusing instead on the trees in front of us, green and filled with shadows. "Technically I'm not on campus."

"Someone saw you go this way." The radio at Jay's shoulder crackled. He muttered something into it that I didn't quite catch, but the gist seemed to be that he'd found me. "You're lucky I happen to be searching this end of the Academic Quad."

"Yep. That's me." I wrapped my arms around myself, feeling both cold and annoyed. "Lucky, lucky me."

To say Jay was attractive was an understatement. His hair, which often seemed black in the perpetually overcast bluish light falling on Astoria, was actually a deep chocolate brown with a hint of reddish highlights that came out in sunlight. He had an olive complexion that gave him a perpetual tan, and his muscular build showed in the way his uniform shirt was a tight in all the right places. He was exactly tall enough that I had to lift my chin a little bit to look him in the eye. Izzy called it "perfect kissing height," a must-have dating criteria in the world according to Izzy, and that was the first thought to fly through my mind as I'd looked him full in the face.

In short, he was beautiful.

But Jay was a cop—okay, Campus Security officer, but a cop by any other name—and a southern gentleman. Maybe that made him the fantasy of every other girl on the hill, but every cell in my body shrieked "RUN!" and pulled me in the opposite direction.

It didn't matter that I'd never wanted anyone as much as Jay.

In fact, that was the problem: I'd instantly wanted him too much. That shiver I got when I felt his eyes on me told me everything I needed to know about what might happen if I gave it half a chance, and I had not moved three thousand miles to live the same life I could have had back home.

I'd made a resolution to avoid Jay like he was covered in toxic mold and set afire, but Astoria was a small campus, too small to avoid anyone for long. Izzy thought the whole thing was so hilarious that at first she went out of her way to drag me places where Jay, Mr. Popular, was supposed to show up. Finally, I started refusing to go places with her altogether rather than get tricked into suffering through another night tongue-tied and flustered, tripping over my feet and spilling drinks and generally being a complete mess every time I was near him. Eventually Izzy got the drift and dropped it.

"What are you doing out here? It's way too cold for only a hoodie."

I snorted. "Of course you think it's cold. You always think it's cold. It's that thin Georgia blood in you. Izzy was exactly the same. She was forever complaining about the weather. 'It's too cold. It's always raining.' I could never figure out why she wanted to come here in the first place. But she…"

I stopped, unable to finish the sentence. In the wake of Izzy's death, the drama of my possibly romantic feelings for Jay, like everything else, had faded into the background. It wasn't that I didn't notice him. It was impossible not to. It was just that, compared to losing Izzy, whether or not I liked him, or anyone, didn't seem as significant anymore.

I stared into the distance, thinking about how much that used to mean something had come to mean so little. Jay coughed, but otherwise sat silently next to me. It was nice to sit with someone and not feel judged.

Jay was there when I found out about Izzy. He'd convinced his bosses to let him come along on the grounds that he knew both Izzy and I and thought I'd find comfort in a familiar face. I knew something was wrong when he came to my room with my hall director, Mike Fuchs, and Dr. Yates. It was too many people at too late an hour to be anything good but even I hadn't come close to guessing the truth as they shuffled in and closed the door. Jay had stood silently as Mike delivered the news in a quiet, even monotone, watching while I'd screamed in anger and disbelief.

Ever since then, Jay found excuses to check up on me, dropping by to make sure I'd registered my bike with Campus Security in case of theft or that the batteries in my fire alarm were working. He'd told me once, in passing, that he'd had two friends die in Iraq. I suspected that was why he was good at handling me. Though I didn't have clear memories of the night Izzy died or the days that immediately followed, the look on Jay's face said he understood as much as I did what it meant that she was gone.

"Dr. Yates called you?"

"Not me specifically. She called dispatch, told us you started yelling during a session and ran out. Then she said what must be her favorite phrase, given how often she uses it—"

"I know," I cut him off. "'High risk for self-abuse.' I've heard it. Several times. At this point I'm convinced it's the only diagnosis she knows."

His smile was quick and stiff. "Yeah. Well, you know what happens when she says the magic words. Every officer starts running around campus, looking to do a threat assessment."

"You'd think they got a gold star every time someone threatened to kill themselves."

"Is that what you did?" He turned to me with troubled eyes. They looked almost black in the growing darkness, making the whites stand out. "Do you want to hurt yourself?"

"No, Jay." I sighed and looked down. "I don't want to hurt myself."

The bottom of my jeans were wet and caked in mud, but I couldn't remember how it got there. Another lost moment of my life. I didn't like blacking out, but I couldn't seem to help it. Did I want to hurt myself? Was it possible to hurt more than I already did? It didn't seem likely.

I continued the recitation of assessment responses in a hollow, sing-sing voice. I'd been through this so many times in the last few weeks I couldn't even pretend to be interested. "I have no plans to harm myself or anyone else. I have no means with which to harm myself or anyone else. I am not currently experiencing any thoughts of harming myself or someone else. I am not experiencing suicidal ideation."

As the words rolled off my tongue, I tried to remember the moment I'd become an expert on suicidal ideation response protocols. Like everything else that had happened in the wake of Izzy's death, it seemed to have come with the package that was life

AI—After Izzy.

I pushed myself up off the bench, rolling my head against my shoulders to ease the knot between my shoulder blades. "Now that we've covered the bases, can you give me a ride back to my room?"

"I'll take you back, but this is serious." Jay ran a hand through his tousled hair, grimacing. "I don't know what's going to happen. I know you're not going to class. When this sort of thing occurs, they tend to send students to the hospital for evaluation."

"Because I ran out of my therapist's office?" I rolled my eyes. "I'm not crazy, Jay. I just can't stand everyone asking me how I am constantly. I'm awful. Everything is awful. How could anyone not get that?"

"I think they do."

"Then why do they keep asking?" My hands curling into fists unconsciously. For a moment I felt full again, like someone had scraped out my guts, mashed them with rage, and stuffed them back into me like the shell of a twice-baked potato.

Jay sat quietly, his face turned up to me. His hair had gotten longer on the top but was closely cropped on the sides, which I now recognized as a holdover from his military days he couldn't seem to let go of. I had several cousins with the same haircut, and I had a sudden impulse to run my hand along the buzzed edges, to see if it felt like touching thistle down like I remembered.

Where did that come from? I wondered for the hundredth time before shoving the impulse into the background. Jay watched me closely, his warm eyes dark and full of concern. All at once the anger ebbed away, taking the last of my energy with it.

33

"I'm sorry, Jay. I'm not mad at you." I hung my head. "I'm just mad. I'm mad at everyone. I'm mad at the world."

Jay eased himself off the bench, dusting his hands on his dark pants. "Let's get you back to your room."

"Right." I rubbed at my face. "Time to face the music."

5.

Jay and I rode in a heavy silence back to my residence hall. It wasn't far, but that didn't stop Campus Security from driving their trucks in slow circles between the library, the parking lots, and the residence halls keeping an overly vigilant eye on the quiet campus. There had been a time when being alone in a truck with him would sent me into an alternating fit of moony-eyed staring and self-defensive meanness. It was a testament to how little I cared about anything anymore that I was sitting less than a foot away from him and wasn't tripping all over myself trying to get away. Instead the ride was stiff and formal, Jay slipping back into his official role as campus shepherd, and me, his wayward collegiate sheep, being dutifully returned to the flock.

When we pulled up to my building, I got out and Jay followed. I didn't try to stop him. I was getting used to people who claimed to have my best interests in mind assuming I had no personal boundaries. I trudged up the stairs and at the top I could see Mike waiting outside my room. I let myself in, Jay and Mike in tow, then sat down on my bed and waited for the obligatory lecture to begin.

The meeting was brief, a replay of most of the encounters I had with people of late. Mike expressed concern, I placated and promised to do better. After assuring himself that I wasn't an immediate danger to myself or anyone else, Mike extracted a promise from me that I would call the Resident Assistant-on-Duty if I felt like I needed help. I agreed, reciting the number I knew I'd never dial.

Through it all, I could feel Jay carefully evaluating my every move, every word, making his own assessment of my mood. After Mike departed, I turned my attention to his way. "And what do I have to promise to get you to leave?"

"What are your plans for the weekend, Callie?"

I blew a long, tired breath through my lips, then gave the same answer I'd given Colin. "I dunno. Clean, I guess. Catch up on my reading. I'm really behind."

"I don't suppose I could convince you to meet me in the library in the morning."

I fidgeted, hugging my arm to my side. After my public display of crazy today, there was no way I was going to sit on display in the library where my every move could be visually inspected and dissected by the AC student body. "No thanks. I'll pass. I study better alone."

"That's what I thought." He adjusted the utility belt hanging low on his waist. "I'll call you at ten to make sure you're up."

"No need. I'm a big girl. I think I can manage to haul myself out of bed."

"I know you can." Jay smiled, a little less Officer Houghton and a little more casual classmate now that his formal duties had been dispensed with and Mike was gone. I'd seen him do this dance while he was confiscating the occasional beer from an underage neighbor or escorting someone home from the library, but it was strange to watch him walk try to walk that line with me. "But I'm calling just in case, so make sure you have your ringer turned on." As if he had been reading my thoughts, Jay gave me what I suppose was meant to be a stern look and said in the authoritative voice he usually reserved for breaking up campus parties, "If you don't answer, I'm coming over here. So don't make me come over here."

I offered him a mock salute. "Sir, yes sir."

"Damn straight." He tipped an imaginary hat at me as he left.

As soon as the door closed I felt the fake smile slide off my face. I puttered around my room, trying and failing to focus long enough to do more than open a book and stare at the words on the page for a few minutes before getting distracted again. I knew there were things I could or should be doing—all those normal, responsible things I kept telling everyone were on my list. Clean room. Clean self. Do homework.

Generally speaking, get it together.

I knew what those things were, but I couldn't do them. Even picking up the clothes off my floor seemed overwhelming. I'd used every ounce of energy I had to get through the day. Instead I sat on my bed, a book in my lap, staring at the blank wall formerly known as Izzy's without really seeing it. How many other students had lived in this very room, had decorated that wall, and then moved on with their lives, unremembered? How many other rooms in other halls on other campuses had seen people come and go, never to return?

How could the most important person in my life be just another statistic?

Occasionally I opened my mouth, a half-formed thought caught in my teeth when I remembered that saying the words aloud wouldn't make Izzy hear them. I was so used to her being there that even now, my first impulse was to talk about my problems with her.

So I studied the wall, keeping quiet vigil, with a mouthful of things I couldn't say.

6.

When I snapped awake, the alarm clock read four twenty-three in the morning. I'd passed out fully clothed, half-sitting, half-lying on the bed. One of my flats had come off, but otherwise it appeared I hadn't so much as twitched in my sleep. My contacts stung my eyes, and I cursed myself for falling asleep with them in again. As I heaved myself up, I noticed the lights over the 2dressers were still on. I tried to remember what had awoken me. I'd felt something— no, *someone*—moving around the room. I sat up quickly, scanning the small space. There didn't seem to be anyone in the room now.

I didn't remember Jay locking the door when he left, so I checked it. Locked.

Shivering against the cold, I got ready for bed. I chucked off my cords and grabbed a pair of light blue flannel pajama pants with bright red cartoon lips printed all over them, pulling them on. Izzy made me buy the pajama set, I remembered with a smile. She'd said the lips reminded her of the opening of *Rocky Horror Picture Show*. Every time I'd put them on, she'd stop whatever she was doing, turn toward me, raise her arms above her head like the live-action performers of the show, and half-yell, "In the beginning, there were THE LIPS!" Then she'd giggle as though it were the first time she'd said it, and I'd giggle in return.

Now I'd never hear her say those words again. I'd never hear her say anything again.

When I finished getting dressed, I walked over to the mirror hanging above the dresser on my half of the room. There were two chest high dressers on either side of the door, one for each person, with a mirror above each. Izzy had added a full-length mirror to the back of the door so she could get a complete view of her outfit before she left every morning. According to Izzy, if you couldn't see the shoes, then you couldn't see the whole outfit. In Izzy's world, it was tantamount to a criminal offense.

Personally, I couldn't have cared less. It was a good day when I bothered to put on a little lightly-colored lip balm and mascara before I left for class, which always irritated Izzy. Izzy subscribed to *Elle* and both American and French *Vogue*. She claimed her one true religion was to worship at the feet of Anna Wintour. She'd always looked upon my lack of interest in fashion as one of the true tragedies of her life.

"Why did I have to be cursed with a best friend who will never fully appreciate all I have to teach her?" she'd lament as she pulled a bag out of the back of her closet and shove it at me while we got ready to go the movies. "Someday, when I'm a fabulous famous designer," she'd say, flipping her stylishly cut red hair, "you'll be sad I'm not around to dress you anymore."

That was Izzy. She never doubted all the things she was going to do it in life—and then one night, some anonymous driver had made sure she never would.

As I fished around in my eye, trying to remove the contact lens without taking a portion of my eyeball with it, the details replayed in my head.

It was two weeks before Halloween. Izzy had gone to an Angels and Demons party. Izzy had, predictably, gone as a demon. If

I closed my eyes, I could still see her outfit: a dark red suit jacket that was low-cut in the front and flared at the waist with a matching mini skirt, a lacy black halter top peeking from beneath the jacket.

Izzy completed the outfit with pantyhose with black seams up the back, impossibly high black heels, a tasteful jeweled lapel pin with rubies in it, and a pair of black cat-eye framed glasses for show. While other girls in our hall had worn the skimpiest outfits they could find, Izzy surpassed them by playing up the stereotypical "hot librarian" look.

Gazing at me over the top of the glasses, Izzy pulled her tiny mouth in an injured expression. "Oh, come *on*, Callie. Don't you want to have any fun in college?" Her carefully mussed hair swung around her face.

"I have plenty of fun, Iz." I twisted around in my chair to look at her. "For example, tonight I'm going to sit here and write this paper for Gender in Popular Literature and Film, which is due Monday and which I haven't even started." Turning back to the keyboard, I tried to ignore the feeling of Izzy rolling her eyes at my back.

"But you have the whole weekend to write it, and the party is only this one time," she cajoled in her sweetest voice. "I'll even help you if you wait until tomorrow. Can't you shelve your relentless work ethic for one night and come with me? I've got clothes you can borrow to be an angel. You'd look great!" Izzy clapped her hands in excitement at the thought of playing dress-up with me as her life-sized, if somewhat flat-chested, Barbie.

"Sorry, but I'm out. You have plenty of other people from the hall to go with, and I need to get this done. Besides, a vicious work ethic isn't something you shelve when you're a scholarship kid."

I opened my notebook pointedly on my desk and began flipping through it. "Neither one of us is going to enjoy it if I have to be subjected to an evening of watching my friends getting drunk and acting like brainless, giggling zombies to get attention."

As I felt her stony silence growing, I knew I'd hit a sore spot. "God, Iz, I didn't mean you. I know *you* aren't stupid. You can take care of yourself. You're not going to drink whatever someone hands you and you're not going to let anyone else do it, either. I just can't deal with it tonight. I don't want to babysit. I don't want to have to get in some jerk's face when he gets handsy with some poor drunk firstie who should know better." She continued to glower at me, but seemed slightly mollified.

"Please?" I begged. "Let me stay here, write my paper, and go to bed early." I gave her a little smile. "Tomorrow I promise to make sure you get up in time for waffles at brunch and you can tell me all about your amazing night."

Izzy dropped her hands from her hips and scowled in defeat. "Alright, fine. I'll go with Gloria and her roommates, but if I don't get my waffles in the morning, no matter how big a pain I am to wake up, you're going to be in deep trouble."

She stepped over and kissed me on the head. "You get back to your boring work," she said as she sauntered toward the door, "and I'll have some actual fun."

That was the last time I'd seen Elizabeth Leanne Miller alive.

I'd managed to get my hands on a copy of the official AC

report by convincing Dr. Yates that I reading it might help bring me 'closure.' I kept the creased and worn pages under my mattress, but I'd read the words so many times I could recite them.

The authorities hadn't discovered the identity of the person who hit Izzy that wet October night. There were four girls who went to the party with Izzy—Gloria, Lauren, and Shannen, first year girls who lived down stairs from us in room 103, and Bethany, a girl from a nearby complex who their constant shadow. All of the girls, including Izzy, had walked to a house party just north east of campus, on a small street that abutted the same wooded park I'd run to earlier.

According to the report, which contained suspiciously similar statements from the girls, Izzy was dancing with some guy in a black suit wearing devil horns and an eye mask around 12:15am.

When they'd looked for Izzy again an hour later as they got ready to leave, the girls couldn't find Izzy anywhere. After what they swore was a thorough search of the house, they broke the first rule of going to a party as a group—never leave anyone behind. They left the party around 1:40am and walked back to campus. All four girls reported being back in their rooms no later than 2:30am.

A hysterical passerby called 9-1-1 almost an hour later when she found Izzy's body by the side of the road. Izzy's tiny Prada clutch lay beside her. The police called Campus Security as soon as she was identified as an AC student.

By the time her body was found, Izzy had been dead at least a half-hour. Sometime between 2:15am, when most of the other students identified as being at the party came back to campus, and the 9-1-1 call around 3:30am, Izzy was headed back to campus in those ridiculous heels when she was struck by a car. She'd been found on a road that winds through the park toward the back of campus instead of one of the more direct routes through the suburbs back to campus, which suggested she had gotten lost on her way back, further supporting claims from some witnesses that Izzy had appeared intoxicated at the party.

The police said, given Izzy's injuries, it was likely she died very shortly after impact, and the driver had probably been intoxicated. Fearing the prison sentence that would inevitably follow, they'd driven away. Though the police had searched local auto repair shops and Izzy's death was all over local news, Izzy's killer had never been found. At this point, almost a month later, it seemed unlikely they ever would be.

Everyone else seemed to have made a sort of peace with that, but I couldn't. It killed me to think of Izzy's last moments being spent lying in a pile of rotting leaves on the cold ground. I couldn't imagine the kind of person who would leave my beautiful, funny, sweet friend with blood seeping through the fabric of her elegant suit. I hated them, whoever they were. Hours passed, then days, and now weeks, but instead of lessening, my resolve to find and punish them grew stronger with every tick of the clock. Izzy deserved better from this world than to die out there in the dark alone. I had no idea how I would find the person who did it, but if I ever did, I resolved to ensure they met a similar fate.

Shaking myself out of my own dark thoughts, I put on my black wire-framed glasses. As I shoved them up my nose, I could've sworn I saw something move behind me. Telling myself it was sleep deprivation, I glanced at the reflection in the mirror to be sure.

Izzy was sitting on her bed, staring at me.

"I'm dreaming," I said to the apparition. "I must be dreaming." I closed my eyes and breathed in and out slowly. "In a few seconds, I'm going to open my eyes and turn around and the room will be empty." Turning, I took another deep breath and opened my eyes.

Izzy was still there.

"I'm losing my mind. I am absolutely losing my mind. Perfect."

Izzy rolled her eyes at me. She was wearing the outfit she'd had on the last time I saw her, down to the fake glasses and the three-inch heels.

"You're not here. You're not real!"

Izzy continued staring at me with a singularly Izzy expression of irritation.

I flopped back on my bed, exasperated. "I don't know why you're here, but from the look on your face I've done something to piss you off. Why don't you tell me what it is so I can finish going quietly insane?"

After a moment or two, I heard a rustle. Moving my arm, I watched as Izzy picked her way through the random crap strewn across the floor. Frowning down at the top of my dresser, Izzy carefully selected a tube of lipstick. I recognized it as one she hated; she complained every time I wore it. She said it made my mouth the color of dried blood. "Who would want to kiss that?" she'd ask.

I watched in stunned disbelief as she removed the cap,

dropping it on the ground, and with a look of deep concentration, slowly turned the tube to reveal the brown-reddish wax. I held myself still as I watched her carefully print two words across the full-length mirror. The lettering was perfectly straight, like all those choir signs Izzy painted in high school.

HELP ME.

I jumped to my feet. "Help you? How, Izzy?" I pleaded. "HOW?"

Izzy leaned over and pressed her lips delicately to the mirror. When she pulled away, a foggy impression of her lips remained, puckered as if to kiss the note in a bright red signature. Izzy turned toward me and raised her fingers as if to touch my face, giving me a sad smile.

Then she disappeared.

A number of options rushed through my mind: I was hallucinating. This was all part of some cruel but elaborate hoax. I was losing my mind. Or…

I reached out, tentatively, touching my fingers to the smeared lipstick, to the imprint of the lips—her lips. It was real.

I rattled the door handle. The door was locked. No way in or out.

Izzy had been here. Izzy needed me.

And this time, there was no way I would let her down.

7.

After a fitful night of little sleep, I rolled out of bed around eight-thirty on Saturday with what I felt were the beginnings, at least, of a plan. My first step in deciphering what happened to Izzy seemed simple enough, if unpleasant. I needed to talk to the four girls who had gone to the party with her.

Lauren, Gloria, and Shannen lived in our building in a quad downstairs that had turned into a triple when their roommate didn't return from Fall Break. Bethany, the fourth girl who'd gone to the party with them, lived in another complex across campus. I wasn't sure of her room number, so I had to hope I could catch her downstairs. Luckily, she hated her own room due to a roommate with a perpetually present creeptastic off-campus boyfriend who was almost twice our age. If I was lucky, said creeper would be in Bethany's room and she would be, once again, crashing on the common room couch in 103.

I knew the girls had been questioned numerous times by both the local police and various college administrators, but I had a strong suspicion they hadn't told anyone everything about that night. Even if they hadn't held something back on purpose, maybe they had left something out accidentally. It was also possible that something they had said in passing, some small detail that held the key to making sense of the story, had been missed by the administrators and cops because they weren't students, who were privy to the *Days of Our Lives* levels of convoluted gossip that tended to run the social engine of our tiny campus bubble.

Either way, I had a feeling there were things the girls hadn't mentioned to anyone else, things that seemed embarrassing or personal, but would be harder to hide from someone who knew them. Plus, I had no idea where else to start, and this seemed like as good a place as any.

I took a shower, letting the almost scalding hot water wash over me as I planned out what I was going to say. I carefully combed out my long hair and blow-dried it, which was something I almost never did, preferring to wash it before bed and let it dry while I slept. I was so absorbed in my muttering I practically tripped over an unexpected visitor when I swung the bathroom door open.

Jay sat on the floor in the middle of the hallway, reading, his long jean-clad legs stretched out in front of him. "Hey," he said, giving me his lopsided smile, a deep dimple appearing in his cheek as he smiled appreciatively at my bare legs.

I yanked at my short robe, feeling exposed despite my habit of strolling the short distance from my room to the communal bathroom in the exact same outfit almost daily. I'd passed tons of people in this hallway, but Jay was the only one who made me acutely self-conscious about my lack of coverage. I didn't have to look at him to feel his amusement, so I stepped over him, pulling my keys from my pocket to unlock the door.

"What are you doing here?"

Jay ignored my tone. "I came to make sure you got up." He stood, extending a large coffee cup toward me.

"As I told you last night, totally unnecessary. Look!" I flapped at hand at myself. "Squeaky clean and ready to work."

He had the decency to keep his eyes on my face as I practically dared him to look at my legs again. "Well, I guess that's something." He held the cup out again.

I was irritated he brought it. I hated the feeling that someone was trying to clean up the mess I'd become. I knew Jay probably had good intentions, but that's what it felt like. I started waking up on my own when I was seven. I'd held my mother's hand and fed her ice chips when she was too sick from her chemo and cancer to move, when even my father couldn't face being in the room with her anymore. I did my father's laundry, not to mention my own. I bought our groceries, fed us both, made our beds. Despite the respite living with the Millers had briefly afforded me, my life had long been about doing, not about being done for.

On the other hand, I was so grateful to see caffeine that, after a moment, I relented and took the cup. Jay's mouth pulled into a self-satisfied grin, but he was smart enough to keep his comments to himself.

"I'm surprised you're here," I took a quick sip of the coffee. "You're usually not up this early on the weekends, are you?"

"No. I work the evening shift on Fridays so I tend to sleep in."

I pushed the door open and placed the coffee cup on the dresser. "So all this is for my benefit?"

Jay leaned casually against the doorframe. "I came to ask, one more time, if you'd come to the library with me."

Jay's presence was mucking up my plans to interrogate the 103 girls. I needed to shake him, quick. "And as I told you last night, I am not the study buddy type."

Jay's gaze flowed past me to Izzy's empty side of the room, but his attention snapped back with an intensity that hadn't been there moments before. I pulled my eyes away from his and ended up focusing on the curve of his full lips, twisted upwards.

"You studied with Izzy."

"That was different," I responded icily.

"Why?"

It took me a minute to realize he was seriously asking. "Because she was Izzy, alright?" I laughed a little at the hysterical notion of Izzy spending her Saturdays in the library. "It was…" I couldn't find the right words. Maybe they didn't exist. "*She* was special," I said finally. "There is *no one* like Izzy."

He sighed. "Can't fault me for trying."

I shifted uncomfortably in my robe. It was starting to get chilly. Why wouldn't he go away? "But I can blame you for not taking no for an answer."

As usual, my ire seemed to bring out the humor in him. "What can I say? I'd prefer you didn't get kicked out of school. You make life…interesting."

"Oh, I'm sure I do. If I wasn't here to make a spectacle of myself, who would they send you to rescue? Everyone loves a public breakdown, right? Isn't that the point of most reality shows?" I tried to laugh at the joke, but it came out hollow and forced.

"No one is rooting for you to fall apart."

"Sure they are." I rubbed at a spot on the carpet with my toe. "They're probably just hoping someone catches it on video when I do so it will go viral."

"Well, not me." His gaze was relentless. I felt pinned down by it, an ant under the sudden glare of a magnifying glass. "I don't think there's anything wrong with you. You've been through a lot. You need to talk to someone about it."

"I'm fine." I bit down on the inside of my lip, desperately trying to control my temper. *He's being nice*, I chastised myself. *He's doing this because he cares. He does not deserve to get his head bitten off in return.*

"No, you're not. But you could be." He cupped the back of his neck with his hand. "You don't have to talk Dr. Yates. Just talk to someone. If you want, you could even talk to me."

"No amount of talking is going to bring Izzy back." I gritted my teeth. "Everyone in the world wants me to talk about it, and the more I do, the worse I feel. I'd be better off if everyone left me alone."

"I think alone is the last thing you need right now."

"And I think you'd prefer if I were helpless and in need of rescuing." I took a step toward the door and Jay backed away in response. "But I'm not pathetic, so I don't need to be saved. Go find some girl who swoons every time you go all real American hero."

I watched all sympathy drain from his face as he abruptly pushed himself off the door frame. "Fine. I'll be in the library if you want me."

I could feel the heat in my face as the words left my mouth. It was a low blow, and given the number of military men in my family, I knew better than to mock someone's service. I tried to tell myself it was necessary. *You need to get going*, I reminded myself. *Helping*

Izzy is what's important right now. Jay turned to leave, his rigid, Marine posture a reminder of my rudeness.

Before I could stop myself, I called after him. "Hey, Jay? Thanks," I gestured with the cup, "for the coffee."

He stared at me for an uncomfortable moment, and I could sense him debating something. But then he just gave me a curt nod and strode away.

I held the door open for a moment, listening to him clomp down the stairs and smack the door open. When it banged shut, I closed my own and placed my head against it. Why did I have to be awful to people who were nothing but kind to me? What was wrong with me?

From the corner of my eye, I could see the bright red words and Izzy's lips, still emblazoned on the mirror to my right. They looked bigger, somehow, from this angle. Their careful print was broader, more desperate in their exactitude.

HELP ME.

It was a good thing Jay hadn't followed me into the room and seen the message. He might revise his assessment of my mental stability. I considered smearing the lipsticked missive with my hand, but couldn't make myself touch the waxy imprint. Even if I had written it while in the throes of some hallucinated dream state, it felt like wiping out a part of Izzy. I couldn't do it, not when it might be real.

Not when I had so little of her left.

8.

Back on task and gearing up for the first skirmish in my battle, I spent what felt like an exorbitant amount of time standing in front of the closet considering my wardrobe choices.

As I got ready, I thought about my approach. Depending on which girl opened the door, I wasn't even sure they'd talk to me. The last time I'd seen any of them was the night she's died. I cringed at the memory; it hadn't been a pleasant encounter. I wasn't anticipating my sudden appearance to be entirely welcome.

"What do you think, Iz?" I murmured as I flipped through the hangers. "What would you pick for me to wear to an Inquisition?"

I eventually settled on a pair of dark jeans that fit tight in the hips and thighs but flared slightly at the bottom of the leg, a dark red V-neck sweater made of material that was warm like wool but soft to the touch like velvet, and a pair of caramel-colored ankle boots Izzy gave me as a back-to-school gift. After putting on a tiny bit of blush and a light coating of reddish lip gloss, I added a pair of grey metal ball studs in my ears and looked myself over in the full-length mirror on the door. Though the clothes were a bit big on me, reinforcing the fact I'd lost a lot of weight in the last month, the sweater brought out the natural blush to my skin and lips and my hair had a shiny healthful glow to it. I left it hanging in loose waves around my face. I looked more like I was ready for a date than an interrogation, but I wanted it to seem as though I was happy and healthy and, more importantly, completely back to normal before I went digging into Izzy's death. I figured that meant putting effort into my appearance, which seemed like a normal thing for a nineteen-year-old girl to do.

It was almost noon by the time I finished, which meant the girls should be awake no matter how late a night they'd had. I knew their habits, which they'd learned mostly from following Izzy, well enough to know this was the best time to try getting something new out of them. If they were hung over, hungry, and not expecting me, maybe I'd catch them by surprise.

I headed down the stairs feeling determined, but when I got to the door, the large dry erase board attached to it read: "Gone to the Mountain, Biatches! BB Sunday –Love, 103." Snow season had finally started in Cascades, and it wasn't uncommon for a group of AC students to get together and head up for the day or even a long weekend of snowboarding and skiing.

Staring at the board, I felt as though someone had emptied all the air from hallway. I heard a sucking sound, like a person trying to control their breath, but it sounded far away. It took a few minutes to realize that the sound was coming from me. I gripped the light grey door frame, suddenly grateful that everyone who lived on their side of the hall was either asleep or already of out the building. Forcing myself to count to ten, I felt my breathing slow until I was no longer gulping for air.

As I walked back to my room, the energy drained out of me. This was so stupid. Izzy wasn't trying to send me messages from beyond the grave. Izzy was dead, and in my insane desperation to believe that my best friend, the person I loved and trusted more than anyone else in the world, was still with me, I'd imagined the note or written it myself in my sleep.

I was so engrossed in my thoughts I didn't see my RA and neighbor, Jenna Stewart, until she was practically on top of me.

"Callie!" she gushed, cornering me on the stairs. "It's so good to see you."

"Jenna," I said, unable to manage even the most minimal of friendly greetings. It wasn't Jenna's fault that she got on my very last nerve on my best of days. It was just her way. Jenna was terminally bubbly, a personality trait that made her my social equivalent of nails on a chalkboard. Even before Izzy died, I'd never been a huge fan of upbeat, and Jenna was a poster child for positivity.

"You look so nice!" she continued in her rapid-fire way. "It seems like you might be going somewhere special. Are you going somewhere special, like to the theatre or something?"

"Yep. High school drama club performance of *The Bell Jar.*"

"Wow, that seems kind of dark for high school, but maybe it will be good, you know?" she continued, clearly missing my sarcastic tone. I rolled my eyes, but Jenna ignored me and babbled on. Jenna was like that—totally unflappable.

Jenna was also obsessed with the concept of sleep hygiene. "I've been thinking about your sleeping problems. You know what might help you with your insomnia? A bigger bed." She waved her arms expansively. "If you turned the beds in your room lengthwise, you could put them together and have a king-sized bed. You'd need to put a foam mattress pad on top to cover the crack, but they aren't too expensive…"

Jenna had finally noticed the look on my face. I was repulsed by the idea of accidentally rolling over in my sleep onto Izzy's bed, which still smelled faintly of Izzy's favorite perfume, a honeyed rose scent by an East Coast perfumer she found on the internet. It was rare and unique and a statement—quintessentially Izzy—and I thought of her every time I caught a whiff. The idea made me want to gag, and it must have shown on my face, because it shut Jenna up for a few seconds.

After a beat, she'd picked right back up where she'd left off. "The first step toward good sleep hygiene," She continued confidently as I stared at her in silent horror, "is to create an inviting and comfortable sleep space."

On that hideously insensitive note, I pushed right past her. I couldn't even muster a response. "We'll talk more later," she called after me. "Have a good time at the play!"

"That girl has all the finesse of a four-year old on a sugar high," I muttered under my breath as I unlocked my door. I stepped inside and slammed it behind me, eyes closed as I tried to block out the mental image of Jenna's giant bed plan.

She's only trying to help, a small internal voice reminded me. I considered all the notes Jenna had slipped under my door while I'd been barricaded in and refused to leave. *She's probably completely normal. I'm the one with the screw loose.* I leaned against the mirrored door, trying to figure out what to do next.

No 103 girls.

No leads.

Nothing.

Maybe it was better. What was I going to say anyway? "I know you're hiding something because Izzy left me a note?" No one would believe me. I'd be better off if they didn't. After all, a psychotic break made way more sense than a dead girl sending me missives in cosmetics. Maybe I was just imagining it all. The thought reminded me of a Patsy Cline song my mom had been obsessed with, and I hummed it a little under my breath. Mentally unhinged, lonely, and blue. That about summed me up.

Then I opened my eyes. "What the…"

I stumbled numbly across the floor. Laid out on Izzy's bed was a little black dress Izzy had picked out for me at the Nordstrom Rack on a weekend shopping trip to Portland, a dress that had definitely been hanging in my closet when I left the room earlier, carefully locking the door behind me.

Next to it was a pair of chunky satin heels with long straps you wound up the ankles. Izzy 'lent' them to me with the idea of never recovering them despite my flat refusal to ever wear anything so impractical. A lacy black shawl that once belonged to my mother was folded next to the dress. My black satin clutch was sitting with the outfit along with a pair of real diamond studs Crystal and Greg gave me for my eighteenth birthday. The earrings had originally belonged to Crystal's mother. I'd tried to offer them to Izzy, or insist they be kept for our younger sisters, but Crystal wouldn't have it. Crystal had simply said, "Heirlooms are for family. You're family." They were one of my most prized possessions.

It was an outfit for a special date.

Or something you'd wear to a cocktail party.

"Or to a really upscale funeral," I swallowed, my mouth dry. "Not exactly what I had in mind this morning, Iz."

This was precisely what Izzy did whenever we went to a party or she dragged me out on some ill-fated double date. Never trusting me to dress myself, Izzy would lay out clothes for me, down to the accessories.

Staring down at the outfit, I felt a little irked Izzy was still trying to dress me. But then again, hadn't I asked her to? Hadn't I stood in front of my closet, wishing she was here to do things like this?

Maybe I could have dismissed the lipstick note as some unconscious desire to reconnect to Izzy so overwhelming that I'd written it myself, but I definitely had not done this. The door was still locked when I came back to my room; I had heard the click when I turned the key. Either someone with a sick sense of humor was messing with me in the most painful way imaginable, or Izzy was trying to reach me, to tell me something about the night she died.

My hands trembled as I fingered the hem of the dress, then ran my palm across the rough lace of the shawl. A collection of clothing inherited from dead women, laid out for the living.

It was a message; it was a mission.

"Okay, Izzy." I picked up the dress and held it to myself. If this is what she thought I needed to do to help her, I was willing to follow her lead. "But just so we're clear: I am still not wearing those shoes."

9.

As I laid the dress back on the bed, my cell phone started ringing. "Hello?"

"Callie?" The voice on the other end hesitated a moment. "Hey, it's Colin."

"Colin? Oh, hey," I sat down the edge of my bed, but I couldn't take my eyes off the clothes. "What's up?"

"You wanted me to call you when I found out about the movie. I know it's kind of last minute, but the people I'm going with wanted to go to an early afternoon movie. Around one-thirty? I wanted to make sure I got in touch with you early enough that you could come with us."

Crap. I'd totally forgotten about Colin and the movie. I wanted to beg off, but I kept thinking about how nice he'd been in the cafeteria the day before. "What movie?"

"The group is pretty evenly split between seeing that new zombie movie, *Zomborific*, and a British comedy, *Rentboy*. I was hoping you could help us make a decision."

I hadn't heard of either movie, but definitely felt unsettled enough to know anything involving the dead returning to life was a bad idea. "*Rentboy*." I tried to force some enthusiasm into my voice. "I vote for funny."

"Great. It's playing at the Gateway. Should I come by your room beforehand?"

"No." The thought of someone else being in the room made me feel panicky. So far, Izzy hadn't done anything weird while other people were around, but I wasn't about to push my luck. "I'll meet you there. Around one-fifteen?"

"Sounds great. I'm really glad you're coming."

"Me, too, Colin." We said a quick goodbye and he hung up.

I clutched the phone tight in my hand and stared at the outfit. Surely Izzy couldn't have known Colin would call. Could she? Was that the sort of thing ghosts knew? It seemed super weird, but then everything seemed weird these days. And even if she had, surely Izzy didn't really intend for me to get all dolled up to go with Colin and a group of other people to an afternoon movie? But if not, what was the point of laying out the outfit? I studied each item on the bed carefully, but nothing seemed to shout, "HERE'S A CLUE!"

"I don't know what you were thinking," I finally said aloud, unsure if I was addressing Izzy or myself, "but there is no way I am wearing that."

After my phantom fashion encounter, I couldn't get out of the room fast enough. I hung the dress and shawl back in the closet and dumped the clutch and earrings on my dresser. I didn't want to face the outfit when I came home because I didn't want to think about what it meant.

I didn't change my clothes, though I felt a little overdressed for a mid-afternoon movie. I snagged my camel-colored pea coat with hood from my closet and pulled it on. I always felt cold in movie theatres and had a tendency to use my coats as a blanket, so I figured between the weather and the movie I'd err on the warm side. I grabbed my phone, iPod, keys, and wallet and left the room, double-checking to make sure the door locked behind me.

It took about thirty minutes to walk from campus to the movie theatre, which was only a little ways down the hill toward the river and a couple of blocks northeast of campus. I could have taken the shuttle that ran from the campus into town to the waterfront or walked to the trolley running along the river's edge where most of the hotels and tourist attractions were located but I needed a break from campus…or at least my room. So I left almost an hour and a half early, deciding to take a walk through town to clear my head before facing Colin and his friends.

As I left the building, I shoved my earbuds in and cranked up a random mix before pulling my hair back over my ears to keep them warm. With a flick of my finger, Sleigh Bells blared into my ears, blocking out everything else. It was a cold day in Astoria, the kind that stripped the last of the leaves off any trees that dared to resist the progression from fall into the beginning of winter. The wind whipped wildly at the edges of my coat but it wasn't raining, so I left my hood down.

The town was set on the tip of the Oregon border, flanked on one side by Youngs Bay and by the Columbia River on the other. Both spilled out into the Pacific out past their junction. Being so close to the water meant Astoria never got too cold temperature-wise, but the wind had a tendency to cut through layers of clothing, dragging water from a mild drizzle with it. I couldn't count the amount of days I'd ended up soaked and frozen to the bone in seemingly mild weather.

As I walked past campus into town, I watched my classmates wandering about with an air of contented purpose. I wondered if Izzy and I had once looked as blithely carefree. It didn't seem possible I had ever been so easy-going. Every time I started to get comfortable in my life, the universe hit me with a loss that cut so deep it made the sheer act of breathing an effort. My mother, my father, now Izzy and the Millers in her wake. I doubted I could ever be like my classmates, who knew nothing of loss or fear or loneliness on the grand scale that haunted my life. The realization made me feel even more isolated by comparison, and I quickened my pace to escape the glow of their happiness.

Pausing on a corner as I waited for traffic to pass, a brightly colored banner featuring a cornucopia snapped in the wind, and I felt my face growing hot. Thanksgiving was less than a week away, and I had not heard a word from Crystal or Greg. Touching my cheeks, I realized numbly I was crying.

I hurried away from the tall, narrow residential homes and into downtown, passing quaint B&Bs, day care centers, auto shops, and the local heritage museum. When I got to the corner of 16th and Highway 30, there was still a half hour before the movie started, so I headed into the older section of downtown to kill time. To my left, the city climbed toward campus. To my right, the river flowed under a large bridge that crossed the Columbia connecting Oregon and Washington in the distance, a long span of steel loops and rivers cutting against the smooth sky like a line drawing.

I was still wandering around when the wind picked up and the sky opened, rain falling in earnest. I ducked inside a restaurant off the highway. A hand-painted message on the dark glass windows boasted "Cherry Pie and Clam Chowder," neither of which sounded particularly appetizing, but place looked dry and warm inside. The door closed behind me with the gentle jingle of an old-fashioned bell. A woman in a crisp white shirt, navy skirt, and a light-blue-and-white plaid apron led me to a small booth in a glassed-in corner that provided views of the water and the traffic traveling up and down the highway. Each table had a paper place mat at each seat with a cartoonish map of Astoria on it and a little paper cup of crayons next to the salt and pepper shakers. I glanced over the menu and ordered a large mocha. When my stomach rumbled in protest, I added a slice of triple berry pie with whipped cream.

As I waited for the food, I reflected on how surreal the last two days had been. Out in the world, it seemed ludicrous to think Izzy was trying to communicate with me.

I didn't want to believe someone was messing with me, that anyone could be so cruel. My classmates might not be models of empathy or understanding, but the proposition that I was being gaslighted didn't make sense. Even if everyone knew about Izzy's obsession with preventing my fashion suicide, no one could have heard me ask Izzy what to wear…unless they'd bugged my room or something. And who would bother? I was doing a perfectly fine job of self-destructing all on my own. Even if someone here hated me enough to want to get rid of me, all they had to do was wait.

And even that wouldn't explain Izzy's appearance. No matter how desperate I was to see her, I could not have conjured Izzy as perfectly as she had been in my room. She'd left me a message, sealed with a kiss. So Izzy. No, I knew she was real down to the core of me, as real as the table I was sitting at. Her message was simple and undeniable: HELP ME. I couldn't turn my back on that, no matter how crazy it might seem to anyone else. That said, it was crystal clear absolutely no one would believe me if I tried to tell them. If I was going to help Izzy, I was on my own.

The pie arrived and I picked at it, trying to work on my plan of attack. Talking to the girls who were with Izzy had to be the first step; they could help me at least establish a timeline for the evening, maybe give me the names of a few more people I could talk to. I grabbed a purple crayon out of the cup on the table and, flipping the place mat over, began making a list of people to talk to.

I added the four firsties Izzy had gone with and then sat back, stumped. I didn't even know who hosted the party. I knew it was a house party for the crew team, and added crew team guys in brackets to my list, but I wasn't confident any of them would help considering they usually couldn't remember their own parties. After a few minutes, I added a notation for the guy Izzy was dancing with. Rolling the crayon between my fingers, I scrutinized the names.

1. Gloria
2. Lauren
3. Shannen
4. Bethany
5-8. <Crew house boys>
9. <dancing devil>

It wasn't much, but it was a start. I flipped the place mat back over and traced a line along the route Izzy would have taken from the upper edge of campus along the winding roads through Clatsop National Park and into the small neighborhood of homes where the upperclassmen who chose to move off campus usually rented. Grabbing a green crayon, I placed an X roughly in the space where Izzy had been found, past a dead-end turn-off that led to the local electric utility station.

"You need anything else, hon?" Startled, I looked up to see the waitress looming next to me, and hurriedly covered the X with my hand.

"No, I'm fine." I must have looked shaken, because her eyes were wide and sympathetic.

"I'm sorry. I didn't mean to startle you."

"It's okay. I'm ready for my check."

She pulled her pad from her apron and tore a small sheet off, placing it face down on the table. "You were friends with her, huh? That girl who died?" She gestured toward the map, and my hand curled reflexively into a fist, crumpling the paper beneath it.

"Yes." I pulled my wallet from my pocket, pretending to be absorbed by counting change. "Here," I shoved a ten toward her. If I overtipped, maybe she would take the hint and go away. "Keep the change."

The friendly smile slipped from the waitress' face. "I'm sorry, hon, I didn't mean to upset you," she said quickly. "It was a real shame, such a pretty little thing. My heart broke every time I saw her picture on the news…"

I shook the bill at her with a glare. "Anyway, you take care now." She eased the money from my hand and turned away from the table.

I turned back to the map crumpled in my hand. Taking a deep breath, I smoothed it out against the table, then folded it up and slipped it into the back pocket of my jeans. I still had a while before the movie started, but all I wanted was to avoid people and their random, empty sympathy. If need be, I could sit in the theatre and watch the commercials they run before the previews. Sitting in silence for two hours seemed like paradise. At least no one would try to talk to me.

10.

The rain fell harder as I stepped outside, wind yanked my hair around my face. I dragged my hood up and dove back into the heavy beats of Dessa as I walked down the highway to the Gateway, traffic speeding by. There wasn't much on this side of the street between the main downtown drag and the movie theatre: a frozen custard place that didn't see too much business during the cooler months, a gas station, and a few empty storefronts.

I turned the corner into the small strip of shops where the theatre was located, crossing the parking lot toward the entrance. Even from a distance and from behind, Colin was easy to spot. He was the only person I'd met who could wear the standard college uniform of grey sweatshirt hoodie and jeans and still look preppy. It was the little touches that did it, the brown shoes and matching belt, the shiny newness of the jeans hinting they were not only clean, but had been ironed and folded before being carefully put away, not shoved in a drawer or left in a heap at the bottom of the closet. Even Colin's hoodie was pristine. The printed letters were clearly readable and fully formed instead of faded or flaking, and the hoodie fit his frame without being overly long or baggie.

Every time I saw Colin, I was surprised Izzy hadn't been won over by his obvious care for his appearance. It wasn't a fussy care implying an ego, but rather an attention to detail that displayed a thoughtfulness and consideration for the small things. It made Colin look put-together, even if it sometimes came off as a little anxious to please. Izzy was the sort of girl who could spend an hour getting her accessories exactly right and tended to launch into lengthy speeches on the plight of fashion vis-a-vis the average American male every time a pair of saggy jeans walked by.

Colin stood near the ticket booth talking to a guy I didn't recognize from a distance. I couldn't see Colin's face, but the conversation looked intense from the hunch of his shoulders and the way he was leaning toward the other guy.

I slowed my pace. How could I have forgotten other people were coming, too? Colin had mentioned friends, but I hadn't bothered to ask who we were meeting. When he called, I was too intent on getting out of my room to care. Now, I felt self-conscious as I wondered about who might show up and what they might say about Izzy or me.

I considered telling Colin I had a headache and fleeing back to school. At that moment, Colin looked up. His face broke into a wide grin as he half-walked, half-jogged across the empty parking lot to meet me.

The ever-present earbuds made me an expert lip reader when it came to conversation openers and I read the word "hi" coming from his lips as he reached me. I begrudgingly removed them from my ears, the roar of the wind off the river rushing into the vacuum. Colin turned and fell in step with me as we headed back toward the theatre together.

"Hi Colin." I forced a weak smile. "Thanks again for the invitation."

"No problem, Callie. I'm glad you decided to come." I could hear his smile even though I couldn't see his face from behind our hoodies.

The small theatre did so little business that it sold tickets from the concession stand so we skipped the empty box office. As Colin and I reached the entrance, I recognized the person Colin had been talking to as Nate Dermott, one of the guys from the crew team. Nate and I had been in our mandatory first-year seminar together and didn't exactly see eye-to-eye philosophically, which led to some tense class discussions. Nate held the door open as Colin and I entered.

"Hello, Nate," I managed with effort as I passed him. Nate gave me a silent head nod in return but didn't look particularly happy to see me. I groaned inwardly. Who else from my non-fan club was here? Surely, Nate didn't count as "friends" in the plural sense of the word. I wouldn't have guessed Nate and Colin were buddies, but AC was small enough everyone knew each other one way or another.

I stood a little bit back from the front of the concession stand, pretending to look over the menu as I debated whether I still had time to make a semi-plausible gracious exit. Colin stood next to me. I glanced over at him, trying to gauge how annoyed he would be if I bolted, but he stared up at the menu. Nate continued past us as if were we strangers, ordering a large popcorn and Coke combo and his ticket. After the girl behind the counter handed him his food and tore his ticket, he cruised toward the theatre without a backwards glance toward Colin and me.

Colin shot me a toothy grin. "Know what you're getting?"

"A Coke slush," I replied. "I only like popcorn when I can mix it with chocolate-covered almonds, but they don't sell them here."

"Chocolate and popcorn?" Colin made a face. "Doesn't the chocolate get oily with butter and kind of gross?"

I chuckled at his obvious revulsion. "It's pretty good, Colin. You have to go light on the butter, but the salty/sweet combination is one of the best to be found. I mean, if you don't mind getting your hands a little dirty," I teased, eying his neat appearance pointedly.

Colin shrugged. "I'll take your word for it," he said, moving toward the counter.

"So is it you, me, and Nate?" My mouth was dry and I swallowed nervously, hugging my arm to my side.

"I guess I didn't tell you who was coming, did I?"

"No, you didn't." Colin's eyebrows drew together in obvious concern. "But I didn't ask, either," I added in an attempt to make peace.

The girl behind the counter began tapping her fingers on the glass display, trying to draw our attention. Colin turned back toward her and quickly apologized. He ordered two tickets and two large Coke slushes before I could stop him, passing a torn ticket and drink back towards me.

My self-possession flared a little. Colin didn't ask before buying my ticket, but I didn't want to start an argument in the middle of the theatre. Instead, I gritted my teeth and took the drink from Colin, who looked entirely too pleased with himself. This was not a date, and even if it was, I'd still want to buy my own ticket and soda. Izzy always complained about Colin doing things like this. At the time, I'd written it off as Izzy being overly sensitive because Colin wouldn't take the hint and back off. Now I could see what she meant. It wasn't only that Colin did proprietary things, but that he simultaneously put you in a position to feel like it was impossible to protest or decline without hurting him. He didn't do it to be pushy, but he wasn't always quick to take a hint. I frowned and made a mental note to be more assertive about picking up the tab if there was another opportunity.

As we headed toward the movie, Colin walked close to me. He looked anxious, as though he was worried I wasn't having a good time and it was his fault. Seeing the obvious concern on his face, I felt like a heel. Why couldn't I accept his generosity? It was like Jay and the coffee. If my own mother had been alive, she'd have been ashamed of my poor graces; I could almost hear her chiding me in my head. I took a long sip of the slush, trying to stuff all of my irritation back down into the box I'd been keeping my unpleasantness in since Izzy died.

Be nice, a little internal voice reminded me. It sounded a lot like Crystal. *You are capable of it, so be nice.*

As we got to the door of the theatre, Colin pulled it open for me and I resisted the urge to protest. Plastering a smile across my face, I tried to restart the conversation. "You said there were other people here. Who?"

Colin ducked his head. I slowed to a stop inside the large entranceway of the theatre where the hallway split left and right around the sides of the stadium-style seats. "Colin?" I narrowed my eyes at him.

"Callie, don't get mad, okay?" Colin picked at the edge of his

71

slushie lid with neatly trimmed nails. "There were other people who were supposed to come, but they ended up backing out…" Colin paused as the door opened and a couple passed between us. A shaft of bright light fell across Colin's face as the exterior door swung open, and I could see he was pink with embarrassment.

"And…."

"Callie, I didn't plan things this way, but Nate is in there with the girl he's seeing, Danielle, and Danielle's best friend Emily came and brought her boyfriend Gabe, so…." He stared at his shoes.

"It looks like we're here on a date," I finished. "And it looks like you set me up so it would be a date without telling me after I explicitly asked you and you said we were going as friends, and you are worried I'm going to kill you where you stand for lying to me."

Colin swallowed hard, his Adam's apple bobbing rapidly. "Yes, but Callie, I really did mean it as a friends thing. There were supposed to be two other guys here and Emily and Gabe weren't coming the last time I spoke to Danielle. I didn't know who was coming until we got here."

"You should have called and warned me."

"Why? So you could back out?" he countered. He obviously knew I'd been on the verge of bolting. "It really isn't a set-up," he pleaded. "You look so sad every time I see you. I thought it would be good for you to get out and do something. I don't want you, or anyone else, to get the wrong idea."

I sighed, wishing I'd turned around in the parking lot when I'd first seen Colin. Then, suddenly, Colin's attitude then clicked into place. "Is that what you and Nate were talking about so intently when I got here?"

He nodded. "Yeah, I was making it clear to everyone that this is not a date and that you wouldn't take any suggestion that was kindly. And I didn't want them to say anything to upset you. I told them that if they so much as mentioned Izzy, I'd clean their clocks."

I felt the anger draining away as I stared into Colin's eyes, so desperate to please and protect me I had to stifle a giggle. "You realize Nate could kick your ass with one hand tied behind his back, right?"

He bit back a smile. "So you're not mad at me?"

"No. You didn't do it on purpose." I punched him lightly in the arm. "Next time, though, if you don't want it to seem like a set-up, you might let a girl pay for herself."

He rolled his eyes as the pinched set of his shoulders eased. "So you'll stay?"

"Yes, I'll stay." I trudged down the hallway into the dark theatre. Colin followed. Thinking of that little Crystal-like voice, I glanced back. "And thank you for the ticket and the drink."

Colin grinned as I squinted, searching the rows of seats for the others. Nate was sitting with Danielle Gomez, who I recognized as the captain of the campus pep squad, in the middle of the row about three quarters back from the screen. Emily Lawrence, another pep squad girl, sat on Danielle's right side, and her boyfriend, Gabe Hudson, another crew guy, sat on the other side of Emily. The boys were leaning back, talking behind the girls' heads. Emily and Danielle leaned toward each other, giggling and chatting as the guys draped their arms loosely around the girls' shoulders.

Seeing the group of them together, they looked…normal. Happy. I knew I didn't belong here, with these people. I felt like an alien, brought along to observe humans in their natural habitat. Lifting my chin, I forced myself up the aisle toward them.

If I'd had the whole student body to choose from, I don't think I could have picked a worse group of companions for my first foray back into the world. Izzy had dated Gabe for about five of the fifteen minutes he and Emily were broken up over Spring Break our freshman year. After Emily and Gabe reconciled, Izzy became a natural enemy in Emily and Danielle's minds and I was identified as the captain of Izzy's personal guard. I hated drama and tried to leave Izzy to clean up her own romance-related messes, but I distinctly remembered having said some particularly unkind things about Danielle and a push-up bra after she'd poured a drink down the back of Izzy's dress at a party last Spring. Gabe was a pretty nice guy when he wasn't with Emily, but they'd been dating since their sophomore year of high school and old habits were hard to break.

I'd complained to Izzy when she'd dropped Gabe that the best thing that could happen to him would be for him to get out from under Emily, and by extension Danielle's, thumb. "It's not my job to rescue him," Izzy retorted. "If he can't figure out he can do better, that's on him." Watching Gabe and Emily cuddle together, I doubted that would happen.

As I got to the end of the row and began scooting sideways down the aisle, I cursed myself for going first, leaving me trapped between Gabe and Colin. The aisle was too narrow to fix it without making it obvious that I wanted the exit seat. I focused on getting to my spot and through the next ten minutes until the movie started, when I could blissfully ignore their existence. Danielle and Emily shot glances at me as I settled into my seat, their heads swiveling up from their phones like perfect mirror images of darkness and light, Danielle's tight dark curls swinging in in tandem with the slick sweep of Emily's straight amber hair.

From their side glances and bursts of giggling, it was obvious the girls were texting about me and Colin. I suppressed the urge to snatch their phones and chuck them at the screen. Instead, I made a show of taking off my jacket and draping it across my legs like a blanket, clenching at the fabric to keep my hands steady. Glancing down at my red sweater and neatly pressed jeans, I was immediately reminded how much time I'd spent getting ready that morning.

A flush crept up my neck. *No wonder they're laughing. They think it's a date and no matter what Colin said, I'm sure it looks like one.*

Thankfully, the lights came down almost immediately and the movie started. The plot was one of those absurdly premised comedies that left little impression ten minutes after it was over, but I found myself chuckling along with the others, lost in the predictable twists. Colin was as good as his word and didn't attempt to hold my hand or touch me unnecessarily, leaning away from me and giving up the entire armrest between us. I was actually sorry when the credits began to roll and the lights went up.

"Wow." Colin said, plucking my empty slushie cup from its holder.

"What?" I smiled. "The movie wasn't that impressive." I

pulled my jacket on as I followed him toward the theatre exit.

"I just can't remember the last time I saw you actually laugh."

I thought for a moment. "Me neither."

I stopped by the bathroom as we left the theatre, and by the time I made it outside Colin and the others were waiting for me. It was only four-thirty, and the group decided to go into town and get some coffee. Colin, ever persistent, tried to convince me to go along.

While the guys were debating various options, I stood off to the side, considering. Back to my room and whatever might happen next with Izzy, or tag along and try to be normal for a few more hours?

Emily, arm draped around Gabe's neck, stopped talking to Danielle long enough to give me a pointed once over. "You should come," she said, voice loud enough to draw the rest of the group's attention. "After all, what's the point of getting all dressed up if no one *special* sees it?" Danielle stifled a giggle and Nate coughed awkwardly.

"No thanks." I smiled, my face stiff with a mix of cold and strain. *Back to the room then.* "I have a lot of homework to catch up on."

Colin, who at least had the decency to look as awkward as I felt, shuffled over to me. "Hey, let me walk you," he suggested quietly. "It's the least I can do after…." He jerked his head toward the others.

"I'm fine." I patted Colin's shoulder with one stiff arm extended, the way you'd pet an unfamiliar dog. "Go have fun with your friends." I gave him what I hoped was a friendly shove in the direction of the others. A small frown passed over his face, but he acquiesced and headed to the group.

With a perfunctory wave, I headed for the far end of the parking lot, planning to cut back through the neighborhood. I'd barely made it out of old Downtown and onto a residential street when I felt, rather than heard, someone coming up fast behind me. I had the earbuds in again, but there was a slight movement behind me as though someone was reaching out to grab me. It was enough to trigger my self-defense training, accumulated through years of conditioning as an urban cop's daughter and an alcoholic's punching bag, and solidified in a women's self-defense class I'd taken the previous semester. I ducked my head to my shoulders and bent my knees as I spun around, extending my right leg in a sweep as my hands pulled my attacker forward, using his momentum against him. I only had a moment to realize it was Colin before he hit my leg and went down.

Colin's face was twisted in pain as he rolled over onto his back, clutching his wrist. I scurried toward him. As I got closer, Colin sat up, cursing under his breath as he pulled away from me.

"Wow, Colin, I am so sorry." I knelt back down next to him, gently touching his shoulder. Colin had managed to use his arms to break his fall, but he had road rash on the base of both palms and holding his right wrist at a delicate angle. I bit my lip. "I really didn't know it was you."

"I was yelling at you the last block," he pouted, a sour note bleeding through his gritted teeth.

"I had my earbuds in," I replied weakly, shoving the dangling cords into my pocket. "I feel awful."

"No, it's okay. It's my fault. I should know better than to sneak up on a girl like that. It was obvious you didn't hear me when you didn't stop." He reached back with to push himself up, grimacing as gravel pressed into his torn flesh.

"Here, let me help you." I grabbed him under one arm, pulling him to his feet.

"Thanks."

"Can I see your hands?"

Colin extended his palms toward me. His left hand looked like it would be okay after it was cleaned and bandaged, but his right had little bits of gravel embedded in it. His hands were nothing compared to his right wrist, which looked terrible.

"We can head back down to the hospital."

He shook his head. "I don't want to go to the hospital for a few scrapes. I can go to the Health Center when they open Monday morning."

"Don't be stubborn. First of all, you need to have that gravel picked out of your hand. Secondly, you may have broken your wrist. You need someone to look at it, and you can't wait until Monday. Let's go to the hospital."

"I can't go to the hospital. Not without a campus referral, anyway. Not unless it is an obvious emergency." He tried to turn away from me, but I tightened my grip on his good arm, forcing him to look me in the eye. What I saw there, hiding underneath the good grooming and polished exterior, surprised me. It was shame.

Colin must have been on the same bare bones college health

insurance I was. It was what you used if you were independent like me and didn't have local insurance to supplement your own, or if your parents weren't getting benefits because they weren't working. From the way his face burned with a deep red that flowed up his neck and into his cheeks, I was betting it was the latter.

"Alright," I pretended to give in. "I'll make a deal with you. If you let me take you to Campus Security and have them look you over, I'll be satisfied. If they clear you to wait until Monday, we'll wait. If they say you need to go to the hospital, then we will go to the hospital— together. Deal?" I could not imagine anything I wanted to do less than go to the hospital with Colin, but I knew if Campus Security referred Colin then the Health Center would make sure his insurance covered the treatment.

He swallowed and nodded. "Deal."

We began walking slowly back up through the neighborhood toward campus, Colin cradling his injured wrist. We walked in silence, and I was surprised to find it wasn't unpleasant. With some people, silence would sit with you, heavy and suffocating; Colin's silence was companionable.

Maybe it was because we both loved Izzy, but I found a solace with Colin I didn't seem to find with other people. It was comforting to be with someone without feeling pressured to talk. Everyone else turned my silence into a problem, a sign I must be in crisis over Izzy. Every second I didn't speak would loom larger and larger until I had to talk to keep from drowning in it. Colin seemed to accept my silence as merely as merely an indication I had nothing to say.

We walked for about twenty minutes, listening to the sound of the wind, the thrum of tires on wet concrete, and our own breathing.

When we were about a block from campus, he finally broke the quiet. "Can I ask you something?"

"Sure," I said, feeling generous after the small bit of peace between us.

"Where did you learn to do that?" I shot him a quizzical glance. He cleared his throat, and tried again. "Where did you learn to fight?"

"Oh! The leg sweep?"

He nodded, seeming both intimidated and impressed. It brought a smile to my lips. "I'm the only daughter of a cop in a huge family of cops, Colin. I grew up in the big mean city, not in some small town with a one-cell jail like you," I teased, bumping his uninjured shoulder lightly with my own. "I think I was eight when my dad started teaching me to stomp an insole and go for the eyes."

I reached into my pocket for my keys, which were attached to a karabiner big for me to fit my hand through. I held it up where he could see it. "I don't carry this monstrosity because I'm afraid I'll end up locked out when I inevitably lose them." He looked dubious. "Okay, fine, I probably would lose them otherwise, but in an emergency this also doubles as a set of brass knuckles." I fit my hand through the metal ring and curling my fingers into a fist, a set of sharp keys lying across the top of my knuckles.

Colin paled and stopped short. He looked so startled that I laughed out loud, deep and full. I shoved the keys back in my pocket. "What's wrong? You suddenly afraid of a little girl with a handful of metal?"

"Did she know how to do that?" My good humor drained out of me like water rushing into a storm grate. I didn't have to ask him who or what; I knew.

"No. Izzy couldn't fight. We weren't really sisters, remember?" The words were heavy and sad. "Izzy was raised to believe the world was a much safer place than I was."

I looked down at the ground, the piles of wet leaves barely visible in the gathering of early dark, and thought of her lying there. I had to swallow hard to keep the tears from coming and washing my strength away, right there in the middle of the street. I turned and started walking again, forcing my feet to keep moving. Colin caught up and fell in beside me. Watching him hold his wrist, I felt angry at him for being there, for coming after me, for getting hurt and making me take care of him.

"Can I ask you something?" I heard the edge in my voice and pressed on, not waiting for an answer. "What possessed you to follow me, anyway?" I didn't stop walking, but I turned my whole head to glare at him.

"I wasn't following you."

He kept his eyes on ground as though he was worried he might trip over something. White hot anger burned in my chest and threatened to burst the dam holding back the tears inside me. For a split second, I loathed Colin. I could not stand that one more person I liked could be so soft and weak in a world obviously intent on dealing out pain and punishment indiscriminately, even if that pain was caused by me.

Then the answer came, so soft it was almost a whisper: "I

didn't think you should be walking back all alone."

It dawned on me then that he had been trying to protect me, to show the care for me no one had shown Izzy. My anger turned inward, and I despised myself in turn, for being callous and ungrateful. That hatred—at Colin, at myself, at the world—squeezed my heart like a fist closing around it.

11.

Colin and I arrived at the edge of campus, cutting between the music building and the library to get to the Campus Security office. His face grew considerably paler as we walked. He kept it arranged in a careful mask of concentration, as though he was focusing all his energy on getting back to campus without complaining. His wrist had swollen up into a lump the size of a golf ball. It was obviously badly injured, but I understood well enough what it was like to be dependent on the Health Center for my own random scrapes and bruises that I knew better than to raise the issue again.

Getting checked out and referred to the hospital by Campus Security isn't going to hurt him any. My only hope was that Colin wouldn't pass out before we got there, because I wasn't up to carrying him or dealing with the attention an unconscious student would bring on an otherwise uneventful campus night.

By the time we reached Campus Security, his face had gone from pale as a sheet to beet red, and the whites of his eyes glowed under the lights in the parking lot. I scurried to open the door for him, standing to one side so he could pass. When he glanced at me, I expected to see a grimace or a smile. Instead, for an instant, I saw a hardness in his eyes that startled me. I sighed inwardly, feeling crushed beneath a heap of guilt and regret. I had a knack for bringing out the worst in everyone around me, even someone as mild and good-natured as he was.

Before I could think about it for too long, I heard a warm deep voice call out to Colin by name. My stomach flip-flopped in

83

response; I'd know that thick accent anywhere. I stepped into the office behind him and found Jay, his face friendly with concern, standing behind the waist-high counter. He was dressed in a Campus Security issue long-sleeved black uniform shirt with dark blue piping, a shield with the words "CAMPUS SECURITY" stitched over the left breast pocket in a gold thread. The heater was on full blast in the office, and Jay had his sleeves rolled half up, which made his forearms look even more muscular under the soft dark hair running down them. Jay didn't normally look muscular drowning in jeans and an oversized hoodie with the rest of us, but in his Campus Security gear he always looked stronger, more solid. I once again cursed my genetic predisposition toward trusting any man in a uniform.

As I stood there, trying to shake the inevitable Jay-related gut check of warmth, he caught me looking at him. A lopsided grin spread up his face, and he winked at me. I felt a slow burn start up my face in response. I quickly glanced over at Colin, who was watching my face with an intense curiosity, making me blush harder. He had obviously seen Jay wink at me, and from the look on his face, Colin guessed something was going on between us. I could feel the blush spread all the way to my hairline and hugged my arm to my side out of habit, trying to vanish from the awkwardness of the moment. Jay's mouth quirked in a self-satisfied smile at my obvious discomfort.

In an attempt to divert attention from the increasing tension, I blurted out, "Colin broke his wrist." The smile vanished from Jay's face as he turned to Colin, who looked as mortified as I felt.

"He fell on our way back to campus," I continued vaguely. I hugged my arm harder. "I was hoping someone could check him out."

Jay bustled through the swinging door bisecting the counter and bent over Colin's hand, examining it with expert efficiency. Colin grimaced as Jay turned the wrist gently in his hands but he managed not to make a sound.

Without looking up, Jay addressed me. "Why didn't you take him to the hospital?"

I shot a look at Colin, who stared blankly in return. He was ashamed of being worried about the money and having to tell Jay, another classmate, about his financial predicament. I knew if anyone on campus would have understood, it was Jay, but I didn't have a way to communicate that to Colin, and I didn't want to embarrass him further.

"We were almost back to campus, so Colin and I thought it would be better to get someone here to look at before we walked all the way back down to the hospital," I lied. Jay nodded absently as he continued to look Colin over. Colin cast a surprised and grateful glance in my direction and I smiled in return.

As Jay worked, I got a better view of Colin's wrist. A large bruise had bloomed on the side, full of reds and purples, and the lump on the back of Colin's hand had swollen to the size of a golf ball.

Jay sighed as he completed his inspection. "The gravel would hurt like hell for me to clean out, but I could do it. The wrist, though, is so swollen I can't tell if it's severely sprained or broken. I don't think you'll be able to tell without an x-ray." Jay scrutinized Colin, who was growing paler by the minute. His face shone with a thin layer of sweat, but I couldn't tell if it was the overly warm office or from the exertion required to keep quiet as Jay examined his injuries.

"You should go to the hospital now, Colin. If it's broken, you need to know sooner rather than later," Jay concluded.

"So you'll give him a referral?" I asked, and Colin shot me a warning look. In an attempt to make it sound like a general question, I hastily added, "I mean, how does he get there? Do you give him a ride? Or do I go with him in a cab or something?"

"We will give him a referral slip. The AD-on-Call usually does the transport if you don't need an ambulance—" Jay turned back to Colin. "You don't, do you? Need an ambulance?"

"No." Colin remained seated, tipping his head back against the wall behind him. He seemed to be growing paler by the minute.

"I'll call the AD," Jay replied. He walked over to the counter and bent across it to grab the phone. As he dialed, Jay gave me a sideways look. "Should I tell them one transport, or are you going with him?"

"Oh, ummm…" I fumbled. On the one hand, I hated hospitals. Being in them reminded me of the months before my mother's death. Sleeping on cold plastic padded benches, the stale air that always smelled vaguely chemical… I shuddered at the memory. On the other hand, I felt like I owed it to Colin to keep him company. It seemed like the least I could do.

I knelt in front of Colin. "Do you want me to go?" I asked quietly. As soon as the words were out, I wanted to kick myself.

How could I be such a wretched friend to the one person who had treated me like I wasn't a pathetic freak? "I'm happy to, if you want me there."

"No," he said dully. "I can go by myself." His tone was expressionless, and there was an emptiness in his eyes that made me feel indescribably sad for him. Colin didn't have anyone else to go with him; he didn't have a roommate and his best friend was attending a college in Portland about two hours away.

"Really, Colin," I pressed, tilting my head up to look in his eyes. I placed a careful hand on his shoulder in an attempt to comfort him. "I'm happy to go with you. You shouldn't have to go alone, and," I lowered my voice and leaned in to keep Jay from overhearing, "I kind of owe you the company, all things considered."

Colin smiled wanly at me and shook his head. "No," he whispered back. "It was my fault for scaring you. This?" He raised the wrist he cradled to his body in his other hand. "This is my penance for being an idiot."

I opened my mouth to protest again, but he cut me off. "You've had a long day. Go home, watch some Netflix, get some sleep. I'll be fine," His tone held a confidence I was sure he didn't feel. He leaned his head toward me, his lips almost touching my ear. "I'll call you in the morning." It was a statement that sounded more like a question, giving me permission to turn him away.

"Alright," I agreed, pushing myself away as I stood. I turned back to Jay, who had finished the call while Colin and I were talking. His eyes flicked back and forth between Colin and me in a calculating way. I met his questioning gaze with my own. "So?"

Jay seemed to shake himself. "Mike will be here in about ten minutes." Jay pulled a first aid kit out from behind the counter. "In the meantime, why don't I clean out your left hand, Colin?"

Obviously taking Colin's silence as permission, Jay dragged a chair around the counter and pulled it up in front of Colin, who was seated on the small bench in the office lobby. Jay then disappeared back into the far recess of the office and returned with a small bowl of water and damp washcloth. He sat the items on the bench next to Colin, then flipped the chair around, straddling the back. Taking Colin's hand and resting it, palm up, on the back edge of the chair, Jay folded the washcloth and began gently wiping at Colin's hand.

Given the small space in the lobby and the green cast tingeing Colin's face, I didn't think it was a good idea to sit down on the bench in case Colin puked everywhere. Unfortunately, Jay's chair didn't leave a lot of room to move around him toward the doorway, and I didn't want to make him stop helping Colin so I could leave. Regardless of what Colin said, it seemed wrong to bail before his ride showed up.

After leaning awkwardly in the corner for a few minutes, I hoisted myself up on the small counter that made a window in the wall. I had to take my coat off to manage the maneuver without falling or kicking someone, but the small office was so stuffy I didn't mind. The counter was high enough that my feet dangled well off the ground.

From this angle, I could watch Jay work on Colin's hand. Colin kept his eyes closed, choosing not to look. After Jay swabbed the hand a bit to loosen some of the dried dirt and mud and gently cleaned it with a towel, the scratches didn't look half as bad. Jay used a pair of tweezers to remove two tiny pieces of gravel that were impacted, then he cleaned Colin's hand again. Finally, he covered the scratches in a thin layer of antibacterial ointment and expertly applied a clean gauze pad to the wounds, wrapping it in place with an ACE bandage. The whole process was completed in a matter of minutes with a neutral efficiency that impressed me.

As Jay was finished, Mike Fuchs came through the office door. Seeing me sitting on the counter, legs swinging back and forth, Mike's face pulled into a disappointed grimace, obviously assuming I was the one in need of a hospital visit.

"Hey Mike," Jay said as he gathered up the first aid supplies. "Your transport is right here." He motioned toward Colin, and I smiled smugly at Mike, who only shook his head at me in response. Mike helped a shaky Colin to his feet and made to open the door for him.

"Bye Colin," I said softly. "Call me and let me know how you are?"

Colin stopped in the doorway. Despite his apparent discomfort, he gave me a genuine smile. "Of course."

Mike snorted as he placed a gentle hand on Colin's back, pushing him through the door and out into the darkness.

12.

"So." Jay's voice pulled my attention back to him. He was staring at me, his eyes serious. I thumped my foot against the wall beneath me nervously as Jay finally took in my nice clothes and makeup, making the seemingly logical leap everyone else had. At this rate, the whole campus would be buzzing about my non-existent date with Colin before the weekend was over.

"I should head home," I said as I tried to figure out how to gracefully get down from the counter without biffing it.

"Here, let me help you." Jay moved toward me, hands extended.

Unfortunately, I had chosen that exact moment to hop off the counter. As I half-landed on Jay's feet, I flailed wildly, managing to knock one of his arms away as he tried to steady me.

Luckily, Jay was more solid on his feet than I was. He threw his other arm around my waist as I lost my footing altogether, pulling me into his chest to steady me. I felt his palm pressed against the small of my back and looked up to find myself staring into his face. As I fought the pull of his warm gaze, I was suddenly aware of the starched feel of his uniform shirt beneath my fingers, trapped again his chest. My heart pounded in my throat, and the sound of my shaking breath filled the empty room.

We stood there, clasped in an awkward embrace, the rise and fall of Jay's chest quickening with my own. His eyes were unreadable, seeking something from me I couldn't put into words. I felt dizzied by our closeness, which immediately turned to anger at my own discomfort. I felt my lips purse together automatically in irritation, embarrassed flames rising up my neck and licking along my cheekbones. Jay's face hardened in response. He straightened instantly, releasing me from his arms.

I'm pissing off everyone tonight. I grabbed my coat and yanked it on. Jay stepped in behind me and took hold of the collar as I tried to get my arm into the second sleeve.

"Thanks," I muttered.

"Don't mention it," he said stiffly as I found the armhole and pulled the thick fabric into place.

I was already flustered by my feelings for Jay, and his coolness left me even more untethered. The only thing I knew for sure was that I needed to get out of the office. Grabbing my purse, I turned toward the door to find Jay opening it ahead of me. He'd managed to get his own coat on while I was struggling with mine, and he had a large set of keys in his right hand.

Jay called out to say he was going on rounds and another officer I didn't recognize emerged from the back of the office. Without a word, I pushed past Jay and heard him follow me out, the door jingling shut behind him. Not wanting to extend the tenseness between us, I immediately headed for my hall on a darkened path next to the building.

"Callie," Jay called after me. My embarrassed anger thrummed in response and I doubled my pace.

"Callie!" he barked, more an authoritative demand than a request, undoing my feeble grip on my irritation.

"What!" I wheeled around to look at him, wrapping my arms

across my chest for warmth. With the waning sunlight and the lengthening winter nights, the air had grown considerably colder while I was in the office. The gentle pat, pat, pat of the light rain falling into pools around me fed the deepening shadows. Jay stood beside one of the Campus Security SUVs, holding the passenger side door open.

"Get in the car." He pointed a finger at the passenger seat. "I'm driving you back." His expression was full of determined self-confidence and it reminded me of my dad and all my cop cousins, who became so accustomed to people doing what they said in their professional lives that they took it for granted that everyone would always jump when they were told to.

Irked at the assumption, I started to say no out of spite. At that particular moment, however, a brisk wind swept up the path, cutting through my thin coat and covering my face in a light mist of rain. I'd taken a deep breath in unconscious anticipation of yelling at Jay at the wrong moment, and the icy air made my chest hurt; instead of a protest, I doubled over coughing. When I managed to stop coughing, Jay was still standing there, holding the passenger door open like an overly patient chauffeur.

I stomped back to the SUV. I knew I was being childish, but I was frustrated, both with myself for being weak and with Jay for always sensing it when I was.

I climbed past him into the dry interior, determined to keep my mouth shut for the handful of minutes it would take to reach my dorm. I noticed the triumphant smirk on Jay's face as he closed my door with a snap. He hopped into the SUV, pulling carefully out of the parking lot and back onto the main road without a word of acknowledgement.

Inside my stomach churned with mixed emotions like a swarm of angry bees. What was it about me that screamed vulnerable? I was used to Jay hovering a bit, but even Colin had insisted on following me back to campus. Why couldn't anyone just treat me like normal? I knew it was because I hadn't been acting like myself since Izzy died, but that didn't mean I wanted to be treated like a child. Even when people were trying to be nice, it was just too much.

They don't share my grief, but they can't accept that I can feel it and yet not need their pity. It hit me that everyone on campus was acting the way my teachers and neighbors had when my mother died. Everyone tiptoed around my father and I for a while, too polite to pretend it wasn't happening, yet simultaneously seemingly untouched by the way it changed our lives. They'd talk quietly if we were in earshot, say apologetic things to my father full of tuts and coos, but then they'd moved on. We never really did move on, though, not as a family. It changed everything for me, but I'd managed to survive, even if he hadn't.

Now it was the same thing all over again, only the teachers had PhDs and I couldn't hide out at home to avoid awkward interventions with the school counselors. But I still didn't want everyone watching me, waiting for me to either give up entirely or move on. Maybe it was that simple for them, but not for me. My emotions were not an A/B test, something I could switch on or off.

If no one else missed Izzy the way I did, that just told me they were idiots. But I still wanted them to acknowledge that everyone, even someone like me who fell down but kept getting back up, could be angry. Could be sad. Could have their heart truly and maybe finally broken by losing another person they loved.

And that I could feel *all* of those things and still be strong.

Part of me knew this was Jay's way of looking out for me, but it felt overbearing in that same tentative way. Like he was waiting for me to fail, to fall down. Like he got something out of being the one who got to pick me back up.

Even if I did think Jay was hot, and he was, admittedly, pretty hot, I didn't want to date someone who thought they had to take care of me, who got a jolt of superiority out of my moments of weakness. I felt confused by Jay's constant mixed messages: did he see me as someone who was his equal, someone he wanted as more than a friend, or as a kid sister he constantly had to drag out of trouble? Why would he want to date someone like that—because it was easier to control them? Well, if Jay thought he could control me, he obviously didn't know me.

If Izzy was here, she'd tell me I was doing my best impression of Amelia, I thought, remembering of the routine tantrums of the preteen Miller middle child. The criticism stung because I knew, in my heart, it was true. I was being stupid and stubborn, acting out of will to prove I still could. I should have been grateful for the ride; instead, I grudgingly pressed my lips firmly together, rubbing my hands against my arms as I shivered in the silent car. Jay automatically turned the heat on in response to my unspoken need, turning both vents toward me. He seemed completely unaffected by my temper tantrum, relaxing back in the seat and stretching one arm along the edge of the window as he drove.

It only took a few minutes to get my building. I hoped he'd drop me off and continue on his rounds, but he pulled into a parking space near the back door and cut the engine. Part of me wanted to jump out right away, but for some reason, I hesitated.

The warm air in the truck slowly cooled as the silence deepened and spread around us, reverberating like waves from a stone thrown into a smooth lake. Normally being with Jay made me twitchy and nervous. Instead, my own exhaustion waylaid me. I laid my head back against the seat and gave into it, waiting for Jay to say whatever it was he wanted to say or for me to give up and get out of the car.

"So, when did you start dating Colin." It was a statement, not a question. I jerked against the seatbelt in surprise. I turned toward him, but Jay stared hard out the windshield. I couldn't catch his gaze.

"I'm not." His eyes rolled toward me witheringly. "We went to see a movie today with a bunch of other people," I spluttered defensively. "He made it very clear it was a friends thing or I wouldn't have gone." I couldn't believe Jay's gall. "Why is it any of your business anyway?"

"It's not," he replied neutrally. I couldn't read his expression from this angle and undid the seatbelt to turn sideways in the seat, facing him fully. His hands were on the steering wheel, working it beneath his grip. "Did Izzy ever talk to you about Colin?"

I was so stunned you could have knocked me over with a feather. What did Izzy have to do with this?

"Sure," I replied slowly. "She complained about him following her around all the time, but that wasn't exactly unusual, you know?" Jay looked at me intently as I searched my memory for anything Izzy had said that seemed out of the ordinary. "Lots of guys chased Izzy. Colin was certainly more persistent than others, which annoyed her, but she never made it seem like a big deal. Why?" I demanded, suddenly suspicious. "What did she say to you about Colin?"

Jay stared hard at me, his dark eyes black and inscrutable in the darkness. "Nothing, Callie." I squinted at him, searching his expression for the slightest change. I was pretty sure he was lying; at minimum, he wasn't telling me everything he knew. "Izzy complained to me about it, too, that's all."

"Complained? Like griped about it to you her friend, or complained like filed a formal complaint with Campus Security?"

"She never filed a formal complaint," he said eventually, frowning at the memory.

"Did she say he hurt her?" I pressed. "Or said something hurtful?"

"No," Jay admitted. "I just didn't like the way he was always following her around after she said no. I told her as much."

"What did Izzy say?"

"She laughed," he admitted with a sigh. "She said Colin was annoying, but he wasn't scary. She said I'd obviously been away from home too long if I didn't recognize a real pursuit when I saw one." He rubbed his hands against his face, and when he pulled them away I could see the tiredness lurking underneath.

"Jay, look," I began, picking my words carefully. I appreciated his concern for Izzy and for me, but I couldn't help picturing Colin's face as he flew over my leg. "Colin can be…overzealous," I said finally. "I know that. I watched him take beating after beating from Izzy and keep coming back for more. But trust me, he couldn't hurt a flea. He doesn't have it in him."

"Are you sure about that?" From Jay's doubtful expression I could tell he wasn't reassured by my assessment. It flummoxed me that Jay saw Colin as a threat to Izzy or anyone else.

"Colin and I have talked about Izzy. Colin felt very sure of his feelings; he was confident he could win Izzy over. It was kind of sweet. A little pathetic, but sweet."

Jay only shrugged in disagreement, and I pressed on. "He loved her, Jay. I think he still does. He wouldn't hurt her," I concluded, feeling sure of my words as I remembered how nice he'd been to Izzy while she was alive. "Colin is one of the only people who hasn't treated me like crap since Izzy died, and I haven't exactly been a pleasure to be around."

Jay nodded absently, seeming lost in thought. "Maybe you're right. I just worry—"

"About me, right?" I pursed my lips. "Don't be. If you thought Izzy could handle Colin, then you *know* I'll be fine." I took his distraction as an opening. "Thank you for the ride," I said, making my exit.

"Wait," he said, unbuckling his seatbelt and opening his door. "I'll walk you in." He seemed calmer again, the easygoing Jay resurfacing.

"Thanks," I said, slamming the door a little as I strode past his side of the car, "but I think I can make it to my room without hurting myself."

"I'm not worried about your ability to walk up a flight of stairs," he said, reaching back to adjust his collar as he followed me. "I'm here for the protection of the greater AC student body. I wouldn't want you breaking anyone else's wrist if they got in your way."

I froze. Casting a sheepish glance back, I was greeted by Jay's trademark smirk. "How did you know?"

"I think the better question is, how did you do it?"

"Leg sweep….and I kind of threw him." I busied myself swiping open the door to hide my embarrassment.

Jay chuckled as he reached over my head, grabbing the door to hold it as I entered ahead of him. "Nice. Did he try something?"

Big brother was obviously back in full-on nosey mode. "No," I hissed, as we climbed the stairs to the second floor and walked down the empty hallway toward my room. "I told you, it wasn't a date. I left the movie theatre alone to head back to campus. Colin decided to follow me. I felt someone coming up behind me, and I didn't think about it. I threw him."

Jay stood behind me as I got my keys out, and I couldn't help but smile wearily when I looked up to find him grinning like an idiot. "The wrist," I said as I turned the key and opened the door, "was an accident. But how did you know?"

"I've seen enough injuries from fights to know what I'm looking at. No way did Colin hit the ground hard enough to do that much damage by tripping. I knew he'd had help from someone, and from your guilty expression I assumed it was you." My face turned scarlet. "I'll be surprised if you didn't break his wrist. That must have been one spectacular throw." He beamed at me with pride, and I shook my head in response.

Jay followed me into the room without invitation as I reached to flick on the lights. I don't know why it hadn't occurred to me Izzy might do something while I was gone. It just hadn't. Then it was too late.

Izzy's side of the room, which had sat bare and empty since her parents took her things away, was awash in colorful decoration. A blanket Crystal made me covered Izzy's small twin bed. A poster of Van Gogh's "Starry Night" I'd kept in a poster roll in my closet was tacked up on the bulletin board above it, and a row of books had been taken from their plastic storage tub under my bed and lined up along the small shelf over Izzy's desk. It wasn't a lot, but all of the sudden it looked as though two people lived in the room instead of one. My first thought was that the Housing Office had moved someone into Izzy's space without telling me.

Once I recognized it was my stuff scattered around the room, the pattern was obvious. Izzy had picked very specific things to decorate with, things that would remind me of her. All of the books were ones she'd given me or we'd bought together. The poster was from the annual campus poster sale the previous fall; Izzy severely mocked me for choosing it after we discovered it gracing approximately one out of every five firstie rooms on campus, which was why I'd kept it stashed away when we'd moved in this year.

The blanket was part of a coordinating set Crystal made for

Izzy and I, hers a bold red with gold binding, and mine a deep blue with silver. They were made to fit our double beds at home, so the blanket fell all the way to the floor. I'd put it away when the weather turned colder in October in favor of my heavy duvet, but Izzy had still been using hers when Greg and Crystal came to pack her belongings. A couple of green throw pillows from my bed were tossed neatly into either corner, giving the bed the appearance of a makeshift couch. The effect was pretty and well put-together, but also reflected my tastes rather than Izzy's. As I ran my fingers along the edge of the bed and felt the satiny fabric crinkle under my fingertips, I could feel the tears gathering my eyes.

"It looks nice," Jay said, startling me from my reverie. I'd been so caught up in Izzy's latest demonstration I'd forgotten he was there.

"Yeah, it does." I shook my head to clear it of tearful thoughts and hugging my arm to my side to cover the aching sob bubbling in my chest.

"I bet she'd like it," he said, and I felt his hand close gently around my arm. Jay stood so close I could feel his breath flutter the back of my hair, and I shivered, but I couldn't tell if it was from his presence or Izzy's handiwork.

"Actually she'd hate it," I replied without turning around. "But she knows I'd like it. I guess that's what counts." A small smile played across my lips. Izzy appeared to be much less critical of my taste in death than she was in life.

"Callie…" I could feel the warmth radiating from Jay in the cold room, a comforting presence. I suddenly felt compelled to tell him everything—about Izzy, about the messages, about how she needed my help. I wanted someone, anyone, to believe me and to believe that Izzy was still here, still real, still waiting to be saved. I knew it sounded insane, but maybe Jay would believe me. No matter how I pushed him away, Jay kept coming back for more, even when I seemed to repel everyone else. Maybe he would believe me. Maybe he was the one person I could trust.

I turned to face Jay and the closeness of his body overwhelmed my senses. I could see the loose thread on the open button at his collar and smell his soap, a warm mixture of fir and sandalwood. He smelled like the giant trees standing outside my window, sturdy and strong and always green with life and purpose, even in the darkest parts of winter.

Wow, did I want to kiss him. Or maybe I wanted him to kiss me. Either way, I definitely wanted there be kissing. And, if I was honest, maybe a little more than kissing…

I felt Jay tense as he raised a tentative hand toward my face, closing his thumb and finger around a strand of hair near my chin. "I should…" Instead of stepping away, his weight shifted closer to me. I could feel the edge of the bed at the back of my knees.

Okay, definitely more than kissing.

Part of the reason I'd never had a boyfriend, or even seriously dated anyone, was that I'd sworn I'd have a different life than the one I'd grown up with. All those missives the old Southern Baptist women in my neighborhood preached about the trap of young love, older men, and innocent seeming kisses that quickly turned to early pregnancy and no education? I'd taken those to heart.

Izzy might have scandalized the fine ladies of the PTA by being good at dating without getting serious, but I knew myself well enough that if I started something, it was likely to stick. It's just who I was. While other girls fought with their friends and called everyone their "BFF," I'd had exactly one best friend, ever. Only one. She was all I'd ever wanted. If I trusted someone enough to let them in and really let down my guard, I knew they'd be there forever.

Jay didn't strike me as someone I could be casual with, if such a thing existed for me. If I gave in and kissed him now, it wouldn't be the last time. Staring up at him, the larger part of me didn't care anymore. I liked Jay. I more than liked him. I always had. Standing together in a room so quiet I could hear our hearts pounding, I was pretty sure Jay more than liked me, too.

Why not give in? Jay was a strong, solid presence, and at this point I needed one. He knew I was fiercely independent to my own detriment sometimes, but he respected my autonomy and my mind. On more than one occasion, he'd commented about how smart he thought I was, and Izzy told me, back when she was trying to set us up, that Jay once admitted to her he thought I was the most intelligent woman he'd ever met. I'd floated on that compliment for a week, all the while pointedly ignoring him. For all his southern manners, Jay had never tried to tell me what to think or how to be. I was pretty sure he never would.

On paper, he was the spitting image of my father, and his father before him. The thought of getting emotionally and physically involved with someone like Jay terrified me for so many reasons, not the least of which being that I didn't know how I'd managed to jump from no serious boyfriends ever to contemplating telling my troubles to someone, let alone Jay specifically. And if I told him about Izzy, if trusted him enough to tell him what was happening, that seemed just as serious as admitting I wanted him. Maybe more. Kissing Jay, however serious, might be dismissed later as a moment of weakness in the face of wild attraction. But telling him about Izzy?

It would be mean trust.

And I was not good at trust.

The thoughts whipped through me in seconds, but it felt as though a lifetime passed while my entire worldview wobbled on its axis. I felt a breath catch in my throat as I looked up into his eyes. In the shadows of the florescent lights they turned a dark brown color that threatened to swallow me with their intensity. If I was going to tell someone, anyone, this was it; this was a person I could trust, maybe with my life…and maybe with Izzy's, whatever was left of it.

"Jay, I…" I looked down, trying to figure out a way to tell him that would sound the least crazy.

"It's fine," he said quietly. "This isn't the right time. I'm happy to see how much better you're doing." He pushed the strand of hair in his fingers behind my ear before stepping away from me, surveying the new décor again. "It's nice to see you taking up space, making the room your own. I think Izzy would be happy to see you moving on with your life."

Reality smacked me hard, shoving all thoughts, romantic and otherwise, right out of my head. Jay didn't think my dorm makeover was Izzy's doing. The thought had never occurred to him. Of course it hadn't. Only an insane person would jump to such a conclusion, and anyone who said it *was* the handiwork of a very dead girl was in need of serious help. Jay had assumed, as any normal person would, that the decorations were an indication that I was starting to put Izzy's death behind me, not as a sign Izzy was still very much part of the here and now.

And why wouldn't he? I thought, looking at the blanket and pillows. *It might make sense if you…if you didn't know what she meant to me.*

Jay was a good guy, maybe even a friend, but nothing more. To see Izzy's hand in this, you'd have to know Izzy and me, *really* know us: what we were like when we were together, what we wouldn't and wouldn't do for each other. You'd have to have *loved* her…or me.

And Jay, good as he was, wasn't that guy.

Jay liked what he thought he saw in me, but it was only his idea of the girl wearing my clothes. I had a lot of secrets I'd brought along to college, and I'd made damned sure no one other than Izzy knew about them. Jay's image me of was picture largely painted by my matchmaking BFF, and Izzy had a habit of making me seem …lighter than I was. More fun; less severe. I think that's who she'd wanted me to be.

Maybe that girl, that imaginary Callie, was someone who would have already claimed all this space as her own. But he hadn't really known Izzy and he certainly didn't know me if he thought I would be so casual about letting her go. Maybe that made me crazy, but that was who I was. I wasn't a person who would have taken Izzy's bed when she'd been dead no more than a month. I wouldn't have taken anything from her, ever, not unless she gave it to me.

I pulled my arm around my middle again, hugging myself against the emptiness crashing down on me. *No*, I thought, giving my head a small shake, *Jay is nice and he makes me trembly down to my toes, but he would never believe me.*

He stood by the door, quietly watching me. The warmth in his eyes had been replaced by a neutral blankness as he took in my change of demeanor, cataloguing it away for some future incident report. He was too grounded, too rational. If I told him, he'd be the first to testify at my commitment hearing. He wasn't a person you could tell your secrets to, and I had too many.

No. I wouldn't talk to Jay.

There was only one person I wanted to talk to now.

And, it occurred to me, that maybe it was possible I still could.

Only moments before I'd been falling into a fantasy of coming clean to Jay; now, I desperately wanted him to leave so I could try to talk to Izzy. I faked a yawn and as I moved across the room and flung myself down on my bed.

Jay glanced at the door, then back at me, "I should get back to the office." He opened and closed his mouth, as though he wanted to say something, then thought better of whatever it was.

"Out with it, Jay."

"Are you okay?" His eyes flicked over my face, puzzled. "A minute ago, it's like you were about to…"

"About to what?"

"I don't know. "He scratched at his jaw absently. "Something."

"I think the word you're looking for is study." I propped

myself up on my elbows. "I still have a mountain of reading to catch up on before finals." When he didn't make a move to leave, I rolled over, picking up a fat textbook off the floor. "Or maybe it was sleep? Seriously, going to the movies was more social interaction than I've had in weeks. And I don't know if you know this, but people? They can be kind of exhausting. At this point, my plans amount to curling up with this boring book until I pass out. I may not even make it to dinner."

Jay eyed me suspiciously, so I made a show of opening the book and beginning to read. After a minute, he shoulders slumped. "Good night, Callie," he said softly as he opened the door.

"Night, Jay," I called after him as the door closed with a quiet snick. I lay still, waiting for the telltale sound of his retreating clomping on the hallway stairs.

As soon as I was sure he was gone, I dropped the book back on the floor. I locked the door, then turned to Izzy's side of the room to examine the display again. I couldn't imagine anyone barging in, but if I was going to try to talk to Izzy, I didn't want to take the chance someone might interrupt us. I couldn't deny that Izzy was trying to talk to me. I had to try to respond, even if I didn't have the first clue where to start.

I stood in front of the bed, trying to discern some hidden message from the set-up. But other than moving stuff around the room, Izzy didn't appear to be saying anything in particular. I turned to the bookshelf. The books seemed to be organized in a haphazard way, but the titles didn't spell out anything I could discern, either by jotting down the first word in each title or even the first letters on a piece of paper I'd grabbed off my own desk. There seemed to be no hidden code, no matter how hard I looked. Feeling disheartened, I picked up a dog-eared anthology of American poetry Izzy and I shared for a class we'd taken together the previous semester. As I lifted the book from the shelf, I felt a jolt pass through me. My eyes closed reflexively in response.

I was in a large room, surrounded by high wooden shelves filled with books in a long aisle. Looking to the right, I could see a familiar unlit fireplace and two large plush chairs at the far end of the room. I realized I recognized the room; I was in the campus bookstore. I somehow knew that I should be there, but didn't know how or why. I had the strangest sensation of being in, but not in control of, my body.

Without intending to, I crouched down and grabbed a large soft cover book off the bottom shelf. Turning to its cover, I could see it was the same book as the anthology I'd been looking at in my room moments before, but it was brand new, the waxed paper cover gleaming beneath my perfectly manicured pink nails. I stared at the book, and my hand, which I knew immediately wasn't my hand.

I heard myself call out, "Callie, I found it," and the soft girlish trill wasn't my own. It was Izzy's.

Then a figure appeared at the end of the aisle. As she strode toward me, I took in her scuffed Doc Martens, worn jeans, and faded Gossip t-shirt. It was as though I was looking in a mirror backwards through time. I gasped with an internal shudder of horror at the scowling girl in front of me.

I was looking at myself.

My eyes flew open and I dropped the book as if it burned me. My left hand tingled and ached as though the nerves were enflamed. The fire licked its way up my forearm into my elbow, which twinged like I'd landed hard on my funny bone.

I stood rubbing my arm with my other hand as I stared stupidly at the book, trying to make sense of what had happened. I remembered being in the bookstore with Izzy the day we'd gone to get our books for the semester, but the memory was hazy and faded, a narrative outline in my mind of the events rather than a clear recollection.

Touching the book, I'd felt like I was there again, in the moment, going through the events in real time instead of flicking through spotty images in my mind, which was more like reading a flip book with sections missing. I knew instinctively that the memory wasn't mine. It was Izzy's. I'd been reliving the moment we'd bought the book, but from Izzy's perspective. I had been inside Izzy, but I wasn't in control. I couldn't move or speak of my own volition. All I could do was experience the moment as Izzy had experienced it, but in perfect detail.

My mind reeled. There was no way I could retroactively be in Izzy's body. It was weird enough to see her in the here and now, but to travel through time? To see myself, and not be myself? It was even more astonishingly impossible than the idea that Izzy might still be haunting me.

I started to reach for the book again but ended up clutching the desk as my head swam. My mouth was dry and, as the whooshing sound in my ears receded, I could hear myself breathing hard, like I'd been running. My arm ached with tiny, receding shocks; I wasn't sure how much more I could take of the sensation, which now ran the length of my arm as though I'd slept on it wrong. I felt weak and trembly all over.

I took a deep breath, exhaling slowly, then another. After a few minutes, I felt steadier on my feet. I bent toward the book, a discarded piled of pulp and glue on my floor. Its spine was broken, and it had fallen open to a section near the back. I brushed my fingers lightly over the text, waiting to feel the shock again.

Nothing happened.

I crouched down and, with another deep breath, placed my palm firmly against the pages.

Nothing.

Frustrated, I picked the book up with both hands, and, after a moment's consideration, closed the book and hugged it directly to my chest. Nada. My fear and my excitement began to morph into desperation. What did the book mean? What message was Izzy trying to give me? She had been here while I was out; where had she gone?

I dove for the bookshelf, touching the spine of the next book, then another, and another. Still, no visions of Izzy danced in my head.

"No," I whispered. I frantically pulled the books off the shelf and, after holding each one for a moment, dropped them in a pile on the floor. I needed to reconnect with Izzy. I knew in my bones she was trying to tell me how to help her or show me some critical piece of information I didn't have, something about the way she'd died, but nothing came.

By the time I'd thrown the last of the books to the floor, I was sobbing. I pulled the chair out from under the desk, ripping the cover off a large volume of Modern British history as I did so, and fell into it, defeated. What was I doing wrong? What had I done right the first time? Why was it only the one book? Was there something in the bookstore I was supposed to see, some clue to her death? I thought through every detail again and came up empty.

Gazing dejectedly at the literary mess scattered at my feet, I raised the chair leg slightly to kick the torn history text out from underneath me before I did it more damage. As the book flopped across the floor, it knocked into one of the chunky black heels Izzy'd put out for me. I'd returned the dress to the closet and put the shawl and earrings carefully back in the drawer where I kept a few sentimental things and my sparse jewelry collection, but I'd forgotten to put the shoes away. I knew the only reason I was keeping the shoes was because Izzy had given them to me. I'd never wear them, even with the large square heel I knew Izzy had chosen because I flatly refused to wear anything I couldn't easily balance on. They were ridiculous shoes, meant to look pretty for others and torture the owner; knowing me, if I ever tried to wear them, I would stain the satin or tear the ankle ribbons or find some other way to destroy them through the mere act of walking.

Beautiful, but impractical, like Izzy.

I was thinking of the day Izzy gave them to me as I leaned over to pick one up...

"Stand up straight," I heard myself say with breathy annoyance in a voice that was familiar but not my own. I leaned my head back up to find a version of me towering above. She frowned dramatically and pulled her back straight.

"I hate this," my doppelgänger muttered. A perfectly manicured hand popped into my field of vision as I reached out and grabbed the girl's ankle.

"Look," I said, pulling her leg out in front of the mirror mounted to the back of a door. Other-Callie grabbed my shoulder to steady herself as I turned her foot slightly so the tie of the ribbon winding to the top of her ankle showed in the reflection. "Look at how sexy that ankle is!" I demanded firmly.

Other-Callie grunted as she tightened her grip on my shoulder. "Though," I added, hearing the frown in the voice that was, and was not, mine, "the whole thing would look a lot better if you'd get a pedicure."

I studied the reflection of the foot in the mirror, focused on the task at hand. Other-Callie squirmed away from my grip, and I glanced up, catching my own image in the long mirror, short red hair sweeping along the side of my face...

When I came out of the memory, I was sprawled on top of the books I had yanked off the shelves. Apparently I'd pitched over on my face after picking up the shoe.

Every muscle in my back and shoulders ached as though I was

getting over a serious bout of the flu. I sat up gingerly and leaned my head against Izzy's bed, closing my eyes against the fluorescent glow of the light overhead. It took several minutes before I could even think about standing, but the light hurt my eyes enough that I willed myself to move. Turning it off, I switched on a small lamp on top of my dresser as I made my way carefully back to my bed. I curled up in the corner, pulling the covers tightly around me as I shivered against the cold that had settled over the room.

The alarm clock read 9:43 p.m. Had I been in the memory that long? Or had I passed out? The building's ancient heating system rattled and wheezed away as I pulled the covers tighter around me, but I couldn't stop my teeth from chattering. Surveying the mess, I'd made scattering the books across the floor, I shuddered at the crystal clear memory of being, and simultaneously not being, Izzy. It was surreal, being in her skin, trapped and unable to act, seeing myself and not being myself.

Spying the long ribbons of the fancy shoes in the pile, I considered my own memory of the day Izzy foisted the shoes on my unwilling feet. I could recall the events only as a hazy piecemeal rendition of the relived memory I'd experienced as Izzy. By contrast, Izzy's detailed account of the event was so perfect that it felt as though she's given me the shoes only moments ago. I could still make out every aspect of the relived memory in crystal detail.

The memory of the bookstore was the same. My own memory of the moment was dim, fragmented. Hers made me feel as though we'd only just returned with our purchases. I found myself unconsciously rubbing my fingers together at the thought of the brand new book in my hand.

As I mentally picked my way back through the afternoon, I looked for the key to unlocking access to Izzy's memories embedded in the objects.

What were the commonalities? I tried to make a list:

First, everything that triggered my transition into Izzy's body and memories was something Izzy had moved, and therefore touched, as a spirit. Second, I had been present for both events, and Izzy had been talking to or touching me during memories, so she was actively thinking of me at the time.

Third, I'd been focused on my shared connection with Izzy to each item as I'd touched it, thinking about our relationship and how the object figured into our shared history. I hadn't been thinking of anything specific when I'd touched the other books. Instead, I'd been so consumed by my frantic yearning for Izzy that I'd grabbed them to grab them. But when I'd focused in on the memory of trying on the shoes, a connection ignited. Maybe that was the key. Maybe I needed to access my own memories to get back inside the moment with Izzy.

But what did it mean? Was there some key to Izzy's death in all these lost moments suddenly regained, or was this merely her way of reaching out to me? I scanned the room for more objects that might bring Izzy's message a little closer but nothing jumped out at me. Izzy's selections seemed arbitrary—a textbook, a pair of shoes.

"How am I supposed to help you, Iz?" I wondered aloud, unsure if I was talking to myself or to her. "What do I need to do?"

I sat in the freezing room, silent, waiting for any sign, no matter how small. The wind whistled at the edges of my not-quite-perfectly sealed window. Low voices murmured through the walls and floors around me. Everything seemed too loud, and yet too quiet. Even my own breathing echoed in my ears as I strained for something, anything, that might guide me to her.

"Are you there?" My words were soft and a little shaky. "Izzy?"

A long moment passed, then another.

Wap! Wap! Wap! A staccato rhythm, quick and loud, sounded against my door.

13.

No, it couldn't be. I stared at the door, frozen. Even now, it was hard to believe that my dead best friend might be casually knocking on my door. The knock came again, slightly more insistent, and I clenched the blanket reflexively.

Then it was followed by a decidedly un-Izzy like cough in the hallway.

It's probably Jay, checking up on me again. I pushed myself off the bed, raking my fingers through my unruly hair in an effort to look more put together than I felt.

Be nice, but direct, I reminded myself as I opened the door. *He's sweet, you're grateful, but he'd never understand.*

"I know, I know, you're just here to verify my continued positive emotional progress," I began, quoting my therapist as I pulled the door open.

There stood Colin, still in his hoodie and muddy jeans, a broad smile on his face. As I gaped at him, he raised a cast-covered arm and gave me a small wave.

"I stopped by to tell you I was okay…" His gaze swept past me.

The room was a disaster. With the books thrown haphazardly across the floor and the blankets on my bed twisted in a pile, it looked like I had redecorated and then began trashing the room. The whole scene made me seem like an unstable loon, and if anyone knew what actually happened, they'd realize their first impression was dead-on. After all, hadn't I just been attempting my own star turn in an episode of *Ghostfacers*, complete with highlights from my best friend's life experienced through her now very dead body?

As the idea hit me, a sob and a giggle bubbled up in my chest simultaneously. I choked hard with laughter as tears streamed down my face. I had to grab the doorframe for support as I trembled with full-bodied exhaustion.

Colin cocked his head slightly to one side as he gazed at me in confusion. Then he took a big step toward me and, without a word, wrapped his arms around my waist. I leaned into him, burying my face in his shoulder as I sobbed. He only pulled me closer, rubbing circles on the small of my back with his good hand. I slid my arms around his waist and clung to him like a drowning woman clings to a life preserver.

What the hell am I doing? I was appalled with myself. Hadn't I been thinking about locking lips with Jay only a few hours ago? Now here I was, hanging on to this poor boy for dear life.

So much for being strong and independent.

Gracious as he was, Colin didn't seem to mind. We stood in the doorway as tears and snot running down my face and onto his hoodie.

Eventually I stopped crying, but I was so exhausted that I didn't let go right away. I turned my head sideways, my nose grazing his jaw I laid my cheek against the now damp fabric of his hoodie and waited for my breathing to slow. With each hiccupping wheeze, I inhaled a clean soapy smell gently wafting from Colin's neck and clothing.

He's so squeaky clean he even smells like detergent. I had to suppress a half-delirious giggle at the thought.

Colin didn't say anything; he held me gently, as though the calm settling over me would break if he jostled me the smallest bit.

It surprised me how much I didn't want him to let me go. It had been a long time since I had let anyone hold or comfort me. It was hard to give up, especially when everyone who loved me always seemed to leave or die or grow so sick inside they'd kill us both. At the same time, I was feeling together enough to realize that Colin, who had no idea what a mess I was, might be getting the wrong idea, which was the last thing I needed right now.

I let go of his waist and took a step back. Colin's arms drop away quickly. He tried to smile, but I could see the concern lurking underneath. I gave him a small smile in return, then swept my arm inward as an invitation. It seemed like the least I could do, given the circumstances. Colin stepped into the room, and I closed the door behind him.

"Redecorating?" His lips quirked.

I squeezed out a shaky laugh. "Something like that."

He gave the room an exaggerated once-over. "I like it. It has a kind of effortless quality. Very of the moment."

My laughter was cut short by the soreness in my ribs. "Exactly what I was going for."

I began picking the books up off the floor and quickly stacking them on Izzy's desk. I was afraid if I touched one for too long or thought too much about it I'd have an episode in front of Colin. I wasn't sure I could handle any more hysteria-inducing out-of-body incidents tonight, with or without an audience.

When the last novel hit the desk, I noticed Colin looking at ticket stubs from various movies, music, and shows I'd been to that were collaged haphazardly on the corkboard above my bed.

"Sorry. I need another minute or two to pick up. I wasn't expecting company."

"Don't sweat it," he replied without turning around. He seemed genuinely engrossed in looking at the stubs, so I turned back to the trashed side of the room.

Carefully picking up the ribboned heels, I began reciting lines from various movies in my head to avoid thinking too much about the shoes or Izzy. I braced myself, waiting to catapult into the past, but the shoes were only ridiculous footwear again. I placed them gingerly inside Izzy's old closet and slid the door closed. Finished with my tidying, I turned toward Colin at the exact same moment he turned to face me. Suddenly the space between us seemed uncomfortably narrow.

"So…" I started, but I couldn't think of anything to say. The air was choking with awkwardness as I studied the continent-sized tearstain I'd left on his shoulder. "I broke your wrist?"

"Yep," he said with a sad chuckle. "The ER doctor asked me if I'd gotten into a fight, and I had to tell him the person who kicked my ass weighed about a hundred pounds soaking wet."

"I weigh more than that!" I protested, crossing my arms over my chest as Colin looked me up and down dubiously.

"After all the weight you've lost? I doubt it."

Since when did Colin pay attention to my appearance? Before I could protest, he'd turned back to the ticket stub mosaic. I moved next to him in order to straighten the blankets on my bed.

"Is this every concert and movie you've ever seen?" he asked, gesturing to the two hundred or so stubs grouped haphazardly together.

"No, only the ones from the last couple of years." I sat down on the bed, then waved a hand, inviting him to take a seat. He settled on the edge.

"I've seen quite a few of these bands," he said casually.

"You have?" It was hard to picture Colin, properly attired in his matching belt and shoes, nodding along in appreciation with a scrubby, obscure-band-t-shirt-sporting crowd. "Where?"

Colin chuckled dryly at my obvious dubiousness and I pulled a little at my sleeve, embarrassed. "I only meant—"

"That you're surprised a small town hick like me knows anything about the indie music scene? We do have the ability to access music in rural America. We use this thing called the Internet." His eyes twinkled as he made air quotes around the words. "It's been described as a series of tubes…"

"I'm sorry," I backpedaled diplomatically. "I just meant I didn't think you'd get many live shows where you grew up."

Colin shrugged off the insult with ease. "We wouldn't have, but there was a small college in the town where I grew up, and we used to sneak into campus shows to see bands we liked."

"Crafty." *And completely out of character*, I added, trying to square the academically focused neat freak I knew with the image of Colin producing a fake ID for the exclusive purpose of rocking out to Pvris, Lambchop, or Bat For Lashes.

I watched him as he cocked his head to the right, then the left, reading each one as though he'd be tested on the contents later. It was strangely attentive and personal. I liked it. No one had ever spent so much time looking at them, but the collection was one of my most prized possessions. I kept the stubs in a box when they weren't on display and putting them up every year, choosing which shows or movies still made the cut and which ones didn't, was a ritual I'd started when I first moved in with the Millers.

"So you came by to tell me I broke you?" I asked, trying to find a graceful way to give Colin the opportunity to leave, even though part of me didn't want him to.

"And to see if you wanted to get pizza. I missed dinner."

My stomach rumbled as I considered the offer. "Pizza sounds amazing."

"We could hang out for a while," Colin ran his good hand down his jeans. "I mean, if you wanted to," he added, staring intently at his sleeve. I guess I wasn't the only one who didn't know how to act after my outburst.

I looked around the room, thinking about how long the day had been. I was tired and emotionally worn out. All I wanted to do was relax and avoid thinking too deeply about anything for a while. Watching a movie with Colin seemed like it would do.

"Sure," I said, trying to act more casual than I felt. "I think I'm going to go wash my face and clean up a little. Do you mind ordering?"

"Nope," Colin said, pulling his phone from his pocket. "I've got Delmonto's Pizza on speed dial."

I grabbed a pair of dark blue sweats with Astoria College printed down the leg and a college t-shirt out of my drawer. I could practically feel Izzy standing there, judging me. *This isn't a date*, I argued with the apparition in my head, *so sweats are perfectly acceptable. We're just hanging out.*

Great. Now we were having imaginary arguments.

I headed for the door and over to the bathroom. I quickly changed into my sweats and t-shirt and moved to the sink to wash my face. I'd cried or smudged off most of the make-up I'd put on that morning, but I took my time to thoroughly wash my face. I took my contacts out and put on my glasses. Looking at myself in the mirror, dark circles still visible beneath my frames, I looked about as non-date-y as possible.

I went back to my room. Colin wasn't there, but his shoes were neatly lined up next to Izzy's closet. He must have gone downstairs to meet the delivery guy. I stood in the center of the room, suddenly caught in the middle of a potential emotional minefield. What else had Izzy touched that might be waiting with a message for me? I eyed the new decorations warily. I had no idea what I looked like when I was caught in the trance of one of Izzy's memories, but I didn't want Colin to be the one to find out. I sat down with my back against my bed, figuring sticking to the bare floor was my safest option.

Colin let himself in, carrying a pizza box and a two-liter bottle of soda. I watched as he grabbed two mugs off a shelf over my desk and then sank to the floor, setting the pizza between us.

"Bon appetit." He poured a full mug of soda and held it out to me. I accepted it gratefully and sipped at the icy drink.

Pulling his hoodie off, Colin popped the lid up on the box. I watched as he nonchalantly folded a huge slice of pizza in half lengthwise, maneuvering it one-handed towards his mouth. The warm greasy smell of the cheese and pepperoni wafted toward me. Suddenly ravenous, I grabbed a slice in my hands, trying not to burn myself as I gobbled down the first piece and reached for a second. As I began shoveling the second piece into my mouth, I caught Colin watching me, eyes twinkling in amusement.

"Wha' so 'unny?" I managed around the food, struggling to swallow a huge bite.

"Nothing." Colin smoothed his face into a solemn expression. "It's nice to see you eat." Feeling self-conscious, I frowned and started to put the slice down. Colin held his hands out in protest. "No, really. I like a girl who eats. I eat! I swear! See?" he said, grabbing another piece and shoving half of it in his mouth.

I smiled. "Don't choke, Colin."

Between the food and the soda, I was starting to feel almost human again. *Maybe I should be eating more*, I mused. I felt a lot less fragile inside, as though I could sense the food spreading through my system, filling me up. A knot of tension inside me relaxed a little as whole minutes passed without any Izzy-related weirdness. Izzy hadn't sent me any kind of message with another person in the room. As long as Colin was here, nothing abnormal seemed likely to happen. It was a relief to feel like I had some control of my surroundings.

Colin and I finished most of the pizza between us. As we ate, we talked about everything and nothing: our classes, campus gossip I'd missed in the last month, movies we liked, bands we hated. At his insistence, I put the remaining two slices in my tiny fridge. It wasn't even eleven, and though I was exhausted, I still didn't feel like being left alone with my thoughts…or Izzy's. Colin looked anxious, too, as though he was sure any second I was going to throw him out.

And I should. I shouldn't keep him here just because I don't want to be alone.

Why? A little voice in my head whispered. *You're having a good time. Why is that bad?*

Because it's selfish. I feel like I'm using him.

He doesn't seem to mind, the voice responded suggestively. And he didn't. Colin was detailing his secret love for a certain country-turned-pop-princess' work. His smile was open and friendly, eyes twinkling as he laughed at himself even as he protested that the root of his affection was for her songwriting skills, not her impossibly long and shapely legs.

Well, I mind. I objected. *Because I don't like him like that, and it would be wrong to give him any other ideas.*

Would it?

Sitting with Colin, laughing and talking easily, effortlessly, maybe I wasn't so sure.

Maybe I was a little interested in him. I felt like a fraud for even considering it. Hadn't I been thinking about doing a whole lot more with Jay a handful of hours earlier?

Therein lay the problem with Jay. I might want him, but I

didn't trust him. Actually, it was me I didn't trust. I took one look at those dark eyes and sly grin, he said one syllable with that butter-melting mouth of his, and I lost all sense. I'd had a grade A example of that when I'd considered telling him about Izzy. Being with Jay might be exciting, but it was no way to live. Not for me.

And then there was Colin. Though I'd known him for almost a year and a half, I was surprised to find how much more there was to him than I'd guessed, certainly more than I'd imagined based on the things Izzy had said. But Izzy and I were different people. Colin and I had a lot of things in common that he didn't share with her, from our love of academics to financial difficulties to stupid stuff like movies and music. He wasn't exactly thrilling, but he wasn't threatening either. He had an easy West Coast casualness and while he was smart and nice and prone to open doors or pay for a girl on group outings, he wasn't ever going give me orders like Jay did.

Thinking about Colin and Izzy reminded me of his feelings for her, and my head spun. What *about* Izzy? Wasn't Colin still in love with her? Wasn't his love for Izzy a big part of why I liked him—because he missed her as much as I did?

Sneaking looks at Colin over the lip of my drink, I didn't feel friendly. I liked the way his neat blonde hair was cut a little too high over his ears, the way it contrasted against the dark brown t-shirt he was wearing. Watching him toy with the hem of his jeans as he talked, I couldn't help but smile.

Being with Colin made me feel better. It wasn't everything, but it was certainly a place to start. I wasn't sure about Colin's feelings for Izzy, but I wasn't sure about my feelings for him either. For now, we were friends, which was probably all I could handle.

Friends.

"Hello? Earth to Callie." Colin waved a hand in front of me, with a slight frown.

"Huh? Oh, I'm sorry." I realized I'd been so caught up in my own thoughts I'd missed whatever he'd asked me.

"I was saying you looked tired." His eyes shifted toward the door. "Do you want me to go?"

"No," I blurted, then blushed a little. "I mean, you can if you want, but I'm fine." A yawn escaped my lips, as if to contradict me. "Seriously, I'm good."

"Okay." We sat for a minute, looking everywhere but at each other.

"So, did you want to do something else?" I asked before I could stop myself. Colin's wide, toothy smile made my stomach do a little flip-flop.

"Sure," he replied. "Wanna…I don't know," he hopped to his feet as he cast around for something in the room to suggest itself. "Wanna watch a movie?" he asked, motioning to my laptop.

"That sounds great," I said as I began digging under my bed. Colin looked at me quizzically. I motioned him out of the way, pulling a large plastic tub out from under the bed, and saw the surprise on Colin's face as he took in the vast collection of DVDs.

"Wow. Maybe you haven't heard of the internet. You know you can download movies now, right?"

I swatted at him. "I like things I can touch."

"Noted." His eyes stayed studiously focused on the box, but he smirked at my unintended meaning.

"I have about a hundred," I said hastily, pulling the lid off so he could read the neatly organized alphabetical titles. "I bought most of them used when DVD rental stores started going under. Then, once I had a bunch, people kept buying them for me. Anyway, I've got a little of everything. What do you feel like?"

"Action? Comedy?" I suggested. "No horror," I added quickly, thinking of the run of zombie and ghost movies I'd acquired over Izzy's objections and how unsettling I found them now.

Colin repositioned the laptop on a desk chair in front of Izzy's bed so we could use it as a couch. It was a smooth maneuver which both impressed and depressed me.

Does that make him a gentleman, or does it mean he isn't interested? I wondered, then chided myself for assuming that just because Colin wasn't trying to crawl into my bed that automatically meant he wasn't interested. One of Izzy's chief complaints about Colin's niceness was that he never tried anything, which she deemed "BOR-RING!" I'd always thought it was a testament to how much he actually liked her.

Colin settled himself onto the makeshift couch, shoving a throw pillow behind his back. He hadn't even looked at the DVDs, but from the smirk on his face I knew he had something up his sleeve.

"What?" I narrowed my eyes as the grin spread.

"Oh," he said with mock innocence, "I was wondering what you had in the realm of vampire romances."

I blushed as Colin sniggered. "How did you know?"

"You've got at least two ticket stubs for every one of those movies on your wall," he said, ticking off the evidence as he went along on his fingers. "They're spread out like you're trying to hide that you have more than one, but I saw them. And I'd wager there are more in that box under your bed." I felt my face grow redder, confirming his suspicion.

"You have a hundred DVDs. I know you have those movies here somewhere. Probably the books, too. Don't even pretend you don't."

I nodded, too mortified to speak.

"Okay," he said, resting his elbows on his knees as he smiled at me. "I've never seen them. Any of them. But," he motioned to the ticket stubs, "you have pretty good taste, generally speaking. So if you like them that much, I'm willing to give it them chance."

I must have looked surprised, because he quickly added, "Let me rephrase: I'm willing to *try* the first one. We'll see how it goes from there."

I dug the movie out from a separate box under my bed, and popped it in the video player. The glare on the laptop from the overhead light made it hard to see, so I turned on the lamp on my desk and flicked off the overhead light. He patted the patch of the bedspread next to him. "Okay, let's get this sparkly show on the road!"

I approached the bed with trepidation. Izzy had put the bedspread there. Did it hold another one of her memories? I touched the fabric with only the tips of my fingers, ready to yank my hand away if the magical mystery dead girl show began, but nothing happened.

Stifling a sigh of relief, I settled in next to Colin as the sweeping exterior shots of the Pacific Northwest rolled across the screen. I shivered a little, hugging my knees to my chest for warmth. Without a word, he slid his arm hesitantly around my back, as though he was waiting for me to shrug it off.

An epic emotional war of guilt, glee, doubt, fear, and hope waged inside me for exactly thirty seconds. Then I settled in against him. I felt him release a happy sigh, and as I turned my head to look at up at him, I found him looking down at me. The space between our faces could be measured in inches. My breath quickened as I felt his knee start to bounce erratically. I stared into his eyes, which shone back at me.

Then, just like that, the moment was over. Colin turned his attention to the laptop and I settled my head against his shoulder.

As the movie I knew by heart played, I drifted in and out of sleep. Even in my half-conscious state, I was aware of Colin's arm around me as he shook with laughter. It was comforting. I hadn't meant to fall asleep, but I felt safe. It was nice to be held. It was nice to feel wanted. More than anything, though, I felt normal. I felt like a regular college girl with typical does-he-or-doesn't-he-like-me problems. I hadn't felt like that in a long time. After the last few weeks, it was a welcome relief.

I woke up to find Colin pulling his hoodie on. "I'm sorry. I guess I fell asleep," I said, sitting up. He had taken my glasses off and put them somewhere, making my view of him soft around the edges. I groped around, shoving them on so I could see him better.

"Yeah, you were pretty out of it," he said as he bent down to pull his shoes on.

"And you sat through that whole movie!" I ducked my head in embarrassment.

He reached out, pulling my chin up so he could look at me. "Actually, it wasn't terrible. The dad is pretty hilarious."

I started to smile back but yawned broadly instead, and covered my mouth. "Wow. I was more tired than I thought. Sorry I'm so boring." I slumped down and pulled one of the throw pillows under my head.

"Not boring." He shook his head, bright eyes suddenly serious. "Peaceful. You looked peaceful."

He walked over to the bed, pulling up the long edge of the blanket and tucking it around me. "Go back to sleep." He gently pulled the glasses off my face, setting them on top of Izzy's empty dresser.

I squinted up at the fuzzy outline looming over me, and a goofy, uncertain smile spread across my face. "Goodnight, Colin."

He leaned toward me, and I instinctively closed my eyes. An eager thrill of dread ran through me, a war between the desperate desire to be kissed and the simultaneous fear it would happen. I took a deep breath as I felt his face close to mine, his clean soapy smell all around me.

Soft lips brushed against my forehead, then pulled away. My eyes slid open as he opened the door and snapped off the lights, his dark outline backlit by the bright hallway fluorescents. "Good night, Callie," he called quietly, closing the door behind him.

I sighed as I listened to his footsteps fade down the hallway. Before I could spend too much time dissecting the evening or the needy mess I was turning into, descended back into an exhausted sleep. But as I drifted off, my last thoughts were of Colin and his smile.

14.

When I woke up Sunday morning, I lay under the blanket for a long minute, startled to find I'd spent the entire night in Izzy's bed. Given that Izzy had redecorated it for me, I found it didn't bother me as much as I would have expected. Her permission somehow resolved my reluctance. If she wanted me there, who was I to argue? I'd slept better than I had in weeks.

Examining my side of the room from Izzy's bed, I noticed the ticket stub collection and blushed. *I am blushing! I am blushing over Colin Turner!* I pulled the blanket up over my head as I giggled at myself. If Izzy could see me now…

I sat up, the blanket spilling down my chest. Izzy *could* see me now. Izzy was here, which meant she knew about Colin and me. My chest ached with the desire to have an actual conversation with Izzy, and it consumed my giddiness.

What did she think? What would she say? I'd never had an any interest in the guys who followed Izzy around, before or after she was through with them. I didn't know how she would respond to me maybe sort of *like* liking her biggest fan at AC. If I decided I wanted Colin—and that was a big if—would she be happy for me? I wasn't sure.

The girls downstairs would return today, but I knew they wouldn't come back until the late afternoon so they could maximize their skiing and snowboarding time. It was only nine o'clock, so I had hours to kill before I could talk to them. In the meantime, I needed to figure out how my new connection to Izzy could help me learn whatever it was she needed to tell me.

The problem with the relived memories, I decided after mentally cataloguing my experiments from the day before, was that I wasn't sure it would work on an object Izzy hadn't touched as a…ghost.

I hated using that word, but what else was I going to call her? A spirit? A presence? However you framed it, it all came down to one thing: Izzy was dead, but I was still communicating with her, and Izzy was using a variety of weird avenues to try to talk to me. But why couldn't she just *tell* me what I needed to know? If she could move my stuff around and leave me cryptic lipstick notes, why couldn't she just draw me a straight line from her death to whomever was responsible?

I didn't know. Maybe there was some weird supernatural prohibition on outing your own killer from the grave. If there weren't, there would be a lot fewer YouTube submissions to *Unsolved Mysteries.* Maybe I was imagining it all.

I gazed at my side of the room again, searching for something that I associated with a strong memory of my best friend but that post-life Izzy hadn't touched. As my eyes fell on the collage of stubs again, I remembered Colin making a comment about me seeing The Mountain Goats five times.

A shiver ran through me as I scrambled off Izzy's bed toward my wall. I hadn't seen the Mountain Goats five times. I'd only seen them four times. My tickets to the last show were a present from Izzy. Despite her general aversion to what she referred to as "music consisting entirely of whiney boys with sad guitars," she'd given in and gone to see them with me as a birthday concession. I had five stubs on my wall, but two of them were from the same show—one for me and one for Izzy.

Removing the pushpins holding them in place, I gently pulled out the two tickets. I took a big gulp of air to brace myself. Then I picked up the first ticket and held it tightly in my hand as I concentrated on my memories of Izzy and I at the concert.

Nothing happened. Feeling disappointed, I tried the other ticket. Nada.

I knew my recollection of that night was clearer than the memories I personally had of the moments I'd relived as Izzy. I could still remember the drive to the show, what we were both wearing, the sickly-sweet tang of some concoction Izzy had talked the bartender into creating especially for me in honor of my birthday, the pulse of the music so loud it vibrated through the floor and up my legs, yelling the lyrics along with the crowd, the words so familiar that I laughed when it turned out Izzy knew them all because I played the songs so much. I felt like I remembered every detail of that night, but I could not get back to the memory for Izzy's perspective.

I sighed. My hypothesis seemed accurate. I could only pull memories from items Izzy touched as a ghost, which presented a problem.

Glancing around the room again, my gaze fell on the blanket Izzy's mom had made me. Izzy had touched it recently, but it hadn't triggered any memories the entire night I'd slept under it.

But then again, a guilty voice added, *you weren't exactly thinking about Izzy while you were with Colin.*

With a deep breath, I spread the blanket flat, then crawled on top of it, stretching out on my back. I thought carefully about the day Crystal gave it to me. It was the weekend before we'd left for our first year of college. Izzy and I came home from buying the last of our back-to-school stuff. I was sitting on Izzy's bed, sorting school supplies into piles while Izzy modeled potential "first day of school" outfits for my approval. Crystal came into the room carrying two large boxes. Closing my eyes, I rubbed my palms against the satiny fabric…

I was standing in Izzy's room. Once again, I had the surreal experience of standing outside myself, watching as Other-Callie sorted a large pack of spiral notebooks into piles. I was Izzy again, but also not Izzy, living through her but somehow apart.

I did a half-turn, glancing at a long mirror behind me. It was strange to look at Izzy through her own eyes, critical and observant. The rust-colored peasant blouse with tiny cream flowers edged in pine green leaves billowed perfectly over the edge of the green suede asymmetrical skirt that fell above my knee on one side and to mid-calf on the other. The outfit made me look taller than I was, especially paired with the vertically ribbed tights and two inch-heeled slouch boots I was wearing, and the creamy flowers perfectly matched my skin. With the right combination of accessories, I was confident the outfit would work for the first day of school. I felt a flutter of self-satisfied pride as I looked myself over again.

Turning back to other-Callie, I felt a small involuntary sigh escape my lips. She was wearing a stretchy red t-shirt she'd found on some Internet site advertising the fictitious La Cafury Beauty School from *Grease*, dark blue jeans, and red Converse. She didn't look bad, just young, thirteen instead of seventeen. I felt myself winding up for a lecture, but as I opened my mouth, my mother glided into the room.

I was always impressed with my mother's natural poise. She could be covered in baby food and carrying a load of laundry, and she still looked like she was ready for her fairy godmother to sweep in at any moment and transform her matronly outfit into a slinky gown so she could tango with a dark, handsome stranger with a rose in his teeth. How she ended up living in suburbia as a boring housewife I'd never know, but looking at her, I made a silent vow for the millionth time that it would never happen to me.

She was carrying two large boxes. Each was gift-wrapped in robin's egg blue paper and tied with a brown ribbon. She was grinning triumphantly, which was how I knew whatever was in the boxes was something she'd worked hard to hide from both Callie and I until it was ready.

"What's this, Crystal?" Other-Callie asked, and I could hear the suspicion in her voice. Even after years of living with us, it was evident Callie still couldn't get used to being given things, nice things, for no reason. With Callie, you knew she always expected there was a catch, some unexpected cost she'd have to pay later, which made it hellish to try to give her anything. I'd complained to my mom about it. She told me after everything Callie had been through, it was a miracle Callie was doing as well as she was and not to give her a hard time. Still, I sometimes wished my friend could loosen up a little, learn to take a compliment or gift with any kind of grace, and maybe take better care of her appearance.

"I know you girls already have everything you need for school," my mom began as she sat down on the edge of the bed near Callie, who was holding one of the packages awkwardly, like she expected it would explode in her face any second. "But I wanted to give you both something that you could have, something you could keep, that would help mark the beginning of your new adventure."

I moved over to the bed, pulling the package into my lap. It was large and on the heavy side, so it couldn't be jewelry, which was my idea of a keepsake, but I was willing to keep an open mind. "I love presents," I heard myself say as I began pulling the ribbons free.

"Open them at the same time," my mom said, and I glanced up to see Callie pulling hesitantly at the ribbon.

No one needed to prompt me, so I began pulling the paper free from the box, which flexed under my hand. *A coat?*, I wondered, as I felt the plain white box give gently. Running my fingernail along the edge of the box, I popped the tape holding it shut and yanked the lid off.

As I stared down at the fabric, I tried to keep the delighted smile frozen on my face. In the box was a large square of fabric, a quilted pattern sewn across it. It was a shiny red that looked like it belonged to a hideous bridesmaid's dress, and I suppressed a shuddered as I reminded myself to be grateful it wasn't actually a dress, which wasn't out of the realm of possibility with my mom. Pulling my gift from the box and shaking it out, I could see it was a large, lightweight blanket. A giant rectangle of the ruby material was bordered with about a foot of equally objectionable light gold material. It was nice, I guess, but so BORING! No decoration, no patterning, just red and a little gold with a little uneven stitching. And so obviously homemade it made me want to gag.

"Thanks, Mom!" I said with as much enthusiasm as I could muster, and she beamed in response. I looked over at Callie, who was holding an equally hideous blue rectangle with silvery grey trim.

God. Bad enough one hideous blanket, but two?

I tried to catch Callie's eye, but she was staring at the blanket, which she had gathered into bunches in her fists. Callie looked up at my mom, and I could tell from the look on her face she was also struggling to say something nice about how ugly the blankets were. My mom tried hard, but she had no sense of fashion.

I gave Callie a sympathetic smile behind my mom's back as I tried to think of a polite way for the blankets to end up in the back of the closet where they could be conveniently forgotten when we left for school. Callie didn't seem to notice me, though; she kept staring at my mom.

"You made this?" Callie asked, her voice a hoarse whisper. "You made this…for me?" Callie looked as though she was about to cry.

"Of course, honey," my mom said soothingly, and I felt stunned as Callie began to sob quietly.

"It's beautiful, Crystal. It's so beautiful."

An icy sensation washed through my stomach as my mom moved over to Callie, wrapping my tiny best friend in her arms and rocking her slightly.

Callie didn't hate the vile blanket. She loved it. She thought it was beautiful. Of course she did. Callie had about as little taste as my mother.

I looked down at the hideous red blanket spread across my lap, then back at Callie, who was laughing now as my mother, *my* mother, wiped the tears from her cheeks. I suddenly felt angry at both of them, at Callie for being perfect all the time, and at my mother, so quick to replace me with my best friend, who was the kind of daughter she'd obviously always wanted…

15.

I hurtled forward, rolling off the bed and onto my hands and knees on the thin carpet. I couldn't believe how angry I felt. Even though Izzy's anger was quickly fading, the memory of it was still fresh and clear in my mind, like it had just happened. And, in a way, it had. I felt sick, like I needed to get the memory out of me the only way available. I grabbed my trashcan and dry heaved until my sides ached.

Izzy hated me. If only for a moment, she'd hated me, thoroughly and completely. Even though I knew, without knowing how I knew, that the impulse had been fleeting for Izzy, it was real. It had happened. Looking at Crystal holding me, Izzy wished she'd never met me, that we'd never been friends and I'd never come to live with them. For a moment, she'd wondered if her mother loved me more than her, and in that instant, fear and jealousy overwhelmed every warm and friendly feeling Izzy had for me, replacing them with loathing and disgust.

Izzy had hated me.

Izzy had wished I was dead.

After a few minutes, I slid down to the floor, pulling my blue blanket down around me. Looking at the handfuls of fabric bunched in my fists, I thought about my own hazy memory of that day, how pleased Izzy seemed by the gift, how she had scrambled over the bed in her ridiculous boots to hug me alongside her mother, telling me I was silly for crying. It was one of my happiest memories of living with the Millers. Now I knew that, for Izzy, it was one of the worst.

Izzy was jealous of her mother's love for me, and I'd never even noticed. Crystal welcomed everybody with a kind of boundless love that always seemed to have room for more; she was forever taking in the random stray friend of one of her girls and caring for them. It never occurred to me it might bother Izzy or her sisters.

Was this the reason Izzy came back? To tell me she was mad at me? To tell me I'd cheated her out of some of the only love she'd had in her short life? My stomach clenched at the thought.

"No," I told myself vehemently, saying the word out loud to ward away the doubt I felt.

Izzy's message was clear. *HELP ME.*

She needed my help. I'd been the one to pick that sad memory, that particular moment to relive, not Izzy. It was my fault I'd seen something I didn't like. I refused to believe Izzy would have shown me that memory by choice. It seemed more likely that some sort of Izzy essence imprinted on the things she touched, with little control on her part as to what those might be. No wonder she kept leaving me clues that lead nowhere. It was hard to give someone direction when you had no idea what you might be telling them. Izzy loved me; she would never have left such a hurtful thing for me, not when I knew she could see how much I was hurting without her…

…would she?

The doubt left me utterly bereft. I thought Izzy was the one person who'd always, unfailingly and without hesitation, loved me, just like I loved her. We were more than friends. We were better than blood. We'd chosen each other as best friends and sisters in a whole world of people, and that made our kinship the truest kind, because it meant we weren't sisters because we had to be. We were sisters because we wanted to be.

Except maybe Izzy didn't. Another wave of shame and isolation rolling over me. I sat on my floor, staring at the small, suddenly claustrophobic room.

"What's the point of all this?" I wondered aloud. "How can I help you, Iz? Or are you just here to torture me?"

Only silence answered as hot tears slipped down my face. Greg and Crystal had packed up and shipped out almost everything Izzy owned. All I had was my stuff, and while much of it was associated in some way with Izzy, it also was not necessarily going to trigger any memory that might help me figure out what had happened to her. I hadn't gone to the party with Izzy, so all of my memories associated with that night occurred, effectively, with Izzy off-screen. Her memories, particularly the memories of the moments leading to her death, would similarly be absent of me. Plus, everything she'd been wearing or carrying that night—her clothes, jewelry, shoes, purse, keys—were all either in a bag somewhere in the Astoria Police evidence lock-up or back in Texas. Even if I assumed I could jump into a memory of Izzy's I didn't also share, one that spirit Izzy had to touch before I could relive the memory, I didn't have access to any item that might store a useful memory from the night she died.

As I thought about the last week and her cryptic, unhelpful missives, I pounded my fists against the floor, suddenly as angry at Izzy as she had been at me. The whole thing was so typical. Even dead, Izzy's drama was still the primary focus of my life.

Why couldn't I mourn my friend and move on? Why was I worried that she was jealous of my relationship with her mother? The Millers had dropped me the moment Izzy had died. Why was I so concerned about what she would think of Colin and me to the point I was considering letting him go? Even if I did sort of like him, it wasn't like she could have him now. Why did I have to be stuck chasing after Izzy and whatever new impossible thing was going to make her happy, over and over?

Was it possible to love someone as much as I cared for this beautiful, unreasonable girl without losing sight of what might make me happy in the process? Or was that the cost of caring so much?

"I guess it's not surprising you hated me sometimes," I said aloud. I didn't know if Izzy was in the room with me, but I needed to talk to her, so I hoped my need to say what was on my mind would be enough to will her into my company. "Because sometimes I think I hate you, too."

I forced myself to my feet and grabbed the blanket, straightening it over her bed. "You are so selfish sometimes! Why can't you leave me alone?" I said, yanking hard at the blanket's corners. "Why can't you move on to some pretty land of harps and angels, or, I don't know, maybe heaven to you is a never-ending marathon of Paris Fashion Week. Why can't you just go? Then I could love you and I could mourn you, and then I could move on."

I dug around in my drawers, pulling out a pair of old jeans and a faded yellow t-shirt. As I grabbed underwear and socks out of another drawer, I heard something behind me. When I turned around, the blanket on Izzy's bed was in a heap in the middle.

"No," I said vehemently. "No, no, *no*. I am not going to touch that stupid blanket. If you want me to help you, you have to help me figure out a way to understand what you're trying to tell me. Until you do," I said, opening the door and lowering my voice to a hiss as someone walked by in the hallway, "Leave. Me. Alone." I closed the door a little too loudly and marched into the bathroom to shower.

I stood under the hot water for a long time. It turned my skin an angry red and my scalp stung, but I never got warm. I couldn't even cry. I stood under the spray with my eyes closed and my arms wrapped around chest, feeling numb. When I was sure no one else was in the bathroom, I got out and pulled on my clothes. I meticulously combed my hair, twisting it into a long wet braid. I brushed my teeth and flossed for good measure. After I washed my face, I applied an exfoliator Izzy foisted on me, then dug out a jar of moisturizer she insisted I use during the winter. I rolled the jar around in my hand, glumly examining the expensive label. In her own screwy way, Izzy was always trying to take care of me.

Izzy and I had fought before, but it never lasted. Would that change now that she was dead? I wasn't sure. Our fights were always over stupid stuff and never took long to resolve. We would both apologize and then split a pint of Chunky Monkey and all would be forgiven.

Despite any hard feelings, she was still my best friend. I needed to say I was sorry. I didn't hate her. I could never hate her, not really. And I knew deep down she didn't hate me either. But I needed to hear it. So what happened when the person you most needed to hear say sorry no longer had a voice?

I knew I was stalling. Part of me was afraid that whatever message Izzy left for me next might be worse. But what did time mean to a ghost? She might be able to wait forever. With a sigh, I hung up my washcloth and walked back over to my room, opening the door slowly as I braced myself for whatever surprise she had left me this time.

The blanket was back in place, smoothed out and tucked at the corners, and the throw pillows were once again arranged in a small pile in each corner but nothing else in the room looked like it had been moved.

"Iz?" If she hadn't touched anything new, then that just left the bedspread, and I didn't want to touch it again. Not right now. As hurt as I was by her memory, my sense of rejection paled in comparison to the guilt I felt over yelling at her. I didn't want her to go away. I'd only just gotten her back. Any Izzy was better than nothing.

My chest tightened and I trembled at the thought of losing her entirely. The space was too still, too empty. I had to get out of the room. I had go somewhere, anywhere else. I grabbed a bunch of books, tossing them in a bag with my laptop. I dropped the bag by the door and pulled on my coat, scarf, and gloves. As I hoisted the bag over my shoulder, I noticed a scrap of paper on the floor.

A torn corner of a note from Izzy lay under the bag. She'd written it at the beginning of the year during a boring hour she'd spent working Orientation check-in alone while I was shanghaied into helping move huge first-day boxes of stuff from the mailroom. Picking it up, I held the scrap of paper carefully in my hands. I didn't even know I'd kept the note or where the rest of it might be.

Studying it, I could make out a handful of words, elegantly written in Izzy's slanted script.

e sorry excuse for a

ck. I would do a much better job of

nd anyone in the world other than you

sorry.

love and misses from the ninth circle of hell,

Izzy

A tear rolled down my nose as I slowly folded the tattered message and tucked it in my back pocket.

"I love you, too," I whispered into the cold room. Then I picked up my bag again and, closing the door with a quiet click, headed to the library.

16.

I spent the rest of the afternoon in the library, hiding from Izzy and trying to figure out how to catch up on the work I'd missed. I'd heard back from all my professors, and while they were sympathetic, none of them were the kind who thought that meant I should get a pass. Looking over my revised study schedule, I chewed on the end of my pen. I needed to really buckle down if I was going to get through my make-up assignments plus everything left on my syllabi before the end of the semester.

After several hours, my back ached and my eyes watered but I had an outline and rough draft for two of my three papers. I made my way back to Spruce in the growing dark, precariously balancing a huge stack of books I needed to dig into for my paper for Dr. Cliff as I stepped carefully to avoid the icy patches beginning to form along the edges of the walk.

When I got back to the room, it was the same. Not a single book or shoe or pillow was moved even an inch. Part of me had been expecting Izzy to have stacked all the furniture in the middle of the room or left a message spelled out in tortilla chips across the floor, something huge, bizarre, and hard to explain. I wasn't sure how I felt about the nothing she'd left in its place.

I unceremoniously dumped the books in a pile on Izzy's bed since her desk was covered and mine would be occupied by my laptop. It was Sunday night, and the 103 girls had to be back by now. Since Izzy hadn't giving me any additional direction, it was time to talk to some of the people involved who were still breathing.

My dad had worked a couple of years in the HPD Gang Unit before he'd become a supervisor in the Auto Theft Division, and one thing he'd complained over and over about was the difficulty of investigating a crime in an insular community. "You have to do so much to get them to trust you, to see you as one of them, that honestly I sometimes wonder if we aren't doing good cops a disservice sending them undercover for this kind of work," I remembered him telling my mom after the local paper had published a story that had, in turn, sparked an internal investigation into corruption in the unit while he was working there. "Sometimes I think we're better off using snitches and flipping people," he'd said, throwing the newspaper in the trash. "It's less reliable, but in the long run better for the department."

I was already an insider, sort of. Admittedly, I wasn't exactly a popular member of the campus community since I didn't usually say a lot and when I did, I wasn't always the most tactful. And okay, yeah, I was a huge subject of campus gossip at the moment, but maybe I could make all that work in my favor. I wasn't looking to get anyone busted for a little recreational drug use while I was hunting for people complicit in my best friend's death; besides, if I was a little looney, who'd ever believe me? It seemed like a workable angle.

I walked downstairs and found the 103 wipeboard clean of notes. Someone was home. I knocked on the door and held my breath. A long moment passed; no one answered. I knocked again, harder.

"Hang on!" an exasperated voice called from inside. I shifted my weight from one foot to another while I waited, trying to ignore the mass of knots in my stomach.

Finally, the door swung open to reveal a small thin girl in a pair of pink pajamas and fuzzy slippers. She was wearing wire-rimmed glasses and her long brown hair was pulled into two light brown pigtails falling around her face. Wiping at one of her eyes behind her glasses, she looked like she had just woken up.

"Shannen," My voice came out in a flat the-facts-and-only-the-facts-ma'am tone my father used to use to interrogate me when he thought I was lying about something. I called it "the detective voice." Until now, I didn't even know I had one.

"Callie?" Shannen sounded as surprised to see me as she looked. "What time is it?"

"Six—at night," I said, and she held the door open a little wider for me. I walked into the room, flopping down on an old beat-up couch covered with a navy blue sheet. I looked around, taking in small changes. 103 was more or less exactly how I remembered it.

The quad suite had a large common room with closets and desks, with a second separate smaller room about the size of a closet containing two sets of bunk beds. The sleep room could be closed off so some of the roommates could sleep while the rest studied or hung out with friends. It was a good arrangement, even better if you could get into one with only three people. Gloria, Lauren, and Shannen lived in the room. Bethany, the fourth-wheeling shadow roommate, was stuck by the Housing-Powers-That-Be in another complex but spent most of her time here. I'd hoped to catch them all here at once.

Unfortunately, it looked like Shannen was the only one home. She closed the door and wandered over toward me, grabbing a blanket and pulling it around herself as she settled onto a small circular purple rug on the floor. She was obviously sick; no wonder she'd been asleep. As she sniffled and blew her nose, I mentally arranged my face in what I hoped was the kind of neutral, detached expression I'd so often seen on my dad when he was in uniform.

"Sorry I woke you," I began, hoping she would cooperate if I started out nicely.

"That's okay," she wheezed. "We haven't seen you in...in a long time." Shannen coughed into her tissue, but it was obvious she was trying to figure out what to say to me. "What's up?"

"Are Lauren and Gloria going to be back soon? Is Bethany coming over?" I tried to keep my tone neutral but I could tell by the way Shannen looked at me she knew what I was after.

"Sorry, Callie." Shannen shot me an apologetic glance as she fidgeted with the tissue box. "Bethany left for Thanksgiving already. Her parents found a ticket cheap enough that she could go but she had to skip some class. Lauren and Gloria went to the mountain for the weekend."

She coughed again. "I was supposed to go with them but I got super sick and I have an exam on Tuesday that I needed to study for, so I stayed here."

She cast a sidelong glance at me as if she was hoping I'd take the hint and leave. When I didn't say anything, she continued. "They went with some super cute cross-country guys. I guess one of them, his parents have a house up there? Anyway, they must be having a pretty good time because they were supposed to come back this morning, but Gloria called to say they were going to stay another night and skip tomorrow. "

"So it's just you."

"Yep," she sniffled.

I bit my lip, debating. I considered coming back later when I could talk to them all at the same time, but a little echo of my father's voice rumbled in my ear, reminding me it was better to question suspects separately. Everyone always said that before he'd started drinking heavily, he'd been an excellent cop. I listened because, in my gut, I trusted those memories. I didn't consider Shannen a suspect, exactly. She was more of a potentially uncooperative witness. Either way, I was here now. No place to go but forward.

"I…" I began, scooting to the edge of the couch to tower over her, curled up in the blanket on the floor. She became immediately immersed in picking at the loose threads in the rug. "I need to ask you about what happened the night Izzy died." The words came out in a rush. So much for cool, calm, and collected.

Shannen huffed a little. "Haven't we already been through this?" she whined weakly.

"No, actually," I snapped, unable to keep the anger from my voice. "Not with me. I sat there and watched the four of you tell that story over and over to other people like you'd rehearsed it." I could feel myself getting worked up, and I struggled to maintain my calm. "None of you ever actually talked to me about it. None of you." The unspoken accusation hung in the air. The girls had been my friends, too, but not one of them had come to see me afterward.

"I'm sorry. I didn't think you wanted to talk to me." Her voice quivered, and I could tell she was upset.

Good, a mean little voice whispered in my head.

"We wanted to. At least, I wanted to." She looked up at me, her lip quivering. "But you were so sad. You wouldn't leave your room. You wouldn't talk to anybody." I could see her eyes growing wet behind her glasses, fat tears threatening to spill down her puffy face. Despite my anger, I felt the tiniest bit sorry for snapping at her. Of the four of them, Shannen was a nice girl, but decidedly on the follower end of the spectrum. If there had been a group decision to avoid me, she certainly wasn't the one who'd made it.

"Besides, we didn't think you'd want to talk to any of us. The last time we saw you, you were screaming at us about how it was our fault." Her chin jutted in the air as she stared past me out the window.

I remembered the scene all too clearly. Out of my mind with grief and rage and sure they weren't telling the whole story, I'd screamed at them in front of the police. Jay intervened, half-dragging, half-carrying me out the door and away from the Counseling Center where it had been agreed the police could talk to students who were willing to give statements. I still remembered the startled and horrified look on Shannen's face over Jay's shoulder as he'd pulled me from the room.

I paused, considering my options before choosing the conciliatory route. "I'm sorry, Shannen. I should never have said that to you. I know it's not your fault."

Her expression softened, so I plowed on. "I need to understand what happened. I think…" I stumbled over the words as they came out. "I think it would help me. I think it would help me move on."

"Alright, Callie." Her gaze moved back to mine. "If it'll help you, I'll talk to you about it." She wiped at her eyes and pushed up her glasses. "What do you want to know?"

"Can you start from the beginning?" My voice cracked with desperation. I was on the verge of tears myself. Face-to-face with someone who been with Izzy the night she died, my emotions were cycling faster than I could keep up.

Shannen pursed her lips together in a grim line. "Fine. The beginning you already know." She took a deep breath and blew it out slowly. "When we got ready for the party, we thought you were coming, too. Then Izzy showed up and said you didn't want to come, that you were going to stay home and be boring." She winced. "Sorry, Izzy's words."

I gave her a small smile and tried to look calm. "Sounds like Izzy."

"Anyway, we were already…"

"Pre-partying?"

"Yeah." Shannen looked a little embarrassed. "Gina got some senior guy she knows to buy us a bottle of Midori, and we'd all had a few shots. We offered Izzy some, but she didn't want any."

I nodded, trying to encourage her along. I remembered the time in high school when I'd made myself uber-sick on shots of raspberry liqueur. Izzy had been the one to hold my hair back. We'd both sworn off flavored liqueurs after that fiasco. I wanted Shannen to tell

152

me something I didn't already know or couldn't have guessed on my own.

"Anyway, we finished getting ready and went to the party. It was packed." She coughed and paused to blow her nose again. "The house is nice and there are like five guys living there, so it's huge, you know?" I nodded in confirmation. "And it's not that far from campus, so we walked. Gloria complained the entire time about having to walk in heels, and Izzy told her to suck it up, that Gloria was going to have to learn to deal with it if she was going to have any kind of social life here."

Shannen looked a little smug, enjoying the memory of Izzy telling Gloria off. I suspected every one of Gloria's roommates wanted to stand up to her, so I wasn't surprised. Gloria was an alpha type, the kind that had to rule whatever social network she was in. I could barely tolerate Gloria, but Izzy thought she was okay and Gloria admired Izzy enough to be on her best behavior around us most of the time. With her roommates, it was a different story; Gloria had them jumping through hoops before the end of the first month of school. From the look on Shannen's face, the bloom was obviously off the rose when it came to the Sisterhood of Spruce 103.

"When we got there, the party was already going pretty strong. The guys all had their bedrooms open. There was a full bar in the basement and kegs in the kitchen. People were everywhere, even in the backyard. It seemed like half the school showed up." The tone of Shannen's voice implied, even now, that she thought the party was awesome. I bit the inside of my lip, resisting the urge yell at her.

"We all split up," she continued. "Gloria went to go find some guy she was trying to hook up with. Lauren made it a whole fifteen minutes before she was on the phone to her boyfriend back home, telling him how much she missed him. Bethany went off to find the guy from her Intro to Philosophy class she has a crush on. I started talking to this cute sophomore on the crew team."

"And Izzy?"

"She was pretty pissed at Gloria by the time we got there, so she took off. She went off to talk to some of her friends, I guess." Shannen sniffled.

My antenna went up. "What friends?" I asked, a little too sharply.

"I don't know." Shannen shrugged, chewing her lip as she tried to remember. "Upperclassmen, I think. I didn't know any of them."

It took everything in me not to strangle Shannen then and there. "Guys? Girls?"

"Both?" she suggested weakly. "I wasn't really paying attention." She twisted a piece of tissue in her hands. "I know there was some guy there Izzy dated last year because he asked me where she was."

Great. That narrows it down to about fifteen people.

"He was pretty drunk, though. I think I saw him passed out on a couch later."

"Would you remember what he looked like?"

"Yeah," Shannen said after a moment. "I think I'd know him if I saw him. But to be honest, I don't know if he ever found her or how much he'd remember. Everyone was pretty drunk, Callie. Plus, you know." Shannen gave me a look heavy with implications.

"Go on." Now I felt like we were getting into territory the girls might not have covered with Astoria PD or campus authorities.

"You know it was a theme party, right?"

"I remember."

"Everybody was in costumes," she said, as though that explained everything.

"Angels and devils." I cut her an inquiring glance, waving my hand trying to elicit more of an explanation.

"A lot of people had masks on. It was hard to see their faces. That was part of what made it kind of…fun?" Shannen looked sheepish.

To me, it sounded like a recipe for ugly hook-ups and regretful mornings, which was exactly why I hadn't wanted to go. I wasn't sure what that had to do with Izzy, though. I realized Shannen was still talking and made myself focus.

"We were there for a few hours. Bethany got bored because her guy didn't show up and she ended up getting drunk, so I had to take care of her. Lauren was ready to leave as soon as she got off the phone. Gloria's guy wouldn't talk to her or something, and she was pissed. We all kind of decided we wanted to leave."

"Okay…" I said, but Shannen stared at me blankly. "And then?"

"Then we went to find Izzy," she said unhelpfully. "This is the part you've already heard." Shannen acted like she didn't want to keep going, but I could tell by the look on her face she was more scared of pissing me off.

"Whatever it is, just spit it out." *Careful*, I reminded myself. I gave her what I hoped was an imploring look. "I need to know what happened." I dug my fingertips into the sides of my legs to keep from gritting my teeth. "Please."

"We went to find Izzy, and she was dancing with this guy. They'd turned the lights out in the living room and things were…" Shannen looked down, obviously embarrassed. "Hot and heavy is the only way I know to describe it. The guy Izzy was dancing with had a mask on that covered over half his face and gave him devil horns. Izzy was all over him."

I glared at the insinuation, and she hurried on. "And he was all over her, too. I mean, it *looked* like they were both having a very good time," she explained desperately. "Gloria went over and told Izzy we wanted to leave, and according to her, Izzy said, 'So go!' and blew us off."

"Gloria was ready to leave right then. I convinced her we should try talking to Izzy again, and I went over to Izzy with her this time. I told Izzy we were all tired, then Gloria reminded Izzy she was the one who'd told us never to leave a woman behind."

Which was exactly what I screamed at the girls in the Counseling Center.

Shannen looked at me like she knew what I was thinking, and her voice rose an octave. "Then Izzy looked at Gloria and said, 'Yeah, I meant for people who couldn't take care of themselves,' which pissed Gloria off."

"I can imagine." Saying Gloria could be temperamental was putting it lightly. Some queen bees, like Izzy, preferred to be loved; Gloria was the kind who liked to be feared.

Shannen shrugged in agreement. "Then Izzy kept dancing with the guy. We went back to Lauren and Bethany, and Gloria said we should leave, so that's what we did."

"And that was it." My words were soft, pained.

Shannen leaned toward me, pleading for understanding. "We didn't want to leave Izzy there. She didn't want to come with us, and she was pretty adamant about not needing us to look after her." Shannen's chin quivered. "I never would have left her there, not if I'd known what would happen. But you know how Izzy was! She was so strong. She was always in control…"

"I know Izzy."

A cacophony of emotions rang through me; it was hard to focus on any one feeling. I wanted to scream. I wanted to cry. I wanted to punch the walls. I wanted to plead for forgiveness. It was too much to register and, having ripped the Band-Aid off the wound, too much to suppress. My whole body shook and I hugged myself trying to keep the flood in.

Shannen was sobbing now, obviously heartbroken. I needed to get out of the room before my temper erupted all over both of us, and the only means of escape were blocked by someone I wanted to punch in the face instead of forgive. Gritting my teeth, I said what was necessary to get away.

"I don't blame you," I managed to choke out.

Shannen bowed her head as she sobbed, wiping at her nose and cheeks with the tattered tissue in her hands. "I'm so sorry, Callie."

"Me, too," I whispered.

I didn't realize tears were sliding down my face until Shannen extended a fresh tissue toward me. We sat quietly for a while, wrapped in our respective misery. Eventually, I pulled myself together, tossing the tissue in the trashcan next to the couch. "I'm surprised Izzy would pick a fight with Gloria…" I muttered, mostly to myself.

"That was the weird thing," Shannen said as she blew her nose again.

"What?"

"Izzy was drunk. And I mean, *drunk* drunk."

I vehemently shook my head. "Shannen, that's impossible. Izzy doesn't get drunk. I've known her for years. I've never seen her drunk. Not once. Ever."

Shannen looked scared, like she didn't want to argue with me, but she continued. "I don't know what to tell you. She seemed pretty plastered when I saw her. But you don't have to take my word for it." She held her hands defensively. "I know for a fact Bethany barely remembers anything, but you can ask Gloria and Lauren. Well, Lauren, at least. I honestly don't know how much Gloria is going to want to talk to you."

Like I'm going to give her a choice. "Thanks for talking to me." I stood shakily and started for the door.

"I hope this helped you." Shannen pushed herself up to follow me.

It hadn't helped at all. In fact, it made me feel worse, but I couldn't tell her that. "It did. Thank you for…everything. I hope you feel better." I opened the door.

"Callie," she called hesitantly. I stopped but didn't look back, my hand on the doorknob.

"It would be nice to see you more." I glanced quickly over my shoulder to see her standing in the middle of the large room. She reminded me of a lost little kid, in her wrinkled pajamas and clutching her blanket.

"Sure," I shot her a tiny, too-quick smile. "We could…" I searched for something appropriately vague and non-specific, "…hang out sometime. Get some coffee."

"Really?" Shannen's lips turned upward hopefully. She obviously believed I'd forgiven her. "That would be great."

"Text me," I said, executing my hasty departure before I could get trapped into making any more promises I was sure I wouldn't keep.

17.

I practically ran back to my room. I was on the verge of a full-scale nuclear meltdown and my emotional targets were changing approximately every fifteen seconds. I was frustrated with Shannen for being too weak to stand up to Gloria or Izzy. I was angry at Gloria for being pushy and mean. I was bitter at Izzy for getting in Gloria's face, and maybe, possibly, though I still didn't believe it, getting drunk. Mostly, though, I was furious at myself for not going to the stupid party because there was no way Izzy would have pulled that crap with me. Better to be alone when I felt like this. At least then the only person I could do damage to was myself.

I sat on my bed, cataloguing the particulars of our conversation. Despite Shannen's warnings, I knew I'd talk to all of the other girls eventually. I'd have to wait for Bethany to come back from break, but since it was unlikely she remembered anything about the party, the delay didn't worry me. I'd seen Bethany drunk; if Shannen said Bethany was a lost cause, she was probably right.

That left Lauren and Gloria, and two days before they would both leave for Thanksgiving weekend. Lauren lived within driving distance, but Gloria lived in LA and was likely to be catching a flight late Tuesday or early Wednesday morning. Gloria could probably also tell me who the guys who threw the party were. Shannen hadn't offered up any names, and I felt confident that she would have if she'd known them. Gloria, always on the hunt for a new boyfriend, preferably one with a car and the ability to buy her liquor, would have made it her business to know.

Without any other leads to chase down, I needed a distraction. I couldn't face more homework. After spending most of the day in the library powered by nothing more than a little sugar and caffeine, my brain was the consistency of tapioca. The only thing I was good for at this point was a little mindless movie watching until I could fall asleep.

The temperature had dropped steadily throughout the day, and the wind and icy rain howling outside my window made my room considerably colder. I took out my contacts and changed into an Astoria College hoodie and thick matching sweatpants to keep warm. I was brushing tangles from my knotted hair when I heard a knock on the door.

Colin stood in the doorway, dripping wet and grinning at me. He was wearing a blue rain jacket with a small tear at the shoulder and his jeans were soaked. He held up two plastic grocery bags with his good hand. "I didn't see you at dinner. Thought you might be hungry."

I could see a bag of chips sticking out of the top of one of the bags; my stomach ached, reminding me how little I'd eaten all day. At the same time, the look on his face reminded me of the way he'd once looked at Izzy. It reminded me of our earlier fight and of the vicious memory of Izzy's jealousy. What if she had decided she liked him after all? Did it make me a terrible friend if I decided I didn't care?

Colin licked his lips nervously, then nodded in the direction of the stairs. "Are you really going to send me back out into the rain?" His little boy haircut, always so carefully combed with every hair in place, hung wetly in his eyes, and his cheeks were ruddy from the cold. I wanted to let him in, even if I wasn't sure what to do about it afterwards.

Then my stomach let out a massive growl, completely betraying me. My face turned bright red as I clapped my hands over my belly.

He laughed. "Guess I showed up just in time."

I swung the door open. "Yes, come in quick! Before I begin devouring the furniture."

Colin shrugged out of his jacket and planted himself in the middle of the floor, calling out items as he unloaded the bags one-handed and laid them out for me. "We've got salt and vinegar chips, spicy black bean dip, mango salsa, microwavable mac and cheese, regular popcorn, kettle corn, lots of ramen, annnd…" He reached into the bag before waving his hand with a flourish "…double chocolate mint ice cream. And two spoons."

"That's my favorite."

"I know." Smiling, he held up a hand, pulling me down to the floor next to him.

"This is great, but you know this is way more food than we can possibly eat, right?"

"I was almost out of food. I decided to stock up before the Campus Store gets cleaned out for break." Colin tried to open the chips, but couldn't get a good grip with his cast.

I stuck the ice cream in my freezer then took the chip bag from him. "I forgot about that. Guess I need to get over there tomorrow if I'm going to have food over break." I sighed as I opened the bag and handed it back to him.

Colin raised his eyebrows in surprise. "You're staying here? I thought you and Izzy always went to her parents'…" He trailed off when he saw the look on my face.

"They didn't ask me."

"So you're spending break by yourself? That sucks." He put a hand lightly over mine. This time it didn't send nervous jolts up my arm; it reminded me of how utterly alone I was.

I shifted my hand out from under his and picked up the jar of bean dip, opening it. "Are you going home?"

"It's only an hour by train. Kind of hard to avoid it when you're this close."

"You don't want to go home?"

He shrugged. "I'll be there soon for Winter Break, and I have so much work to do before finals. I never get anything done when I'm home. My mom makes me look after my brothers, and all my cousins show up, so the house is full of kids jacked up on caffeine, screaming and running in circles." He grabbed a handful of chips. "Plus, my high school friends aren't really my friends anymore, you know?"

"It was the same for Izzy and me. It was okay last year, I guess, but when we went back for the summer it was obvious how much had changed." I didn't add that Izzy had immediately fallen back into the swing of things, dragging me to an endless string of summer parties and beach trips where I was reminded repeatedly of how little I had to say to people I'd gone to school with for twelve years.

"I still like all those guys, but…" He paused and I noticed the adorable way his eyes narrowed slightly and his nose scrunched up when he was deep in thought. I'd seen him make the same face plenty of times in class, but now a warm glow swelled in my chest.

"My town? It's kind of small. So maybe it isn't like this for you. But like, we have one stoplight. One." He held up his index finger for emphasis. "I've lived there my entire life. Astoria probably seems tiny to you, but the entire concept of public transportation was completely new to me when I got here. And when I go home, so many of the guys I hung out with in high school are still there. They never left and they aren't really doing anything."

"That makes sense. Houston's not small, but our neighborhood was. It's the same. I go home and go to the grocery store and I run into people from school and nothing has changed. It's like time—"

"Stopped," we said in unison.

"So," Colin gestured to food packages scattered in front of us. "Ramen or mac and cheese?"

"Mac and cheese."

Colin passed me two containers and I went to the hall kitchen to use the microwave. On my way back to my room, I passed two girls coming out of a neighboring room, and I found myself beaming at them. They exchanged a look before politely returning the smile. "Back to the land of the living," I muttered to myself.

Colin was still on the floor where I left him. He'd pulled out my movie box and was rummaging through it. I stood in the doorway, noticing how at ease he seemed, more than he had when he had visited Izzy. He looked completely comfortable riffling through my stuff. I was failing utterly at my 'take it slow and figure things out' plan. And yet, I couldn't imagine sending him away, especially when I knew he would be gone soon.

He held up an action flick. "Feel like watching something?"

"I don't know if I'm going to be awake much longer." A shadow of disappointment passed over his face and I felt a little thrill zing through me.

No! I chastised myself. *Stop that now!*

This was getting out of hand.

"How about TV instead? We can watch a couple of episodes and if I'm going to pass out, at least you won't be trapped for two hours while I snooze."

"I don't feel trapped with you," he responded quietly and I froze. If he was about to make some sort of declaration, things were going to go very, very badly.

Maybe.

"I feel…" he inhaled deeply, and I braced for the emotional impact. "Better." He raised his eyes to mine and I willed my face not to show how much his next few words mattered to me. "When I'm with you, I feel like all this bad stuff that has happened matters. Izzy was here, and she was real, and she was beautiful. I loved her for over a year. Even if she never loved me, I loved her."

He might as well have punched me in the stomach. Colin loved Izzy. He loved Izzy and he spent time with me because I was the next best thing, just with like the Millers.

Colin didn't appear to notice. "I loved a girl and she died. That's a huge deal, even if everyone acts like it isn't." He swallowed hard. "I can't do that. I can't pretend it didn't happen, or that I don't still miss her. But when I'm with you, I can feel everything I felt for Izzy, but I also feel like I can finally start getting over it."

Do not cry, do not cry, I admonished myself. *Do not let him see how much this is hurting you. You weren't even sure you liked him!*

"So, how about…" He held up a DVD box. "Bad '90s sitcom?"

"Sure!" Colin scrambled up to set my laptop up. I put the unopened food back into the bags for him, clearing the floor as I picked up our trash. Colin settled on the makeshift couch. I grabbed a blanket off my bed and sat down next to him, leaning back to keep a safe distance between us.

Colin frowned, but didn't say anything as he started the DVD. As the show started, I remembered the last time I'd watched this show. I could practically hear Izzy's laughter, remembering how we'd stretched out on overstuffed couches in her parents' living room under a slow-moving fan, hiding from the summer heat. Who knew it was possible to simultaneously love and miss and resent someone so much at the same time? I tried to focus on the show, but all I could think about was what he had said.

Colin *loved* Izzy. He'd actually said it.

Loved.

L. O. V. E.

Of course he did. Everyone loved Izzy, including me. She was beautiful and glamorous and filled with the promise of adventure. I, on the other hand, was too serious and too plain, with a bad attitude and a mouth to match. Colin spent time with me so he could hang on to Izzy, the way a toddler holds onto their favorite blanket after it's nothing more than a scrap of fabric. He found me…comforting.

The thought hurt.

I *liked* Colin. I didn't know why I'd never noticed it in the year and a half I'd known him. Maybe it was because he was so focused on Izzy, or because I'd always been focused on avoiding my feelings for Jay. Maybe his willingness to keep Izzy's memory alive made me see him in a way I hadn't before. Whatever the reason…

I liked him.

I liked his bad haircut that made him look like he was twelve and his earnestness. I liked his smile that showed too many teeth. I liked that he laughed at stupid things and had good taste in music. I liked that he was kind. I didn't care that he always seemed like he was trying too hard to impress. I liked that he tried hard. And I wanted to be someone who was worth that kind of effort.

I was still sulking when the first episode ended. Colin leaned forward to start the next and his hand brushed my leg. I pulled my knees to my chin in response. The room grew colder as the rain outside turned to sleet, slapping hard at my window. I pulled the blanket tighter around me. Colin crossed his arms, rubbing them with his hands.

"Do you want a blanket?"

"No, I'm good."

I bit my lip, trying not to laugh at his attempt at manliness. He was obviously freezing. "Could I share yours?"

"Sure." I held out the blanket. Colin pulled it over him, fluffing out the blanket so we were both covered.

The laugh track on the sitcom kicked in, but I hadn't been paying enough attention to remember to laugh. My breathing had unconsciously slowed to match his, and as our chests rose and fell in time, I felt wonderful and terrified and sad. Even if he was using me to stay close to Izzy, maybe that was enough for now. Wasn't that one of the reasons I liked him? Because Izzy was important to him, too? The episode ended, but neither of us moved to start the next one.

"Look…"

I headed him off. "It's okay. I get it. I love Izzy, too. I'm just glad we can be friends."

I turned my face toward the window, where the sleet mixed with hail pounded insistently. It sounded like my heart, pounding against my ribcage.

"Hey," Colin turned toward me, his arm brushing mine. "I don't think you understand," He wrapped his fingers lightly around my wrist, pulling my attention to him. "I said I loved Izzy. Loved." He squeezed my wrist to emphasize the word. "Past tense. And I know, no matter what you say, that she never loved me." He chuckled, low and sad. "I'm not sure she even liked me."

"I don't think that's true," I said weakly. This was getting harder and harder. I felt like I was betraying Izzy's confidence, but I didn't want to lie anymore.

"When I'm with you…" His palm grazed mine as he laced our fingers together. "I'm happy. Happier than I ever was with Izzy. Not that I ever was, you know, *with* Izzy. Not really." He licked his lips. "I like you. I like you a lot."

Our faces were so close together I could see the translucent freckles across the bridge of his nose. "Me, too," I whispered. The words hung in the air.

Part of me was crushed by the weight of my betrayal: of Izzy, of our friendship, of my stupid inability to cope alone. But then a glowing smile lit up Colin's face. Instantly, his lips were on mine, hesitant at first, then crushing against me, and everything else disappeared. His lips were a little dry and chapped from the cold but tasted sweet and salty and wonderful.

A wave of giddiness rolled over me. His fingers tightened briefly around mine and then released my hand as he ran them along the edge of my face, brushing my hair back from my neck. They trailed a warm line of electricity along my jaw to the tip of my chin. He bent his head forward and the kiss deepened. I found myself suddenly thinking about how good a kisser Colin was and how much Izzy had missed out—

There was a loud sound like a bomb exploding accompanied by a vicious *crrrrack!* from my window. Startled, Colin yanked me toward him as I threw the blanket up at the last moment. The peace of the room broke as the window shattered, raining ice and tiny shards of glass on us.

Sleet and hail poured through the window, its metal frame still shaking. The floor was glittered with broken glass. Huddled together, I trembled and Colin wrapped his arms tightly around me, his cast poking into my side.

Before I could say anything, the door burst open. Jenna barreled into the room, RA-on-duty bag flapping behind her. She stopped short when she saw the glass, casting her gaze wildly about the room. I'm not sure what surprised her more, the broken window or the sight of Colin and me on top of one another under a blanket. Either way, Jenna stared at me, horrified hand over her mouth.

As absurd as it seemed, I was more worried about getting a humiliatingly well-intentioned safer sex lecture from Jenna than about my broken window. "We're fine!" I scrambled up, throwing off the blanket. As the fabric fell away, I heard a wave of the glass hit the floor. Jenna inhaled sharply, and I said a silent thankful prayer that I hadn't been cut to ribbons.

I turned to check on Colin. He was staring at me, mirroring Jenna's stunned expression. I reached up to touch my face and felt something sticky on my fingers. When I pulled my hand away, it was covered with blood.

Memories of my dad's rages flooded my mind. The blood that bloomed into bruises, the accidents that were never really accidents. Uncomfortable looks from teachers that mirrored Colin and Jenna's. That unsettling feeling of a hot, white spotlight shining down on me, slick with sweaty fear and shame.

Get through it, a little voice in my head instructed. I instantly clamped down tight on my emotions, turning them off like the flick of a switch.

"Well, this sucks." I licked at my lips and tasted blood. "Guess I'll have to get a new blanket." My voice came out flat and eerily calm as I responded to my own emergency with a practiced efficiency. "Jenna, can you grab me a pair of shoes from my closet?

I don't want to cut my feet. Also, can you get me some paper towels out of the bathroom?"

Something about the tone of my voice jolted Jenna out of her stupor. She kicked into crisis response mode, grabbing a pair of Converse and tossing them in my direction. They landed next to me on the bed and I pulled them on as Jenna disappeared out the door. Feet covered, I gave Colin a once-over. "You okay? Did you get cut?"

Colin peeked at me and flushed a little green. He shook his head delicately side to side.

"Good. Stay there. I don't want you to step on any of this."

"My shoes—"

"Are full of glass." I tried to smile but hissed at the pain that came from my cheek. "Give me a minute."

Jenna reappeared, holding a handful of damp paper towels. I took them from her gingerly made my way toward Izzy's dresser mirror. "Can you help Colin?" I asked, but Jenna was already moving.

Good. One less thing to worry about.

I turned my attention to my face. My back was mostly turned to the wall and I was covered with the blanket except where it had slid down, so the right side of my face had taken most of the damage. I had a large rounded cut on my right cheek where I had turned toward instead of away from the sound, along with several smaller cuts along my scalp and a speckle of tiny cuts along my jaw. The smaller cuts would heal okay, but I was definitely going to need stitches for my cheek. I pressed a handful of paper towels to it, wincing as I tried to slow the bleeding.

"Trust me, it looks worse than it is." I muttered, trying not to move too much. "I'm a bit of a bleeder." Jenna nodded numbly at me but didn't say anything, ducking out again.

Small pieces of glass sparkled in my hair. I shook my head gently and watched several fall to the ground. I grabbed a comb and began to gently pull it through my hair, careful not to pull too hard and cut myself again. My shirt stuck to my back and, turning around, I could see a few places where the glass had gone through my hoodie and shirt and into my right shoulder, blood seeping through and turning the hoodie an ugly brown.

I tried to pull the hoodie off but my right arm burned when I tried to raise it. Lowering it, I heard voices in the hallway. Trailing behind Jenna was an older Campus Security officer I vaguely recognized and, of course, Jay, who looked supremely pissed. Didn't he ever take a night off?

"Brighton." Jay jerked his head toward the broken window. As the older officer began examining my room, Jay turned to me. His furious gaze wandered from cuts along my forehead to the bloody towels pressed to my cheek as he catalogued my injuries. When his eyes met to mine, he looked ready for a fight.

Well, if he wanted one, I'll give him one. I couldn't believe he was angry at me for something that was in *no way* my fault.

"You missed some," I hissed at him, turning slightly to show him the glass still stuck in my shoulder.

"Son of a…," Officer Brighton muttered under his breath, and Jay silenced him with a look. His head tilted to the side as he reached slowly for my shoulder, as if to turn me.

Colin coughed. "Umm, can someone pass me my shoes?"

Jay stiffened and his hand fell away. Colin was still sitting on Izzy's bed surrounded by a mass of crumped sheets, looking scared but otherwise the picture of health. A vein pulsed in Jay's jaw as he glared at Colin, who stared back at him bewildered.

When no one else moved, I picked up Colin's shoes and handed them to him. "Here." While Colin shook glass out of his shoes, I turned my attention back to Jay.

"Well, officer, what's the verdict?"

He cocked his head to the side. "You're going to need stitches."

"I know," I said, trying to match his disinterested tone. The cut on my cheek burned and my right shoulder ached. The adrenaline was obviously starting to wear off. I knew from experience that this was when the sucky painful part started. I did not want that to happen while everyone was watching me because I would start crying soon, and I could not deal with the humiliation of bawling in front of an audience on top of everything else.

Jay and I were still scowling at each other when Officer Brighton broke the silence. "So you two were, uh…"

I turned my back to Jay. If I pretended he wasn't there, maybe he'd leave. "We were watching TV." I pointed at the laptop, still sitting on the chair, and Brighton had the decency to look sheepish. "All of the sudden the window shattered, like something hit it from the outside. I was sitting closest to the window and had that blanket wrapped around me." I pointed to the blanket. "It shielded me from most of the glass."

Officer Brighton occupied himself taking notes on a small pad. "Did you hear or see anything before the window broke?"

"Nope."

Colin shook his head, too. He had his shoes on and was sitting on the edge of the bed, ready to bolt at the first opportunity. I couldn't blame him. Being caught in flagrante by an RA and two Campus Security Officers wasn't my idea of a good time either, even if we hadn't been doing anything.

"I remember the wind was loud and the window was rattling a lot because of the hail," I offered.

Brighton examined the window frame. He let out a long, low whistle. "This glass is broken like something big hit it." Only a few fragments of glass remained around its edges. "If it had been something small, like a B-B or pellet, I'd expect the hole to be smaller, But the whole window if gone. Sheet of glass this big…" He shook his head. "I don't know, especially with you on the second floor. It's like someone took a bat to it, or maybe a tree branch?"

As Officer Brighton and Jay look around the room for some explanation, my head started to spin. I pulled the paper towel away from my cheek to find it soaked with blood. I sat down on the edge of my bed with a thump that jarred my shoulder. "Ow."

"Hey! Callie!" I didn't even know I'd closed my eyes. I forced them open. "Look at me," Jay instructed as shone a small flashlight in my eyes. The light made my head feel worse, so I closed them again. A whooshing like the ocean sloshed around in my head, making everything else sound far away. I was so tired. It had been a really long day. Someone shook my arm, but I ignored it.

I knew why the window was broken. One minute, I was kissing a guy who was supposed to be Izzy's while I was sitting *on her bed.* And the second I thought about her? Boom.

This wasn't a freak accident. It wasn't a tree branch or the storm. Izzy was pissed at me for making out with a guy she kind of had dibs on. I'd finally found someone who made me happy, and Izzy, jealous, angry, very-dead Izzy, had blown up in response. Kind of literally.

But there was absolutely no way I could tell anyone else that.

18.

I hate hospitals.

I hate the florescent lighting that always makes your skin look grey. The antiseptic smell that burns your nose. The persistent buzz and whir of machines that only serve to emphasize how no place so full of people should ever be so quiet.

I also hate how much they remind me of my mom. Whenever I get a whiff of that awful medicinal scent, I immediately see her in my head, tiny and frail, a scarf wrapped around her head to hide her bare scalp.

I hate that. My mom wasn't like that. She was a beautiful woman with a big smile. She lit up a room. She doesn't deserve to be perpetually tied in my head to something that reeked.

When she died, I'd made a vow that I'd never willingly enter a hospital again unless it was absolutely necessary. Unfortunately, it had been deemed exactly that after I'd gotten a little lightheaded. Whether from a loss of blood or the sight of too much of it, my eyes closed for the tiniest second, and the next thing I knew, here we were.

Shitgri-la.

I opened my eyes then closed them, trying to block out the noises, the smell. A pair of cool, rough hands closed over mine. "Did you bring me here?"

"I rode with you in the ambulance," Jay replied, his voice rough and low like he'd just woken up.

"I take it I'll live?"

"You'll live. You lost a fair amount of blood, though. The cut on your back was worse than I thought. I couldn't tell because of the hoodie." He sounded angry at himself. "You had to have over thirty stitches in the back and another couple in your cheek. The doctor doesn't think your face will scar much, maybe not at all."

I opened my eyes again, squinting against the overly bright light. "I guess there goes my modeling career."

I felt his hands pull away from mine abruptly. "I wish you wouldn't do that." His voice was quiet and serious, irritation boiling just under the surface.

"What am I doing exactly? Look at me, I'm not in good enough shape to do anything," I folded my hands across my stomach to keep them from shaking.

"It isn't a joke. You could have been hurt a lot worse, or even died."

I resisted the urge to ask him why he cared. It was obvious. Jay treated me like a bird with a broken wing. He wanted to fix me. I might be completely screwed up, but I wasn't broken. I didn't need a hero.

"I am well aware of my mortality. Mine and everyone else's."

Jay scrubbed at his tired face with his hand. I kept thinking he was going to get up and walk out, but instead he sat quietly, waiting for me to say something.

"How long have I been here?"

"About six hours."

"Do I have to stay?" I couldn't, wouldn't, stay in that hospital a second longer than I had to. If nothing else, I absolutely couldn't afford it. I might have campus insurance, but it was minimal, at best. The only way things would get worse was if I had a huge medical bill to contend with.

"They wanted to keep you the rest of the night for observation. You'll get out soon."

"You don't have to wait. I can walk back."

"You're kidding, right?" He laughed. "You're on so many pain meds right now you'd be lucky to find your shoes, forget finding your way back to campus." He changed tack before I could argue. "One of the ADs was here earlier. She wanted you to know the college would pick up any medical bills you had. She already talked to someone at the hospital and it's taken care of."

"So they can bill me later? Great."

Jay shook his head. "Everyone is seriously freaked out by the way your window broke. She didn't say it, but I think they're worried you'll sue the school."

The flood of relief was enough to push me over the edge. Once the tears started, they wouldn't stop. I sobbed uncontrollably, my back twinging with every shake of my shoulders. It hurt so much I thought I might pass out, but I kept crying.

Jay stood over me, gently pushing the hair back from my forehead and making shushing sounds. It was the same thing my mother had done when I was a little girl and I fell of my bike and skinned my knee or when I got sick, so sick that I cried because my whole body hurt. The gesture made me cry harder because I had forgotten she did it and now that it was happening, it was like living it all over again. I could see her face, feel her cheek pressed against the top of my head, remembering the way she would wrap her whole body around me, all five feet of it, and rock me gently. Sometimes she'd brush all my hair up into her hands and twist it up off my neck, allowing the cool air to dry the sticky sweat that was always lurking beneath it in the Texas heat.

The motion was an act of love, ingrained a hundred times over, and I had forgotten it until that moment. I hated that. I hated how frail my memory was, how easy it was to forget all the little things that someone you loved could do or say that made them real and showed they loved you in return.

Sometimes it seemed like Death came suddenly, a thief in the night to take your loved ones from you. But the real curse Death left you with was the way a person could die slowly inside you, memory after memory taken while you weren't looking. I had lost so much of my mother already, lost things I didn't even know were gone.

It made me grateful Izzy kept coming to me, even if she was angry and blamed me for her death or jealous that I was alive when she wasn't. I would accept whatever she gave me, because it kept her alive in the world, alive inside me.

It was strange to feel so much love for someone who had tried to hurt me, but after my dad it wasn't exactly a new experience. It was more proof to me that even monsters have people who loved them, who never truly forgot them. And I would not give up on Izzy; I would not stop trying to help her as much as I could.

Eventually I stopped crying. Jay stood next to my bed, his fingers leaving a cool trail across my forehead.

"Thanks." My words were muffled and stuffy as I wiped my

cheeks with the back of my hand.

"Here." He handed me a tissue from the box by the bed. I was genuinely grateful he'd stayed and smiled at him.

I was about to thank him for his kindness, but he pulled his hand away abruptly, dropping back into the chair next to me like nothing had happened. He leaned back, kicking his legs out in front of him in a practiced position that made him look relaxed. I'd seen it enough times to know it meant he was trying hard to look like what was about to happen wasn't all that serious.

"So. You and Colin are dating."

"We haven't talked about it, but yeah, I guess we are." I shrugged to cover my discomfort, then hissed as my shoulder pulled. Jay frowned, but said nothing, like he was waiting for some further explanation. Like he deserved one. "Not that it's any of your business."

"I'm making it my business. You shouldn't be dating anyone right now. You're in bad enough shape as it is without getting hassled by some creep."

"He is not some creep! He's an incredibly sweet guy who cares a lot about me." Jay snorted derisively, but I ignored him. "Just because he doesn't get all alpha-male caveman on me every fifteen minutes doesn't mean he isn't a wonderful person. Not everyone needs to be in control of everything all the time."

"Oh, is that the appeal? He's all sensitive and caring? I bet he sends you little emo songs, you know, songs about pretty, cruel girls who always pick assholes, who never give nice guys like him a chance?"

"You know what, Jay? For someone who is supposed to be all worldly and mature, you sure can be a judgmental ass. Yes, I like that he's different. I like that he's thoughtful and sensitive and that he listens to me when I talk. I like that he probably doesn't know how to change the oil in my car and that I can probably beat the crap out of him blindfolded. I like that he isn't afraid of me being too smart or too strong."

Jay shot up, his ramrod straight Marine posture kicking in as he sat forward. "What about Izzy?"

How did he always know exactly what to say, good or bad? "What about Izzy? She's dead, Jay. She's dead and I'm not and Colin likes me now, not because I am Izzy's best friend, but because he likes *me*. And even if he only likes me because of Izzy, I don't care. I like him. I want to be with him. And that's more than Izzy ever gave him." I fell back against the pillows and clamped my jaw shut to make it clear the conversation was over.

Jay gave me a long, hard stare. I could see the muscles in his jaw clenching and unclenching as he bit back about a half dozen responses. He seemed to be deciding something, but I didn't know what. I stared right back, not wanting to be the one to look away first.

Eventually I won. He stood up abruptly and headed for the exit. He was half-way out the door when he turned back to me. "I'm going to go see if I can find something to eat, or at least get some coffee." I pretended like I didn't hear him. It was stupid and childish, but for the moment I was too annoyed and tired to care.

"Do you want anything?" I gave him the briefest head shake.

"Fine," he sighed, and began pulling the door shut behind him. "I'm sure he likes you, Callie. I get that. Here's what I don't get. If Colin cares so much about you, why isn't he here?"

The door closed with a muffled shwoosh. I sat here, stewing. I wanted to ignore everything Jay had said, write it off as meddling or jealous. The problem was that he had a point.

If Colin cared for me, why wasn't he here? Why hadn't he come with me in the ambulance? Why did Jay have to be the one who guessed how awful I would feel waking up in the hospital alone? Why couldn't the guy I wanted know me at least as well as the guy I wanted to avoid?

I didn't want to think about it, any of it. Not my dead mom, not my equally dead best friend, not my absentee kind of boyfriend, not my overbearing not-boyfriend. I grabbed the button that fed the painkillers into my IV. I pressed it once, then again for good measure. The machinery clicked and whirred as I waited for the meds to kick in and carry me away.

19.

I woke up as one of the nurses came in to check on my IV. As she straighten the blankets over me, I started to ask her what time it was. Before I could get a word out, she pressed a finger gently to her lips and nodded toward the corner.

Jay was stretched out on the bench beneath the window. He looked like he was out but I guessed he was probably like the rest of the military men I'd known—able to fall asleep anywhere, then become immediately alert at the first small sound. One of my cousins told me it was a skill you picked up before you even made it out of Basic. Once learned, it wasn't something you could turn off.

I pointed to my wrist, silently asking the time. In a barely audible whisper, the nurse said, "It's about eight-thirty. Dr. Tabor will be in around ten to give you the once over. I think they'll probably send you home then."

She tilted her head toward his sleeping figure as she adjusted the pillow under my head. "I don't think he's had more than an hour's sleep. I've been on since midnight, and this is the first time I've seen him shut his eyes. You ought to let him rest while he can."

She finished fiddling with the bags that fed my IV and turned to leave. "You still have a few hours. Try to rest." She looked over at Jay again, and a tender look passed over her face. "You've sure got a sweet boyfriend." She closed the door before I could correct her.

I drifted in and out, watching Jay between naps. Asleep he looked much younger than he ever seemed awake. His brow was furrowed and he seemed smaller, somehow vulnerable without his persistent hyper-vigilance. Awake he was always in control of the situation, all pistons firing, ready to defeat the villain and save the day with a wink and a smile. Sprawled on the bench, he looked like someone who needed saving himself.

Dr. Tabor arrived a little after ten. He went about his work with a brisk business-like air. After briefly inspecting my forehead and changing the dressing on my shoulder, the doctor pronounced me fit to be released. He went over some instructions with me.

"Try not to get your shoulder wet if you can help it."

I looked at him out of the corner of my eye. "Have you ever seen the AC showers?"

Dr. Tabor ignored me, continuing to make small notes in my chart. "I'm prescribing you some antibacterial cream. You'll need to change your bandages daily."

"Daily?" I couldn't figure out how I was going to change the bandage by myself, but I figured I'd manage somehow. In a worst case scenario, I could always ask Jenna.

"She can get help from the Health Center if need be," Jay interjected. I hadn't even noticed he was awake. I grumbled but didn't bother arguing. At least he wasn't insisting he play nurse himself. Dr. Tabor gave me some release papers and left a nurse to remove the IV. She offered to help me get out of bed and put my clothes on, but I politely declined.

I grabbed the plastic bag containing my clothes and jewelry. Glancing through it, I saw the EMTs had cut my shirt and hoodie off to get a look at the glass in my shoulder.

I held the ruined shirt up with one hand. "I don't suppose you have an extra t-shirt or something hidden on you."

Jay frowned. "No. I should have thought of that, though. Do you want me to run back to campus and get you something?"

At that moment, the door opened and a huge bouquet of balloons squeezed through the doorway. They were brightly colored and covered in sayings like "Get Well Soon" and "Thinking of You." The largest featured a cartoon of a black cat and said, "Hope you get back on your paws soon!"

Colin emerged from behind them. He was carrying a paper bag in his good hand. I giggled when I saw his gigantic smile, and he reddened in response. "I guess I went a little overboard." He unwrapped the balloon string from his cast and set the little sandbag weighing them down. Then he held out the bag to me. "The essentials."

"More food?"

"Clothes, actually. I called to see when visiting hours started and they told me you were being released today. I figured you'd want something to wear. It's some jeans and a button-up shirt, so you won't have to raise your arm, plus socks and underwear."

I blushed at the thought of him going through my underwear drawer. Colin seemed to read my thoughts. "I hope that was okay," he stammered. "I wasn't trying to be nosey. I thought…"

"It's more than okay," I offered him a warm smile. "It's exactly what I needed."

Colin reached out, gently brushing the hair back from the right side of my face with a frown. "I'm glad you're alright."

"How'd you get into her room?" Jay's deep voice rumbled

from the bench and I flushed. I'd almost forgotten Jay was there.

"Oh! Hey, man." Colin ran his hand down his jeans. "When did you get here?"

"How'd you get into her room?" Jay repeated firmly.

"Well, I was going to have Jenna let me in, but the door was unlocked when I got there." Colin shrugged and turned his attention to me. "I wanted to get here before they released you, and I figured you would need your clothes."

"Her room was locked." Jay's eyes narrowed. "I locked it myself when we left."

Colin's cheeks puffed as he blew out a long stream of air. "I don't know what to tell you, man. It was unlocked when I got there."

"If he says it was unlocked it was unlocked. Drop it, Jay."

Colin's glance swiveled between us, lips pursed. "Wait." His brow furrowed as he turned to Jay. "Were you here…all night?"

I shot Jay a glance of warning, but he ignored me. "Where else would I be?"

Colin's jaw tightened. "Meaning what, exactly?"

Jay smirked. "Nothing."

I suddenly felt overwhelmingly tired of both of them. I pushed the covers back, easing myself out of bed. As Colin took a step back to give me room to maneuver, Jay began crowding past him to get to me, hands extended. I couldn't believe his gall.

"Stop," I said batting Jay's hands away. "I'm a little sore, but I'm fine. They already released me. I think that means I'm capable of getting out of a bed and putting on my clothes."

Jay stepped back, crossing his arms over his chest. Colin

looked from me to Jay and back again, a confusion and hurt mingled on his face. I gently took the bag from him, praying that the back of the gown was tied tight enough for me to make it into the bathroom without flashing both of them the back of my underwear.

When I reached the blessed privacy of the bathroom, I closed the door and flipped on the lights. Splashing water on my face, I caught a glimpse of myself in the mirror. My hair was sticking out in all directions. I had small bandage along my cheek covering my stitches. The rest of that side of my face was covered in small raised cuts where tiny shards of glass had hit me. The weight I'd lost and the general lack of sun in the Pacific Northwest made my already pale skin ghostly, emphasizing every mark against the pallor of my slightly hollowed cheeks. The dark circles of sleep-deprivation beneath my eyes were like bruises.

"I look more like a ghost than you do, Iz," I whispered, fleetingly wondering if she was with me even here.

I took the clothes out of the bag and pulled them on slowly, taking inventory of my physical limits with every ache and pain. Then I ran my fingers through my hair until it was more or less straight. My shoulder pulled as I did it, and I winced.

When I came out of the bathroom, I found Colin leaning against the edge of the hospital bed, his head bowed as he flipped through tracks on his iPod. He gave me a tight smile and removed the buds from his ears, stuffing everything into the pocket of his hoodie. Jay seemed to have disappeared in my absence.

Small blessings. Maybe I was being unkind after he'd spent the entire night by my side, but I was relieved to only have to deal with

187

one of them.

I eased myself onto the bench to pull on the socks and Doc Martens Colin had brought me. I winced when I dragged the first sock on and propped myself against the wall while I waited for the blood to rush out of my head. The world flowed in and out of focus; the pain meds were obviously still affecting me.

"Want some help?" His words were clipped and closed.

"Yes, please. If you don't mind." I knew he was angry but I didn't quite understand why. Yes, Jay had spent the night in the hospital with me, but it wasn't like I'd asked him to. And yes, Jay had been a jerk when Colin showed up, but I didn't have a lot of control over that either. Jay did what he wanted, whether I liked it or not.

Colin busied himself with getting my left foot into the boot, tying it, and moving to the right one. It wasn't easy with his hand still in his cast, and I reached down to tie the first boot while he worked my foot carefully into the other.

"I would have come with you if they'd told me I could," he said quietly.

"I know. He was here when I woke up. I didn't invite him."

"You didn't ask him to leave, though, did you?"

"No, but—"

"I don't like him being here."

I turned my head slightly toward him. Though our faces were only inches apart, Colin kept his gaze studiously trained on my foot, refusing to meet my gaze. "Colin, I'm sorry. I didn't mean to hurt you."

"You don't need him. You have me."

"Okay," I said, unsure of what to do. Colin seemed to think I'd asked Jay to come to the hospital instead of him, and it didn't seem like anything I could say would change his mind.

When Colin finished, I watched as he stepped back and tilted his head to one side, as if examining his handiwork. He held a hand out to me, and I smiled slightly.

"What's so funny?"

"Way to get that slipper on, Prince Charming." The blood rushed to my head again and I wavered slightly. Colin reached out and pulled me into his arms to steady me.

"Prince Charming, huh?"

"Absolutely." I bit my lip.

His eyes sparkled like chips of blue sky reflected in clear water. "I think I like that," he said, gently tipping my chin up as he bent to kiss me. Right as his lips were about to touch mine, the door opened behind us.

"Ugh, Jay!" I practically shouted, jumping back from Colin. One of the nurses ducked her head and closed the door.

"He went back to campus." Colin voice was smooth and cold as glass. I turned around and was startled by the angry look on his face. Did he think I had wanted Jay to be the one kissing me?

"Good. I wasn't sure I could take any more of him today." I closed the distance between Colin and I again, wrapping my arms loosely around his waist. After a long moment, he relaxed into the embrace, pulling me close and resting his chin on my head as I buried my face in his shoulder. "Jay took off while you were in the bathroom. I offered him a ride, but he said he'd rather walk."

I pulled back to look at Colin. "Since when do you have a car?" I narrowed by eyes. "Have you been holding out on me?"

"Ha! No." He smiled. "I've got a friend who lives off campus. I called and asked if I could borrow his car. He lends it out sometimes. I told him I needed to pick my girlfriend up from the hospital, and he agreed to let me use it in exchange for a chance to meet any girl who'd be stupid enough to date me." Colin rolled his eyes. "His words, not mine."

Girlfriend. I rolled the word around in my head. Colin had called me his girlfriend. A couple of days ago, he'd been just one more guy following Izzy around, someone who was only ever available as a friend. I'd never considered if I'd wanted him until she was gone, and now I wondered if I'd always kind of liked him but couldn't admit it to myself. What good would have it done as long as he was attached to Izzy? Sure, this seemed like they were happening kind of fast with Colin. But hadn't I more or less said the same thing to Jay last night?

Boyfriend.

I, Callie McCayter, had a boyfriend.

I'd never done more than go on a random date here or there, so the word felt like it marked something distinct. Momentous. Historic.

"Well, Boyfriend," I said, trying the word out. It sounded good. I picked up the ridiculous balloon bouquet. *My first bouquet.* A goofy grin spread across my face. "I guess you'd better get me home then."

"After you, my lady." He swept his casted arm toward the door in a princely way. "Your chariot awaits."

"Is it made of pumpkin?" I took his arm in my hands.

"No, but…" He wrinkled his nose. "It does kind of smell like the inside of one."

Despite my exhausted, aching body, I laughed. Colin beamed like he'd won a prize from a rigged game at the county fair. "I love that sound," he whispered in my ear. "You have the best laugh." I flushed in response and pulled him a little closer as we walked.

So far this boyfriend/girlfriend thing?

It didn't suck.

20.

When I got back to my room, the glass was gone and the window had been replaced. I had three voicemails from various campus offices offering me any support I needed as well as handwritten notes on my door wipeboard from both my RA and AD. Jay's assessment appeared dead-on. The college had obviously gone into full-scale damage control mode at the vaguest possibility of a potential lawsuit.

As if I have a lawyer. I dumped my things in a heap on my bed. *I don't even have a dentist.* I wondered belatedly if the Millers *were* suing the school over Izzy's death. I wondered if anyone would tell me if they did.

Colin offered to skip class and spend the day with me but I declined. "Go to class."

"You sure?" Colin stood in the doorway, watching me closely. His fingers kept tapping against the frame. "I've already done the reading. I won't miss much."

"No. One of us should be there so we both get decent notes." As much as I wanted him with me, what I wanted more was sleep. "Tell Dr. Cliff I am sorry for missing more class and that I will be at our meeting tomorrow."

Colin chewed at his lip. "Okay. I'll go. But I'm coming back."

I walked over and placed my hand in the center of his chest, fingers curled around the fabric between the buttons. "Good." I kissed him lightly. "I want you to. But for now…" I pushed him into the hall by his shirt. "Go. You know how Dr. Cliff feels about lateness."

Colin pulled my fingers from his shirt and with a quick squeeze, let me go. I closed my door and stood for a moment, savoring the memory of his hands and lips on mine. Then my stomach issued an angry protest, reminding me I hadn't eaten yet. I was still queasy from the pain meds, but I figured food might help. I didn't want to eat two-day-old pizza, so I made myself face the cafeteria.

It seemed like everyone on campus had already heard about the window, though from the snatches of conversation I caught over Jenny Lewis pouring through my headphones at top volume, the stories appeared to mostly confirm that I was a grade-A basketcase who had smashed the window and threatened to jump. A girl standing next to the fruit table insisted I had to be talked down by Campus Security and possibly the Astoria SWAT team.

The tale was beyond ridiculous. I was pretty sure there wasn't a SWAT team anywhere in Oregon outside of Portland, and certainly not in all of Clatsop County, but it underscored how small our campus was. Not only had news of my most recent disaster had time to make it all the way through the student body, there was sufficient interest to blow it wildly out of proportion. I could feel their eyes on me while I wolfed down a large square of lasagna and a serving of green beans.

As soon as I was done, I marched back to my room. Izzy and I needed to have a talk; I knew I couldn't put it off any longer. The more out of control her outbursts became, the less likely it would be that I stayed under the radar while I dug into her death.

The sensible part of me couldn't believe my concrete plans for the day included having a difficult heart-to-heart with my dead best friend, but that was my life now. I had a real, honest-to-goodness boyfriend and I was in a fight with a ghost. I wasn't sure which one I found more implausible.

I paused a moment at my door, steeling myself, then swung it open wide. It bounced against the dresser with a *thwump!*

Everything was the same as I'd left it. No new evidence of an Izzy tantrum. Closing it quietly behind me, I sat on my bed, gripping the edge with my fingers.

Just get it over with already, a voice in my head whispered. *She probably knows what you want to say anyway.*

"Izzy?" My voice cracked. I took a deep breath and tried again. "Iz, are you here?"

The silence was deafening. I felt like a world-class tool. For all I knew, I was about to deliver a deeply emotional soliloquy to myself. "Izzy, if you're here, give me some sign, please. Preferably one that won't send me back to the hospital."

I sat facing Izzy's side of the room, shoulders tense, waiting. The seconds stretched out like hours, and I felt like an even bigger moron as each passed without a response. After three minutes ticked by on my alarm clock, I heaved a sigh and reached down to try to untie my boots, moving carefully to avoid pulling at my stitches. As I worked the knot out of the bow on my left boot, I saw a book fall from Izzy's desk out of the corner of my eye, landing on the carpet with a thump.

I jerked up straight, ignoring the pain. "Izzy?" I asked

cautiously. Ten long seconds passed and then another book flicked off the top of the stack on the desk, landing next to the first one.

"You're here." I swallowed, my mouth dry. "Are you still mad?" I tried to force myself to sound natural. "Umm, knock another book off if you're still mad." I waited; nothing happened.

"Good, because we need to talk." I cleared my throat, then aimed for what I hoped was a light and breeze delivery. "I'm dating Colin, Izzy." A book thumped off the desk, banging hard against the floor. Then another, and another, each coming a little faster than the last.

"Stop that!" The thumping stopped abruptly. "I know you don't like it. But I like it. I like him. I think…" I pressed my lips together, summoning the courage to say everything I needed to. "I think maybe I did even, you know, *before*. Hell, maybe you knew it before I did." Nothing moved so I forced myself to keep going. "But I know it now. I like him. A lot. I might even be falling in love with him. And frankly, I don't care if you're upset. Because it's happening."

The entire stack of books still sitting on the desk fell to the floor as if they'd been shoved, landing in a heap, covers bent and spines cracked.

"I'm sorry, Izzy." I was angry, but also so sad. I hated hurting her; I just couldn't see a way around it. "I'm sorry it has to be him, and I'm sorry if that hurts you. I'm not trying to take him away from you. But I don't want to be alone anymore. He's good to me and we have so much in common, more than the two of you ever did. If you could see that, you'd understand."

As I spoke, the room grew colder and colder until my breath fogged out in front of me.

"Why can't you be happy for me?" I choked back a sob. "I want you to be happy for me. I'll still help you, I promise. Maybe Colin could help…"

The books on the floor flew into the air. They froze in place for a moment, then began swirling as if caught in an invisible cyclone. More books rose from the shelf above Izzy's desk, feeding the churning mass, spinning faster and faster. Suddenly, one book flew out of the whirlwind, slamming against the wall to the left of me. Before I could really process how close it had been, a second book hit the wall even closer, this time to my right. It was boxing me in. I tried to move left, and the next book narrowly missed my head. Turning right, I scrambled in a crouch to the door as the assault continued, a hail of books chasing me across the room. I flung the door open and threw myself into the hallway—and into Colin's arms.

Colin looked at me, bewildered. "Callie, what—"

A book hit me square in the back, then another, and I stumbled against him. Colin's eyes shot past me, catching sight of the swirl of books before I got my fingers around the knob and pulled the door closed. We stood wordless and clutching each other as the books peppered the door with a whomping *rat-tat-tat*!

Tears streamed down my face. Colin eyes were practically falling out of his head, horror and confusion mingled on his paled face. I wrapped my arms around him, hugging tightly. He pulled me closer in response, holding me fully against him as if he could protect me with his body. The door to the bathroom swung open as a junior who lived down the hall sauntered out wearing nothing but a robe, a towel wrapped around her head.

"Jeez, get a room," she snarked as she edged around us.

Colin opened his mouth to speak, but I covered his lips gently with my fingers and shook my head.

"Not here." Taking his hand, I pulled him away, down the hall and out of the building.

21.

Colin was quiet as I led him past the residence halls and down the trail into the park beyond campus. I could tell he had a lot of questions but to his credit he didn't voice them; apparently he was willing to follow until I was ready to explain.

It was a clear day, the kind that left the air crisp and much colder than when the skies were blanketed in clouds. Walking such a long way made my whole body ache to the point where I was gritting my teeth, but I was too upset to stop. If I could have, I would have kept going forever. I wanted to take Colin and walk until we were so far that no one and nothing could hurt us.

But how far is far enough to escape the inevitable?

Eventually we arrived at a small gazebo hidden inside the edge of the park. Releasing Colin's hand, I curled up in the corner on the benches around its interior, wrapping my arms around my legs and pulling my knees up to my chin.

Colin stood in front of me, his hands shoved awkwardly in his hoodie pocket. I knew he needed an explanation, but now that I had him here, I couldn't figure out where to start. How did I tell him I'd been communicating with a dead person who, by the way, was also his ex?

What happened if he didn't believe me?

Worse, what happened if he did?

I waited for him to sit down next to me, but he kept shifting his weight back and forth, rubbing his hands on his jeans or tugging at his sleeves. He paced away from me, like he was leaving, then back, over and over, like he couldn't decide if he was going to stay or go. It made me feel tainted by association; somehow Izzy's rage was my fault, her presence the result of my own failure to look out for her in life. The idea that Colin didn't want to be anywhere near me overwhelmed me with sadness. Tears formed in my eyes but I blinked rapidly, trying to keep them at bay. I distracted myself by rolling a small pile of dried pine needles beneath against the wood until they were crushed and my hand was slightly stick with sap.

Eventually he ran out of steam, collapsing on the bench close enough that my toes touched the side of his leg. "What the hell was that?"

As much as I might be afraid to admit what was happening, I was more afraid of failing Izzy. I couldn't let that happen again; not when this was all I had left to give her. If that meant letting someone in who could help me hide her outbursts and figure out what really happened to her, then that was what I had to do. I had to tell someone, someone I could trust, someone who loved Izzy as much as I did.

Colin wasn't the best choice; he was the only choice.

"That was Izzy." The words came out simple and matter-of-fact, like naming a bird for a child seeing one for the first time.

"What do you mean, that was Izzy?" His voice was strained, the words full of careful consonants. He seemed like he thought I would snap if he pushed me. He was probably right. Underneath the calm exterior, I sensed his fear, but I didn't know who he was afraid of—Izzy or me.

"Izzy has been contacting me." The words gushed out. Now

that I'd decided to tell him, I needed to get it out before I changed my mind. "She asked me to help her figure out who killed her, and that's what I'm trying to do. I haven't been able to get very far, though, and she's mad. About that, and other things…"

I let the confession hang in the air. I could feel Colin's eyes on me, but I couldn't meet his gaze. It was bad enough he probably wasn't going to want to be my boyfriend anymore. But if he didn't believe me, it was off to a state hospital for sure. A girl who talks to ghosts? Crazy with a capital C.

I kept my attention focused on the mass of trees around us, which were full of wavering shadows and hushed sounds punctuated by the occasional cry of a gull. They were the same woods Izzy died in. She was alone, she was scared, and she needed help. None had come. No one deserved to spend their last moments on earth like that, waiting for a savior that never arrived.

If he thinks I'm nuts, then let me be. Better than Izzy being gone for good.

With a touch, Colin closed the distance between us. The fingers of his good hand wrapped around my ankle, pulling my attention to him. "How do you know she wants your help?"

"You believe me? You believe Izzy is talking to me?" If I were in his shoes, I wasn't sure I could be so accepting.

"I'll be honest with you. If you'd asked me that question two days ago, I probably would have made a beeline straight to the Counseling Center to insist they get you professional help. But—" he squeezed my ankle gently "—after the window last night, and the books today… The world is weird. I can't believe half the stuff that shows up on Reddit on a daily basis. Given what's happened right in front of me, how can I argue with you?"

"You believe that I am talking to a ghost because you've seen gifs of mice riding cats riding roombas?" I managed a small smile.

"I believe you are talking to Izzy because I believe there are a lot of things no one really understands. And…" Colin ducked his head down to try to catch my eye. "I believe *you*. If you say Izzy is here, and that she talks to you and needs your help, then I believe you." He squeezed my ankle again for emphasis, and I pulled his hand into mine.

"You believe me." I felt so relieved. "I didn't think anyone would. When I first saw her, I thought I must have gone crazy, like certifiably crazy."

"You actually saw her?"

"I think so?" I searched my memory. "I mean, I think I saw her. I feel like I saw her. She was in my room; she wrote a note on my door asking for help. But I haven't seen her again, so maybe not? I don't know."

He frowned. "Did she say anything? About that night or who hit her?"

"No. She didn't talk. I think she would have if she could." I shrugged. "At first, I thought maybe I was doing it all, that I was blacking out and not remembering it. Part of me still wonders… But all the stuff in the last two days, I didn't do any of that. I know I didn't."

Colin's took a deep breath through his nose. "Like those books."

"And the window."

Colin's head jerked toward me, and I nodded, confirming it was her. "If those things happened, and I've got the injuries to prove they did, and I didn't do them, then I think it must be Izzy. I'm not imagining it. She's here—well, she's in my room at least—and she needs my help."

"You said she talks to you. How exactly does she talk to you?"

I swallowed hard. "She doesn't talk exactly. I don't hear voices or anything. It's sort of tough to explain…"

I described every interaction I'd had with Izzy, from the first time she'd walked across the room and written on the mirror to the book cyclone that afternoon. He paid close attention as I rambled about the different ways I knew how to reach Izzy, how I'd experimented with the stuff she'd touched, and what I thought I should do next to try to figure out the identity of the person who hit Izzy.

"And that's it?"

"Yep." I brushed the needles I'd been picking at with my free hand onto the floor of the gazebo.

"Is there anything in particular that seems to set her off?"

"No. Nothing specific." Except my relationship with him, but I wasn't about to tell Colin that.

Colin put his head back against the wood railing. I chewed at my lip as I watched him processing everything. Even now, in the midst of revealing my terrifying secret about Izzy to Colin, I couldn't help notice how the greenish light that filtered down through the canopy of the trees fell on his face, giving his features an angular look. I could imagine what Colin would look like in five years, or ten, as he grew into his frame and lost some of the boyish roundness in his face. Colin was cute now, but I could see how handsome he would be as he got older. He was still holding my hand, and it was soft and warm in contrast to the growing cold.

I had no idea when I'd gotten in so deep with Colin, but the idea of losing him shook me to my core. I had been lost in a sea of misery and Colin pulled me out. I found the idea of breaking up our only days-old relationship suddenly unbearable.

"What I *don't* understand is why she doesn't just tell you who did it. She wrote on the mirror once, right? Why doesn't she do it again? Mystery solved."

"I wondered that, too. I don't think she can." I thought again of Izzy, of the slow careful letters she wrote. "It seemed like it was really hard for her."

"Like she couldn't remember how to communicate?"

"No. More like it was taking a lot of her energy or something. I got the feeling from the look on her face it was taking every ounce of strength she had to send me that message."

Colin had a far away expression, like he was trying to work something out in his head. "Maybe she only has so long she can last or something."

"Maybe?" I made small circles against the back of his hand. "Most the stuff she's moved or changed happened when I wasn't not there, or when I wasn't not looking. It's like it's easier for her if I'm not watching her directly. Also, it doesn't seem like she always has a lot of control."

"Well, her decorating seems deliberate." He chuckled. "Only Izzy would use her magical ghost skills for a dorm makeover."

I rolled my eyes. "Well that was obviously deliberate. I more meant that I think sometimes things are happening, other things, that she can't help."

"Like the books today?"

"Yeah." I hesitated, shifting away from him a little. "And other things. My point is, I don't think she meant for me to get hurt yesterday. I don't think she meant to hurt me today. I think she got super mad, and it just sort of happened." I shrugged and gave him a rueful smile. "I'm not exactly an expert at this. I think if she could write me a note, she would. I've noticed she almost never interacts with anything technological. No computers, no mp3 players, no cell phones, nothing. She doesn't even move them around, which, again, makes me think she can't for some reason."

Colin studied my face. "There's something you're not saying."

I ducked my head. "You think she's mad we're dating, don't you? That's why she broke the window, right?"

"Maybe. Maybe not." I'd wanted to sound more confident, but I couldn't bring myself to lie to him. "I think so. I think that's why she got upset today, too."

"God, I am such a jackass," He pulled his hand away from mine and folded it in his lap. "Poor Izzy, all alone, and here she is watching me put the moves on her best friend..." He pressed the bottoms of his palms against his eyes. "She must think I forgot all about her."

"Don't be so hard on yourself..." I began, but I couldn't think of anything to say. The truth was, I wanted to be with him so much I didn't care if Izzy hated it, even if that made me the worst friend in the world. Was it horrible I wanted him to feel the same way? Isn't that what any girl wants to happen to her new boyfriend's old flame, even if the dreaded ex happens to be her best friend? For them not to care what their ex thought?

"Do you, ummm, do you want to…"

"Do I want to what?"

Colin looked away from me, out toward the path back to school. At the end of it, I could see a tall, dark-headed girl jogging by, a small dog galloping beside her. It was such a normal, everyday-in-the-park scene that it made our discussion more macabre by comparison. I was still staring at the girl when Colin started talking again.

"Do you want to keep dating? If it upsets Izzy so much?"

I tried to keep the pain from showing on my face. Was this the same boy who had called me his girlfriend only a few hours earlier? But that was before, when he thought Izzy was gone for good. Now that he knew she was still here, still watching…

I guess he felt like he was cheating on her. I could understand that. I felt like I was betraying her by being with him. Why wouldn't he feel the same? As my stomach tied itself into balloon animal shapes, Colin's gaze turned toward campus again.

Back to Izzy. He'd already made up his mind and was ready to go fight another battle to win Izzy's affection, even if it was too late to save her. And what did that make me?

I already knew the answer. Nothing more than a consolation

prize. Next to Izzy, that was all I'd ever be. I focused my attention on my shoes, trying not to remember him tying them for me at the hospital.

Colin's voice broke me out of my sadness spiral. "Callie, there's something I have to tell you."

This is it. My chest tightened but I tried to keep my face blank. *This is where he tells me he can't be with me as long as I'm being haunted by my dead best friend.* "Okay." I jerked my head in agreement. "Go ahead."

Colin licked his lips nervously. "I was there, that night, at the party. I saw Izzy the night she died."

22.

"What?" The word popped out of my mouth, taking my breath with it.

"I was there," Colin repeated quietly, his head hung so low with the admission that I couldn't see his face, only his crown of blonde hair shining darkly in the late afternoon light.

"You didn't tell anyone. I know who the police talked to." He kept quiet as the words spilled out of me. "I saw the list. Jenna showed it to me right after it happened. She wasn't supposed to, but I begged her. I told her it would help me to know who on campus had tried to help Izzy, so she got a copy of the internal report off the Res Life hard drive. It listed the names of everyone who talked to the police and gave a summary of what they said." I stood up, needing to put space between us. "Someone from AC sat in on every interview. Your name was *not* on that list."

He continued to stare at his lap in a numb silence. Part of me knew I was being awful, especially after he had been accepting of my secret, but I didn't care. "How could you not come forward? Did you see her? Did you talk to her?"

"Yes."

I crossed my arms over my chest, hugging myself to keep from hitting something. "When and where, exactly?"

"I went to the party because I'd heard Izzy was going to be there. One of those firsties in your hall told me." He picked at the bandage on his cast, flexing his fingers against the hard edge. "She wasn't returning my phone calls or emails and she kept avoiding me on campus. I knew it was pathetic, but I wanted to see her. I needed to know why she'd stopped talking to me."

"And?"

"She was there, and she looked amazing. She always looked amazing." He glanced at me and blushed but I merely pressed my lips together, waiting for him to continue.

He licked his lips. "I, uh, I tried to talk to her a couple of times, but she…she said some stuff, and I got upset. So I started drinking. Then later I saw her dancing with this guy. Izzy was all over him and he had his hands…" Colin took a gulping breath. "I tried to stop her, but she told me off. Loudly. And in detail."

He shrugged, as if trying to roll the memory off his shoulders. "Anyway, after that, I started doing shots. I normally don't drink much, but I was already drunk when she screamed at me, so it didn't seem like a bad idea at the time. I guess I passed out." Colin swallowed rapidly, obviously trying to keep it together. "I woke up on a couch in the basement and everyone was gone. It was super early the next morning, like around four, so I walked home. I was so hungover I felt like I was dying. I actually had to stop to puke twice. When I got back to my room, I took a quick shower and went to sleep. I didn't hear about what had happened until I woke up that afternoon."

He was obviously so sad. I thought he might actually cry any minute. But I swallowed the rising feelings of sympathy when I remembered the way Izzy had been left in the dirt and darkness. I needed to hear his tale, each ugly detail from beginning to end. I had to know if Colin held the key to unlocking whatever it was Izzy was trying to tell me. Maybe that was why she was always so angry when his name came up. Instead of getting the truth from him, I kept making out with him.

I pushed the thought away. So far, everything about his story matched up with what I'd already heard. I remembered Izzy being particularly irritated with him in the weeks right before she died because instead of complaining about the attention—which was how you knew she secretly liked it—she'd simply treated him to the coldest shoulder I'd ever seen Izzy give anyone, and she wouldn't tell me why when I'd asked her about it. "Why didn't anyone else mention you being there?"

"I don't know why. Maybe it was because I passed out early. Maybe everyone they talked to was as drunk as I was or left before we got in a fight or something."

"You knew! Why didn't you come forward when they asked for witnesses?"

He looked at me with a pleading expression. "I didn't know anything someone hadn't already told them. I still don't know who she was dancing with. I was so drunk I wasn't sure of half of what I remembered anyway. I didn't think I knew anything that could help anyone…"

I flung my hands in the air. "Who are you to decide that?"

"I'm sorry, alright? I was embarrassed. I didn't want to tell anyone the things she'd said to me or that my solution to being rejected was to do five shots of tequila. I swear, Callie, if I thought I knew something, I would have gone straight to the police station."

I turned my back to him, unable to look at him for one more

second. I could tell how badly he needed me to believe him, to forgive him. Hadn't I just been asking for the same thing? I struggled against my anger as I thought how much I had needed someone to believe me about Izzy, to confirm I wasn't insane. Colin hadn't hesitated when I needed him to trust me. Why couldn't I do the same?

I felt as he came up behind me, touching my arm gently to let me know he was there. It was such a delicate touch, full of apprehension, that it broke the tense thread of composure holding me together. I knew how it felt to long for forgiveness you felt you had no right to expect. I'd felt that way with my dad a hundred times, and I hated making anyone, especially Colin, feel as worthless as I used to feel.

I turned toward him, and he put his arms around my waist, pulling me close with his casted arm. I buried my head against his shoulder and cried, long wrenching sobs. Colin cried along with me, his tears falling against the space where his cheek pressed against my forehead.

"I had to tell you, especially now." He spoke the words against my hair. "I didn't want you to think I was hiding anything from you. I don't want anything to wreck…whatever this is." He pushed me back a little, forcing me to look at him. "I'm sorry I couldn't help her, and I'm sorry it bothers her we are together, but I don't want to stop. I want us to be together. And I'm sorry I didn't tell you sooner. I'm so, so sorry."

"I know. I'm sorry, too. I don't blame you." I wiped at my face with the edge of my sleeve. "I guess I thought if anyone could have kept her safe that night other than me, maybe it would have been you."

"If you knew how many times I've thought that…" He shook his head like he was trying to shake off a bad dream. "Especially because she was so out of control the last time I saw her. I tried to talk to her, but she just wouldn't listen."

I frowned. "You know, every person I've talked to has insisted Izzy was trashed that night. I've never believed any of them. But you're different."

"It was bad."

"Then maybe…" If Colin swore Izzy had been drunk, maybe she had been. Maybe that was the clue I'd been missing. I had been so sure I knew Izzy better than anyone that I had automatically dismissed that part of the story out of hand. Looking back, it seemed like a huge mistake. "I hadn't wanted to believe it. I thought…"

"You thought you knew Izzy." Colin's words echoed my thoughts as if he'd heard them. He pulled me toward the bench and we sat down, still clinging to one another. "Look, I know she doesn't drink. I know she doesn't get out of control. So you have to believe me when I tell you this was a whole new side of Izzy, one I'd never seen."

He bent forward, resting his elbows on his knees and rubbing his eyes. "The guy she was dancing, or whatever, with? She was halfway out of her jacket when I tried to break it up and the shirt she had on wasn't much of a shirt. Half the guys at the party were watching them and catcalling like it was a striptease. She was laughing the whole time, like she loved every minute of it."

I shuddered at the thought of her, half-naked and laughing as some stranger felt her up in front of a room full of people she went to school with. It was completely unlike her. Izzy was always the poster girl of poised perfection; she used to say it was her mission in life to never have an embarrassing photo of herself posted on the Internet. "What did she say to you? Exactly."

"I kind of grabbed her arm. I was trying to pull her away from that sleaze she was dancing with. She just laughed in my face." He stared at his shoes, his voice low. "She called me a pathetic stalker. She said I was ruining her good time. She said she already had a daddy and he definitely didn't look like me. She told me to go find some desperate girl to follow around. She said I was a loser and that I had no life. Then she walked back over to that dude she was with and stuck her tongue down his throat."

"Wow." That was it. I didn't know what else I could say. Colin's account lined up with everything else I'd heard, and it was even worse than I'd guessed.

"Do you believe me?"

"Yes." I took a long breath and blew it out slowly, trying to mean it. I didn't want to believe any of what people said about Izzy's behavior before she'd died. But if I was going to help her, I needed to accept that she was completely messed up at the party. Colin's account more or less clinched it. That meant I had to reevaluate everything I'd assumed about any unaccounted time during Izzy's last night. Rolling this new information around in my head, the irony of Izzy's insults hit me. I suppressed a chuckle.

"What's so funny?"

I leaned my head against his shoulder and sighed. "You did what she told you to. You went out and found a desperate girl who doesn't mind if you follow her around. Unfortunately for Izzy, it's me."

"Maybe that's why she's so pissed." He interlaced his fingers with mine, squeezing them gently. "I did exactly what she asked, and she's still stuck with me all the time."

He choked back a snort, but it only made me laugh harder. "Menace."

"Traitor." He froze as soon as the word left his lips. "I was kidding. I didn't mean that."

"No, you're right." I sighed. "Maybe I am. But I still love her better than anyone else."

"I know you do." He was quiet for a moment. "It's why I wasn't sure if you'd...you know..."

"Go out with you?"

"Yeah."

I didn't answer right away. All of it was so hard take in. By blowing off Colin that night, Izzy probably turned away the only person at the party who cared enough to try to save her. "Are we crazy?"

"Yes?" He smiled. "And no. It depends on your scale, I guess. Historically speaking, we seem completely sane."

"Really?"

"Comparatively. We're not, like, Marcus Antonius and Cleopatra."

"Hmmm," I thought for a moment. "Or Ines de Castro and

Peter the First of Portugal."

"Andrew Jackson and Rachel Donelson."

"Ooh! Alexander Hamilton and Elizabeth Schuyler."

He kissed me lightly. "I love it when you talk history to me." I blushed. "And yes, this whole thing is kind of absurd. But measured against the sum of history, we're not as weird as we could be."

"Well thank goodness for that." I nudged him with my shoulder. "So we're good?"

"Yep." He took my hand firmly and pulled me up with him. "We're more than good. Now," he narrowed his eyes, "the real question is can we think of a couple crazier than Alexander and Eliza?"

I thought for a moment. "Hamilton and John Laurens?"

Colin burst out laughing, and I laughed with him. And we kept laughing as we walked back toward the dorms, holding hands and debating historical figures with love lives far more jacked up than ours. It seemed so strange to laugh. But how could we not? We were together, Izzy was haunting me, and somehow, Colin was still bugging her by proxy. So we laughed because we were both tired of crying and tired of fighting, both haunted by a girl we loved and couldn't forget.

23.

The lights were beginning to come on along the winding cobblestone path as we made our way through the academic quad. We passed the large reflecting pool and a flock of birds rose up off the surface and turned toward the ocean in the distance. They were large, elegant and graceful, but their dark shadows against the grey flat sky seemed to hint at an unknown darkness, and I shivered. Colin noticed and pulled me to him, looping his good arm around my waist.

I slowed to a stop as the back door of my hall came into view. Colin dropped his arm in response. "You okay?"

"Yes. Just…thinking." I started chewing on my nails, a bad habit I'd broken after years of being dragged by Izzy to a manicurist every other week. If it were a "super stress emergency," which usually coincided with finals or dealing with my financial aid, Izzy would even do them for me, carefully clipping and shaping each individual nail, then painting it a bright color with an insipid name like "Bubble Bath" or Red Light District Red," something I would never choose for myself, as repayment for making her engage in manual labor. Now the instinctive habit returned as I wondered what to do.

As much as I hated to admit it, I was scared. I didn't know what to say to Izzy to make her stop trying to hurt me. Was she jealous because I was dating her ex? Or was it because I hadn't been there to stop her that night at the party?

Or was it Colin she was after? Were her outbursts because he had been at the party, but hadn't been able to make her listen? Or was it because he hadn't come forward and admitted he'd been there?

Maybe she meant to hurt us both. But was it because we had found each other in her death, or because neither one of us had tried harder to help her, the two people she'd needed most?

Colin reached up and gently pulled my fingers away from my mouth with a small smile. "You know she hates it when you do that," he said, resting his forehead against mine.

"I'm afraid to go back up there."

Colin focused his attention on the door as though he was trying to see through it to what might be waiting for me inside. After a moment, he shrugged. "You could always come stay with me tonight."

"Ummm…" *Spend the night? All night? In his room?* "I don't know."

"I don't have a roommate, remember? I have an extra bed you can sleep in." He gave my hands a squeeze. "To my knowledge, Izzy's never materialized in my room and no one has been throwing my stuff around, so you're probably safe there, at least for the night."

I licked my lips. I'd never spent the night in a guy's room before, but I wasn't sure if Colin knew that. Though Crystal and Greg were firm in their stance that no daughter of theirs, blood or otherwise, was going to be shacking up with some guy before marriage, it didn't change the fact that AC had a casual attitude toward sleepovers. Everyone pretty much slept wherever they liked as long as it didn't cause roommate problems. Sexile your roommate once too often, and you were likely to end up in mediation with your RA. Otherwise, it was kind of a free for all. Izzy availed herself of this option on occasion; I never had.

"No pressure." He ducked his head to catch my eye. "I'm not trying to use Izzy as an excuse to put the moves on you. I just wanted to make sure you knew you had other options."

"I kind of…snore," I confessed, heat creeping into my face.

"I kind of already knew that."

Mortified, I covered my eyes with my hands. "Well, it would be terrific if the ground would open up and swallow me whole right now…"

"Oh, come on." He pulled my hands from my face and smiled. "You've fallen asleep with me in the room before. It's not so bad. I think it's kind of cute."

"Well," I said slowly, testing the words in my head before I said them, "I guess I could stay tonight. I have to figure out a way to deal with this long-term, but right now I'm too tired."

"Then it's decided. Go get your stuff. I'll go home and clean up a little." Colin brushed his lips against my forehead and turned back down the path. As I turned toward the door, I heard him call out to me: "Bring your stuff for British Empire and History of the American West and we can get our reading done." I nodded and swiped into the building as Colin jogged off in the direction of his hall.

When I got to my room, the books were stacked on the desk as though they'd never spun through the air like a bibliographic hurricane, wailing on me. I thought I'd feel relieved, but instead I was irritated. Why couldn't Izzy make up her mind? Either she was pissed at me or she wasn't. She couldn't try to pummel me one minute and then pretend like it never happened the next.

I didn't want to have another confrontation, so I took my time packing in order to stave off my nervousness. I threw my books into my backpack, then dug through my drawers for clothes. After critically considering my limited sleepwear choices, I settled on a pair of purple-and-white plaid pajama pants and matching purple scoop-neck tank top with white lace edging the borders and straps. It would be hard to put on over my head without pulling at the stitches in my shoulder, but I decided it was worth it to look cute for my first boy-girl sleepover.

Izzy would be so proud. I stuffed the items into the bag. Even now, when I flinched at every floorboard creak and door slam in the hall, I still wanted her approval.

I grabbed the DVD set Colin and I had been watching the night before when all hell broke loose, then packed the pain meds the hospital had given me and the bag of ointment and bandaging so I could get Colin to help me change it. I went into the bathroom and gathered my toothbrush and assorted toiletries.

I stuffed everything into the backpack along with a clean towel. At the last minute, I decided to bring my pillow with me. It seemed silly but having it with me made the whole thing seem innocent, like when Izzy and I went to slumber parties at other girls' houses when we were young. I stood in the middle of the room, hugging the pillow for a minute as a swarm of butterflies battered at my ribs. I was nervous, but also absurdly happy, which came with a heaping side of guilt.

"I can't believe I'm going to spend the night with a boy," I whispered. The only response was silence, but I felt Izzy was there, anyway. I couldn't explain how, but I always knew. I could feel it like a tingle across my skin; the quality of the quiet changed in her presence, seeming heavier and more pointed in its absence of sound.

"I'm glad you're here," I continued, "I can't imagine going off to do this without you knowing about it first." I slung my backpack over my good shoulder and walked to the door, hesitating with my hand on the knob. "I love you, Izzy. You're my sister. And even if you don't like it, or you don't like him, I'm glad you know about me and Colin. I'll see you in the morning."

I walked out and shut the door, locking it behind me. As I headed down the hall, I thought I heard the sound of sobbing through the door. I knew it was Izzy, but I couldn't bring myself to go another twelve rounds with her. Instead, I tightened my grip on my pillow and kept walking.

As I trekked across campus to Colin's building, I felt like there was a huge spotlight shining directly on me. You could never forget AC was a small school where everybody knew everything about everybody. I hadn't even known there was an opposite of the "walk of shame," but the "walk of going to get some?" To me it felt equally obvious, and far more likely to attract attention. I'm sure the fact that I was blushing every time I caught someone looking in my direction didn't help. The walk from my complex, Forest, to Calhoun, where Colin lived, normally took less than ten minutes, but it seemed an eternity passed before the building loomed into view.

Of all of the counter-intuitively-designed architectural mazes that comprised AC's various campus residence halls, Calhoun was the king. Because it was built along the downward slope of a ridge at the wooded back edge of campus, Calhoun was designed to go with the environmental challenges through an interlocking series of two-to-four-story towers that, thanks to the sloping, didn't quite line up together. Two parts didn't even connect at ground level due to the slope; the only thing connecting the building's sections was a glass sky bridge. Even the kids who lived in Calhoun couldn't always find their way around it, and I spent one long night there during our first year with Izzy dragging me up and down the stairwells while we tried, in vain, to locate the night's "epic" party.

Luckily, Colin's room was on the bottom floor of H tower, and there was an external door at the bottom of the H/I stairwell across from the C-Store just underneath the skybridge. I didn't exactly relish the idea of walking past the C-Store to get to his room, but it seemed better than going to the main door and then wandering through the Calhoun labyrinth for hours.

I clutched my pillow harder and headed toward the H/I stairwell door that was covered with a big green laminated sign reading" H/I! Come on in!" As I passed one of the small picnic tables outside the C-Store, I heard snickering and looked over to see two guys I didn't know smiling knowingly at me. Notoriety had its disadvantages and this was plainly one of them. I figured anyone else at school would have attracted *some* attention but being Izzy's roommate made me a hot topic of conversation and the broken window hadn't exactly helped. Catching my eye, the larger of the two gave me a knowing wink, and my stomach churned. Why was this the one time I had to forget my stupid earbuds? Trying to ignore them, I focused on the H/I! sign and marched resolutely onward.

I am an adult. I am an adult, I repeated in my head. *It is perfectly normal for me to sleep over in a boy's room. It happens all the time here.* Especially *here. I have no reason to feel embarrassed.*

Still, I couldn't help feeling very far from home and my family. My dad would have had a shotgun ready for any boy who'd even dared to think of spending a night in a room alone with his only daughter, and Crystal and Greg were every bit as strict in a nicer way. They'd been perfectly polite to every boy Izzy dated and every friend of those boys I'd tolerated escorting me to some dance Izzy wanted to attend, but you could tell they were a nice family, and they were raising nice girls, who did not do things like sleep with boys while they were in high school.

Izzy didn't mind because she never got serious enough with anyone to let them get very far, though plenty wanted to. For my part, I had never liked anyone enough for it to matter. Even if I had, I wouldn't have done anything to hurt Crystal and Greg after they'd taken me in. So this? Completely new territory.

I was so lost in my thoughts about the monumental step I was taking that I wasn't looking where I was going. And then I ran smack into Jenna and Marissa, the other RA in my building, as they were coming out of the C-Store.

"Sorry!" I exclaimed as Jenna juggled to keep hold of her bag of groceries.

I managed to hang onto the pillow, but the bag on my shoulder slid down my arm with a jolt. I watched in horror as my bag of toiletries fell out on the ground, the zipper breaking open as my sundries scattered. I scrambled to reclaim them.

Jenna handed my deodorant back to me. "Here."

"Thanks," I muttered, shoving it back into my bag.

"Are you going somewhere?" Jenna peered at me with a look of concern. "Is there something wrong with your room?"

Yes. I'm in a roommate conflict with my dead BFF over whether or not she will let me have boys sleep over, particularly someone she used to date. Did they train you how to mediate conflicts between the living and the dead?

"No, nothing's wrong." I shuffled my feet and looked everywhere but at Jenna. "I'm…"

"She's headed over to Colin's room." Marissa sauntered over to us, carrying my small bottle of face soap. "Here," she said, handing it to me with a smirk, "this was making a break for the bushes."

"Thanks." I focused my attention on shoving the bottle deep into my backpack.

"Colin's cute," Marissa batted her thickly mascaraed lashes at me in faux innocence. "I mean, if you're into that whole preppy thing. Good kisser, though," she whispered conspiratorially. Jenna glanced back and forth between us.

"Compared to what? Your boyfriend pillow?" I twisted my hands around the strap of the bag so hard it dug into my shoulder. Marissa just tossed her dark chestnut hair over the shoulder of her black cardigan and a laugh.

How would Marissa know? She acted like she had first-hand knowledge. When had Colin had time to date her? He's been chasing Izzy for as long as I'd known him, but I guess that wasn't until Spring last year. And how did she know anything about Colin and me?

Jenna cleared her throat, and in a moment of classic Jenna-ness, did what she always did when things got uncomfortable—babbled to fill the empty space. "That's great, Callie. I mean that you're getting out and doing…stuff. Not that you're doing stuff. But it's okay if you are. I mean, that would be good, too. I guess. I mean, not that I know. About Colin, I mean. You're being safe, though, right? Because there are condoms in a basket in our bathroom if you—"

Oh. My. God. I wanted the clouds to part and lightning to strike me dead right there. Bonus points if it managed to take Marissa with me. But Jenna just kept yammering away about the finer points of lubrication while Marissa watched me with a look of increasing self-satisfaction.

Finally I had enough. "Jenna! Stop!"

Jenna's jaw closed with a snap, as she looked at me with a mixture of renewed horror and embarrassment. I pulled myself up to my full height, strangling my pillow in my grasp. "I'm fine. I'm completely educated in…those areas." Marissa stifled a snigger behind a set of perfectly French-manicured nails, and I turned my gaze toward her. "If you'll excuse me," I said, glaring as I stepped past them, "someone is waiting for me."

Holding my head high, I clutched my bag and the last of my pride as I strode over to the H/I tower door, swiped my access card, and yanked the door open wide with a flourish just in case they were still watching. This was high melodrama for me, but I liked to think Izzy would be proud. In fact, I was so incensed by the scene with Marissa that I wasn't really thinking about what came next when I knocked on Colin's door.

The door swung open instantly, as though he'd been standing on the other side waiting for me to knock. For a long moment we stared awkwardly at one another, but the thought of him pressed against the door in anticipation made me giggle, breaking the tension between us. Colin grinned shyly in response.

"Come on in," he said with an exaggerated sweep of his cast-covered arm.

I dropped my bag on the floor and began wandering around the small room, taking it in. His room was similar to mine in a lot of respects—two beds, a pair of desks, matching bookshelves. Instead of built-ins like mine, though, the furniture here was freestanding, which meant the room could be rearranged in a myriad of combinations. With no roommate to accommodate, Colin had taken advantage of the situation, lofting one of the beds so he could fit a small brown loveseat underneath it. The walls were mostly bare, though a large poster here and there sporting '90s alternative bands and album covers broke up the empty white space.

I trailed my fingers over a small pile of textbooks sitting on his desk. A newish-looking laptop sat next to a weathered iPod. The entire room was neatly kept, almost to the point of austerity. It didn't look empty, exactly. Instead, it seemed like the good stuff, the stuff that made a person unique, was kept carefully filed away in drawers or hidden behind the door of the small walk-in closet in the corner of the room.

Kind of like Colin, I mused. *It might appear bland on the surface, but if you looked deeper, you'd find something wonderful.*

Colin was quiet while I inventoried his room, like he thought I might bolt in fear if he made any sudden movement. I turned to find him seemingly engrossed in the fraying hem of the grey t-shirt he was wearing, the red Atari logo printed across the chest -=faded to a dull pink. Feeling me watching him, Colin shoved his hands in his pockets and the slightly too small shirt sleeves strained a little over his upper arms. I'd never noticed Colin's arms before, but like so much of him, once you noticed something, it was hard to ignore.

I flushed, and Colin smirked a little. "So…" He took a step toward me, closing the space between us. He took my hands in his, the tips of our fingers touching below the edge of his cast.

"So." I replied, unsure what to say. His fingers were warm and soft holding mine. His slightly chapped lips were almost rosy. I could see the blonde tips of his eyelashes. My heart hammered in my chest, and I chewed on the inside of my lip.

Colin, seemingly encouraged by my nervousness, took another step toward me, so that our bodies were almost but not quite touching. "What do you want to do first?"

"First?" I swallowed hard. Was there a first? What came second? For someone loudly proclaiming to be completely educated in the ways of love a mere ten minutes earlier for anyone in the general area of the C-Store to hear, I felt like I'd missed some critical lessons. "I…"

I trailed off again, breathing in a heady dose of the soapy scent that was entirely Colin. It was still a clean, preppy smell, but now it had a slightly floral sweetness around the edges, and underneath lurked a mixture of earth and the taste I remembered from chewing on dandelion stems in backyard as a little girl. It was a rich and textured smell; I knew that when I kissed him, that kiss would taste like he smelled, but better. My head spun with the thought, stirring the rabble of butterflies in my stomach.

"Hey," Colin's light eyes were dark and serious as they bore into mine, "you don't have to be scared of me."

"I'm not." I could feel my face growing hotter.

"Mmm," he murmured, the sound rumbling from his throat. As he began to lean toward me, closing those last few inches between us, Marissa's self-satisfied face loomed in my memory like a creature from a bad 1950s horror flick. I jerked back, pulling my hands from his.

His mouth twisted into a grim line. "What is it now?"

"Nothing."

"It doesn't seem like nothing." His chin jutted out. "It seems like something. Is Izzy here?"

"What? No!" I swept my arm wide, gesturing to the empty room. "Dead or not, I'm still not interested in an audience."

"Then are you uncomfortable for some other reason?" When I didn't answer, he pressed on. "If you're not cool with this, that's okay, I guess."

"Your tone doesn't make it seem okay."

"Give me a break, Cal." He threw up his hands. "You're kind of sending me massive mixed signals here."

"When did you date Marissa?" I crossed my arms, hugging myself against the storm brewing between us.

"What?" He blinked several times. "What are you even talking about?"

"Marissa Engleton, the RA in my building?" He nodded slowly in acknowledgement, but still looked confused. "I ran into her and Jenna outside the C-Store. She knew I was coming to see you." I stared, challenging him to respond. Colin returned my glare with an irritated look of his own, making me angrier. "She seemed to have a pretty good idea of what would happen when I got here. She also expressed a pretty high opinion of your skills."

"And?" He asked dryly. I could see the muscle along his jaw twitching.

"Does she have a reason to know?" The words were out of my mouth before I could stop them. I wanted to kick myself for ruining yet a potentially wonderful moment, but the part of me that could never stop being the child of an alcoholic would not let go of a perceived lie, even by half-truth or omission. I'd been lied to plenty in my life; I wasn't going to accept any more from people who claimed to care for me.

He exhaled noisily. "Yeah, she does."

"Oh." My stomach turned. He frowned at me, but I only glared in return.

"What do you want from me, Callie?" He ran his hand through

his short hair, pulling at it in frustration. "We met during Orientation. She was my group leader. We went out a few times last fall. Yes, we made out. No, it never went anywhere. For one thing, she wasn't exactly my type. She thought Arcade Fire was a videogame." I rolled my eyes. "For another, I met Izzy, and then I wasn't really interested in anyone else."

Colin, seeing the doubt my face, pressed his advantage. "You've got to stop doing this. I'm not lying to you or trying to hurt you. Whatever happened in the past is the past. I want *you*. I don't want anyone else."

He moved closer to me, hands up and palms facing me in a sign of surrender. When I didn't wave him off, he stepped in and slid his good arm around my waist, my arms still crossed between us.

"Marissa was boring. Booor-ing. She couldn't hold a decent conversation to save her life." He pressed his forehead gently against mine, forcing me to meet his gaze.

"And the kissing?" I tried to pull away, but he tightened his arm around my waist.

"Terrrrible. Seriously. It was like she was trying to eat my face."

I choked on a laugh and loosened my arms, letting my hands fall to my sides.

"You, on the other hand..." He gently tipped my chin up toward him with the edge of his cast "...could win an Olympic gold medal." He pressed his lips to mine. "You have nothing to worry about with Marissa, or anyone else for that matter."

He feathered kisses across my cheek, skimming his nose along my jaw as he leaned over and whispered in my ear. "Not anyone—alive or dead," he whispered firmly, burying his head against my collarbone as he kissed my neck.

"And if she wasn't dead?" He stiffened against me, and I immediately regretted asking. "I just mean—"

"Callie." He said my name like it was some kind of warning. "I was joking. It's not a competition." His good hand moved from my waist, his fingers sliding up my arm until his hand cupped the back of my neck, holding me in place and forcing me to look at him. "I was an idiot not to see it before. You're the one I should have been with all along. I choose you. Okay?"

I swallowed. "Okay."

"Good." He smiled. "Then stop bringing her up."

Before I could say anything else, he pressed his lips to mine. The kiss was hard, insistent, as if he intended it to end all doubt or discussion.

"I'm sorry," I said in a small voice.

"I know you are. So can we stop with the theatrics?" He tried to make his voice light, but I could see he was serious. I nodded mutely, swallowing as tears welled up in my eyes.

"I hate being like this," I buried my head against his shoulder. "I can't help it. My dad…"

Your dad? A small voice shrieked in my head. *Wow, Callie! Talk about killing the mood.*

"I know," Colin murmured into my hair, so softly I almost missed it.

"Wait, what?" Surprised and shaken, I tried to step away but he

229

only tightened his grip around me in response. "Let me go," I said, feeling suddenly exposed.

"No." His voice was almost plaintive, his cast poking into my back and his arms tightened further. It was exactly the wrong thing to do. I wiggled harder, trying to pull away.

Sighing unhappily, he released me. "I only know a little. Izzy talked about it sometimes. She told me how your mom died and things got bad with your dad and that it was why you had to live with her family."

"She wasn't supposed to tell." Even though I knew at some level that my abuse wasn't my fault, I felt embarrassed and ashamed. As it turned out, even though I'd run two thousand miles, it wasn't far enough away to escape my past after all.

I turned away from him, moving to curl up in a ball against the arm of the loveseat. "We talked about it before we left," I said in a small voice, wishing that—just once—I could see what it was like not to feel like a victim, or an outcast. "Everyone at home knows. I hate that. Izzy promised she would keep it a secret when we got here. So that I could," I swallowed hard against the lump in my throat, "I could start over."

"I'm sorry. I could sort of tell you didn't want people to know, but I didn't know it was a secret." Colin sat down next to me, pulling my legs across him. Part of me wished he'd stop crowding me, but it seemed to make him less frustrated with me, so I didn't say anything. I reached down to untie my shoes, but Colin swatted my hand away and began working the knots out of the laces one-handed as I tried to find the right words to explain the mess that was my life. Setting my boots on the floor, Colin hugged my knees to his chest, but his mouth was tight and angry. "I hate that she's always getting in the way."

"Don't say that!"

"Ugh, you know what I mean." He threw back his head in frustration. "I thought telling you I knew would make things better. Instead I repeated something she said, and now you're upset again."

"It's just…the whole thing is complicated." He waited quietly for me to continue. "The thing you have to understand is that it wasn't all hell or high water. Things were good, even great, when I was little. But when my mom got sick, it was like the center fell out. I didn't know how much she held my dad together until she couldn't anymore." I thought back to the day I'd walked into the living room to find my father, a bear of a man, curled up in a ball and weeping into the back of our couch, his whole body shaking.

"Why didn't anyone help you?"

"At first no one noticed, I guess." I paused, thinking back. "Or maybe they felt sorry for him. Here he was, all alone, with this little girl to raise. Maybe they gave him a pass for a while." I shrugged. "Why doesn't really matter to me anymore. The point is, for a long time, people seemed to know. I could just tell by the way they wouldn't look at me, or how they pointedly avoided asking certain questions."

"I did my best to cover for him, but by sophomore year of high school, it was kind of obvious. I'd come to school in dirty clothes because the water or the electricity was cut off when my dad drank all our money away. I lost count of all the times Izzy suddenly decided she was having a fat day and needed to try some new fad diet just so I could have lunch."

Colin rolled his eyes. "Izzy didn't believe in fad diets."

"No, she didn't," I smiled sadly at the thought. "She used to say a love of double pepperoni pizza was what separated the designer from the runway model. She just couldn't stand to watch me go hungry."

"Your dad is an asshole," Colin muttered, eyes glinting with a deep kind of anger.

"No," I shook my head as I tried to make him understand. "He just couldn't accept my mom was gone. He'd always been a heavy drinker, but it was different, after. From the moment he woke up until the moment he passed out, he had a drink in his hand. And when he was drunk…"

I swallowed hard trying to gather my courage. I'd talked about my dad before, but mostly to therapists and, at night when things were so bad I couldn't sleep, I'd had Izzy. She would listen to me tell her the most horrible things, and she would pat my hair and tell me over and over it was okay. I'd never gone into depth with anyone else, not even Crystal. "When he was drunk, he'd blame me. He used to tell me I was the reason she got sick, that my mom would still be alive if it weren't for me. Then he'd hit me."

Numbness descended as I said the words, my unconscious instincts working to block out the terror I felt as a barrage of memories flooded in—him pinning me to the ground and choking me as he screamed red-faced, me hiding under the bed as he raged drunkenly through the house, calling for me, telling me what he would do when he found me.

A tear ran down my cheek, and I wiped at it. Colin's watched me with a blank expression. "It was a terrible way to live, but he was my dad. I protected him. He needed me and I did my best. Then, one day, I couldn't hide it anymore." I shrugged noncommittally. "Izzy's parents took me in. I never saw my dad again. I don't know where he is now."

Colin's expression was a mixture of sympathy and muted anger as he rubbed comforting circles on my knee. "My dad was a good man, Colin. He was a good dad, a good husband, a good cop. I'd loved him my whole life and then, all of a sudden, he wasn't the person I'd known at all. It was like this other person was always there, lurking beneath the surface, and I had been too blind to see it." I shook my head, trying to break free of the memories threatening to flood in and overwhelm me. "And it wasn't just me. My teachers, our neighbors, friends, their parents…no one seemed to see it."

"Or they didn't want to."

"Maybe," I admitted. "Except for Izzy and her parents. Izzy always saw me."

Colin harrumphed. "Yeah, well, they waited long enough to help."

"But they helped," I insisted. "When no one else would, the Millers helped."

"It just seems like everyone kind of…failed you."

I nodded. "Maybe. Or maybe, like me, they thought he would get over it and get better." I bit my lip, trying to hold back the tears. "But he never did. When something like that happens, it's hard to believe in the goodness of people. At the end of the day, I guess I just feel like everyone is capable of becoming a monster under the right circumstances."

"Is that why you never had a boyfriend?" Colin asked quietly. I hadn't told him, but I guessed if Izzy had spilled the beans about my parents then she'd probably told him that, too.

"No," I sighed. "Yes. Maybe?" I laughed hollowly. "My parents were in love, like real honest-to-goodness, eternal, let's-die-at-the-exact-same-time-like-the-end-of-*The-Notebook* kind of love. When I was a little girl, I'd look at them and think, 'That's what I want when I grow up.' After I saw what losing her did to my dad…"

I shook my head. "I guess I thought, if that's what it could cost you, maybe love wasn't worth the risk. Yeah, my parents had a blissful life together for about eleven years, but my dad hasn't had a moment of happiness since the day she was diagnosed. He couldn't be in the room with her near the end. I took care of her. She hadn't even died yet, but he was already gone."

Colin brushed his fingers across my cheek, drawing my attention to him. "I know it's hard. It's scary to care about someone, to trust them. But doesn't it seem worth it? I mean, think of how happy we are…at least, some of the time." He gave me a rueful grin.

"You mean when I'm not first conductor on the express train to Crazytown?"

"No," He shook his head emphatically. "I mean we're only at the beginning of whatever this is, and already I'm so much happier with you than when I'm away from you, all I can think about is when I'm going to get to see you again. I can't believe that's a bad thing, even if it means taking the chance you might hurt me. I think that's worth it. Don't you?"

I sniffled a little as my heart thumped erratically at his words. "Yes," I whispered.

"Then let's try to go easy on each other. You know, my family isn't perfect either. Did you know my parents aren't really my parents?"

I cocked my head to the side. "What do you mean? You're adopted?"

"Yeah." A shadow fell across his face.

"I didn't know that."

"No one knows that. No one here, anyway. Not even Izzy," he added pointedly. "My parents adopted me when they thought they couldn't have any kids of their own. Then, when I was eight, surprise! They had my brothers, who are twins, and a year later, miracle of miracles, another little boy. I have three brothers, but they're not really my brothers, you know?"

"Well, Izzy wasn't really my sister, but that didn't mean I loved her any less." I took his hand and smiled, trying to be encouraging, but Colin only frowned in response.

"My parents, they're good people, and they try, but it's obvious I was the substitute kid. I was the kid they got because they couldn't have real kids. When they did, it didn't leave a lot of room for me." He shrugged, and I squeezed his hand in sympathy.

"Do you know anything about your real parents?"

Colin shook his head. "I think about my real mom all the time. When I turned eighteen, I contacted the adoption agency, but it was a sealed adoption. My mom, whoever she was, hadn't contacted them since she gave me up. I gave them my name and phone number so if she contacts them they can tell her I want to meet her. But I don't know if I will ever get to. I don't know if I will ever know why she gave me up."

Hearing the longing in Colin's voice made my heart ache. I would have done anything to make him feel better, but I knew when it came to familial wounds, even the most well-intended sympathy could make things worse. I held his good hand in my own and gripped it as tight as I could, as though I could squeeze the sadness out through his fingers.

"The point is, I can't say I understand what you've been through, but I do understand what it feels like to feel unloved and unwanted, Callie. I know how it feels to think you're broken and everyone you love will leave you." Colin's eyes shone. "That's why we have to try. Because that's not going to be us, not if we don't want it to be."

Colin stared into my eyes with a sad and angry look, but I saw it for what it was—a glimpse into the heart of a boy who felt, at his core, the deepest sense of rejection, and who was willing to try to love someone despite all the pain it might cause. This was the part of Colin Izzy could never see, for the same reasons she had never truly understood me. Colin and I might be damaged goods, but we fit together the way puzzle pieces do. By filling in the missing parts, we might be exactly the right people for one another.

Only a month ago, I would have sworn Colin was madly in love with Izzy, but now...maybe this was what it was like, though.

Maybe sometimes you didn't realize what was right in front of you. Despite everything I'd been through, here was someone who seemed determined to care for me no matter what. Wasn't that what everyone searched for? Someone who would love you despite everything that was awful about you? Someone who would love you forever? Colin was right. To be loved like that had to be worth the risk even if the intensity of his feelings for me seemed a little overwhelming.

Letting go of his hand, I crawled over him until I was sitting in his lap. I pulled his casted arm across my lap and wrapped my arms around his neck, ignoring the ache in my shoulder. I looked Colin straight in the eye and took a deep breath, inhaling the wonderful clean smell of him. It was all there in his eyes, hope and fear intertwined. I was sure they looked like my own. Then I said the scariest words I could think of.

"I think...I love you." A look of relief and happiness broke over Colin's face. "I do. I love you, Colin. And I'm not leaving you."

"I love you, too, Callie," Colin said hoarsely, pulling me tight against him. He pressed his lips against mine hungrily, as if he were trying to seal the promise between us. "I love you, and I'll never leave you," he whispered between kisses, each one deeper and longer than the last. I gasped as he tilted my head back, peppering feathery kisses along my cheekbone and the curve of my ear. "We won't let anything or anyone come between us."

"Umm-hmmm," I murmured, tightening my arms around his neck. Colin skimmed his nose along my jaw, pulling me upright so we were eye-to-eye. "No one," he said fiercely.

Thinking fleetingly of Izzy, alone and crying in my room, I hesitated for a moment. *In for a penny, in for pound, sugar*, I heard my mother say in my head.

"Nope," I pecked him on the lips as punctuation. "Not anything." I kissed him again, and let my lips linger a little longer. "Or anyone." I kissed him again, and he responded in kind, parting his lips slightly as our tongues tangled together.

We stayed like that for a long time, lost in our respective heartaches and the ways our love for one another was, inch by inch, repairing us. We kissed until our lips ached, snuggling down into the worn fabric of the secondhand couch together, wrapped around each other in our own little world, as we giggled and laughed and talked. I was practically bursting with happiness, maybe for the first time in years. Eventually we drifted off to sleep together, holding each other, crammed on the tiny loveseat.

When I woke up the next morning, I hadn't done my homework or taken my pain medication. My shoulder ached, my head throbbed, and I had a terrible crick in my neck from sleeping at a weird angle.

It was, without a doubt, the best night of my life.

24.

When we got up the next morning, Colin and I realized we only had about a day and a half before he left for Thanksgiving weekend. I was all for skipping classes for the next two days to spend as much quality time together as possible, but he was having none of it. "You've missed enough class already," he lectured as he moved around the room in a burst of energy.

"Yes, but *I* don't have class until eleven. That's *hours* from now," I argued, attempting to marshal whatever feminine wiles I possessed to convince him to skip his early class and stay with me. I wasn't having much luck, but I felt my heart skip as I mentally catalogued the way his nimble fingers fed a brown belt through the loops of his jeans, the edge of his untucked polo shirt riding up to reveal a triangle of skin where his hip bone jutted slightly below his narrow waist.

Colin shook his head and smiled, but kept moving, occasionally stopping to offer up another platitude seizing the day and the dangers of procrastination. At one point, I couldn't even make out what he was saying because his face was buried in a thick hoodie.

"Sorry. Did you just say, 'Mur face shun in importance?'"

He emerged, looking pleasantly annoyed. "I *said* education is important."

I rolled my eyes. "Yes, I am well-aware. And last time I checked, my GPA was better than yours."

"Then you haven't checked in a while."

"Hey!" I tossed a pillow at him. "I was ahead in all my classes, you know, before." I faltered. "Technically, I'm just incomplete on some assignments."

"Uh-huh." His grunt indicated that he was not at all convinced, and I made a mental note to make sure to get any missing assignments in as soon as possible. I smiled as I watched him carefully try to flatten his hair in the mirror a few times, then shrug and give up.

Yep. As soon as possible…which could mean after break, right? Maybe if I kept trying, I'd get the chance to muss that hair a little more. "Then how about you give a girl a chance to catch up?" I batted my lashes at him. "It's very cold over here without you."

"Awwww." He grinned and came closer, for a moment making me think I'd won. Then he picked up a blanket from the edge of the loveseat and tucked it around me. "Better?"

I scowled a little. "Not what I meant. You *always* go to class. Can't you miss this once? "Puh-leeeeeeeeeeaase?" I stuck out my lower lip as I hooked my finger through his belt loop and tried to drag him back onto the loveseat with me.

"Nope. I *always* go to class because if I didn't, I would never be able to keep up academically with my intensely competitive girlfriend." He unhooked my fingers, kissing the tips before letting them go. "I'm going class. You are going class. You also have a meeting with Dr. Cliff at two."

I pulled the blanket over my head. "I completely forgot." I moaned.

"You, of all people, forgot about Dr. Cliff?" Colin snorted. "If

I didn't know better I'd have thought you had a shrine to him in your closet."

"I know, I know. I'm the worst." I mentally cursed myself for collapsing into a puddle of lovey dovey gooeyness. I was forgetting about a lot of things this morning, I realized with a pang of guilt.

Focus, Callie. You are staying in school so you can help Izzy. You remember Izzy, right? Your very best friend in the entire world who needs you now more than ever? Izzy first.

Colin pulled the blanket off, kissing my forehead, my cheek, then my lips. With every feathery brush of his mouth, the words receded a little. I had to admit it was hard to remember my priorities when Colin was kissing me. I wrapped my arms around his neck, pulling him toward me, but he only smiled and pulled my hands away so he could put his shoes on.

"How about we meet for a late lunch at the HUB after your eleven o'clock class?" he suggested. The HUB was the campus alternative to the dining hall. It was open all day to serve sandwiches, burgers, pizza, and other quick lunch and dinner options to faculty and commuter students who weren't on a regular meal plan.

"That would be great. If I bring my outline for Dr. Cliff's paper, will you look over it for me before my meeting?"

"Sure," he muttered, shoving his books hastily into a backpack. He glanced over at the clock. "I have to run or I'm going to be late."

He gave me another quick kiss, pulling away reluctantly as I hung on. I giggled as he wagged a finger in my face, mockingly authoritative. "Go to class."

"Yeah, yeah, yeah." I sighed, throwing the blanket off my legs and stretching as he hustled out the door.

I showered and changed in the co-ed bathroom on Colin's floor before I left. I got a few stares from Colin's floormates as I went back and forth to his room getting ready, but I didn't care. My shoulder ached and my neck was still sore, but I hummed to myself as I brushed my teeth.

I still didn't know what I was going to do about Izzy, but I knew we would figure it out. She couldn't stay mad at me forever. Maybe, with Colin's help, I could make faster progress on talking to people from the party. Then she would see that we both still cared about her, that our being together didn't mean we were forgetting her.

I needed to run back to my room to grab my outline before class, so I left everything but my books at Colin's. I stopped by the Health Center, where I let Nurse Nancy cluck and fuss over me while she changed the bandaging on my shoulder and, for good measure, the one on my cheek, too.

"Child, you look like someone ran over your face with weed whacker," she said with a grimace.

"Is it really that bad?"

"Compared to your shoulder? No." She dabbed ointment on a couple of my tiny cuts along my hairline. "The bandage on your face can come off in a couple of days, but that one will take a while." She sighed, leaning back to look at me. "It's just such a shame. You have such pretty skin…"

"Maybe I'll start a new trend," I quipped, feeling a little stung.

"Patchwork chic might be totally in next year."

She stripped off her gloves and tossed them into the trash bin. "Don't worry about it." She patted my arm as she peered at me over the edge of her glasses. "Gives you character."

Yeah, because that's what I need, more character. But I kept my retort to myself and even mustered a polite thank you as I left. My momma would have been proud.

Despite Nurse Nancy's observations that I now resembled Frankenstein's monster, I felt strangely pretty. I never thought of myself as pretty, but spending an evening with someone telling you in detail how beautiful each and every part of you is could have that effect, I guess. While I was at the Student Center, I made an appointment to see Dr. Yates the Tuesday afternoon after break. Word of my hospital visit must have reached the Counseling office because Ms. Bloom didn't comment on my appearance. She just seemed surprised at my suddenly sunny disposition.

The weather had turned frigid overnight, which wasn't unusual for the Oregon Coast in winter and spring, but I didn't have a hoodie. I'd left it at home because my shoulder hurt too much to pull anything over my head. My residence hall felt very far away as I hurried past my bundled up classmates back to my room, hugging myself for warmth.

When I reached the building, I ran up the stairs two at a time. I heard someone following me from the lounge, but didn't pay much attention as I unlocked my door. Stepping in, I sighed with relief that everything appeared as I'd left it. I went over to the desk and began digging around for my outline. I was so absorbed that it took a minute for me to notice Jay leaning against the doorsill. I could tell from the tight set of his mouth that he was angry at me, but I didn't know why. I didn't really feel like fighting with him so I just ignored him, hoping he'd take the hint and go away.

"Where have you been?" I could practically hear him grinding his teeth from all the way across the room.

"What are you, my warden?" I shot back, turning to face him. I couldn't believe he was spoiling my good mood. Jay's brown eyes were flinty and cool, but I held my ground and stared back at him defiantly.

"Sometimes I think it would be good if I could lock you up somewhere."

"Wow, I bet all the girls looove hearing that. You're quite the sweet talker."

"I asked you where you were." He took a step into the room, abandoning any pretenses of a casual chat. "I came to check on your shoulder late last night when I got off shift. I got worried when you didn't answer."

"I spent the night at Colin's."

He flinched ever so slightly. "As in—"

I gave him a harsh smile. "As in *with* Colin." I was overstating the case, and I knew it, but I was tired of having the same fight over and over. Jay was not my keeper. If hurting him was what it was going to take to make him leave me alone, so be it. We stood glaring at each other, neither one willing to back down. Without breaking eye contact, Jay reached back and swung the door closed with a thump.

So not the reaction I was hoping for. "I did *not* invite you in."

"Too damned bad. I have something to say to you, and you're going to hear it." Jay stood in front of the door. I obviously wasn't getting out of the room until he'd said his piece.

"Fine." I waved my hand in a gesture of defeat. "Get it over with."

"Colin is bad news."

"Says who?"

He hesitated. "People."

I rolled my eyes. "That's it. That's all you've got? 'People' say he's bad news?" I threw up air quotes for emphasis. "Tell me something, Jay. What do 'people' say about me?"

When he didn't respond, I laughed mirthlessly. "Yeah, that's what I thought. I guess that means Colin and I are a perfect match."

"You have to trust me on this. You cannot keep seeing him."

"I *cannot*?" My hands balled into fists, "Who made you the boss of the universe? You can't tell me what to do, Jay. It's getting ridiculous. You have to stop. I know you're jealous, but—"

Jay barked out a laugh. "Jealous? Is that what you think? You think you know about the world, about the horrible things people are capable of? You don't know anything. I don't care who you sleep with. I'm trying to keep you safe."

Despite my feelings for Colin, it felt like all the air had been sucked out of the room. Rejection hurts, no matter who it comes from, and Jay's words tore a little hole in my pride. *It doesn't matter if Jay doesn't want me*, I thought to myself furiously. *Colin does.*

"I can look out for myself," I replied, struggling to keep my voice from betraying the sting I felt. "Colin loves me. He isn't going to hurt me. He takes care of me."

"Did he tell you he was there the night Izzy died? He did a bang-up job of taking care of her, didn't he?"

It was a low blow, even for Jay, and the look on his face said he knew it. I struggled against the urge to throw something at him.

"Yes! As a matter of fact, he did tell me. He told me everything. Which apparently is more than I can say for you." I wanted to scream at him. *But screaming means more attention,* I reminded myself, dropping my voice to a harsh whisper. "If you knew he was there, why didn't you tell me? You've never told me anything about what happened. I had to find it all out for myself."

"I told you what I could." He caught my withering look and tried again, invoking a tone of authority. "I told you what you needed to know."

"Yeah, well, it's good to know you stick to those high-minded principles right up until you think you can use it to get what you."

"You think this is what I want?" His shoulders sagged and his voice was low, like he was talking more to himself than to me. "None of this is what I want. I'm trying to protect you. That's all."

His admission made me feel sorry for him. But I didn't want to feel sorry for him. I wanted to stay angry. I wanted to be mean. I wanted to be mean enough that when this fight was over it could be the last one. Then we could get some distance. In time we'd be nothing more than polite classmates, instead of something too close to be friends and too far apart to be more.

"Yeah, well, thanks for the info, but Colin beat you to it." I turned my back to him to let him know that as far as I was concerned, our conversation was finished. I opened my backpack and threw in my outline along with a few other notes I thought I'd need for my meeting. When I heard the door open, I kept my back turned until it closed again.

I thought about all the fights Jay and I had had lately as I pulled my pea coat out of my closet. After losing Izzy, it hurt like hell to think about cutting someone else out of my life, but things between Jay and I kept getting uglier and uglier, and I didn't like the idea of Colin getting caught in the middle. Tears rose in my eyes at the thought of actively avoiding contact with Jay, but I didn't like hurting him and he couldn't seem to help hurting me. Maybe it would be better if we didn't talk at all.

Pushing the thought away, I grabbed my iPod and shoved it into my coat pocket, jamming the earbuds into my ears as though I could block out my problems with the music if I cranked it loud enough. As I headed back out into the cold, Neko Case blasted in my ears, crooning about killer whales and man-eaters, about those naturally inclined to destruction, and the naive surprise of their inevitable prey.

25.

Even before I made it inside the HUB, I saw Colin waving like an idiot at me through the glass walls, grin flashing. I smiled and hustled inside, dropping my bag on the chair as I leaned over to kiss him. Colin reached up and pulled me into his lap, deepening the kiss until I pulled away, feeling embarrassed.

"Stop," I giggled as Colin place a row of kisses along my neck above my coat collar. "We're in public."

"So?" he whispered, pushing my hair back and moving toward my earlobe.

"So not everyone enjoys watching us make out while they eat greasy pizza." I extracted myself from his arms and moved into a chair next to him.

"How was your morning class?" He dipped a large fry in ketchup and shoved it in his mouth.

I sighed. "It was fine. I met with Dr. Bolkin about my paper before class. She told me I can have until early January to finish it because grades aren't due until after that and she's going to be out of town for the holiday anyway." I grabbed a fry and nibbled at it. "As long as I do my ten-minute presentation during finals like everyone, she says I can still finish with a high B or an A. I was ahead in the reading, so I only have one more response paper left."

"Of course you do." He smiled. "Who doesn't love following up a lot dense reading by writing long-winded responses?"

"I do." I chucked a napkin at him and he laughed. "You should be glad I'm such an overachiever. Getting a lot done early means

I'm not nearly as behind as I should be."

"That," he rolled his eyes, "and the faculty loves you."

"That is not true! I work super hard."

"Yes, you do," he nodded in mock seriousness. "Which is *why* they love you. Come on, Callie. Every history major knows you're the department pet. You're the only sophomore they've said word one to about graduate school."

I scowled. "You're exaggerating."

"No, I'm not." He wiped his hands on the napkin I've thrown at him and then reached across the table to take my hand. "And, for your information, I like that about you. My girlfriend is hot *and* smart. I won the girlfriend lottery."

"Well, since you're so excited by my academic prowess…" I dug my outline out of the top of my bag and passed it to him.

While he read, I went to the counter and bought two pieces of cheese pizza. When I came back, the outline was sitting on the table. Colin was staring out the window, a strangely blank expression on his face.

"So what do you think?" He was quiet, which worried me. "What's wrong with it?"

"Nothing."

"Your tone doesn't say nothing." I glanced over the top page. "I know it still needs work." I gave him a hesitant smile. He was acting so weird. "That's why I wanted the help of my equally brilliant boyfriend."

Colin crossed his arms. "It seems like you've got plenty of ideas of your own."

His tone was so reserved that it shook me. He'd been so warm and sweet just a few minutes before. "Did I miss something? You seem kind of mad at me."

"I guess I just think your hatred of stay-at-home moms is kind of uncalled for."

"What?" I asked in surprise, flipping through the outline. "I don't hate stay-at-home moms."

"That's what your outline says. How did you put it?" He reached over and pulled the pages from my grip. "Ah, here it is," he gestured toward me as he read aloud from my notes. "The inherent isolation and lack of professional or social opportunity for these women generated a widespread social malaise. And no wonder— their lives were confined to the care of others, inherently tied to their role as 'wife' and 'mother.' Social forces coalescing created a framework that denied the suburban housewife a sense of personal accomplishment or public praise as individuals, relegating them to the role of caretakers." He opened his hand, letting the outline drop to the table. "Sounds like you hate them to me."

"I do not," I argued. "My paper is on the medical diagnosis of feminine hysteria in the 1950s and 1960s. Which, yes, touches on the creation of suburbia, the concept of the nuclear family, isolation, and okay, yes, stay-at-home mothers, but only peripherally."

I watched as he stabbed another fry in the ketchup. "You're not seriously upset about this, are you?" I tried to catch his eye, but he wouldn't look up. "It's a stupid paper."

"Yeah, well, some women really like being moms. They like staying home and taking care of their families. You know, my mom is a stay-at-home mom and she thinks it's great."

"I'm sure she does. My mom was a stay-at-home mom and she was happy doing it. Crystal is a stay-at-home mom, and she's awesome. But they had a choice…mostly." I paused, trying to choose my next words carefully. "It's is a *history* paper."

Colin snorted. "I know. I'm a history major, too, remember?"

"Right. And you know history hasn't always been all that kind to women." I gathered the pages carefully, slipping them off the table and into my bag. Maybe if I moved the outline out of the way, we could stop arguing about it. "After WWII, a lot of working women wanted to keep working. They didn't get to."

"Because veterans needed jobs," he countered, in a cool, clipped tone.

"Yes," I nodded as I tried to calm him down. "But that didn't mean they liked it. And women who weren't happy being moved far from their families and cut off from financial independence were often diagnosed as having mental health problems when what they wanted was to have a choice in what they did with their lives."

His lips, pressed in a thin line, twitched. "Says you."

"And Betty Friedan. Or, going back even earlier, Charlotte Perkins Gilman."

"So all women who don't work are unhappy? There's not a single woman out there who feels grateful to have someone love them and take care of them? "

"I didn't say—"

He kept talking cutting me off. "When you love someone, that's what you want to do. You want to give them everything. Why is that wrong?"

"It isn't." He was so upset. I'd obviously hurt him but I didn't know how. I paused, trying to figure out how to explain what I meant without making things worse. "Lots of women are happy with that. I'm just saying, women want to have a choice. And historically, sometimes their desire to have a choice, and their unhappiness with their options, was treated like a physical ailment instead of a social disease." I looked at him imploringly. "I'm writing a paper about that. That's all." He nodded curtly, but didn't say anything.

"You don't think women...*belong* in the home, do you?" I felt suddenly sick at the idea that I might know his answer, and I wasn't going to like it. "Like, exclusively?"

"Well, yeah." He shrugged. "I mean, maybe." I must have looked as appalled as I felt, because he rushed on. "Look, I think, you know, I had a lot of friends in high school whose parents both worked all the time, and it caused them problems. Maybe if there had been someone around to take care of them, they might have had an easier time. When you decide to have kids, you have a responsibility to put them first, even if that means making some...sacrifices."

"And those sacrifices have to be from a mom?" My voice was getting kind of loud and screechy as my shock slowly morphed into something much closer to anger. I inhaled a long breath through my nose, trying to stay calm. "Why can't it just as easily be a dad?"

"I dunno." Colin traced a pattern on the tabletop as he looked anywhere but at me. "It seems weird."

"And you think that's a good enough reason?"

"It's just the natural way of things." He glanced at me. "Women are better at that stuff."

"That's complete bull. Women are trained from a young age to 'better' at caregiving. While girls are given dolls, boys are given trucks and race cars."

"So?"

"So maybe girls want to be race car drivers. Maybe girls want to build things. And maybe we'd be better at those things and boys would be better at caregiving if it was okay for each of us to have both." I pushed my pizza away untouched. I'd lost my appetite. "Stay-at-home dads only 'seem weird' because of ingrained institutional sexism."

Colin crossed his arms. "You're entitled to your opinion, I guess."

I gritted my teeth, balling a napkin up in my hands. I couldn't believe this was happening. What happened to the sweet guy I knew, the one who never tried to control me? How was it possible we'd been all over each other last night, and now he was calmly eating fries while telling me how, in his ideal world, I'd be barefoot in the kitchen with a baby on my hip for the rest of my life? Maybe Jay was right. Maybe I didn't know Colin as well as I thought I did.

Glancing up at a clock on the wall, I was relieved it was almost two o'clock. "Look, I've got to go see Dr. Cliff." I scooped up my uneaten pizza, tossing it in the trashcan nearby. "I'll see you later, I guess."

"If that makes you happy," he said in a tone that made it clear my happiness was the least of his concerns for the moment. I grabbed my bag and hurried out of the HUB.

My mind whirled as I tried to process what had happened. I knew Colin and I had come from different worlds, but his words spun me.

On the one hand, what he said made sense. If you loved someone, of course you wanted to give them the world. And wasn't that what every girl was looking for? Wasn't that what my dad had done for my mom? And Izzy's dad, too? It seemed to have made my mom and Crystal happy. There were even girls I had grown up with already posting photos of rings and baby showers on Instagram.

But I wasn't Crystal or my mom. I wasn't even Izzy, who might have been happy running a fashion line backed by a wealthy husband. It might have worked for them, but I wanted…more.

I wanted options. I wanted control. I wanted my own money, my own career. I didn't know if I ever wanted to have kids. Maybe I would, some day really far away, but not until I'd done lots of things and been lots of places.

That was why I'd come to AC. To become something outside the confines of the world I'd grown up in. I loved Colin, and I wanted to be with him, but I wanted to be more than someone's wife and someone's mother. From the way he seemed proud of my academic accomplishments, I'd thought he understood that.

When it came to romance, though, Colin seemed to believe things only worked one way. It felt so…*limiting* was the only word I could think of. Couldn't I have the world in my own way? Couldn't I give him as much as he gave me? Was that too much to ask for?

I didn't want to believe that, but from the way Colin had looked away from me when I left him in the HUB, I was starting to wonder if I was wrong.

26.

My meeting with Dr. Cliff was brief, but productive. He approved my outline, gave me some additional sources to incorporate into my paper, and we briefly discussed a couple of short assignments I could do to make up for quizzes and response papers I'd missed. It was a lot of work, but it was manageable.

Three of my four classes were now back on track. I still needed to meet with my last professor, but from the emails we'd exchanged I was pretty sure I was fine there, too. I was surprised how easily I was going to keep my grades out of the toilet.

Maybe Colin was right. Maybe it wasn't hard work that had earned me so much leniency. Maybe I was our teachers' pet.

I should have been happy to know I could stay in school at Astoria, but I kept mentally returning to the arguments I'd had with Jay and Colin. It seemed like, no matter which way I turned, I was burning up all my bridges. I couldn't stop myself from picking fights, especially with people who cared about me.

I wandered back up to my room in a funk. Shrugging out of my pea coat, I started digging through my backpack for the pain meds the hospital gave me, then remembered I'd left them at Colin's. This morning I had been so sure I'd be spending the night in Colin's room again I hadn't thought twice about leaving my things there. Now I wondered when I'd get them back.

I fell back on the bed in a fit of pique, wincing as my sore body hit the mattress. The light hurt my eyes, and the stitches in my cheek itched.

"Izzy?" I listened for a moment. "Are you here?"

There was no response. Only silence. "I'm so confused. I wish you were here so I had someone to talk to…" Trailing off, I covered my face with my pillow and wondered if I'd be able to take a nap for a while in spite of my shoulder pain.

I was on the verge of dozing off when there was a knock on my door. I pushed myself up and walked over it, steeling myself for a second round with either Colin or Jay, whichever one had come back for more. I swung the door open, braced for the inevitable.

"Lauren?" I rubbed the sleep from my eyes. "What are you doing here?"

Lauren took a tiny step backwards, like she was about to bolt. "Shannen said you wanted to talk to me about what happened to Izzy."

A wave of guilt rose up and crashed in my chest. I'd completely forgotten about talking to the girls because of Colin. No wonder Izzy was pissed at me. I couldn't manage to make anyone happy, alive or dead.

I nodded and opened the door wider, allowing Lauren to enter. She was wrapped in a cream-colored trench coat that was slightly too large for her frame and cinched so tightly at the waist the bottom flared around her like the open petals of a flower, revealing a blush-colored knee length skirt and patterned tights beneath. As she stepped into the room, she stared at the side of the room that used to be Izzy's, taking in the empty closet and the bed-turned-makeshift-couch. I sat down on my bed, gesturing for Lauren to sit on the other one, but she shook her head, shifting from one dainty foot to another in the middle of the room.

"I want you to know that I think about Izzy every day," Lauren began slowly, her normally perfect diction exaggerated by her grief. I could tell this was a speech she'd rehearsed over and over, so I didn't interrupt. Truthfully, I respected her for coming to see me rather than making me hunt her down.

"If there was any way for me to go back and change what happened that night, I would. I would do anything to make sure that Izzy made it home." She let out a shaky breath, her fingers curled to tug at the edges of her sleeves. "I cannot imagine how awful it must be for you here without her. I want you to know that I looked up to Izzy and cared about her. She was my friend, too, and I miss her. I'm sorry I left her there. I'm sorry we didn't call you to come get her." Lauren, normally as smooth and composed as her carefully coordinated outfits, raised a shaking hand to her face and wiped at her eye. "I'm sorry."

"I know." I rose and wrapped my arms around her, hugging her as hard as my shoulder would allow. She began weeping openly then, but I couldn't cry. The part of me that learned through my mother's death to be strong in a crisis kicked in automatically. Numbness froze my insides in place as Lauren clung to me. I patted her lightly on the back, waiting for her to finish as I stared off into space.

I wondered if Izzy was watching us, this weeping china doll confessor and me, her stoic, wooden absolver. *It's probably exactly what Izzy wants*, I mused. *Lots of wailing and gnashing of teeth.*

But I couldn't afford to give Izzy any more of my grief, at least not now. If I started crying again, I might never stop, and Izzy needed me to hold it together long enough to find out what Lauren knew. I hoped she understood that.

Eventually Lauren collected herself and sat down on the edge of Izzy's bed. I handed her a box of tissues and she took one. "Shannen said you had questions."

"A few," I admitted. "I think Shannen covered most of it. Shannen mentioned a guy who was looking for Izzy. Do you know who it was?"

Lauren tapped her perfectly manicured nails against her arm. "I'm not positive, but if I had to guess, I'd say it was Colin. He was there, and he was always looking for Izzy. I spent most of the night on the phone, so I can't be sure," she added apologetically. "I saw him come in with some people, but I didn't see him after that."

I nodded. Shannen said Izzy had gone to talk to friends, plural, who included an ex from our first year. After talking to Colin, I'd had a pretty good idea he was the ex Shannen had spoken to. Lauren's confirmation settled it. "Who was he with?"

"Gabe Hudson and Emily Lawrence, Danielle…"

"Gomez."

"Right, and that guy she's dating."

"Nate Dermott."

Lauren nodded. "Colin was alone," she added in a way that implied she'd already heard we were dating.

Stupid tiny campus, I fumed. At least that cleared up one of my lingering questions, "Did you know the other guy, the one she was dancing with when you left?"

"No. None of us did." Lauren looked around at the side of our room that had once been Izzy's. "Honestly, I wasn't even sure Izzy knew who it was."

I sighed. Sooner or later, I was going to have to find someone who could tell me that devil's name. Then he and I were going to have a little chat. "So I'm guessing you're going to confirm she was as drunk as everyone else says she was."

Lauren paled a little, but nodded. "Yeah. And the weird thing is, I don't know what she could have been drinking that would have gotten her so drunk so fast."

"What do you mean? I got the impression the place was awash in a sea of free booze."

"Yeah, that's true. When we first got there, I walked around for a while and there were drinks of all colors, shapes, and sizes. But I never saw Izzy with one. I mean, I got a beer and nursed it most of the night, but I don't remember Izzy getting a mixed drink. When I was with her, all she was drinking was Coke."

I looked at her sharply. "You don't think Izzy was drinking?"

Lauren shook her head. "No, I didn't say that. She was smashed when I saw her before we left, so she must have been. But she was so drunk I figured she must have downed a fistful of shots or done a massive keg stand while I wasn't paying attention, and that doesn't really seem like Izzy to me."

"No, it doesn't," I said, mostly to myself. I was frustrated by the conflicting stories. None of this fit. I felt like I was missing something obvious, but for the life of me, I couldn't see it.

"Was anyone else overly drunk that night? Anyone seem way

more wasted than usual or anything?"

As she mulled the question over, I racked my brain for the last time I'd seen Izzy drink. *Maybe the reason Izzy drank so rarely was because she was some kind of super lightweight*, I mused. But I didn't remember anything like that from few times I'd seen her drink, although maybe I'd always been too preoccupied with my own shenanigans to notice.

Finally, she looked at me and shrugged helplessly. "Honestly, Callie, I don't know. There were people drunk everywhere. I know Danielle Gomez had to be dragged out by her boyfriend, but I didn't know anyone else well enough to know if it was unusual for a typical Friday night. Plus, Bethany was a handful. Shannen and I had to half-carry her to get her back up the hill."

"I thought Gloria was with you."

"She was. But do you think she was going to risk Bethany puking on her Gucci's? No way. All she did was berate Bethany for getting drunk. Honestly, Beth hasn't been around much since then. Gloria cornered her in the bathroom a couple of days later and told her she was too embarrassing to hang out with anymore."

"What a crappy thing to do. Why do ya'll let Gloria push you around?"

"I dunno. It was easier with you and Izzy around. Gloria never tried to pull that crap with you. But with Izzy gone and you..." she pulled off tiny tufts of tissue with her pale pink nails "...unavailable, it's been a lot harder. You know how it is here. Three weeks into school, everyone already has their groups formed. It's kind of hard to make new friends. I've been spending nights in Bethany's room occasionally so she doesn't have to deal with Gloria."

I gritted my teeth, kicking myself. Taking them under our wing hadn't been my idea, but I knew Izzy would be disappointed by how little I'd bothered to be support Bethany and Lauren after she'd died. They weren't helpless, but Gloria was a handful and the others were new to being on their own.

"It's like being in a sorority," Izzy had told me when I'd asked her why we'd taken on teaching four random girls we didn't know what campus life was like. "A sorority of womanhood," she'd added, placating my strenuous objections to any reference to a Greek system. "They're young, they're away from home for the first time, and some of them have never been to a party before. Do you really want them out there on their own? What if something happened to one of them? How would you feel?"

I knew how I'd feel, which is why I'd agreed to befriend them, but I'd never invested in it the way she had. Maybe it was because Izzy had grown up with younger sisters and I hadn't, but at the time I'd resented being asked to take care of someone else. Now I wished I'd taken it more seriously; I might have been able to save Izzy in the process. Looking at Lauren's puffy eyes, I realized it wasn't too late to help the girls, and that I owed it to Izzy to at least try.

"Lauren, I know I haven't been there for you lately, but that's going to change."

"Really?"

In for a penny, in for a pound, right, Iz?

"Really." I bumped her with my shoulder. "It's probably time I start doing more than just sitting in this room. I'm caught up, mostly, in my classes. I definitely will be when Thanksgiving break is over. I know it's going to be hectic heading up to finals, but do you think we could all get together for coffee or a movie?"

Lauren's lip quivered as she broke into a smile. I thought she was going to cry again, but instead she threw her arms around me, hugging me so tight her fingers dug into my shoulder. Despite the pain, I didn't pull away.

"Thanks, Callie!" She released me. "We've missed you so much." Then her smiled faded again.

"What's up?"

Lauren reached into the pocket of her coat, slowly withdrawing her fist. "Izzy leant these to me the night off the party." She opened her hand, revealing a pair of tiny earrings. They were enameled roses, dusty pink buds with a pale gold edging along the petals.

I held out a shaky hand and Lauren tipped hers slightly, rolling them into my palm. "These were some of her favorites. Izzy's sister gave them to her before we left for school, as a going away present. I remember Izzy was so surprised she almost cried." I could barely swallow around the lump in my throat. "She told Amelia that at least someone in the family had taste as good as hers. I've never seen Amelia so proud of herself."

I closed my fist around the earrings. "Izzy must have trusted you a lot to lend these to you."

"I thought you should have them. They belong to your family."

I sucked in a breath at her words.

Your family.

I wasn't sure it existed without Izzy.

Lauren stood to leave. "Maybe you could talk to Gloria about Bethany? I really hate sleeping on that floor." She gave me a hopeful look.

"Oh, Gloria and I are overdue for a talk," I said, my attention still focused on the earrings.

"You know Gloria left for break already, right?"

I glanced up at Lauren, forcing a brittle smile. "I can talk to her next week." *And oh, what a talk it will be*, I added silently. *I'll have to bring her up here so Izzy has a chance to see it.*

As Lauren pulled the door open, I called out to her. "Lauren?"

"Yeah?"

"Can you let me know when Bethany comes back from break? I'd like to apologize for being such a crappy friend."

"Sure, Callie." Lauren had brightened considerably, like a load had been lifted from shoulders. I felt glad I'd been able to help her. "Have a happy Thanksgiving," she sang, fluttering her fingers as she glided through the door. It fell closed with a quiet click behind her.

I walked over and carefully sat the earrings on top of Izzy's barren dresser. I stood in front of the mirror, staring at the reflection of my bandaged and scabbed face behind the glinting jewelry.

Thanksgiving. A day for giving thanks.

For what?

For my dead best friend, who might hate me now that I was dating her ex?

For my almost parents, who didn't even care if I was home for the holidays, or the little sisters I wasn't sure I'd ever see again?

For the tattered remains of my broken and neglected friendships?

For my not quite cemented and already imploding relationship with my first real boyfriend?

I sat down abruptly, banging my lower back on the closet as I dropped to the ground and buried my head in my hands. My shoulder hurt, but not nearly as much as my heart. What did I have to be thankful for, exactly?

You're alive. I reminded myself again that Izzy would probably have given anything to have my problems.

At that moment, though, it didn't feel a lot like living. It felt like going through the motions of a life out of instinct instead of desire, as though something inside me had died when Izzy did, but I kept going. If she was a ghost, what did that make me?

A zombie, my snarky internal monologue supplied.

"Now there's a holiday special no one's making, Iz," I mumbled, chuckling hollowly. "Zombtastic and Ghostly's Thanksgiving: The Remains of a Boo-tiful Friendship."

I wanted to hear her groaning laugh over one of my bad puns. I needed to hear it, just once, even if it was a trick of my imagination. Then I would know I wasn't as alone as I felt. "Get it? Because it's the end, instead of the beginning?"

The room didn't say anything in response.

27.

I feel asleep on my floor, curled in a ball in front of Izzy's closet. When I woke up, I felt strangely calm. Talking to Lauren had given me a renewed sense of clarity and purpose. Boys might come and go; Izzy was still with me, and she'd *died*. I needed to stop crying and focus.

I dug through my pile of dirty laundry until I found the crumpled list in the back pocket of the jeans I'd worn to the movies. Picking up a pen, I read down the list, editing as I went.

~~Shannen~~

~~Lauren~~

~~Colin~~

1. Bethany – Sun/Mon
2. Gloria – Mon/Tues
3. Nate Dermott?
4. Gabe Hudson?
5. Emily Lawrence / Danielle Gomez??
6. <Crew house boys> ?
7. <dancing devil>

Chewing at the end of the pen, I nodded at my revisions. My list was getting longer, and the more names I added, the less sure I was that the people involved would talk to me. Still, I should probably try, in the interest of thoroughness if nothing else. Someone had to know who the dancing devil was.

Despite her purported drunkenness, I decided I would talk to Bethany first. Maybe she could help me, maybe she couldn't. Either way, I wanted to hear about her issues with Gloria before we faced off. That way I could deal with Gloria all at once.

"I know I've been distracted, Iz," I said aloud without removing my eyes from the page, "but I haven't forgotten my promise. I will find out what happened to you."

I jerked as a sharp rap rang against the door. It took a minute to register that it wasn't Izzy reaching out to me. "Come in." I hastily crammed the list into my desk drawer to protect it from prying eyes.

"Am I interrupting?" Jenna stuck her head in the door, frowning when she saw me sitting alone at the desk. "I thought I heard you talking to someone." She stepped into the room.

I hastily grabbed a book off my shelf, holding it up. "Just reading. Sometimes if I'm having trouble concentrating, I read aloud. It helps me focus." Jenna continued eyeing me, so I added, "I'm working really hard to catch up on my classes."

"Oh! Yeah, you really need to." Jenna perched on the edge of the Izzy's bed. "I've heard reading aloud helps with proofreading." I nodded, looking at her expectantly. Maybe she'd take the hint and leave. Instead Jenna cocked her head and smiled back at me brightly, her curls bouncing crazily as they fought to escape the low pigtails she'd used to restrain them.

"So…" I said as she continued to grin at me. "I guess I'll get back to it?" I raised the book again.

"Right!" Jenna glanced down at the paper in her hand as if only she'd just remembered it. "Well, I wanted to come by, say hello, see how you're doing, if you're getting out more. Though obviously you are, since I saw you last night." Her brow furrowed, but she rambled on without pause. "Though I guess you weren't so much going out as staying in. Not that you had to stay in. Maybe you went out, then stayed in. Either way, you're doing better?"

I was forever amazed Jenna could say so many awkward things in the same breath.

"Yes, much. Was there anything else?"

"Are you staying for break?" She pulled a hidden pencil from behind her ear out and held it poised over the paper. "I'm supposed to get a floor count."

"I'll be here." I hoped my voice sounded neutral. It must have worked, because Jenna sprang from her seat in the direction of the door, obviously on her way to confirm the other Thanksgiving losers.

"Oh! Cool! Any plans? I think some people are having an off-campus dinner or something if you need a place to go."

"No, no," I responded immediately. "I have plans." The excuse sounded vague and weak, but Jenna, distracted by her paperwork, didn't seem to notice.

"Remember, if you're planning to stay for Winter Break, you need to let Housing know right away," she lectured, pausing at the door, "because they have to approve you and put you on a list so Campus Security doesn't turn off your card access. Though you're not staying for Winter Break, are you? I'm sure you're not. That would be *so* depressing! I hear there are hardly any people here. You're probably going back to Texas, huh?"

I bit the inside of my cheek, trying to keep a polite smile on my face until she stopped jabbering and went away, but Jenna barreled on. "The idea of going home must be *so* hard without Izzy. But I bet it will be good for you. Hey, maybe you could visit Colin for part of it! You two are so cute together. Not that I've seen you together, but I can picture it in my mind—" she paused, scrunching her face as if to create a mental picture "— totally cute! Anyway, I'll see you next week. Have a great Thanksgiving!" With a quick wave, Jenna left, closing it behind her.

Winter. Break.

Alone.

I shuddered. An entire month of being stuck on campus, eating chips and peanut butter sandwiches alone in my room because Campus Dining was closed, hanging out with the handful of international students who couldn't afford to go all the way home or travel during the break, and slowly going more insane with Izzy as my primary source of companionship.

The possibility overwhelmed me. I struggled against the spreading numbness that usually preceded a panic attack, the edges of my vision blurring. In the weeks after Izzy's death, I'd had them so frequently they were coming two or three times a night when I tried to sleep. It was one of the only reasons I'd agreed to set foot inside the Counseling Center in the first place. I was willing to take anything that would help me sleep through the night, even though taking the anti-anxiety meds also made it impossible for me to focus, drowning me a calming disconnectedness. I'd had to stop taking them so I could wake up for classes. Now I regretted my decision.

When I finally got a grip on myself, I dug my medication out of the back of my underwear drawer. Like so many things in my life, I'd hidden the pills in the hopes that if I didn't see them, I wouldn't have to deal with them.

Out of sight, out of mind, right?

Those words took on an entirely new meaning when you had an invisible friend.

After a few tries, I managed to get the child-proof cap off. I swallowed one of the pills, coughing a little as it crumbled down my throat.

I thought about going to look for Nate or Emily, but I didn't have the first clue how to find them or if they'd still be on campus. I knew Colin could put me in touch with them, but I couldn't bring myself to call.

I couldn't believe I hadn't heard from him. Where was he? Why hadn't he called *me*? Was he still mad?

I pulled out my cellphone, frowning at it. At the very least, I needed to get my pillow and pain medication back before he left for break. The fight seemed so stupid in retrospect. So we didn't agree on everything—what couple did? I couldn't stand the idea of him going away with us mad at each other. It would be almost a week before we saw each other again. Given this was our first real fight as a couple, it seemed somehow important we resolve it face-to-face. At the same time, being the one to call felt like giving in, and I couldn't do it. Colin wasn't leaving until the next day. I could always call him later.

Instead, I tried to read as I'd told Jenna I would, but my mind kept straying back to Lauren and Izzy's last night. I pulled the list from my drawer, smoothing the rumpled paper against the edge of the desk. How was I going to find all these people, much less get them to talk to me?

There was a loud crack as something smacked against the wall, and I jumped, glancing wildly for Izzy's latest freak-out. The room was still and quiet. Crack! The sound was coming from outside. When I peeped through the blinds, I saw a couple of guys throwing tiny rocks at a room on the first floor. I couldn't make out what they were saying, so I cracked my window.

"Theresa! Therrrrrrr-eeeeeeeeee-saaaaaaawhhhh!" an obvious drunk guy bellowed. "Come to the paaaarty!"

"Shut up, dude!" his slightly sober friend hissed. "The RA might hear you."

"Theresa!" Super Drunk continued in a singsong voice, stumbling as he threw another pebble. "Come on, T! Don't you want to paaaaar-T?"

A window below slid open, and an unseen female's voice echoed into the darkness. "Shut up, you idiot! I told you, Theresa already left for break!"

Super Drunk stumbled toward the window, squinting. "I want her to come to the crew party."

"She's not here! Now go home, jackass."

The window slammed closed. "Let's go, dude," Slight Sober whispered to his friend, who was still mumbling something about Theresa, as he dragged Super Drunk away from the building.

I closed my window, fuming as I watched them stumbling

toward the road. A crew party. A fucking crew party. The same drunk idiots who'd hosted the last party of my best friend's life had waited a whole respectful minimum of a month before getting back to business as usual.

I should call Campus Security, I reached for my phone. *It would serve them right.* I couldn't believe it. Izzy was in the cold ground, but apparently the party stopped for nothing, even death.

The same...drunk...idiots...

I picked up the list, staring at it. It was a stupid idea. I mean, a truly stupid, reckless, most likely entirely pointless idea.

But...

I closed my eyes for a long moment, then spoke the words I never imagined I'd say again.

"Okay, Izzy. You get your way. Time to go to a party."

28.

By the time the crew house came into view, my stretchy blue velvet skirt kept riding up and my arms were freezing under my thin excuse for a cardigan. I'd drawn the line at uncomfortable shoes, opting for my eighteen-hole Docs and thick socks over patterned tights. At least the bottom of me was relatively warm. I'd pulled my hair into a high ponytail with a sparkly hairband and added some heavy makeup and pale lipstick, all courtesy of Izzy, to try to balance out my casual look with something that said, "Here to party!" I figured the first step to getting anyone to talk to me was looking like I didn't secretly hate everyone I saw stumbling around near the entrance to the old two-story. Luckily they all seemed too preoccupied with making out or breaking up or getting holiday bombed that no one paid much attention as I made my way up the long walk, climbed the sagging porch, and wandered inside.

Loud music hummed from speakers scattered throughout the large room off the entry, thudding with a persistence that demanded less talking and more dancing. I could see why anyone trying to talk had wandered into the front yard. Dim lamps threw shadows across the living room, where the shabby furniture was pushed back. A few couples swayed lazily to the beat, but I didn't recognize anyone so I pushed deeper into the house, looking for people I knew.

I worked my way backward, through a dining-room-turned-video-game-room where a bunch of people were playing some loud shooting game I didn't recognize, then into the large kitchen. The house must have been nice once, the kind a couple with a group of kids would need to raise them all, but those days were long past. Generation after generation of Astoria College students had passed the house down as a rental, until the walls were more poster tape and spackle than sheet rock, and the entire place smelled vaguely of old sweat and stale booze.

As I'd predicted, the kitchen was awash in a sea of solo cups and liquor. I found a cup that looked clean, then filled it halfway with the remnants of a bottle of cheap red wine. I had no intention of drinking it, but if I was going to fish around about Izzy, it seemed like a good idea to at least pretend to drink something.

A door off the kitchen was propped open, and from basement I could hear the occasional roar of cheering and booing. Seemed like most of the party was downstairs. I squared my shoulders. I wasn't looking forward to having a conversation with anyone about Izzy under these circumstances, but now that I was here, it seemed stupid to leave without trying. *Time to find our hosts and get this over with.*

The rickety stairs were steep and the only light came from a flickering bulb. I couldn't believe someone hadn't managed to fall and break their neck yet as I hugged the wall, scooting down one step at a time as I balanced the drink in one hand and groped my way along with the other.

I'd been right to follow the noise. The giant basement, which ran the full length of the house, was packed: people crowded onto couches talking, people lined up along the wall next to a pool table where it appeared some epic game was happening, two guys playing foosball in a corner surrounded by a cheering, and sometimes jeering, crowd, and a large bar against the far wall packed with people waiting for more booze. The sheer number of bodies made the basement stuffy and hot even in the middle of winter, and the smell was a pungent mix of alcohol sweat and bad body spray.

Part of me wanted to puke from nerves and anxiety. An even larger part of me simply wanted to flee. I closed my eyes for a moment, took a deep breath, and plastered a huge fake smile on my face. *You can do this*, I told myself. *You have to do this. For Izzy.*

I opened my eyes and took a confident step forward…

…and sloshed my drink right down the front of Gabe Hudson's shirt.

"Oh shit!" I covered my mouth with my hand in an effort to hide the hysterical giggle that erupted as I watched him stare down at his chest in horror. "I'm so sorry." I cast around for something he could use to dry off. "I didn't see you."

"Yeah," he grunted sourly. "I kind of guessed."

"Are there towels or anything?" I tried to figure out a way to help him as he twisted the wet fabric between his hands. I'd come all this way to find someone I could ask about Izzy, and then managed to royally piss off the first person I'd managed to find who might be able to tell me something.

"Don't worry about it." Without missing a beat, Gabe pulled the t-shirt off, ran it over his stomach, and tossed it in a corner near an ancient washer/dryer combo. I had to give Emily credit; Gabe might not be a straight-A student, but he definitely made up for it in the chiseled chest department. "I'm staying here for break, so I can wash it later." He ran a hand through his hair, squinting at me in the dim light. "Can't say I expected to see you here."

"Oh, ummm yeah," I stalled weakly. "Well, you know how it is. Holiday week." I shrugged. "Last chance to party before finals."

"You don't party."

I could tell by the way Gabe was staring at me that he wasn't buying my story for a second. Caught between the proverbial rock and Mr. Hard Abs, I blurted out the first thing that popped into my head. "Colin and I had a fight." I glanced over Gabe's shoulder, pretending to scan the crowd. "I thought I might find him here."

Gabe stared at me for a long minute before his shoulders relaxed. "No Colin tonight," he sounded surprisingly sympathetic. "He hasn't been to a campus party since the night…"

"Oh."

I must have looked as forlorn as I felt, because suddenly Gabe fell into friendly, helpful mode. "Let's get you another drink." He tossed a friendly arm around my shoulder, dragging me toward the bar. As much as I wanted to shake him off, I figured my best bet to get him talking was to go along, so I let him. I was surprised to see the crowd part a little as we approached, making space for me at the makeshift bar. Gabe leaned over it and grabbed a bottle of wine from underneath, extending it toward me. Since I wasn't about to drink out of an open bottle, I shook my head. "How about something a little less dangerous to everyone around me?" I suggested, faking a laugh to play off the refusal.

Gabe leaned over the bar again and this time came up with a bottle of tequila and two shot glasses. "Come on, we can share." He poured a double that was almost to the brim before I really had a chance to protest. The one and only time I'd done shots in high school had led to epic puking, but from the way Gabe was smiling and pushing the glass toward me, I didn't think I could really say no.

One shot, I told myself. *One won't hurt too much. Then he'll feel like he can trust you, and you'll be able to ask him about Izzy.*

I picked the glass up and held it out to Gabe uncertainly. "What should we drink to?"

"How about to pretty girls, and the boys whose hearts they break?" There was sadness behind his smile.

"To Izzy, then." *And to hoping you're a talkative drunk.*

Gabe chuckled. "I was thinking of Emily, but yeah. To Izzy, too." He tossed back the drink and I followed, trying not to gag as the cheap liquor hit the back of my throat and burned its way down into my stomach.

I sat the glass back on the bar, pushing it away from me. I was definitely not doing that again; I was already regretting the first one. Gabe didn't notice, eyes closed as he filled his glass and threw back his second shot.

"I take it you and Emily are fighting again?" I asked, trying to steer the conversation back to an opening.

"When aren't we?" Gabe poured himself another. "I feel like we spend more time broken up than together lately. Sometimes I don't even know what we're fighting about." He picked the glass up and stared into it, as if looking for answers. "I think we're having a conversation about something completely normal, and the next thing I know, she isn't speaking to me."

"I know the feeling," I muttered, but Gabe didn't seem to notice.

"Why do girls do that?" He tossed back his drink. "Seriously. I want to know. And you're a girl, kind of."

"Gee, thanks."

"No," he huffed, "I just mean, you're a girl, but you're not girly. You know? You stomp around in those boots and stare at people with your scary laser death eyes and they run away and stuff. And you're like, really mean to everyone, but you don't play games with them. Nate said it was because you were a lesbian, but I told him he was just being stupid, that it was because you're just like…a dude. Like a girl dude."

"Thanks. I think." I was surprised Gabe Hudson had bothered to think about me at all, much less talk about it with Nate. "And to answer your question, I don't know why anyone fights with anyone, male or female. I'm just as clueless as you are. I think we all feel that way."

"Izzy didn't." He stared hard at the floor.

"No." I swallowed. "Izzy always seemed to know what she wanted and how to get it."

We stood in silence for a moment, lost in our own thoughts. *Now or never.*

"Gabe, can I ask you a question?"

"Yeah." He poured himself yet another shot.

"Did you see Izzy that last night? The night she was here?"

Gabe sighed, and I could smell the liquor on his breath even before he downed his next drink. "Yeah, I saw her."

At the rate he was drinking he was going to be useless to me pretty soon. Maybe it was the heat, or maybe it was the shock of finding myself feeling sorry for Gabe Hudson, but my head felt full of cotton and my stomach was already roiling. I needed to get info out of him, and then get the hell out of that room. "Everyone keeps telling me she was drunk. Was she?"

"Yep."

"How drunk?'

"So drunk she hit on me in front of Emily," he said flatly. "If Emily hadn't been so distracted taking care of Danielle, she probably would have tried to scratch out Izzy's eyes. We had a huge fight about it, and then later when Nate and I were trying to carry Danielle out, Izzy was all over some other guy. I got screamed at for two hours, and I didn't even do anything."

"So you don't know who the guy was?" I pressed. "The one she was dancing with?"

"No. I mean, I've seen him around, but I don't know his name."

"Did Nate?"

"I dunno." Gabe put a hand on my shoulder, pulling my face toward his. "It should have been me."

"What?" I swallowed hard, trying not to puke from the smell of his breath. "What should have been you?"

"The guy she was dancing with." Gabe grabbed the bottle and did a shot straight off it, grimacing as he swallowed. "If it had been me, she wouldn't be dead now."

Tears pricked in my eyes. "You don't know that," I managed, too stunned to do much other than parrot Dr. Yates' words to me toward the sad boy standing next to me. "What happened was an accident. It isn't anyone's fault."

"Yes, itis." Gabe slurred. "Is'my fault. Is'yer fault." He gestured broadly with the bottle. "All o'us." He took another swig. "We killed her."

My stomach lurched. "I…have to go." I pushed myself off the bar, stumbling through the crowd toward the stairs. My vision swam as the floor pitched beneath me. I was drunk, very drunk, and I'd had exactly one shot. What was wrong with me?

The pills. I'd taken meds to stave off the panic attack. I wasn't supposed to drink with them, and here was I was, doing double tequila shots. I threw my hands out, trying to steady myself, and managed to practically hit a girl sitting nearby in the face. "Sorry!" I yelled, stumbling forward. I heard laughter behind me, but I ignored it and focused on getting to the stairs and the suddenly very important wall they were connected to.

I was still trying to get up the steps when Gabe caught up with me. "Lemme help you," he breathed, practically pushing me along as we made our way up and out of the basement.

I immediately turned toward the front of the house, cutting through a side room to get back to the living room, moving in the direction of the dance music I knew signaled I was close to the front door. Gabe kept following me, yelling something I couldn't hear over the throbbing beat. When I reached the door, the cold air hit me like a slap, helping me stave off the dizziness.

"Callie, wait!" Gabe called after me, grabbing my arm. "You can't leave."

"Lemme go," I complained, trying to pull free. I was having a harder and harder time focusing. "I wanna go."

Gabe grabbed me as I stumbled down the front porch steps, pulling me back toward the house. "You're drunk. No one leaves drunk. Those are the rules now."

"I'm not drunk," I protested, wriggling in his grip. My shoulder hurt, but I pulled harder anyway. "I wanna go home." I hammered my fists against his bare chest, but Gabe just gripped me tighter.

"I'm not gonna let you get hurt," he yelled, pulling me up a step against my will. Even drunk Gabe was surprisingly strong.

I managed to get one hand free and was rearing back to punch Gabe right in his six-pack when there came a most unexpected and awful sound: the telltale wail of a Campus Security siren. Gabe dropped my arms and put his hands up, swearing colorfully as he turned in the direction of the bright light now shining on the front of the house, spotlighting both of us.

"Evening, officers," I heard Gabe slur in greeting as people began pouring out of the house around us. Sensing the opportunity to make my exit, I stumbled down the stairs and across the yard, moving as fast as my unsteady legs would carry me. I heard someone coming up fast behind me, and I doubled my step, almost tripping over my own feet as my heavy boots slowed me down.

"Not so fast," a familiar voice grunted as two hands grabbed my shoulders from behind.

"Lemme go!" I pulled hard against his grip, but my captor held firm. "Let. Me. Go!" I stomped hard behind me, trying to smash my captor's feet. Instead I lost my footing and pitched forward, almost losing my balance.

I felt the stiff fabric of a uniform through my cardigan as tight arms wrapped around my waist. The familiar scent of sandalwood and firs surrounded me as warm breath huffed against my ear. "Callie, it's me. Would you stop trying to hurt me?"

I twisted around to face him. "Jay, what are you doing here?"

"My job." I winced as he shone his flashlight in my eyes. "You're drunk."

"Am not."

"Yeah, you are." Jay shoved the flashlight back in his belt holster. "Come on. Let me take you home."

"I can walk."

"No," Jay said sharply, shaking me a little in frustration. "You are not walking home in this condition." He closed his eyes for a long minute. "Please don't do this to me. Don't argue with me." Jay opened his eyes, and he looked so sad. It reminded me of the look on Gabe's face when he was talking about saving Izzy. "Just shut up and get in the truck."

"Okay." I swallowed hard. "Okay." I dragged my feet toward the truck. Jay followed close enough behind that he could catch me if I started to fall, but he didn't touch me again.

He helped me in and closed the door before walking back up to the front of the house, where Gabe and the crew guys who lived there were waiting. While Jay had been chasing after me, the crowd had almost entirely dispersed and the thudding music no longer echoed across the lawn. Apparently I'd given all the other underage attendees time to escape.

Eventually Jay climbed back into the truck, muttering something into the radio before pulling back out onto the road. I closed my eyes and tried to focus on not puking before I got back to my room.

Jay broke the silence first. "You are really stupid, you know that?"

I raised my head and opened my eyes, turning to meet Jay's fuming gaze. Seeing he had my attention, his focus shifted back to the road. "I can't believe after what happened to Izzy that you were about to walk back to campus in the dark. How could you do that? How could you be so unbelievably stupid?"

"I'm not drunk," I protested weakly, then closed my eyes as we went over a pothole that bounced the contents of my stomach up into my throat. "I only had one drink." I waved my finger at him for emphasis. "One."

"So how do you explain your current condition?"

"I forgot something."

"Which was?"

"I took the pills the Counseling Center gave me."

Jay slammed on the brakes and pulled the car off to the side of the empty road, tossing me against my seatbelt. "You mixed alcohol and anti-anxiety medication?"

"Not on purpose."

Jay dropped his head for a long moment, and I could see the muscles in his jaw working in the glow of the dashboard light. After a long moment, he opened his eyes and continued driving back to campus. I kept waiting for him to start yelling at me again, but he didn't. He just stared directly ahead and drove in silence, which somehow felt worse than being chastised.

When we reached the backdoor of Spruce, Jay didn't pull into an empty parking spot. He put the car in park but left the engine running as he hopped out and walked around the car to my side. He yanked the door open and held out a hand, offering to help me. I ignored it, unbuckling my seat and wiggled out, cursing the too-short, too-tight skirt as it rode dangerously high up my thighs.

"Where's my ticket?" I asked as he slammed the door shut, pointedly ignoring me as I pulled my clothes into place.

"What?"

"You're supposed to write me a ticket," I held out my hand. "I'm underage. I'm drunk. I was at a campus party. You're supposed to write me up, Officer Houghten."

Jay threw his head back and laughed, hard and loud, breath steaming out in warm puffs under the parking lot lights. "You're a piece of work, you know that?" He grabbed my outstretched hand, pulling it down so I stumbled toward him. "If I write you up, what do you think will happen next?"

"I'll have a hearing," I muttered, refusing to meet his eyes.

"Yep. And since you're already on probation, what do you think will happen next?" When I didn't answer, Jay put his hand under my chin, pulling my gaze up to meet his. "Promise me you won't do it again?"

"I won't," I whispered. "I promise."

Jay stared into my eyes for a long moment, as if trying to see whether or not I was lying, before he gave up with a shrug and let me go. "Drink a lot of water before you go to sleep." He didn't give me a second glance as he walked back to the driver's seat and climbed in.

I knocked on the passenger window, and he rolled it down. "Are you going to get in trouble?"

"Do you care?"

"Of course. You can write me the ticket. I can deal with the consequences, whatever they are."

"Maybe you can, but I can't. Good night, Callie." With that, he rolled up the window and pulled away from the building, leaving me alone in the parking lot, watching the truck disappear into night.

I got undressed slowly, then made myself drink an entire Nalgene full of water before crawling into bed. Whether Jay believed me or not, I'd meant what I'd said. I wouldn't be going to any more off-campus parties. The entire evening had turned out to be a horrible idea and a complete waste of time. I hadn't found out anything, really, other than that Colin and I weren't the only Astoria students who blamed themselves for what happened to Izzy. Izzy's death had touched a lot of people, more than I'd realized. Though I found it oddly comforting to know Izzy still mattered to people like Gabe and Lauren, it didn't help me much. I also knew Gabe and his friends were dead ends, investigation-wise. They were almost always together and had all the same friends, same classes. If Gabe didn't know the guy, it didn't seem likely Nate or their girlfriends would.

Worse still, if Gabe was good enough friends with the crew guys to be crashing at their house for a week, it seemed increasingly unlikely any of the crew guys knew the dancing devil either. Other than Gloria and Bethany, I was running out of leads. At this point, I had to face the prospect that Izzy's dancing devil might not even be an Astoria student. He might have been a friend visiting campus or a random townie crashing a campus party. It didn't happen often, but the more times I struck out trying to identify him, the more likely it seemed.

"Sorry, Izzy," I mumbled as I pulled the covers tight, feeling thoroughly discouraged. "Guess that wasn't my finest hour. I'll think of something else tomorrow." I realized belatedly that the light was still on, but before I could get out of bed, it flicked off.

"Night."

Though there was nothing but silence in answer, I could sense she was there. For the moment, that was enough.

29.

The pounding on the door was so loud, it sounded like someone banging their fist on the back on my eyelids. My eyes were on fire from my contacts, which I'd fallen asleep in again, and every part of my body was sore.

"One second," I slurred as I shook myself awake, the aftereffect of the anti-anxiety meds hitting me hard. Note to self: if alcohol was my dad's Achilles heel, then prescription drugs were obviously mine. As I stumbled to the door, I noticed the clock read seven-thirty. Who would be knocking this early?

I yanked the door open to find Colin looking grumpy and holding all my stuff. I immediately regretted the decision to sleep in my clothes. Also, there was a strong possibility my hair resembled a dead cat and I was pretty sure I had pillow creases on my face. Why did he have to stop by now?

"Here," he said gruffly, shoving the pillow at me. "You didn't come back last night, but I figured you'd need it over break. This, too," he said, dropping a plastic bag with my toiletries and clothes inside the door.

"I didn't think you wanted me to come back," I said, blinking hard against the searing pain in my eyes. "Did you want to come in?"

"I can't." The finality in his tone made my heart drop into my stomach.

"Oh." My voice sounded small and weak, but I couldn't help myself. I scrambled to fix things. "Maybe we could meet up for lunch?"

"Actually, I'm leaving right after my morning classes. A friend is driving me to the station so I can make my train."

"I thought you weren't leaving until this afternoon." I was practically begging him to stay longer, but I couldn't help myself. Why was this so hard? Why couldn't I say I was sorry? He looked gorgeous, standing under the flickering hallway lights in a long-sleeved, forest green t-shirt with a banded collar, two buttons open so I could see the curve of his Adam's apple, every strand of his golden hair perfectly in place.

"Plans changed." Colin shoved his hands into the pockets of his perfectly pressed dark jeans and glanced down the hall, like he couldn't wait to escape. I couldn't blame him. I was pathetic.

"Okay." *Don't cry, don't cry*, I admonished myself. "I guess I'll see you after break." I pressed my shaking palms against my legs to keep from reaching for him.

"Sure," he replied brusquely and turned to go. I couldn't believe he was leaving things like this. No hug, no kiss. He hadn't even said he would call.

"Colin," I called after him. He hesitated, then turned back. I wanted to beg him to skip class and stay with me, to apologize for our fight, but I couldn't remember what I had done to make him this angry. I could see it in the set of his mouth, the glint in his eye. I couldn't figure out what to say to make it right, and for one split-second it felt like a hundred terrible fights with my dad: me trying to appease him without knowing what I was atoning for. The pain was the echo of years of hurt, filed down to a point and shoved, like an ice pick, through my chest.

"I hope you have a happy Thanksgiving," I managed to whisper, the words so soft I didn't think he would hear them. He gave a curt nod of acknowledgment, then turned abruptly and walked away.

I stood in the doorway, watching until he disappeared into the stairwell.

He never looked back.

I closed my door and slid down it. Even with medication, I couldn't hold back the panic anymore, the endless looping certainty that I would crush, kill, or otherwise destroy everything and everyone I ever tried to love. I pulled my knees up and ground my eyes against them, trying to block out a world that was always punishing me for some crime I didn't remember.

I stayed that way for a long time.

30.

I only managed to leave my room once on Wednesday. I slept in super late, until I sure almost everyone had left for break, then snuck over to the bathroom. After a quick shower, I pulled on my Happy Bunny pajamas, dragged my hair into a ponytail, and fled back to my room. I forced myself to eat a bowl of cereal so I could take my pain meds without feeling nauseous, then put in one of my favorite movies and climbed into bed. I angled the laptop on the desk so I could see the screen, but I didn't really watch it. Instead I stared across the room at Izzy's bed, thinking of the time I'd spent huddled there with Colin watching videos.

I couldn't believe Colin and I were still fighting over something like a stupid paper. He'd been so upset about it he'd even moved up his train ticket to get away from me. If this relationship was any indication, I was apparently as big a failure as a girlfriend as I was a daughter and a best friend. I didn't have any new ideas on how to help Izzy until people came back from break, so there wasn't a lot to do other than sleep, study, and watch old movies on my laptop.

Thanks to the pain meds, I drifted in and out most of the day and through the night. When my alarm went off at nine the next morning, it was Thanksgiving. Listening to the loud beep echoing in the unnatural quiet of the empty residence hall, I shut it off and pulled the covers over my head, trying to block out the terrible day for as long as possible. I needed to go out to get food but couldn't face the holiday crowds. There would be lots of harried, cranky people running around, trying to wrapping up last minute errands so they could get home and be with the people who loved them…

They would never know how lucky they were.

The thought was enough to make me consider raiding the common kitchen for leftover food. At this point even a little communal culinary theft seemed better than facing the holiday hordes. I was still in bed, contemplating a foray into petty crime when there was a loud rapping on the door.

Who would be knocking on Thanksgiving? I wondered. The hall was empty when I'd ventured out for bathroom visits. If I wasn't the only one left in my building, I was close. My visitor knocked again loudly.

Maybe it's Colin. I doubted Colin could have gotten out of a holiday with his parents, but maybe he had changed his mind and left on the later train after all. Or maybe he'd driven back to campus to see me. Maybe he was sad about our fight, too, and had come back to see me so we could make up. He lived close enough; maybe his parents had let him drive back for a visit. Maybe he'd even take me with him. Colin was the only person I could imagine coming back for me, so it had to be him.

"One second," I yelled. I paused to evaluate myself critically in the mirror as I ran my hands through my mussy hair. Not great, but Colin had seen me in a bedraggled state before. I didn't have time to change, but hoped the pajamas were endearing in a snarky way.

Smile, Callie, I told myself, taking a deep breath. *Be nice, be apologetic, and be happy to see him.*

"Hi!" I said brightly, swinging the door open wide.

"Hi!" Jay replied with mocking enthusiasm, his lips curved in his trademark smirk as he leaned against the opposite wall.

"Oh. It's you."

"You were expecting someone else?"

Ignoring the jab, I turned back toward my bed, leaving the door open. "Here to give me another lecture?"

"That depends." He cocked his head to the side, studying me. "How are you feeling?"

"Fine." I kept my eyes trained on the floor. "A little embarrassed."

"Then there's no reason for a lecture is there?" Jay strolled into my room with a relaxed air that annoyed me. He dragged Izzy's desk chair into the center of the room and parking himself in front of me.

I pursed my lips. "Last time I saw you, you were reading me the riot act."

"Do you want me to yell at you? Because I can do that."

"No. I know I deserved it, and way worse. Thanks, by the way." I added belatedly. "For not writing me up."

He shrugged stiffly. "Don't mention it."

This conversation was getting more and more awkward. "So what *do* you want? I mean, if you aren't here to lecture me, why are you here?"

Jay shifted immediately back into charming mode. Whatever he wanted, he thought he'd need to sell me on the idea. "I came to rescue you from your pathetic holiday." He put his hands behind his head and stretched out his legs, looking pleased with himself. "I hear you don't have any plans."

"Where'd you hear that?"

"A little birdie told me." His grin widened.

Jenna. "That little birdie has a big mouth," I retorted, hugging my pillow tight to my chest. When my shoulder screamed in protest, I winced.

A look of concern passed over Jay's face. "Is your shoulder hurting?" He sat forward, all casualness discarded.

I almost lied to get him to leave me alone, but I knew, somehow, he'd see through it. "Yeah," I admitted. "It's been getting worse."

"Have you been putting the ointment on it and changing the bandaging?"

I frowned. "I got Nurse Nancy to change it Monday, but I forgot yesterday."

"They're closed for break. Do you have someone to change it for you? Colin, maybe?" Jay tried to keep his tone light, but his expression was unreadable.

"Colin went home for break." I suspected Jay knew this since he knew I was alone. Typical Jay, bringing it up to needle me. I held his gaze steadily, unwilling to show how much Colin's leaving hurt me.

"He didn't take you with him?"

"No," I explained with strained politeness, refusing to rise to the bait. "We haven't been together long. We agreed it might be a little awkward." I was stretching the truth a bit, but I didn't see any reason Jay needed to know that.

Jay rubbed his face with his palm. "Things are so different

here. Back home, you could bring anybody, you know?" He sounded genuinely perplexed.

The truth was, I did know what he meant. In the South, people treated complete strangers as if they were life-long friends; you never turned anybody away on a holiday, especially if they didn't have somewhere else to go. As much as I resented home, sometimes I longed for the meddling way people tried to care for one another. That was why Jay was in my room, trying to save my holiday. I should have been grateful. Instead, it only served to remind me how alone I was.

Jay continued wistfully as I stewed. "I can't believe how many kids get stuck here for the holidays. No one takes them in and AC doesn't organize something for them. It don't seem right," he finished, his accent falling thickly on the last few words.

I shrugged noncommittally. "I guess we're not in Kansas anymore, Toto."

"Ain't that the truth?" He laughed. "Anyway, that sorta leads me to what I came here for. I think you should come with me for Thanksgiving."

"Like on campus?"

"No. There's a veterans' rehab center not too far from here that does a big Thanksgiving celebration every year for the soldiers who have to stay and their families so they can spend the holiday together," he explained. "They ask local vets and their families to bring a dish or volunteer to serve. I've been going every year since I got here. I usually leave around noon and serve the early shift from two to four. Then I hang around and eat with the late dinner crowd so I can watch football and spend time with the guys who don't have family to visit them. I was wondering if you'd like to come."

I was stunned by the offer. Of course, Jay would give up his Thanksgiving to help other people. Of course, he'd find a way to turn his own loneliness into something that could benefit someone equally lonely and in far worse shape. And, of course, he'd picked an activity I absolutely wanted to do. Much of my extended family had been in the service, and I knew first-hand about the difficult holidays when they were deployed, the tear-filled joyful scenes at the airport when they returned. I couldn't imagine coming home, injured, and not having someone to care for you. It was such a sweet gesture that it completely undid any residual anger I felt toward him. Not only was Jay spending his holiday doing a selfless thing, but he was rescuing me from a truly miserable Thanksgiving in the process. Moments like this made it impossible to hate him, even if he was forever being nosey and controlling.

"I'd love to go," I said, surprised by my own enthusiasm. "I don't have anything to bring—"

"I've got that part taken care of. I've got two turkeys I deep-fried this morning and a couple of pans of stuffing. You're more than covered."

I giggled. "You deep-fried turkeys? You deep-fried turkeys *this* morning?"

"Hell yeah! Best way to cook a turkey," he replied, lying thickly into his drawl. "You ain't lived til you've had a deep-fried turkey." He rubbed his hands together for emphasis.

"Can't say I've had the pleasure. You can only die of a heart attack once, right?"

"That's the spirit." He stood up and held out a hand. "Shall we?"

"What time do we need to leave?" I ignored his hand and pushed myself up, grimacing as I put weight on my bad arm.

"Not for another hour or so." He crossed his arms, frowning. "Would you mind letting me look at your shoulder? I don't like the way it's bothering you."

I paused, considering. I didn't like giving in, but with the Health Center closed, I didn't have a lot of choices unless I wanted to go back to the hospital. "I guess?" I motioned toward my pajamas. "I'm not exactly decent under here."

He nodded thoughtfully, eyeing me as blood rushed to my face. Was Jay actually considering using an injury as an excuse to get me naked?

"You should go in the bathroom and change."

Apparently not. I blushed harder at my assumption.

Jay didn't seem to notice. "I'm gonna go down to the truck and see if Floyd has a first-aid kit. If not, I'm going to run over to the Campus Security office and get theirs."

Intent on getting past my momentary awkwardness, I busied myself getting ready. I was fishing out a tank top buried underneath a pile of long-sleeved t-shirts when I realized he was standing in the doorway, watching me. "What?"

Jay smiled broadly. "I'm real glad you're coming with me." Before I could respond, he turned and strolled down the hallway.

Since I wasn't expected to bring anything, I decided the least I could do was make myself presentable. After two days straight of lying in bed feeling sorry for myself, I was a rank, disgusting mess. I took a quick shower, not worrying about the bandage on my shoulder since Jay was going to change it for me. When I took the bandage off my cheek, there was only a small thin scab where the larger cut had been, so I didn't bother covering it up. Most of the other tiny nicks and scratches were fading. To my relief, they were almost unnoticeable under a little makeup, and I mentally thanked Izzy for making me buy the expensive cover-up I almost never used.

I pulled on a burgundy tank top and a pair of beige slacks. I had a matching cardigan that was cream at the top but was dip-dyed so that it flowed to a deep burgundy at the wrists and waist. It was something I could throw on after Jay looked at my shoulder without a lot of additional pain or inconvenience.

Jay still wasn't back, so I puttered around my room, clipping my hair back from my face with tiny barrettes and digging out a pair of earrings and a necklace I hardly wore. I didn't want to get too dressed up since I'd be serving, but I also wanted to make sure I was respectful of the veterans and their families. I was slipping on a pair of ballet flats when Jay appeared carrying a large first aid kit with the words CAMPUS SECURITY scrawled across it.

I noticed Jay had changed clothes as well. He was still wearing jeans, but they were newer than the ones he usually wore, and from the shine I could tell he'd starched and ironed them. He had on a dark blue button-down shirt tucked into his jeans that contrasted with his olive skin and brought out the reddish highlights in his neatly combed hair. The sleeves were rolled up to his elbows,

297

the top two buttons open at the throat. He was freshly shaven and the scent of aftershave mixed with his usual earthy smell as he passed me.

Jay moved around my room with a purposeful air, pulling the chair in front of Izzy's bed and gesturing at me to take a seat. I sat on the edge, back ramrod straight.

"Sit back, Callie," he said softly.

I jumped as his fingers pulled the strap of my tank top off the top of my shoulder and Jay chuckled a little in response. His hand grazed the back of my neck as he ran his palm under my hair, pushing it over my other shoulder and out of the way. I felt overly aware of the path of his fingers as they ran across the top of the tape holding my bandage in place.

What is wrong with you? I chastised myself. *You have a boyfriend!*

"Let me know if I hurt you," he murmured, clearly focused on the task at hand as he pulled my old bandage away slowly from my skin.

"You've really pulled on some of those stitches." His breath warmed my neck where my cool wet hair had been moments before, and I shivered involuntarily. "You need to take better care of yourself."

I bit the inside of my lip and tried to think non-romantic thoughts as he expertly began cleaning the wound. You were supposed to think about sports, right? That's what they told guys. I liked sports.

Baseball. America's pastime. Take me out to the ballgame.

Nachos. Soda. Hey-batta-batta-batta-saw-wing-batta! Bryce Harper. Bryce Harper's butt. Crap! I am terrible at this!

I started saying the alphabet backwards in my head. Definitely nothing sexy about the ABCs. I was just finishing my third pass at H-G-F-E when he finished. "There you go." He smoothed the tape across the top of the new bandage.

I jumped out of the chair, pulled my sweater on, and reached into my closet to get my pea coat. "Thanks," I said, more to the closet than to Jay.

"Anytime." He put everything back in the first aid kit and snapped it shut. "You really should get that checked more often."

Every microbe of attraction I'd been fighting moments before drained out of me like water rushing down a drain. "Yes, thank you *so* much. I do love being constantly told how incompetent I am," I muttered, yanking the coat on and shoving my arm through the hole. I managed to pull at my stitches as I did so and was rewarded with searing pain in response. I grabbed the painkillers off the dresser, shoving them in my pocket without turning around. In my other pocket went my cell phone, and I ignored a pang of loneliness when I noticed I had no missed calls or texts.

When I turned around, Jay was staring at me, gripping the first aid kit. He was as irritated with me as I was with him, and I wondered for the umpteenth time if we'd ever be able to go for more than fifteen minutes without an argument. I really needed to stop antagonizing the only person who could stand to be around me for a holiday.

I slowly counted to ten in my head as I grabbed my purse. *Time to be the bigger person.* "Thank you very much for taking me with you." The words sounded stiff and formal. "I appreciate the invitation."

Jay gestured toward the door. "After you, ma'am." I walked out into the hallway and he followed. "Got your keys?"

I bit back a sarcastic remark and nodded, watching as he locked the door behind me. Maybe if we could keep our answers to nods and grunts, we would make it through the day without killing each other.

31.

Jay borrowed a truck from a classmate who was gone for the weekend, and pretty soon we were loaded up and heading south. The longer we drove, the more the quiet stretched out between us, empty of words but full of the unspoken.

"So are you going to tell me what you were doing at that party the other night?" Jay asked eventually, breaking the tension.

I shrugged noncommittally, feeling trapped. "I was bored."

Jay snorted. "You're lying."

"I am not," I responded hotly.

"Yeah, you are." He frowned, looking sour. "I don't know why you are, but you are. You don't go to parties."

"I've been to plenty of parties."

"Only under duress." He shot me a sidelong glance. "Izzy dragged you to a lot of parties, but you didn't go willingly."

I couldn't really argue that point. Jay was right; I went mostly because Izzy wanted to, and I'd wanted to make her happy. I knew I couldn't tell Jay the real reason I'd gone without him blowing up, so I decided to tell him a slanted version of the truth, and hoped he'd let it slide. "I went because I miss Izzy," I said slowly, dragging out the words, "and because it seemed like the kind of thing she'd want me to do."

"And you think Izzy would want you to wander off from some party on foot, drunk out of your mind?" Jay's knuckles whitened on the wheel. "Somehow I doubt that."

"It was stupid, okay? I know it was stupid," I fumed. "Trust me, it won't happen again."

"Good." Jay rolled his shoulders, as if trying to ease tension on them. "Then I just have one last question."

I crossed my arms, feeling grumpy. "If I'd known this trip included an interrogation, I would've stayed at school."

"All I want to know is," Jay turned his dark eyes on me, "why didn't Colin go with you? What kind of guy lets his girlfriend do something so incredibly stupid by herself?"

"Colin doesn't 'let me' do anything," I countered, throwing sarcastic air quotes up with my fingers. "I don't need his permission and I can take care of myself."

Jay pinched the bridge of his nose in frustration. "Of course you don't need his permission. That's not what I meant. I doubt he could stop you from doing anything you wanted anyway."

"But you could?"

"No," he said sharply. "I just meant…" Now it was Jay's turn to choose his words carefully. "After what happened to Izzy, I'm surprised he didn't want to go with you. I'm surprised he didn't want to be there, just for his own peace of mind."

I turned my face away, staring out the window. I didn't want to tell Jay I hadn't told Colin I was going to the party, that I wasn't sure he'd have gone with me even if I had told him. It wasn't Jay's business. "Colin trusts me," I mumbled, trying to cover my sadness and frustration. "And anyway, I'm not going to do it again, so what does it matter?"

"Okay," Jay said quietly. After a long tense moment, he switched on the radio, tuning it to a local country station. I kept my mouth shut despite my deep loathing for modern country, cataloguing the hundreds of different ways Colin and I would make fun of this moment if he was here. Occasionally I discretely slipped my phone from my pocket to make sure I still had service and hadn't missed a call from him, but there were no messages. The longer I didn't hear from Colin, the sadder I felt, until I found myself mentally agreeing with the singer crooning, "Am I blue? I'm so blue, for you…" on the radio.

If Jay noticed, he didn't show it. He drove along quietly, occasionally tapping along on top of the steering wheel in time with the music. Lost in my own self-pity, I barely noticed when he pulled over at a roadside stand.

"Wait here, I gotta get something." He slid out of the truck without waiting for a response. When Jay returned, he shoved a large bouquet of brightly colored flowers at me, and gently placed two large pies in plain paper boxes on the bench seat between us. The flowers were a mixture of pinks, reds, and yellows and were surprisingly fragrant for late November. I recognized gerbera daisies and chrysanthemums, but there were a number of small broad-lipped flowers in pale yellow and snowy white. They had a scent I couldn't identify as it wafted gently toward me, and I inhaled deeply, smiling.

"It's freesia," Jay said, answering a question, once again, that I hadn't asked.

"They're beautiful!"

"Yeah, well, don't get excited," he said blandly as shifted the truck into reverse. "They're not for you."

"Oh! I didn't…" I turned my hot face toward the window,

trying to hide how sad and embarrassed I was at having thought they were for me. I held them carefully for the rest of the drive, taking in their delicately soapy smell and wondered what kind of girl Jay would go out of his way to buy flowers for.

She was probably a pretty nurse who worked at the rehab center, someone friendly and good at taking care of people. Jay probably didn't feel like he had to act like an overprotective big brother with her; she probably took care of him.

Without intending to, my mind began to create a pretty little rodeo queen for Jay, with dark wavy hair and skin-tight wranglers like the ones the FFA girls back home wore in high school. In my mind I saw her riding horses and baking pies and mending wounded soldiers by day, then two-stepping her way around a dance floor with Jay by night.

The more I thought about it, the grumpier I felt. Even Jay had a sweetheart to spend the holiday with. I was the just charity case he'd brought along for the ride. I suddenly wished I'd never gotten out of my Happy Bunny pajamas.

The rehab center turned out to be a small and unassuming set of brick buildings located to the southwest of Portland. The squat structures sat in a clump around a neatly-trimmed lawn. Tall pines lined a wide driveway and the edges of the small parking lot. Except for a stone marker reading "Beckham Veterans Rehabilitation Center" near the entrance, it could have been mistaken for a high school campus.

Jay parked the truck near a door in a small side parking lot labeled "Staff Only." He jumped out of the truck and pulled a large cooler from the bed. I got out, careful not to drop the flowers as I juggled them with the pie boxes. As I attempted to balance everything, I heard the door open.

"Jayden Houghton, you are late!" a female voice roared in a decidedly Midwestern accent. A large woman in an apron stood framed in the doorway, hands on her hips and an ireful expression on her face. Her brown hair had streaks of grey running through it and was pulled back from her ruddy face in a bun at the nape of her neck. She wore a long white apron covered in food stains over jeans and a checkered shirt with the sleeves rolled up.

Jay set the cooler on the ground and walked toward the woman wearing his most charming smile. "Am not," he protested as he hugged her. After a moment, the woman's stern expression broke into a tired smile and she embraced him in return. "And if I am," he said, arranging his face into an expression of mock innocence, "it's clearly her fault."

I approached them slowly, feeling shy and out of place. It suddenly seemed like I was crashing some other family's reunion. Jay swept the flowers out of my hand. I fumbled the pies in the exchange, almost dropping them in the process.

I scowled at Jay's back as he presented the flowers to the woman with a small flourish. "These are for you, May."

May grabbed the flowers from his hands, chortling hard enough that her whole body shook. "Well, aren't you sweet!" She swatted at Jay affectionately. "Though I see your manners are still lacking." She wiped a meaty hand on her apron and extended it to me. "Hi there, sugar. I'm Maryweather Lewis."

"You're kidding," I blurted before I could stop myself.

Jay scowled at me, but the woman only laughed in response. "What can I say? My papa loved Oregon history. Everybody calls me May."

I took her hand and she shook mine. "Callie McCayter."

"How'd he shanghai you into helping today?" She squinted over the bouquet as she sniffed at the flowers in a self-satisfied way.

"Oh, he didn't! Shanghai me, I mean," I stammered. "I have a lot of family in the service. I wanted to help."

May's smile slipped a bit, and I could see the sadness and loss in her eyes. She hugged her flowers to hide the moment of weakness, and Jay and I politely looked away. As I studiously took in my surroundings, I felt a strange sense of relief. There was no rodeo queen, only a woman old enough to be my grandmother, and Jay's, too.

Though I had no right to be jealous, I was glad all the same. It bothered me. I had no claim on Jay. What did I care if there was someone waiting for him? I should want him to be happy. Besides, I had Colin.

At least, I thought I did.

"Where do you want this stuff?" Jay picked up the cooler and looked at her expectantly.

May's smile returned with renewed strength, like someone had replaced a weak battery in a flash light. "You can put the turkeys in the kitchen and take the trays out front and set them along the buffet."

"And what you got there, sugar?" May examined the pie boxes

critically and seemed to recognize the small white label in the corner indicating their origin. "You put those on the counter in the kitchen with the other pies." Then she turned toward the kitchen, gazing at her flowers and humming softly as I followed.

May found an apron for me and put me to work helping her rotate various trays of food out of the refrigerator, into the oven, and then out to a long row of tables lining one side of a small dining room. She reviewed the dinner schedule with me and confirmed Jay and I would eat with the second shift. May barked orders in a friendly way as more volunteers trickled in. Everyone fell into step, setting up tables and chairs, organizing plateware and cutlery, like a well-coordinated dance performance.

Most of the volunteers appeared to be in their late-forties and early-fifties, and I got the sense from our brief conversations they did not have anyone at home, so they came in regularly to volunteer. Others arrived with young children in tow, military spouses whose loved ones were deployed around the world. All of the women seemed to know Jay, and I watched as they hugged and doted on him like a favored nephew or grandson.

"It's awful sweet of y'all to drive down here to help us," May said as she pulled a large aluminum foil pan out of the oven and pushed it onto a counter. "You know he comes out here almost every holiday?" She waved an oven mitt toward Jay, who was chasing a couple of little boys around a wide space in front of the check-in desk. "I think he misses his family, but he never lets on." She sighed quietly. "I can't believe his momma let him go to school so far away after she got him back, but you know boys. You can't tell them anything."

At that moment, another group of volunteers walked in through the kitchen door, all carrying various trays and crockpots. May swept over to them to take inventory, leaving me to watch Jay as he rolled around on the dining area floor while the boys tried out their best wrestling moves on him.

Was Jay lonely? He never seemed that way at school, always winking and joking as he charmed his way across campus, but as I watched him play with the kids and dutifully accept the attention of the female volunteers, I wondered if he felt as alone as I did. Astoria was a place with few older students and even fewer veterans among its student body. Maybe Jay felt as isolated by his wildly different path to Astoria as I did.

Jay caught me watching him as one of the boys flung his arms around Jay's neck. He grinned at me as he spun the boy in a circle, and I couldn't help grinning back. Then May called me to help her, and I left Jay to his miniature WrestleMania.

Around two, the diners began arriving. It seemed like everyone in the early group was meeting some friend or family member, and there was a steady stream of hungry people lining up in front of the table where May set me to serving heaping spoonfuls of mashed potatoes. Jay was stationed at the other end of the line, carving a parade of donated turkeys with an expert hand. May moved around the room like a cruise director, coordinating servers, replenishing food stations, and directing other volunteers to clear plates for washing.

When another volunteer came to relieve me around four-thirty,

I was exhausted and starving. I surrendered my apron to May, who handed me a heaping plate in exchange. Jay was still slicing away, so I grabbed a seat at the end of a long table and dug into the food. Everything was delicious. Turkey, mashed potatoes, sweet potatoes, broccoli cheese casserole, Parker House rolls, and real cranberry sauce swam together on my plate.

Distracted by my hunger, it took a while before a giggle pulled my attention in the direction of two little girls sitting a few seats away. I glanced at them, and the younger girl sucked at the tip of a long pigtail and averted her eyes in response. The older girl, who I suspected was around ten, stared back, as though challenging me to look away first. It was a tiny assertion of power, so fearless and self-assured, that I had to struggle to keep from giggling.

"You're supposed to chew your food," she stated in an all-knowing tone, nodding solemnly to emphasize her point.

"Really?" I asked, attempting to keep my tone serious. "I can't swallow it whole?"

"You could choke." Her expression was grim, as though she could see it all happening in her mind's eye.

"Are you sure?" I asked, gently lifting the whole plate toward my mouth. "I can't suck it all down in one go, like a vacuum cleaner?"

The younger one giggled, and the older girl, who realized I was giving her a hard time, pressed her lips together. "You could try. But then someone will have to give you the Heimlich moonover," she declared, crossing her arms over her chest.

"Maneuver, Haleigh," said a pretty woman with matching light brown hair and eyes as she slid into the seat next to mine. "Not moonover. Man-ooh-ver." The woman sounded tired, but I couldn't tell if it was irritation at her daughter or simple exhaustion. As she turned toward me, I saw the dark circles under eyes and decided it was the latter. "Sorry about that. Haleigh never met a fact she didn't like sharing with a complete stranger." Her mouth quirked in a half smile and she extended her hand. "Mallory Blessfield. And this, as you know, is my daughter Haleigh. And that little thing is my sweet Clara." She pointed to each of the girls in turn. Haleigh grumbled, embarrassed about being corrected, and Clara continued to suck on her hair as she stared at me with big eyes.

"Clara, get your hair out of your mouth and eat something," Mallory said, digging her fork into her own food. "You have to try a little of everything okay? If you at least try everything once and eat all your turkey, then you can have pie." Clara nodded and began working on cutting her turkey carefully into tiny pieces. Haleigh scowled at her plate, deeply engaged in finding a way out of eating a bite of everything, particularly the green bean casserole squeezed in between the mashed potatoes and caramelized carrots. I watched as she attempted to get a tiny spoonful that consisted entirely of mushroom soup and fried onion topping, quickly swallowing it while pinching her nose.

"Nice try, Haleigh," her mother said wearily. "It doesn't count unless you eat at least one green bean, and you know it." Haleigh's eyes grew wide and she drew in a deep breath in preparation for a loud protest, but the look Mallory gave her froze her in her tracks.

"Fine," she muttered huffily, but turned her attention to the turkey as though she could not bear another bite of green bean casserole for the moment. I tried hard not to laugh, knowing from personal experience of my own childhood Thanksgivings that waiting would make it worse. Instead, I focused on my own plate as I contemplated whether I wanted to try seconds or go straight for the pie.

When Mallory finished her own plate and declared the girls sufficiently fed with "real food" to the extent they'd earned their dessert, she turned her attention toward me. "So, you don't seem to be visiting anyone," she said as she wiped her mouth on a napkin. "Are you volunteering?"

I nodded. "We got here around noon," I said around a small bite of pumpkin pie with cinnamon whipped cream.

Mallory watched as the girls returned with dinner plates covered in tiny slices of various pies and cakes, easily more food than they'd started out with during the meal portion of the afternoon. Without ceremony, she reached across the table to Haleigh's plate and stole a forkful of carrot cake, ignoring Haleigh's vigorous protests. "We?"

I pointed over to Jay, who had finally relinquished carving duties and was going down the food line to fill up a plate of his own.

"You came with Jay," Mallory stated, an approving tone in her voice. "Good for you."

"Jay!?!" Haleigh squealed indignantly. "Jay brought you here? He never brings anyone here." Haleigh narrowed her eyes at me, face flushed with jealousy.

"Oh, hush." Mallory clucked her tongue at the girl. "Haleigh has developed quite the crush on Jay in the last two years," Mallory whispered under her breath, but I could tell Haleigh heard her from the way she slammed her arms across her chest again.

"Well, we're friends," I explained, shooting a sideways glance at Haleigh who was intently pretending to ignore our exchange while drinking in every word. "We go to school together, and he knew I didn't have anywhere to go today so he offered to let me come with him."

Mallory nodded at me. "Their daddy is based out of Camp Pendleton, but he's deployed right now, so we decided to come out help out, spend some time with the other families. Didn't we, girls?" she turned back to her daughters, and Clara nodded solemnly. "But he comes home in a few months, right?"

"Not before Christmas," grumbled Haleigh, her eyes serious and sad as she stared at her plate of sweets, suddenly disinterested.

"No, not before Christmas," Mallory replied, equally serious. "But before your birthday, right?"

Haleigh nodded, and seemed cheered by the idea. "Before my birthday," she said quietly, like a cross between a bedtime prayer and birthday wish.

"You go to Astoria College?" Mallory asked and I nodded as I swallowed another bite of pie. "Good school."

"I was lucky to get in…"

"You must not be from around here."

"No, I'm from Houston. Last year I went home for Thanksgiving," As I said the words, highlights of my last Texas Thanksgiving ran through my head, Greg carving the turkey while

Crystal spread food all over the living room as a revolving door of guests wandered in and out. It seemed like someone else's life.

"You're a long way from home."

I nodded. "This year...it was too far to go," I pushed the plate away from me, pie half-eaten.

Mallory must have noticed my change of mood from the way she was eyeing me, but she didn't say anything. Instead she reached over and stole a forkful of chocolate cake off Clara's plate. "Well, it was nice of you to come out here to help. Nice of Jay to bring you."

"And he's *not* your boyfriend?" Haleigh blurted out in a challenging tone.

"No, ma'am," Jay answered, settling into the chair across from me. Caught out, Haleigh turned positively purple with embarrassment.

Jay smiled down at her. "How could I possibly date anyone when there are girls as pretty as you out in the world?" He winked at her, then gave an exaggerated sigh. "If only I weren't so old..." Jay looked down sadly at his plate, as though it might reveal the secrets to reversing time.

"You're not *so* old," Haleigh said breathily, and I heard Mallory choke back a snort as she sipped her water. "Maybe you could waituntillgotolder." Haleigh rushed, batting her eyes up at Jay, who gazed down at her with such a serious face I wanted to kick him under the table to make him stop.

"Do you think so?" he asked. Haleigh nodded, not taking her eyes off his face.

Mallory leaned toward me and whispered, "If her daddy was

here to see the way she was looking at him—" she nodded toward Jay "—I don't know which one of them would be in more trouble."

Clara, who'd been virtually silent the entire dinner, suddenly perked up. "Maybe if you get that magic elixir you are always pretending to find when you play with your Ken and Barbie, you can marry Jay like you want." Clara grinned at Haleigh happily, as though she'd discovered the secret to solving world hunger.

Haleigh turned a mottled puce. "That was a secret!" she yelled, then burst into tears and ran from the table. Clara, startled by her sister's reaction, also began to cry.

I glared at Jay as Mallory moved around the table to comfort Clara, pulling the sobbing girl into her lap. "Way to go."

"What'd I do?" he asked, mouth half-full of food, and I shook my head at him.

"Do you need help finding Haleigh?" I asked Mallory.

Mallory hugged Clara, who was gently hiccupping and sucking on her pigtail again. "No. She's hiding in the bathroom. She's *always* hiding in the bathroom." Mallory rolled her eyes at me as if to say "oh the drama" and I nodded sympathetically. "We need to get going anyway."

Mallory gently sat Clara on the floor and gathered up their plates. "Phil is supposed to try calling around eight, and I'd like to have them ready for bed before then." She smiled wanly at me. "It was nice meeting you."

She turned to Jay, poking at him with the end of a plastic spoon, "And you, Mister. Stop tormenting my poor daughter, or her daddy's gonna come looking for you with the business end of a rifle when he gets back."

Jay grunted, flexing his jaw in response. Mallory reached out to ruffle his hair affectionately before heading off in search of Haleigh, Clara trailing behind.

"You people are a lot of work," Jay grumbled as he shoved a heaping forkful of food into his mouth.

"You people?" I teased, raising an eyebrow. "As in, you female-bodied people? Or you sentient people in general?" He chucked a napkin at me, but I saw a glimpse of a slight smile before he swallowed another forkful of potatoes.

A few minutes later, a couple of young men wandered over to us. From their sweats, I could tell they were the patients Jay told me he came to spend time with, the guys who didn't have family close by to visit, or maybe any family at all. *Like me*, I mused as I watched them turn their chairs toward a huge flat panel TV. I hadn't noticed it earlier, but as the families packed up and left and the early volunteers dwindled, the crowd grew increasingly smaller and filled with young veterans who were staying full-time at the center while they worked on their rehabilitation.

There wasn't a lot of talk during the game. Instead of the boisterous cheering and groaning I was used to accompanying watching back home, these young men, most of them my age and already carrying their experiences etched in the lines of their faces and across their bodies, sat in a kind of communal silence that reminded me of church. A cloud of palpable loneliness at having no one to visit them hung over the room, an unspoken circumstance which, combined with their combat experiences and lingering injuries, bound them as tightly to one another as the visiting families. No one asked who I was or how I knew Jay; in fact, most of them acted as if I wasn't there.

After a while I got up to clear plates, taking them into the kitchen where May was still holding court. I lent a hand while she directed the last of the volunteers where to store leftovers and supervised the dishwashing. As I stacked the last of the dishes in a large drying rack next to the double sink, I reached up to rub my shoulder and was surprised to feel two hands replace my own, rubbing gently. I could tell without turning around it was Jay, and I closed my eyes and tried to relax my arms and ignore the ache in my shoulder.

"Are you ready to head back?"

"Yeah." I dropped the towel on the counter and turned toward him. For a moment, we were too close, close enough that I could almost count the dark eyelashes lying against his cheek. Then Jay stepped away, off to say his goodbyes. I pulled my coat on and waited by the door, feeling suddenly out of sorts.

When he returned, May was with him, their heads were bent toward each other in low conversation. I watched a deep chuckle shake May's whole body as she swatted his arm. It was strange to see Jay in his element here. There was so much of his life I didn't know anything about.

May smiled when she saw me watching them. "Well, Callie, it was real nice of you to join us this year."

"Thanks for having me. The food was wonderful." I smiled. "I had a great time."

"Good." She beamed at the success of her event. "Maybe we can convince this one to bring you back sometime," she glanced meaningfully at Jay, who nodded. Satisfied with the response, May ushered us toward the exit. "You kids drive safe," she called after us as we climbed into the truck. "It's a long drive."

May stood in the doorway, the light of the kitchen glowing around her, waving as Jay headed out of the parking lot. She looked like a woman from a war movie, waving us off to battle as she waited at home, keeping the proverbial fires burning. I waved back at her until we turned onto the main road and she disappeared from view.

"How do you know May?" I asked as I settled back into my seat.

"She was volunteering at the rehab center when I was there."

"You were in rehab?" I turned toward him so I could watch his profile in the flicker of passing headlights.

"Yep. Blew out my knee yanking a buddy out of the line of fire on a mission." His tone was distant and clinical. "Big hero I was. I could barely walk. Almost got us both pinned down. Poor bastard had to half-carry me back to the transport."

"Wow. I had no idea." I cleared my throat, trying to figure out what I could say. "That was a brave thing to do."

Jay shrugged it off. "I was near the end of my tour, so they sent me back. My company was based out of Pendleton so I came here for rehab. I didn't mind. I like Oregon. I actually applied for AC while I was at the center, working on my knee. I never expected to get in."

"Why?"

He paused for a moment, his hands working a little on the wheel. "Kids where I come from don't go to fancy, expensive private colleges. Most of my friends went to JC, if they were lucky."

"I get that. Everyone back home couldn't believe Izzy and I wanted to pass up A&M or UT to go to a school so far away no one had ever heard of." I smiled a little. "That's part of why she liked you, you know. She used to say you were as much a fish out of water here as I am."

Jay gave a nod of acknowledgement. "Anyway, May was volunteering when I was in rehab. She showed up that Fourth of July. She lost her only son in the First Gulf War and her husband died of a heart attack a few years ago. She says she'd go nuts without people to take care of. By the time I got here, she was basically running the place on the holidays, which means the regular staff can spend them with their families."

I thought about May, about the sense of loss I'd caught a glimpse of floating beneath the brisk happy surface. "She must be so lonely."

Jay must have noticed, because his response turned light and jovial. "Naw. She's got a whole passel of us to look after now. You know they all keep in touch with her? She brings in the postcards sometimes to share with the guys who are still hanging around."

I turned toward the window, thinking about loss, both May's and mine. You could rebuild a family from the ruins of one you'd lost. I knew that to be true enough. But I wondered how many times you could lose a family and start again before you couldn't bring

318

yourself to do it anymore.

I thought of all the families I'd seen that day, some of them missing people who would never come home. I thought about the determined look on Haleigh's face when she said, "before my birthday," Clara's big saucer eyes, Mallory's exhausted smile, and I said a prayer to the universe that their father was alright, would continue to be alright, and would come home to them healthy and whole before Haleigh's birthday. I prayed for his safety, and the safety of my cousins, who I hadn't talked to in years and hoped were with their loved ones tonight. And I prayed for May and the young men at the rehab center who would never be quite whole again, and for Jay who I'd never have guessed was one of them.

Then I prayed for all the families separated by violence and strife, and for all the victims everywhere.

And last, but especially, I prayed for Izzy.

32.

I must have nodded off on the way back to Astoria, because the next thing I knew we were crossing the long flat bridge that leads into town. It was well past dark, but the ever-present clouds had cleared away. The night seemed bright and open by comparison, covered in glittering stars reflected back in the waters below, a rare and beautiful night along Oregon's north coast. The air was crisp enough that the truck's heater had to work to keep the cold at bay. I leaned my head against the glass, watching it fog under my breath.

In front of us, the town rose in ridges up the hills, twinkling like a coil of tiny holiday lights. It was easy to forget how breathtakingly beautiful Astoria was when you saw it day in and day out. You'd become immune to the way the Victorian-style houses perched on the hill like silent pastel sentinels guarding the Northwest Passage against intruders, or you'd forget the chime of the trolley passing along the waterfront, and then you'd suddenly catch yourself in a moment like this and fall in love with Astoria all over again. I gazed in silent appreciation as we crossed the bridge, drinking in this place that was becoming my home.

"You're awake." Jay's voice startled me.

I stretched a little, rolling my head across my shoulders as I tried to shake out the kinks. "It's nice tonight."

Jay nodded in agreement. He didn't seem much for talking, so I settled back and let him drive as I gazed out into the peaceful darkness. I was so relaxed it took me a while to notice Jay had passed the turn off for school. I didn't know where we were going, but I didn't care. It had turned out to be a much better Thanksgiving than I could have imagined. I wasn't ready for the day to end. Wherever Jay was taking me, I was willing to go along if it meant a few more minutes away from campus, where my real life and its problems waited.

Thinking of my problems conjured up an image of Colin, and my heart ached at the thought of his too big grin and sparkling eyes. I pulled my phone from my pocket for the hundredth time. Seeing the phone's blank screen felt like being kicked in the stomach. No message from Colin, or anyone else for that matter. In a world of ceaseless instant communication, the silence felt like an overwhelming affirmation that, while I might be missing them, no one was missing me.

I thought back to last Thanksgiving, when Izzy and I were in Houston surrounded by family and people from high school while college friends sent "Happy Holidays!" texts from their own far-flung locales. Izzy and I sat in the living room as it filled, emptied, and filled again with a constant rotation of relatives and guests, texting one another in a silent running commentary of the proceedings: me talking about how fake everyone's over-enthusiastic reunions seemed, Izzy providing a blow-by-blow critique of every new haircut and fashion faux pas that walked through the door. Izzy and I were together so much sometimes that losing her felt like I'd lost half of myself. Greg and Crystal used to tease us about it, wondering aloud how two people who were in constant company could have so much to text that their fingers might fall off from the effort. "Thank the good Lord we're on a family plan," Greg would tease, "or you'd be texting us out of house and home!"

Things were so different now.

I groaned to myself; Greg and Crystal had continued paying my cell phone bill. After my mom died and my dad fell apart, it had all rested on me—keeping our house going, paying the bills, buying the groceries. After Crystal and Greg took me in, I guess I started taking things like the having a cell phone for granted. It was one more thing I'd need to work out. Money for a cell phone, a place to stay for Winter Break… I really needed to find a job next semester. I sighed heavily at the prospect, trying to figure out how I could fit it in with my coursework.

"You okay?"

"Yeah. Trying to figure out my life." I laughed weakly and stretched again, reminding myself to take the painkillers again before bed as my shoulder throbbed in protest. "Where are we going?"

Jay grinned, the light of the console glinting off his dark eyes. "It's a surprise."

"You're full of surprises today, aren't you?"

He said nothing, tuning the radio to the local alternative rock station and humming along to the quiet music filling the cab.

Wherever we were headed, it was northeast of campus, up in the forested hills behind the college. The darkness felt fuller, almost alive there. The trees pressed in on either side of the narrow road, so that the sky, studded with stars, was a strip overhead mirroring the road.

Eventually we turned left as the road curved, then curved

again, winding in circles up a large hill. The trees fell away and a small guard house came into view as we made a sharp turn near the top. Standing beyond it was a giant cylindrical structure, lit from the base so that it glowed gently in the night. It had to be at least ten stories tall, and its beige sides were scrolled with dark brown reliefs. It was a strange and stunning sight, a tall thin beacon rising out of a clearing ringed with trees. Jay pulled into a spot in the tiny parking lot and turned off the car, but he left the music playing.

"What is that?"

"That is the Astoria Column, Miss History Major." Jay leaned back against the seat. "Don't you know a historic monument when you see one?"

"Monument to what?" I asked, unbuckling my seat to lean forward, tilting my head as I peered up.

"The Lewis & Clark expedition. Westward expansion," he mused. "Exploitation in the name of discovery?"

I climbed out of the truck to get a closer look, walking slowly toward the giant monument. Up close it was strange and imposing. Words and images spiraled up the tower, telling the story of explorers' first contact with native peoples through the Corp of Discovery and the settlement of the west, ending with the railroad arriving in Astoria in the 1880s. It was a little on the hokey side and definitely conjured memories of gender studies lectures about the phallic aspects of monuments to domination, but it was also…captivating.

"It's weird, but really beautiful," I said as Jay came to stand next to me.

"Weird?" Jay folded his arms over his chest. "Like 'why the hell did you bring me here' weird?"

"No," I paused, considering. "Like, 'cool' weird. Unique weird." I bumped his arm with my shoulder. "Awesome weird."

"I can't believe you've never been here." He walked back to the truck, then pulled down the gate and sat down on the edge. "It's a major local landmark."

"I don't get off campus much." I took a seat next to him. "I study a lot. I haven't had time to do touristy things."

"Maybe we can make a day of it some time." He let the suggestion hang between us for a moment. "During the day you can see for miles into Washington and Oregon. This bluff looks down on the whole town, and all the way out to where the Columbia meets the ocean."

"Are you working for the Astoria Chamber of Commerce?"

Jay rolled his eyes at me. "There's a lot of cool stuff to do on the north coast. But hey, if you're not interested in learning more about the place you live in, who am I to rip you from your self-imposed ignorance?" He raised his palms in a gesture of helplessness.

I laughed in spite of myself and turned my attention back to the column. The moon hung in the clear sky to the right of the column, as though the heavens were shining their own spotlight on the strange icon to manifest destiny. It was a lovely fall night, crisp and clear, and wind through the pines shushed and sighed around us.

The cool night cut through my thin cardigan and I rubbed my hands absently against my arms to warm them. Jay leaned back behind me, and when he sat up again he was holding a large faded quilted blanket. He draped one side around my shoulders, then pulled the other side around himself, scooting closer as he did so.

"Very smooth." I cut him a look from the corner of my eye. "If I didn't know better, I'd say you planned this."

Jay snorted derisively. "If I'd planned this, it wouldn't be freezing and the blanket wouldn't be covered in sand."

I chuckled. "Alright then. I supposed your intentions are honorable."

"I thought it might make you happy." Jay was quiet for a moment, and when he spoke again, his tone was serious. "I like making you happy."

I didn't know what to say to that. From inside the cab, the music played on, reverberating through the night. A slow and melodic cover of David Bowie's "Modern Love" spilled out into the night. "I love this song," I said, trying to cover the awkwardness of the moment.

"Me, too." We were sitting so close together I felt the words rumbling in his chest.

There in the dark, as the singer's voice wove its gentle spell around us, the moment seemed abruptly filled with peril and possibility. Despite everything that had happened and was still happening with Colin, Jay had a kind of gravitational pull I could never quite break free from. Every time I thought I was far enough away, he'd say or do the perfect thing, and I'd be pulled back in again. Most of the time I found it infuriating; in this moment, it felt right. That certitude confused me more than ever.

A breeze kicked up, blowing loose strands of hair in my eyes. Jay reached for them at the same moment I did, his fingers brushing against mine. A shot of electricity seared through me, and I froze, breathless, as he gently tucked the hair behind my ear. The tip of his finger grazed my cheek as he grasped my fingers in his and lowered our hands, now clasped, between us. I could feel the warmth of his breath against my forehead, and I knew he was looking down at me. If I turned my face up to his, our lips would almost be touching.

Every part of me knew this was a bad idea. Jay and I couldn't go fifteen minutes without fighting. And yet...

Despite all the things I knew in my head, things I told myself repeatedly when it came to Jay, my heart refused to be swayed by reason or common sense. I felt myself turning toward him before I knew I'd made a decision.

A few moments earlier, we were two people who'd spent an easy afternoon together. Without warning, we'd crossed an unseen line in the darkness. It seemed like we were headed for a collision I somehow wanted and simultaneously fought to avoid, our breath coming out in little puffs as we silently dared the other to close the gap between the possible and the actual, once and for all.

Jay's eyes were black in the moonlight, the glimmering lights from the column reflected in them like the bright stars above us.

Focusing on my tattered resolve, I tried to stop us from doing something we'd both regret. "We should go," I whispered and began to pull away.

"Callie..." A shadow fell over Jay's face. He pulled at the blanket, leaning toward me. Some part of me knew I should stop him, but that part seemed small and distant compared to the gallop of my heart. He tilted his head, never breaking the gaze between us, and I raised my chin and closed my eyes, unwilling to witness my own betrayal and unable to stop it all the same.

A shrill sound whistled through the night, startling us both. We sprang apart, the blanket falling back into the truck bed. Dazed by competing waves of utter relief and crushing disappointment, my phone rang a second time before I recognized the sound.

Extracting it from my pocket, I hit the answer button without looking. "Hello?"

"Callie?" I recognized Colin's voice immediately, and a tidal wave of shame crested over me. "I'm glad I got you! I thought you might be asleep. I didn't wake you, did I?"

"No." I took a deep breath, trying to calm myself. "I'm still up."

And about to cheat on you. Because I'm a horrible, horrible person.

"I'm sorry I didn't call sooner." Colin stumbled over his words in his rush to apologize.

Jay, stared at the ground, lips pressed in a thin grimace. I freed myself from the blanket and moved away from the truck, trying to clear my head and focus on Colin.

"As soon as I got off the train yesterday, my mom packed us all off to my aunt's for Thanksgiving," he continued. "My aunt is eight months pregnant, and they didn't want to travel so the whole family went to their house. She lives out in the middle of nowhere Idaho. I didn't have any cell reception until now. I've been going bonkers trying to get to a place where I could call you." His voice was warm and sincere.

"I missed you, too," I managed, so sick with guilt I thought I'd vomit on my shoes.

Colin, oblivious to my tone, kept talking. "I'm so sorry we fought. After spending two days trapped in the house with my cousins, I don't see how any person, male or female, can manage to stay home full-time and not lose their minds. I was such a jerk. I should have apologized before I left."

"Colin, it's fine, really." Jay slammed the gate of the truck shut behind me and I winced. As happy I was to hear from Colin, this was not a good time to have this conversation. "It was a stupid fight. Forget about it." I tried to forced myself to sound natural. "Can I call you back in a little bit?"

"Sure," Colin replied immediately. He seemed relieved I'd forgiven him so easily. As though he was the one who needed to be forgiven. "I've been thinking about you all day. Did you have an okay holiday? What did you do for dinner?"

"I had a good day, actually." I hazarded a glance behind me. Without a word, Jay climbed into the truck, yanking the door closed and starting the engine. "I volunteered at a rehab facility for veterans, serving dinner for them and their families. I know it sounds depressing, but it was wonderful."

Really, really, wonderful.

Right up until this last part.

"I didn't know there was a rehab center in Astoria."

I walked slowly toward the truck, worried Jay was about to

drive off without me. *Which you deserve*, I chastised mentally. "There's not." I placed a hand on the door handle. "It's out near Forest Grove."

"Wow, that's far," Colin said. I peeked in the truck, waving my hand to indicate I was hurrying. Jay ignored me, gripping the wheel with both hands. "Was it through the volunteer services office?"

"No. Actually…" How could I say this in a way that didn't sound worse than it already was? "Jay took me."

There was a short pause, and I knew, however you were supposed to tell your boyfriend that you'd spent an entire holiday alone with another guy that you maybe kind of hated but also kind of crushed on, I'd done it wrong. Colin had been around for at least some of Izzy's campaign to unite Jay and me, and I cursed Izzy again for her matchmaking attempts. "Colin?"

"Well, I'm glad you didn't have to spend the day alone." The warmth in his voice had diminished considerably.

Jay shoved the passenger door open from inside the cab. "Are you almost done? I need to get the truck back."

I nodded, climbing into the cab. "Colin, I really need to go."

"Wait. Are you still with him?" Colin sounded decidedly unfriendly now, which was exactly what I deserved for getting almost smoochy with another guy.

"We're almost back to campus." I barely managed to snap the seatbelt in place before Jay threw the truck in reverse and began a speedy descent down the hill. "Can I call you when I get to my room?"

"If it's not too inconvenient for you."

"Of course not," I protested into the phone and the truck jerked to the left. I shot Jay a dirty look but he didn't acknowledge it, pulling out onto the road so fast the tires of the truck skidded beneath us.

"Okay then. I need to talk to you."

"Me, too."

"I love you." I could hear the desperate question lingering on the edge.

I glanced at Jay. His jaw worked in silent effort with his hands, kneading the wheel angrily. If I didn't say it, Colin would be hurt worse than he already was. He didn't deserve that. Yes, we'd had a fight, but he was my boyfriend. I did love him. Why was I afraid that if I said it in front of Jay, the world would come apart?

"I love you, too," I whispered into the phone, knowing Jay still heard every syllable. "I'll call you back soon."

33.

The drive back to campus was a wordless, tense disaster. I kept waiting for Jay to yell at me, to call me a plethora of names, all of which would be reasonable. I wanted him to yell at me; anything would be better than the lecture I was giving myself.

In the span of ten minutes, I had come close to hurting the only two living people who seemed to care about me at all anymore. As it was, I'd completely taken advantage of Jay's kindness and repaid him in rejection and cruelty. I also knew that if Colin got the details of our outing, he would decide close counted in kissing, right alongside horseshoes and hand grenades.

And that was what it felt like—as though a bomb had gone off. How could I be so thoughtless? I had a boyfriend. My very *first* boyfriend. What kind of person did it make me if, after being alone forever, I cheated on him almost immediately after we started dating? I was the lowest of the low—untrustworthy, dishonest, and mean-spirited. Caught up in my own need to feel pretty and wanted, I'd let my guard down with Jay, and this was what came from it.

Jay and I could never be alone for more than a few hours at a time, in large part because things kept getting screwed up between us. It didn't matter if we had great chemistry. We were headed in different directions. This yo-yo crap sucked enough when it only involved the two of us. Even before Colin and I had gotten together, I'd known I couldn't keep playing "do I dare, and do I dare?" with Jay.

Colin's love for me made the right decision clear. He didn't deserve to be jerked around, especially given how supportive and understanding he'd been about my problems with Izzy. Jay and I were going to have to keep our distance; that was all there was to it. It made me unspeakably sad to think of avoiding one of the few people who always seemed to be on my side, but I couldn't have them both. I'd made my choice. I needed to stand by it.

The truck jerked to a stop in front of my building and I scrambled out. I was praying I could get inside without Jay and me getting into another huge fight. It would be easier to stay away from him if I didn't feel a lingering need to apologize.

I wasn't fast enough. Jay jumped out of the truck, hot on my heels. Before I could get to the door, he grabbed me by my good shoulder, spinning me around to face him.

"No way." His breath puffed in the cold night. "You're not getting out of this that easily."

I threw up my hands. "I'm sorry, Jay." I hated the way he was looking at me, his eyes glowing with hurt-fueled anger.

"For which part?" he spat, almost shouting. "For acting like you want me or pretending like you don't?"

I hugged my arm to my side, staring into the darkness. "It's complicated."

"No, it's not. One minute you're about to kiss me, and the next minute you're telling some other guy you love him. Which is it?"

My face grew hot under his scrutiny. Out of the corner of my eye, I saw a blind twitch in the window. I wondered if there were people in the rooms facing us, if they could hear every humiliating word. Just what I needed—more gossip.

"Look," I said evenly, taking a step toward him and lowering my voice. "What almost happened back there was a mistake. I love Colin. He's a good guy. I'm sorry you don't like him, but I do."

"Cheating on him is a great way to show it."

The words fell like a blow. My stomach churned as I fought back tears. "You're right. You want me to feel awful? I do. I'm a terrible girlfriend." I saw a flicker of satisfaction cross his face, and my jaw tightened.

"But what about you? It took both of us to make this mess. It's not like I haven't told you, again and again, that I am with someone else. Going after someone else's girl certainly isn't honorable, either." Jay flinched, but I barreled on. "Besides, if I'm such a crappy girlfriend, why would you want me anyway?"

"Because you're all I think about." Jay's voice was rough as he grabbed both my arms, pulling me toward him. It was almost the same thing Colin had said on the phone minutes earlier, and it shook me, emphasizing the complete catastrophe this day was turning out to be.

"I wake up in the morning, and I think about you. I go to bed at night, and I think about you. I worry about how lonely you are, if you're making it to class, if you're sleeping well or eating. I tie myself in knots, wondering if you're safe, if you're happy."

He was so close, too close. The warmth of his hands seeped through my coat and my heart lurched in response. I had to get away. I fumed, summoning anger from every corner of my emotional landscape. I was angry. I was angry at Colin for leaving me alone, at Jay for trying to save me, at the Millers for abandoning me, and even at Izzy for dying and sticking me without someone to share my holidays with. I was a spinning vortex of fury, and Jay made for an excellent target.

"You don't sound like a boyfriend. You sound like a parent."

Jay dropped his hands. "Sometimes I think you need one."

"Well, they're all either dead or they don't want me anymore." Despite my best efforts, my eyes filled, and I was too angry and hurt and sad to stop them.

Jay's face softened. He cast his gaze helplessly toward the dark trees. "I'm sorry. I shouldn't have said that."

"I am so tired of fighting with you." I wiped at my face. "You don't want me. You only think you do. You're looking for someone to save, and I am never going to be that girl, Jay. Not if I can help it." I gathered my resolve to deliver the final blow, even as part of me screamed I was making a mistake. "You don't have any claim on me. We're friends. That's it. That's all we're ever going to be." I turned and headed for the door. I needed to escape while I was still clinging to my shaky conviction.

"I don't believe that." His words were so soft I barely heard him. Deciding it was better if I didn't, I kept walking. When I got to the building, I swiped my card through the card reader and pulled the door open. I hated leaving things like this, especially after he'd saved me from what could have been my worst holiday ever.

Turning to face him, I held tight to door for support. The light from the hallway fell across his face, and what I saw almost undid my resolve. Jay didn't look strong and confident. With his hands shoved in his pockets and the forlorn turn of his lips, he looked like a

334

lost little boy.

No, I told myself. *You are going to do the right thing, as much as you are capable.*

"Thank you for taking me with you today. I appreciate that you thought of me and didn't want me to be alone. It was more kindness than I deserve." He opened his mouth to protest, but I kept talking, afraid if I didn't, I wouldn't get the words out. I mustered what I hoped was a serious and unyielding gaze. "I think it would be better if we didn't talk for a while."

Jay looked like I slapped him. "If that's what you want."

"It is." My tone came out firm but my legs quivered beneath me. Score one for my self-control. "Goodnight, Jay."

I dragged myself into the building, letting the door fall closed behind me. I managed to walk up a few steps until I was sure I was hidden from view. Clinging to the railing, I dropped the emotional barrier I'd been using to shield me from the worst of the storm inside me. It felt as though the ground beneath me had fallen away. From the moment Izzy died, Jay had been there, providing a foundation for me to rebuild on. He'd held me when I cried, stood by me when I made mistakes, taken every abuse I'd heaped on him. I wasn't sure how I would keep going without him. Getting through a day without knowing, at some level, he would always be there to call if I needed him, seemed impossible.

It was only realizing how much I'd come to depend on Jay that kept me from running back through the door and begging him to forget everything I'd said. If my life had taught me anything, it was that needing someone too much was a liability. No matter how much you loved someone, or how much they loved you, eventually everyone went away. I needed to be able to live my life without relying on other people. I needed to be able to stand on my own. If I could, then no matter how many people I loved disappeared or died, I could survive. It was the only way I could get out of bed another day and deal with a world so indifferent to heartache.

After a few minutes, I heard the truck start up and pull away. I took a shaky breath, then another, and forced myself up the stairs.

I needed to put Jay behind me and focus on Colin. I needed to do the right thing, for Colin, for Jay, and for me. I didn't want to be the person this was making me. I told myself to keep going, resolve forged with each additional step.

My head knew what I needed to do. If only logic could stop the wild beating in my heart, fill the aching wound in my chest.

34.

My head was pounding when I got to my room. I changed into my pajamas, an old pair of sleep pants and a faded baseball t-shirt emblazoned with the words "Hermiston Hummingbirds." My shoulder screamed in protest as I pulled my hair into low pigtails. I grabbed the bottle of painkillers off the dresser and walked into the bathroom to fill my water bottle. I downed two pills, then took a third for good measure. If I was lucky, I could sleep through the rest of the weekend. Then I'd have two weeks of classes and five days of finals to get through. It was hard to see beyond the end of the semester, and I didn't bother trying. Even another day seemed impossible.

The lack of generic campus noise in the building accentuated its emptiness, every creak and moan a hundred times louder than normal. I needed to call Colin like I promised, but the pain meds kicked in almost immediately. I laid my phone next to my pillow, telling myself I'd call Colin to at least say goodnight to him before I passed out. As I climbed into bed, I saw the glint of something fly across the room, clicking as it hit the bottom of Izzy's desk.

One of the earrings Lauren had returned glittered at me from the floor. My head swam as I leaned to pick it up, and I regretted taking the third pill. I blinked hard against the dark shadows around the edges of my vision. I didn't think about what could happen when I touched the earring until my fingers closed around it.

"Isn't this awesome?" A girl in a white halter top sucked hard at a straw, her head bent so her face was obscured by a mass of blonde red curls topped with a light blue plastic halo. "This party is huge!"

Bethany is such a lush! I watched as she stumbled over toward a skinny, nervous looking firstie sitting by himself on a couch. He seemed thrilled to have the curvy girl practically fling herself in his lap. I rolled my eyes as she threw her arms around his neck.

God, she has terrible taste.

Lauren bounced up to me, phone in one hand and red plastic cup in the other. Her hair was terrible. She'd attempted sultry waves of the Veronica Lake variety, but instead it looked like she hadn't washed or combed her hair in a week.

Another make-over emergency. All these girls are a dis-ast-er. Sometimes I wonder why I bother.

"Your costume is totally cute!" I tried not feel irritated that Lauren's outfit looked vaguely similar to my own. At least she was trying. If Callie were here, she'd probably have worn jeans and a t-shirt with angel wings printed on it and insisted she was dressed up.

I pursed my lips together at the thought. *I love my girl, but she is so boring! Who studies on a Saturday night? Plus, if she was here, she could run interference for me with Colin.* My nose wrinkled in disgust at the thought. *How did he always seem to know where I was going to be?* I hated how he followed me around all the time. It would have been creepy if he weren't so pathetic.

Lauren was rambling about something. I wasn't listening,

but as long as I smiled and nodded occasionally, she usually couldn't tell the difference. She was sweet, but not all that bright. I'd fix her up with Colin if she weren't so hung up on her sorry excuse for a high-school boyfriend.

One project at a time.

"You should pull your hair back," I cut Lauren off mid-sentence.

"You think so?" Lauren touched her disastrous waves tentatively. "Dave always tells me how much he likes it down."

I tried not to grit my teeth. "Well, Dave's not here, is he? So let's try it," I replied in my sweetest voice. I sat my cup down on the edge of the table behind me as I turned Lauren around. "You have a great neck, has anyone ever told you that?" I pulled her hair back, twisting it up.

"No." Lauren's voice warmed. "I do?"

Holding her hair in place with one hand, I pulled my clutch across the table and dug around in it until my fingers closed on some bobby pins. "Yep, and now it's time to show it off." I held the pins in my mouth as I finished twisting the hair into place, securing it along the edge one pin at a time. I pulled a few wispy curls loose along the bottom, then turned Lauren to do the same around her face.

Holding her at arm's length, I surveyed my work.

I am freaking amazing.

"Perfect!" I smiled encouragingly at her. "Much more angelic. Oh!" I dug through the purse again, pulled out a pair of earrings, and carefully inserted one in each naked lobe.

"There you go. Ready for heaven," I clapped once appreciatively. The earrings, cheap little things my sister foisted on me before I'd left for school, looked surprisingly good on Lauren.

Maybe I'll let her keep them, I mused. *God knows I'll never wear those tacky things.*

"Thanks, Izzy. You're the best!" Lauren leaned in and gave me quick hug, cell phone still in hand. If she didn't learn to put the stupid phone down once in a while she was going to have to have it surgically implanted.

"Any time," I said generously. *Remember that next time you talk to your titan of the fashion world mom,* I added mentally.

I picked my cup up and took another sip of soda. I'd figured out a long time ago that if you put a little cherry juice or lime juice in your coke and added a little fruit, everyone would assume you were drinking like they were. It was amazing what people would reveal when they were drunk, and it was much easier to flirt with someone else's boyfriend if you could blame it on the liquor. The drink tasted a little funny, but I'd watched Gloria open the can herself when she poured the drink, a peace offering for being such a monumental pain on the way here. I sniffed at the limes floating on top and realized they reeked of Everclear.

Injecting fruit with alcohol? Nice try, guys, I fished the lime wedges out and dropping them in the trash.

I turned back toward the main room, surveying the mass

of people swaying to the heavy beat thumping through the speakers. Yep, Lauren was already on the phone to her boyfriend. I could see her working her way toward the door, finger stuck in her other ear.

What a waste of a perfectly good updo. Maybe she's a lost cause, I mused, wishing for the hundredth time Callie had come. *I should have given her more grief. There are absolutely no cute guys here. At least we could have snarked at everyone together.*

At that moment, two guys walked in the front door. The first one was nothing special, but the second guy—hel-lo gorgeous! He was wrapped in a tight black long-sleeved t-shirt that hugged every chiseled muscle in his chest and strained over his buff arms. His fitted black jeans showed off his incredible butt. I didn't recognize him, but he was obviously in great shape. He had on a dark cloth mask that covered most of his face, small horns jutting out of his forehead below a shaggy mop of dark hair.

As he surveyed the room, I did a quick mental check of my outfit. Yep, every curve accentuated, straw playfully poised between my lips. I felt a little thrill as his eyes settled on me and he gave me a cocky grin. Without breaking his gaze, I smirked back, never looking away. As he headed across the room toward me, I was suddenly glad Callie hadn't come after all. Tonight I was feeling devilish, and it looked as if the devil himself had delivered.

"Well, well, well," he purred as he closed in on me,

leaning his weight on a muscular arm he placed on the table next to my waist. "Are you an angel or a devil?" His eyes were intense, penetrating.

I flicked my tongue across my ruby-stained lips. "Devil in disguise?"

He chuckled slightly, leaning in so his lips almost touched my ear. "I'll bet you are. Wanna dance?"

"If you think you can keep up," I said, draining the cup and setting it on the table. Needing no other encouragement, he took my hand and led me toward the dance floor.

The music throbbed as he wrapped his arms tightly around my waist. I guess there were a lot more people on the dance floor than I'd thought, because it was really hot in this part of the house. I unbuttoned my jacket, and the Devil grinned slyly at me, working it slowly down my shoulders to reveal the lacy camisole underneath. I took the jacket and tied it around my waist as we moved together, grinding our bodies against one another.

The song was slow and heavy, and as he trailed his fingers along my arms and down my sides it felt like sparks were shooting from them, blazing a trail along my torso. Every touch was intoxicating, excruciating in its sensual subtext. I felt overwhelmed with sensation. I closed my eyes against the shimmer of a strobe light that began to pulse slowly in time with the music.

"What's your name?" I felt his hot breath on my neck as he trailed his lips along it, dragging my arms around his neck.

"Izzy," I breathed against his hair as he bent down, trailing kisses along the line of my shoulder. I tilted my head back, gulping for air. The sensation of his lips against my bare skin was almost unbearable, and it shook me a little.

Why did I feel so out of it? There must have been more alcohol in the fruit than I thought. I was such a lightweight I avoided drinking as much as possible, since vomit never made for a good accessory, but seeing that the damage was done, I decided to go with it.

Maybe this time Callie will have to hold my hair up. I felt dizzy as the beautiful boy slid his leg between mine and rocked my hips in time with his own.

"What's your name?" I moaned a little as he nipped at my earlobe.

"Will," he whispered, and the music swelled around us. He pressed himself hard against me, and my entire being glowed with sensation. I could no longer feel where his body stopped and mine started.

I tried to open my eyes, but the world rolled and dipped around me. I wasn't sure I'd be able to stand if he let go of me. Part of me was screaming that something was wrong, that I didn't act like this, that I was too drunk too fast. That part of me seemed very far away and the music faded strangely in and out, like someone was playing with the volume dial.

Will turned my face up toward his, and I tried to pull away, but his caress was insistent. I opened my eyes and found him staring down at me, the curve of his lips almost predatory as he lowered his face to mine, running his tongue along my lower lip. I opened my mouth and he invaded me, the world exploding into spinning stars. I knew I should pull back, that I was slipping away faster and faster, but I couldn't let go.

Then the world went black and empty, a dark universe where even the last constellation, burning and eternal, had faded into nothingness.

35.

I was lost underwater, swimming through rivulets of deep blues and greens. I couldn't breathe, but I didn't seem to care. I kept pumping my arms, a feeling of determination pushing me on despite the burning in my chest. I was looking for someone. Who was it? I needed to find them before time ran out, before it was too late. The world shook unexpectedly, the ground below and the water around me reverberating. I jerked left, then right with the rapidly changing currents. I had to keep swimming. There was someone here, someone who needed me to find them.

There! I'd seen a flash of something, a pale slender hand with a wide silver bracelet. I recognized the bracelet but I couldn't remember whose it was. I only knew that my destination was a girl and I had to reach her. My lungs ached and screamed, but I swam harder and faster, thrashing against the current as it held me back, slowed me down. I was normally a strong swimmer, but here the water was a Jell-O consistency, thick and heavy against the beat of my arms. The outline of a large boulder emerged from the shadows, and the white hand disappeared behind it in the current. Grabbing the top of the boulder, I propelled myself forward, reaching for the hand before the tides could rip it away. My fingers wrapped around the wrist, and it jerked away from me. I tightened my grip, pulling the unknown body toward me. Out of the dark blue green mist, a face appeared.

Izzy. It was Izzy. I'd found her.

I kicked hard, trying to pull her with me in the direction I thought was up, but she fought me. I yanked at her arm, and she pulled against my grip. I turned my head toward her, starting to yell her name, but my mouth filled with foul-tasting water. I struggled to spit it out before I started coughing. If I couldn't make it to the surface, we'd both drown. Izzy shook her head no, her short hair floating around her head in a fiery crown.

I kicked again, and this time she came toward me. It was the first time I'd gotten a good look at her. The top half looked like Izzy during our last trip to the beach in Galveston, aquamarine bikini top glowing against her pale skin. But as she swam closer, I noticed her legs were replaced with a tail covered in iridescent scales that shimmered in the filtered light.

Alarmed, I gestured toward her body. Izzy returned my gaze with a kind of sad detachment, as though her newfound mermaid status was something she'd long ago accepted. My arms ached, and I treaded water unevenly, struggling to keep my limbs moving. The water was cold and penetrating, an icy cocoon. I couldn't remember why I was determined to get away. I was so tired, and Izzy was here. My arms began to slow, my legs a languid swish beneath me as my eyes fluttered open and closed once, then twice.

"No!" Izzy grappled with my arms, floating akimbo. I heard her voice not through the dense liquid, but clear and loud inside my head. Izzy grasped me by the shoulders and began pushing me, harder and harder, backward and upwards to where the water was clearer.

"Fight, Callie! You have to fight!" she screamed frantically as her long nails, painted a shimmering aqua color, dug into my skin.

She shoved me toward the light, propelling us both with her powerful tail. "You're not safe here. You have to go." The water was almost clear now. We were very close to the surface.

"I don't want to go," I mumbled, brackish water dribbling between my clenched, chattering teeth. "I want to stay here with you." Even though we were underwater I could feel warm tears spring to my eyes. I tried to bring my arms around to hug her, but my limbs refused to respond.

Grimacing, Izzy shook her head and gave me a final fierce shove. I tried to grab for her, but her fingers slipped through my hands as I floated up and away from her. I fought against the current, twisting and flipping as it overwhelmed my efforts to get back to Izzy. A sad smile on her lips, Izzy undulated in place as she waved to me, her figure growing smaller and more obscure as the current pulled me further and further away...

"Callie!" A frantic voice called my name, shaking me hard. A rough hand slapped lightly my face. My head lolled at the impact; even though my eyes were closed, glowing spots burst against the darkness. Another blow fell, harder and more insistent.

No. Not him. Not again.

"Stop!" I clawed at my attacker as I tried to open my eyes. Strong hands weighed heavy on my arms, pinning them to my sides.

I flailed against them. "Get away from me. Please don't! Stop!" I sobbed, scrambling backwards under the edge of the desk as I tried to protect myself. How had he found me? He was supposed to be thousands of miles away. Who told him I was here? The room was pitch black except for a rectangle of light from the hallway outlining his looming presence.

"Don't touch me!" My hands curled into fists as I struggled against the dazed fog in my head, trying to figure out how to best protect myself. It had been years since I'd fought my dad, but the memories were so fresh and real my defensive instincts came back as easily as breathing.

Make yourself small, a harsh voice in my head commanded. *Protect your head and abdomen. Tuck your chin!*

I lowered my hands and wrapped my thin arms around my body protectively. If I could hold him off long enough, he'd pass out or come out of it. I waited for one of his meaty hands to swing at me.

"Callie," the voice was quieter now, but still choked with urgency. "Callie, it's me. It's Jay."

I heard the words, but they didn't register. Jay wouldn't hit me. It was my dad. My dad had found me. He was angry again. I had to protect myself. My breathing grew shallow and my legs trembled.

You have to calm down, I told myself as I gulped for air. *You have to maintain control.*

"It's okay. You're safe." The dark shadow was backing away from me, hands extended, palms up to show there was no threat. I huddled against the wall. The overhead light flickered on, throwing everything into sharp relief. I blinked hard against the pain it caused, knives in my eyes.

"I'm not going to hurt you." I knew that voice; it wasn't my father's. Jay stood in the doorway, his face pale with worry and fear.

I sucked in air, trying to make the word come out. "Jay?"

"It's me." His tone was soothing as he moved slowly toward

me, pausing after each step to make sure he didn't startle me.

"You were hitting me! Why would you hit me?"

"You were screaming and thrashing in your sleep. I couldn't wake you up," he said softly, still edging closer. His eyes were dark points in his ashen face. He looked as terrified as I felt.

"I. Thought. You. Were. My. Dad." I managed haltingly, choking on each word. Adrenaline abruptly flowed out of me as my body belatedly registered my safety. My arms fell limp to my sides and I closed my eyes, trying to block out the all too familiar sensations flooding me as my brain ran through a relentless montage of memories, overwhelming me with images I worked hard to keep carefully bricked up in a part of my mind I never touched—those worst days with my father, when I would pass out while he was hitting me only to wake up and find him choking me into unconsciousness again.

I was dimly aware of Jay easing himself down next to me. He wrapped his arms carefully around my shuddering frame and I turned toward him, letting him pull me into his lap as I continued to struggle for control. His hands made small circles on my back as he took deep breaths in and out, in and out, whispering to me to breathe with him.

"In and out."

His chest swelled and contracted beneath my useless hands.

"In and out."

I hiccupped and coughed my way through one deep breath, then another. The shaking subsiding as my breathing slowed, but the memories kept coming. I gritted my teeth and shook my head against them, trying to make them stop. It seemed like an eternity before I could breathe normally. Jay held me tight, his cheek pressed against the top of my head as I clung to him. When it was over, I still couldn't make my limbs respond. Instead I sprawled limply in the triangle of his crossed legs, and Jay cradled me in place. We sat together for a long while, slowly breathing in time.

A phone vibrated, and Jay shifted me a little to remove it from his pocket with one hand as he held me against him with the other. I clung to his neck, unwilling to let go as I tried to sort through everything that had happened, or that I thought had happened, in the last few hours.

"Hello? Yeah, Colin, she's fine. She had…an episode."

An episode.

Such a clinical word for a living nightmare, one I never seemed to escape.

Jay gestured the phone toward me, and I shook my head. I was still working on breathing normally. Having another discussion with Colin about Jay wasn't something I could handle at the moment, especially while I was still in Jay's arms.

Jay took the hint. "No, she can't talk yet. I'll have her call you when she can. No, it's no problem. Thanks for calling me. You were right."

Jay snapped the phone shut, dropping it on the ground as he wrapped his arms around me again, tucking my head beneath his chin. "You okay?" His flat tone told me he'd make the judgment for himself no matter what I said.

"No," I admitted weakly. "I'm not okay. I don't think I ever will be."

Jay pushed me away from him to better see my face. "Callie, I've seen reactions like this before. I know a fight or flight response when I see one." He picked at clumps of hair matted to my face with sweat and tears, looping them carefully behind my ears.

"My dad used to hit me," I said simply. "He'd come home at night, drunk, and I'd be asleep, so I wouldn't see him coming. When you grabbed me, I got confused. I thought you were him."

My shoulder hurt and my foot was falling asleep, so I extracted myself from his arms. He let me go, and I crawled onto Izzy's bed, bracing my back against the closet and hugging one of the throw pillows. I was starting to recover my equilibrium, and humiliation was creeping in alongside it. I didn't want anyone to see me like that. Not ever.

"Were you dreaming about him?"

"No," I said, thinking carefully over the vision and the dream. "I was dreaming about Izzy. I haven't dreamed about my dad in almost two years."

"But you used to?"

"Yeah," I nodded, squeezing the pillow as though I could wring the discomfort and fear from the memories. "It happened a lot when I first moved in with the Millers. Crystal took me to a specialist. I had to see her every week until the last semester of my senior year. She said I had…" I hated saying it out loud.

"Post-Traumatic Stress Disorder?"

I winced at his words, not wanting to confirm it.

"I'm a soldier, Callie. You think you're the first person I've ever known with PTSD?"

"It's not uncommon among victims of domestic violence, especially children." I shrugged, trying to play off my discomfort. "That's what my therapist in Houston told me."

"I've heard that. I also know it's nothing to be ashamed of. You'll get better with time."

"I haven't had an episode in over a year, especially one this bad. Did I hurt you?"

"You got me pretty good with your nails," he turned his arms to show a row of angry red half-moons marching down the backs of his biceps. "You were thrashing around so much I was more worried you were going to hurt yourself."

"I'm sorry," I buried my warm face in my pillow.

He pushed himself away from the wall and plopped down on the bed. "I've had worse. It's fine. Really." I raised my head and he gave me a small smile, which I tried, and failed, to return. "It's okay. You're okay."

"I'm really not."

He ran his palms down his jean-clad thighs. He was still wearing the same clothes he'd had on when he'd dropped me off. "You had a dream about Izzy?"

I nodded. "I was swimming underwater, trying to find her. I thought she was going to drown and I needed to save her. But when I found her, she was a mermaid." Images of Izzy, glowing in the dim watery light came back to me. In dreams and in death, she was always beautiful, her hair waving gently in the water. "It turned out she was trying to save me. I guess I wasn't a mermaid, and she kept telling me to fight so I wouldn't drown."

He patted my foot. "If that isn't a metaphor, I don't know what is." I looked at him quizzically. "Izzy has moved on, to a new place. She's something else now. She lives in a different world. No matter how much you miss her, you have to let her go. If you try to follow her, you're going to end up getting yourself killed."

I gaped at him, and he chuckled. "Hey, I took Psych 101. Everybody's got to fill their social science requirement somehow."

I considered his suggestion for a moment. His interpretation made sense, except for the part where Izzy was still here, leaving me messages and asking for my help. But Jay didn't know that; I suspect it would not help matters if he did. The thought startled me back into reality.

"Why are you here? What made you think you needed to check on me?"

"Colin," Jay said blandly. "You were supposed to call him; you never did. He kept trying to reach you but you didn't answer. He was worried, so he called Campus Security and demanded to talk to me. He was completely freaked out. He swore something had to be wrong. He made me promise to check on you." He rubbed his eyes. "When I got here, I couldn't get you to answer the door. At first I thought you were being stubborn, but after I pounded and yelled and you didn't open it, I thought…"

He thought what? That I'd tried to hurt myself? Jay took a shaky breath, and I knew that whatever he'd been thinking, it wasn't good.

"I was supposed to call Campus Security, or at least an AD, but

I wasn't really thinking." He grimaced. "I kicked in your door."

It was a tribute to how emotionally unhinged I had been when Jay arrived that I only now notice that the frame on the door was split and hanging to one side. The door knob was bent door hung slightly askew in the frame.

I covered my mouth with my hands, horrified and ashamed. I knew how scared Jay must have been to do something so drastic. "I'm sorry," I whispered through my fingers.

"No, *I'm* sorry. I overreacted." He gave me a small smile. "You tend to bring out my overprotective side. When I saw you lying on the floor…" He shook his head. "Terrified doesn't begin to cover it. I shook you and yelled your name, but you didn't wake up. I slapped you, and you seemed to come around a little because you started fighting me, so I hit you again." He grabbed my hand, pleading for understanding. "I was desperate. I'd never purposely hurt you, Callie. I hope you know that."

"It's okay," I extracted my hand from his. "I know you were trying to help me. I'd have freaked in your position. You didn't know how I would react."

Jay rubbed his face. "Yes, I did." I narrowed my eyes at him, and he backpedaled. "I didn't know exactly, but I should have expected it. I knew about your dad. Izzy told me."

My face hardened at his words, the mask slipping back into place. "Well, that's just…great."

Thanks, Iz. Way to talk about me behind my back. Were you hoping I'd get a pity date out of it?

Jay sighed. "She didn't tell me much," he continued, trying to reassure me. "Only enough to know it had been violent, that it started when your mom died, and that it went on for a long time before you went to live with her family."

I gritted my teeth, resenting Izzy and her big mouth. It was not her place to tell people about my family or my past, but it hadn't stopped her. But then, this was the same girl who had apparently been working one of her supposed friends for a connection to said friend's mom. The more I discovered about Izzy and her attitudes toward other people and their choices, the more confused and angrier I felt.

On the one hand, there was Izzy-the-Mermaid, desperate to save me. But I couldn't think of her without comparing her to Izzy-the-Devil, whose only interest seemed to be whether other people could be useful to her—her career, her reputation, her social life. The dreams, the visions, the memories were jumbled inside me, until I couldn't remember which part was my sister, my friend. Had she always been a shallow, vapid person and I'd somehow missed it, or was she the sweet, fun, caring and careful girl I thought I remembered?

Would the *real* Izzy Miller please stand up?

I set the question aside for the time being. I'd have to work out my feelings for Izzy when Jay wasn't sitting on my bed, studying me as though he could see the wheels in my mind spinning.

"I should call Colin," I said, trying to restore the emotional distance between us. I felt raw and frayed around the edges, as though my insides were a shattered piece of glass, hastily glued back together. One harsh blow and only fragments would remain. Part of me was so embarrassed by our closeness that I wanted Jay to leave, but I was also aware enough of my own fragility that I knew there was a strong possibility I'd have another panic attack if he left me alone.

"Okay. You do that. I'll go call Campus Security. And I'll take responsibility for the door when they get here."

I started to protest, but he waved me off. "This is on me. I'll pay for the damages. But Callie, you have to tell me if you took anything, or if you're thinking of taking anything else tonight. I know you weren't asleep." Anger and concern mingled in his eyes, and I realized he still thought I'd been trying to hurt myself.

"I took two of the painkillers the hospital gave me for my shoulder." I protested. "When it didn't help right away, I took a third one." Jay groaned. "I know. It was stupid. I won't do it again."

Jay scratched at his stubble-covered cheek. "That would explain it." He searched my face. "It wasn't on purpose?"

I shook my head, blushing again.

"You have no plans to hurt yourself?"

"No," I met his gaze. "I just wanted to sleep. Honestly? I hate those pills. They give me the craziest dreams, and I wake up feeling hung over."

He scrutinized me for a long moment. Then, as if he'd decided something, he pushed himself off the bed. "I'm going out to call Campus Security." He touched the splintered wood along the door frame with a regretful shake of his head.

"Will you come back? Just for a little bit?" I sounded as pathetic as I felt, but I couldn't help it. Between the visions and the dreams and my panic attack, I was in no condition to be left alone.

A flicker of something like pain crossed his face. "If that's what you want." Then he disappeared down the hall.

If that's what I wanted.

Even if it hurt him, he'd come or go, if that's what I wanted.

I sighed and buried my face in the pillow to hide the tears leaking from my tightly closed eyes. I was a manipulative, weak person, and Jay deserved better than me, but I needed someone for the moment, and he was available. Even though I knew I was being unfair to him, even though I knew I shouldn't keep him, I wondered if I really had any intention of ever letting him go.

36.

I went into the bathroom and washed my face. A quick glance at the clock told me it was three in the morning. It seemed really late to call Colin, but I didn't want him to worry. Knowing it was Colin, hundreds of miles away, who'd realized something was wrong made me feel awful for my almost-kiss with Jay all over again. Colin had sent someone he knew I would accept help from, even though Jay treated him like crap every time they saw each other.

I dialed Colin's number, and he picked up halfway through the first ring. "Callie?"

"It's me. I'm okay."

"Are you sure? I tried your number over and over. When you didn't answer, I panicked. I thought Izzy had done something awful, but I couldn't exactly tell people I thought your dead roommate had attacked you."

"Not an unreasonable assumption," I mused. "Actually it was kind of Izzy's fault."

"What do you mean?"

"My shoulder was killing me so I took a couple of painkillers."

"Did you pass out?"

I laughed weakly. "Kind of. Jay couldn't wake me when he got here, and he freaked. I'm fine."

"Thank God," he said with relief. "I was going out of my mind." There was a long pause before he spoke again. "If anything happened…" Colin let the words trail off, but we both knew what he meant. "I can't lose you, Callie. I can't."

"I'm not going anywhere," I responded solemnly, silently vowing to keep my promise no matter what happened with Jay. "Except maybe to sleep," I added, trying to keep my tone light. "You should sleep, too."

"Yeah, I am kind of tired. Do you need to keep talking? I can stay on the phone with you until you fall asleep." He was being super supportive, totally unaware I'd already asked someone else to keep me company. Why hadn't it occurred to me to call Colin?

Because you're turning into a cheat and a liar. You haven't crossed the line yet, but you're practically skipping rope with it.

"I'll be fine. I can't wait to see you after break."

"Me, too." Colin yawned sleepily into the phone. "I'll call you in the morning. I love you, Callie."

"I love you, too," I whispered into the phone, pledging to be a better girlfriend tomorrow.

As I hung up, I heard the sound of a throat clearing. Officer Brighton stood in the doorway, awkwardly shuffling his feet. Jay's face was visible over Officer Brighton's shoulder.

I closed my eyes for a moment, feeling sick of myself. "My door is broken," I said by way of greeting.

"I see that. You just can't seem to keep the men away, can you?" Officer Brighton's fat belly jiggled as he silently ho-ho-hoed to himself.

I'm glad one of us finds all this funny. I avoided Jay's flat gaze. Officer Brighton busied himself examining the damage to the door, still clucking to himself, as Jay and I stood on either side of him, gazing at each other awkwardly. Every time his eyes flicked to mine,

I glanced away.

After an impossibly long time, Officer Brighton heaved himself back to his feet with the help of what remained of the door frame. "Weeeell," he grunted, "we're going to have to get Physical Plant out here to fix up your room again. You're a destructive little thing, aren't you?" Officer Brighton guffawed.

Jay's hand clenched and unclenched at his side. "I told you, I did it."

Jay's words were hot enough to sear the paint off the walls, but Officer Brighton didn't seem to notice. "Might not be able to get to it until Monday, though I'll see what we can do to get approved for a little O.T." He let out a low whistle and turned to Jay. "Gonna be a pretty penny, you know that, right? No one works for cheap on a holiday."

Jay gave Officer Brighton a curt nod and I felt even worse. Jay didn't make much as a student officer, and we both knew it. I wanted to offer to pay for it myself, but I didn't know where I'd find the money.

"You gonna be okay to stay here if we can't secure the door 'til then?" Officer Brighton asked.

Panic fluttered in my chest like a frantic bird, but I swallowed hard, determined not to make a bigger nuisance of myself than I already had. I opened my mouth to tell him I'd be fine, but Jay cut me off.

"She can stay with me." I shot him an incredulous look, but Jay barreled on. "I'm in a double apartment by myself. There's an extra bedroom with its own locking door, so she'd have her own space until they fix the door."

I shook my head in protest, but Officer Brighton ignored me, nodding his approval at Jay. "Sounds good."

"Not to me," I mumbled, knowing it wouldn't make any difference. An empty dorm room was an empty dorm room. They could legitimately move me anywhere they wanted as long as they had a bed empty.

I grew increasingly irritated as they discussed plans to get me a key and details about the door repair as if I wasn't there. Apparently what I wanted didn't matter one wit to these two men, who had decided they knew what was best for me. After a few more minutes of discussion, Officer Brighton said goodnight to both of us and left.

Taking in my expression, Jay sighed and rubbed his fists against his eyes. When he pulled them away, the sadness there was palpable. "I know the last thing you want is to spend more time with me, but you need somewhere to stay until they fix this. I have one of the only unoccupied rooms left on campus. We won't have to get the Area Directors involved, which means less embarrassment for both of us. Can you please accept this is the plan without us having to go five rounds about it first? Just this once?"

"Fine," I said through pinched lips. "I'll get my stuff." I snatched the bag I'd taken to Colin's from the floor and began chucking things into it.

"Seriously? No argument?" I didn't have to turn around to know he was sporting his signature cocky grin.

"Don't push your luck," I said through gritted teeth. "Hand me that?" I gestured to my pillow.

Jay handed it to me, and our hands brushed as I took it from him. He was trying to keep his face neutral, but the crinkling around his eyes gave him away. I'd asked him to come back, yes, but I'd only meant for him to stay until I calmed down. Now I was going to be sleeping just one thin wall over? This had gotten out of hand fast.

I slammed the closet door open, yanking out my coat and pulling it on over my pajamas. I slipped my feet into a pair of ballet flats, and turned around, determined to be appropriately polite and grateful for the place to stay while simultaneously distant and cold enough to send a message.

Jay, ever the gentleman, already had my bag on his shoulder. "Ready?"

After a quick glance around the room, I followed him out. Jay stood in the hallway, looking positively serene. At least his smugness was doing wonders for my resolve. At the moment, I had absolutely no desire to kiss Jay. Kicking him in the shins, on the other hand, seemed more appealing with every strutting step he took.

"You know," he mused as he held the exit door open, allowing me to pass through in front of him, "if I'd known this was all it took to get you to spend the night with me, I'd have broken your door ages ago."

I stopped dead in my tracks, whipping around to face him, too stunned to speak. Jay burst into laughter, but the humor drained away as he grabbed my arm and pulled me toward the truck. "Relax. It was a joke." He worked to keep his tone light and jovial, but hurt was buried in it, like unseen shards of broken glass. "I know I'm not the one you want to spend your nights with."

I shook his hand off my arm. "Look, I'm —"

"Don't say 'sorry.'" He pulled the cab door open.

"But I am, you know." I climbed into the cab. "Sorry."

"Do you have anyone else to stay with?"

I thought for a minute. Everyone I knew had gone home for break, even Jenna. "No."

"Do you want to be alone?"

No."

"Then just say thank you."

Then he closed the door before I could reply.

37.

Jay swiped me into the bottom floor of his building and led me down a long hallway of polished concrete and light brown paint with dark green trim. He stopped, unlocked his door, and stepped through into the apartment without ceremony. I had enough time to catch a glimpse of three or four notes in different handwriting, accented with smiley faces, stars, and hearts on the large whiteboard beside the door before I followed. Jay already had his head in the fridge.

"Drink?" He pulled open a cupboard and grabbed a large mug. "I've got juice, milk, and water."

"Water." I was distracted by the sheer amount of stuff crammed on every flat surface, bookshelf, and table in the tiny living room. Jay's apartment was the complete opposite of Colin's room. Colin's room was neat, if a little bland. Jay's space was a riot of color, each random item standing in stark contrast to the next.

Jay handed me a mug of water. "It's a lot to take in."

"I thought you Marines were all about the minimalism," I teased, unable to focus as my attention shifted from a small oil painting of a mountain range at sunrise to a large Japanese scroll.

"We are," Jay leaned against the arm of a plush brown chair. "At least, I was. I spent years traveling around the world serving my country. I saw things the people I grew up with will never see, good and bad. At the end, all I had to show for it was a couple of scars. It seemed like a waste. Now I don't worry about being able to drop everything and be ready to ship out with no notice. I don't have to."

He sipped at his cup. "I have a home here. At least, I'd like to.

So I decided to act like it." He gestured broadly. My gaze followed his hand around the room, settling on two tall bookshelves. Every row was full of worn hardbacks and paperbacks of all shapes, sizes, and colors.

And genres. I stepped closer, cocking my head sideways to read the titles of the books lying haphazardly across the tops of already full rows. Sci-fi, classics, religious texts, biographies, pop history books, and technical manuals pressed side by side.

"There isn't much to do when you're deployed. Waiting for the enemy can be incredibly boring. Some guys played video games. I read a lot."

"How did you get so many books over there? Or get them back here?"

He shrugged. "They didn't all come from my deployment. I was in the rehab center for a while, remember?" He moved to stand next to me, his arm brushing my shoulder. "I dunno. Some were gifts, some I swapped for. And Amazon really does deliver everywhere, as long as you've got a couple of months to wait."

Being this close to him was like closing a circuit, and even though I was exhausted I could feel the undercurrent, sparks of electric attraction arcing back and forth between us. Time to make my exit. "Where's my room?"

"Tired?"

I nodded, looking down to escape the tenderness in his eyes. *This was a terrible idea.* I needed to get into that bedroom, lock the door, sleep until daylight, then go to Campus Security and insist they fix my door immediately. I'd find the money to pay for it, but I needed to get away from Jay, for both our sakes.

Two doors opened off the tiny living room. Jay opened the one on the right to reveal a bedroom the size of a large closet with a desk, chair, armoire, and single bed. All the furniture was made of blonde wood so new its waxed surface shone like plastic in the florescent light.

Jay sat my bag down on the desk behind me. The bed was lofted to the topmost position, level with my chest. I looked at it in dismay. There was no graceful way to get into it without jumping or pushing myself up, which was going to kill my shoulder. Jay disappeared into the apartment and came back as I placed a small stool next to the bed and climbed atop it.

"Here," he said, dumping a blanket and set of sheets on the bed as he leaned toward me. "Let me help you."

"No thanks, I got it." I moved faster, hopping onto the stool to get to the bed. Jay was already hovering over me, and my leg shot out, kicking him in the chest as he reached for my waist. I missed the bed and almost fell off the stool, windmilling my arms for balance. My hands landed on Jay's shoulders as he managed to get his fingers around my hips, steadying me. Standing on the stool, we were exactly the same height, our faces inches apart.

We stared at each other, and the hurt and anger and longing and sadness built up over more than a year filled the narrow gulf between us. His eyes were the color of good chocolate, his lashes were dark and perfectly even, the planes of his face were long and speckled with shadow. He wasn't beautiful so much as he was handsome, in a sweep-you-off-your-feet-and-carry-you-up-the-stairs

366

kind of way. I couldn't break the spell of our unexpected embrace. My pulse raced as I felt his fingers tightening, pressing into my skin. I was out of excuses, out of resolve.

To my amazement, Jay was the one to save us from ourselves. I watch his Adam's apple bob in his throat as he swallowed hard, shaking his head a little, as if shaking off sleep. Then he lifted me gently, set me on the bed, and took one giant step back. Embarrassed, I pulled my legs under me and picked up a pillow, hugging it to myself. Running a hand across his stubbled chin, he offered me a weary grin. "We really are a comedy of errors, you know that?"

I managed a weak smile by way of apology. Jay sighed and eased himself out of the room, turning out the light as he went.

I woke too early and lay in the narrow bed, staring at the weak light filtering through the blinds. The apartment was quiet. Jay must still be sleeping. I wondered what he looked like when he slept, if his sheets were pulled so tight you could bounce a quarter off the bed, the way my father made his, what kind of pajamas he wore.

Maybe he doesn't sleep in anything at all, I thought suddenly, scandalized by my own curiosity. I rolled over, burying my head under my pillow as I tried to block out visions of Jay in boxers, then briefs, then decidedly less, all competing for my attention.

There was a sharp knuckled rap on the door. I sat straight up, feeling exposed. Jay was already dressed in a tight blue t-shirt and jeans. He extended a cup toward me, and the rich, slightly bitter scent of black coffee wafted from it. I grabbed the cup and sucked down a couple of long sips. It was so hot it burned my tongue, but I didn't care. After the night I'd had, it tasted comforting.

"You're up." The coffee worked its way down into my middle, warming me from within.

"For a while." He shrugged. "Some habits are harder to break than others. Brighton spoke to the carpenter on call. They can get someone in to fix your door today. I also talked to Mike."

"What did you tell him?" I worried I was about to have another round of mental health interventions.

Jay gave me a knowing look. "I told him you were asleep but that I couldn't get you to answer, and I overreacted."

I sighed with relief. He hadn't told Mike about the accidental medication overload or the episode I'd had. I could live with the rest of it.

"Mike said, given the circumstances, he understood. He told me the college would cover it, but he made me promise in the future I'd call him before I started kicking in doors. You'll be able to go back to your room today." He paused and took a sip of coffee.

I should have been relieved. Instead, I felt a stab of disappointment, followed by a healthy dose of guilt.

"I put out some clean towels by the sink for you." He motioned in the direction of the bathroom. "You can shower before you leave. I'll look at your shoulder." I started to protest but he was firm. "There won't be anyone in the Health Center until Monday. Unless you want to go back to the hospital, you need to let me change the bandage."

"Fine." I sounded like a spoiled child who'd agreed to eat all her eggs if it meant she could then have pancakes. "Thank you," I added in what I hoped was a more adult tone. He dipped his head in acknowledgment, but his eyes never left my face.

I eased myself off the bed, grateful he didn't try to help me. It wasn't the most graceful dismount with a mug of scalding liquid in hand, but I managed not to faceplant or pour coffee all over myself.

I dragged my bag into the bathroom and turned on the water. The lingering effects of the pain meds left me feeling half-hungover. I took my time getting my clothes off, turning and turning in the hot water until my shoulders were loose and relaxed. By the time I was done, the tiny bathroom was steamed up like a sauna, but I didn't care. It was holiday break, and this was as close to a vacation as I was going to get.

I put on my favorite pair of maroon stretch cords, but when I pulled out the butter-colored scoop-necked t-shirt I'd brought, I cursed myself. I hadn't been thinking about my shoulder when I'd grabbed my clothes the night before. There was no way I could put the shirt on and still change the bandage.

"Stupid, stupid, stupid." *At least this is one of my nice bras*, I mused, promptly chastising myself for the thought. *I am a terrible girlfriend.* The glum face staring back at me seemed to agree.

Wrapping the towel tightly around my chest so it bunched under my arms, I opened the bathroom door and poked my head around the corner. Jay sat in a chair reading a paperback, long legs stretched before him. Quiet music filled the apartment, giving it a warm and homey air. A blue first aid kit sat on the small coffee table.

"Jay?" He glanced at me, and I felt my face flush. "I forgot to bring a tank top. I only have a t-shirt." It was obvious he didn't see the problem; I stepped into the living room, revealing my towel-wrapped body. "I need you to change my bandage so I can finish getting dressed."

"Uh, sure." He gestured to the futon next to him, book in hand. "Have a seat."

He stood and stretched as I walked to the futon, his t-shirt rising to reveal a thin dark trail of hair below his bellybutton that stood out against his well-toned abdomen. The tiny living room was suddenly microscopic. I dropped onto the futon facing away from him to hide the telltale redness of my cheeks.

Jay opened the first aid kit with a business-like air, piling various bandages and ointments on the coffee table next to it. He gingerly brushed my hair to one side. I braced myself for his touch, trying to remind myself it was a medical procedure. Jay was tending my wound. I knew there wasn't anything exciting about the way Jay would touch me. But it was Jay, and he was touching me, and I was topless. No matter how hard I tried, our connection was hard to ignore.

He took a sharp breath, and I wondered if he was thinking the same thing. "Callie?"

"Is it infected?"

"Where did you get these finger marks?"

"What finger marks?"

"You have bruising all along your shoulders, like someone grabbed you and shook you."

"What?" I pulled my shoulder forward and craned my neck,

trying to get a better look. There was a row of dark purple bruises along the backs of both my shoulders. In some places there were half-moon cuts where the skin was broken. They were the same marks I'd left on Jay's arm last night.

"Did Colin do this to you?"

"What? No! Of course not!" I half-turned to look at Jay. "I haven't seen Colin since Wednesday, remember? You changed the bandages yesterday. Don't you think you would have noticed?"

"Then where…" His tone turned frantic, demanding. "Did I do that to you last night?"

I put my hand on his arm. "No. You definitely did not do that. I never let you get that close. I did more damage to you than you did to me, remember?"

Jay nodded, but his face said he wasn't so sure. I knew he hadn't done it. So where had I gotten them?

The memory of her digging her mermaid fingers into my shoulders sprang into my mind and I blurted her name. "Izzy!"

"You think Izzy did this?" Incredulous did not begin to describe the look on his face.

Lost in my own thoughts, I waved a hand absently. "It's from the dream. It's exactly where she grabbed me when she was trying to save me." Had it been real? Was Izzy a mermaid now? If so, why was she still hanging around campus?

"Izzy can't bruise you. She's dead."

Fuuuuuuuu… I groaned, furious with myself. In my surprise, I'd totally forgotten. Telling Jay I was communing with Izzy's spirit was a one-way ticket to a mental health intervention. It was written all over his face. Jay cared for me, which meant he'd have me committed to protect me from myself if he knew the truth.

Colin, on the other hand, would understand completely. As the wheels turned dizzily in my head, Jay studied me with a mixture of concern and suspicion. I needed to fix this, and fast.

"Except when she visits me in my room at night dressed as a member of the Insane Clown Posse, right?" I kept a perfectly straight face for two seconds, then faked a burst of loud laughter, waving my fingers in the air and rolling my eyes around.

Jay pursed his lips, but he no longer seemed worried about my sanity.

"No." I sobered enough to seem serious, though inside I was walking a careful emotional tightrope. I didn't want to give Izzy up, even for pretend, but I needed to get through this speech convincingly. "I don't think Izzy touched me. I meant it was similar to the way she'd grabbed me in the dream. Maybe that's why I dreamed it." I half-shrugged dismissively.

Jay was still staring at me with a calculating look; he knew I was hiding something. I hated hurting him, but I couldn't think of another way out of it. Frowning slightly, I tried to appear pitying. "Maybe you did do it," I dragged out the words as though I wasn't sure I believed them.

The color drained instantly from his face. He believed it was his fault; no matter what I said now, he'd keep believing it. "It's okay," I patted his arm awkwardly. I felt like a grade-A tool trying to comfort someone I'd just lied to, someone I'd made believe he hurt me to protect my secret. "I know it was an accident. You were trying to help me."

Jay swallowed hard. "I should some put some ointment on those while I do your stitches." His hands shook slightly as he reached for the anti-bacterial cream.

I turned my face to the wall as he ministered the wounds, his touch delicate, as if he thought he'd break me with the slightest contact.

Well, it's official, I told myself. *I am definitely going to hell.*

38.

As Jay finished taping the bandage on my shoulder in place, there was a knock at his door. Jay walked over and opened it. He did it without thinking and without hesitation, and as it swung open I scrambled to pull the towel tighter, jumping up to scurry into the bathroom.

Standing on the other side of the door was Colin.

A heretofore unknown level of self-loathing hit me like a freight train as I watched his face cycle through sadness, anger, and suspicion. In the world championship of crappy girlfriends, I reigned supreme.

"I went to your room." Colin addressed me as though Jay wasn't standing directly in front of him. "Some repair guys and that fat Campus Security officer were there. They told me you were staying here." Accusation dripped from every word as his gaze swept around the room, taking in my wet hair, my bra straps peeking out above the towel, Jay's rumpled appearance, my guilty face. "I came back early to surprise you. Guess I shouldn't have bothered."

I felt like he'd slapped me. "No, Colin, Jay was—"

"Helping you out of your clothes?"

"Hey, that's totally uncalled for! She didn't do anything wrong." Jay took a step into the doorway, looming over Colin. Colin didn't budge a millimeter.

"Did I look like I was talking to you, Jarhead?" He glowered at me. "I was talking to the girl who's supposed to be *my* girlfriend."

"Colin, he was helping with my bandage."

"Which required you being half-naked?"

I sucked in a breath, fighting back tears. "I…forgot to bring the right kind of shirt." The words were reasonable and forceful in my head, but said aloud they sounded pathetic and defensive, a pitiful cover for something else.

"Sure you did." Colin took a deep breath, and it looked as though he was holding back angry tears of his own. "You know, I thought you were different, but you're not. You're just like Izzy."

Before I could respond, Colin stormed off. I dropped abruptly onto the edge of the loveseat, tears flowing freely down my face. Jay closed the door with a quiet click. He turned back to face me, his eyes glowing with anger.

"He had no right to say that. Neither you or Izzy have done anything wrong."

"No, he's right. When it comes to Colin, we're exactly alike."

"You can't actually believe that. Besides, there was nothing wrong with the way Izzy treated Colin. She tried dating him, didn't like it, and told him she was moving on. That's perfectly acceptable."

"She jerked him around, just like I'm doing now." Jay took a deep breath in preparation for counterargument, but I cut him off, standing up. "She was always pushing him away and then pulling him back in. You weren't around for that part, but I had a front row seat. She liked the attention so she wouldn't let him go, even when she didn't really want him. I saw how much it hurt him. And even if I hadn't he's told me in detail since we started dating. I knew how this would make him feel. I knew better."

"You're being too hard on yourself."

"Thank you, Jay. Thank you for everything." I held my head up, digging deep for whatever decency I had left. "I appreciate the way you've looked out for me. Thank you for letting me stay here. But I was right last night. We need to stay away from each other."

"You're overreact—"

"I am through hurting Colin, who has never been anything but kind to me. I am through hurting you, when you're only trying to help me. Mostly, though, I'm through with acting like a confused, unscrupulous twit. I made my choice. I'm happy with Colin and I want to be with him, despite any actions that might have given an impression to the contrary."

Pulling the towel tightly around me, I wove around the furniture in the direction of the hallway, careful to stay at arm's length of Jay. "I am going to get dressed. Then I'm going to find Colin and fix the mess I've made."

I walked into the bathroom and grabbed my things, carrying them past Jay back to the tiny bedroom. I changed quickly, scooping up my belongings as I did. Jay was still standing where I left him. His arms were crossed over his chest, his face awash in pain and anger. For one short moment, the urge to go over and hug him and tell him everything would be alright was almost overwhelming. I took that urge, wrapped it in all the sadness and regret it came with, and packed it down deep inside me where I hid everything else I was ashamed of—my background, my poverty, my insecurity, my past. As I reached the door, Jay took a step toward me.

"No," I practically shouted, startled at my own forcefulness. "If you care anything at all for me, you'll stay away." Then I closed the door between me and Jay and everything that might have been, promising myself that, from this point forward, I'd keep on the straight and narrow path that led me to Colin and away from Jay.

39.

To say the rest of Friday sucked like a world-class Hoover would barely scratch the surface of my crappy day. I stopped by Colin's on my way back to my room, but he wasn't there. When I got home, my door was fixed. It was still unpainted, but at least it closed and locked.

I called Colin several times, leaving increasingly desperate missives of explanation, apology, and affection when he didn't pick up. It was pathetic, but groveling seemed more than fair considering the circumstances. As I waited for a response that refused to come, the hours stretched into late afternoon.

I tried to study, read, watch DVDs. Mostly I lay on my bed, feeling sorry for myself. As predicted, I'd managed to hurt and drive away the two remaining people who cared about me. I was an awful person who took advantage of the good nature of others and used them to make myself feel better about my crappy life.

I flopped over on my belly and pulled my pillow over my head. I was callous. I was cruel. I was incapable of loyalty and completely untrustworthy. I deserved to be alone, and I always would be.

A book fell from Izzy's desk, smacking against the carpet. Then another, and another. "I know, Izzy. You love me. You'll always love me. But you're dead, remember? And besides, you can't really contradict me. You can't even talk."

There was a loud *snick* as something hit the wall and dropped to the bed next to me. Lifting my head, I saw one of Izzy's enameled rose earrings lying next to me on the bed. I stared at it, thinking back to the images I'd seen through Izzy's eyes.

"I can't believe you hate these earrings. I totally thought you loved them." I remembered how excited Amelia was when she gave them to Izzy, and how little Izzy seemed to care about Amelia's feelings when she considered giving the earrings to Lauren. I moved my hand toward the earring, then stopped myself. I hadn't liked what I'd seen of Izzy at all that night, and I felt no impetus to relive it all again.

I bolted upright.

The party.

In the midst of my post-traumatic, mermaid-dream-distracted, panic attack-induced freakout, I'd completely forgotten about the vision. I'd seen things happen at the party even though I hadn't been there. Izzy had finally managed to show me a memory that didn't have me in it, an important one.

I'd seen Izzy's devil, danced with him, heard him whisper his name in her ear.

Will.

He was tall, dark, and handsome, and his name was Will. And, most importantly, I'd recognize him if I saw him again.

I scrambled off the bed, opening my laptop to cruise through every online social media network Izzy forced me to join. I searched every combination of Astoria College and derivative of the name William for over an hour, until I gave up. I guess no amount of Googling was going to magically make the devil appear.

Maybe I could ask someone who'd been at the party?

I could ask Colin to help me find Will, but that would require convincing him to speak to me. Right now, I couldn't even get him on the phone. I could try asking Gabe, now that I had a name to go with a physical description, but that seemed risky, and depended on Gabe being as broken up about Izzy when he was sober and Emily was speaking to him as he was when he was drunk and fighting with his girlfriend. The girls downstairs didn't seem to know the guy, and if they did, they'd already lied to me about it. The odds of them being any help seemed even slimmer than Colin or Gabe.

I flung myself down on the bed, feeling frustrated and angry. I didn't want to lie here, thinking about Colin and Jay and the mess I'd made of my romantic life. I wanted do something good, something real. I wanted to help Izzy.

There had to be another way to find out who the devil was, one that wouldn't potentially give him a heads up that I was looking for him. If there was still incriminating evidence in his possession, I didn't want him to have a chance to get rid of it. I had to find a way to confront him that made him think I knew everything already, that trying to hide whatever clues might remain was pointless. I needed a sneak attack.

I knew somehow that he was tied to Astoria, as a student or an employee. I didn't know how I knew except that Izzy had known it when she saw him, and she was certain, which made me feel it had to be true. What she knew I knew, at least when it came to the information I accessed through her memories. I'd seen enough of our shared time together to know what she'd sent me might contain only her perspective on the moment, but it was an accurate representation of her knowledge, thoughts, and feelings at the time. It was a gift, to have so much access to her internal workings, even for a few minutes, and one that required a great deal of trust on her part.

Realizing once again that, even in death, Izzy loved me and had faith in me, more than anyone ever had in my life, gave me a sense of purpose and self-worth. So she was a ghost. She was still my best friend. I'd find the people who hurt her, and I'd make them pay for taking her from me, for preventing her from having the life she'd deserved.

The problem with looking for Will online was that not everybody used the same sites, and some people limited their profiles so only their friends could see them. More and more students had been locking down their information since the college started checking online before they hired students for leadership positions and campus jobs. It was supposed to prepare us for the real world, where employers were incorporating the same tactics into background checks. For my purposes it made it hard to find someone online if they were being careful.

Where could I go to find a complete list of AC students along with their photos? The answer came to me like a lightning strike: Campus Security would have access to a list like that. They took the photos for student ID cards and kept them in their computer system so they could print new cards when people lost them. Jenna told me sometimes the RAs used that database to identify students who gave the RAs fake names or ran from parties when they were being written up.

Unfortunately, I wasn't an RA. Jenna was gone for break, but even if she had been in the next room, I had no idea what I could have said to convince her to help me. I couldn't tell her I'd seen the unknown guy Izzy was dancing with in a vision and needed to look at the database so I could find him and shake the truth out of him.

I suddenly regretted everything that had transpired between Jay and me over few last weeks all over again. If I hadn't told him to leave me alone only a few hours ago, maybe I could have asked him. But even if I did, I'd having to tell him why I needed to know. Jay certainly wasn't going to help me once he knew what I was up to.

I'd have to think of a way to get a look at the Campus Safety's student list, some way that wouldn't tip anyone off to my real reasons for being there.

Delving back into Izzy's memories one more time, I forced myself to go over every detail, scouring those moments for anything else I might have missed. The color of the drink cups, Izzy's commentary, both internal and external, the way her feet cramped in her shoes. As I flinched my way through Izzy's last night, I felt her—myself—start to lose my focus. After mentally cataloguing every detail of Izzy's memory of the party until I'd committed them to my own, I was positive about two things:

Will, the dancing devil, was a member of the Astoria community, probably a student, and had never been identified and questioned about the incident. He was wrapped up in this in some way, and I was going to find him and force him to tell me.

And finding Will was critical, because whatever had happened to Izzy that night, it involved more than alcohol. Reliving the moments Izzy's sober thinking slipped away from her, I couldn't help but notice that it wasn't like being drunk. It was more than that.

Even if Izzy didn't realize what was happening to her at the time, I'd been stupid drunk a couple of times in high school. Those poor attempts on my part to prove I was nothing like my dad stuck with me enough to know that what happened to Izzy was more than a few too many shots. What had happened to Izzy was more similar to what had happened to me when I'd taken one double shot of tequila with Gabe, one small drink of liquor that happened to be mixed with a bunch of medication.

Izzy had been drugged. Unlike me, she hadn't stupidly done it to herself. It didn't take a genius to realize that people usually got drugged as precursor to something worse. Everyone I'd spoken to had commented on how hot and heavy Izzy and Will were at the party. Though Izzy had thought Will's interest was entirely physical, I was starting to wonder if Will hadn't set Izzy up so she wouldn't, or couldn't, resist his advances. I had a strong feeling that if Will didn't do it himself, he had a pretty good idea who might have. Given Izzy's penchant for teetotaling, it seemed impossible she'd consciously done a number on herself and her memories confirmed that.

No, someone else had drugged Izzy. Maybe they'd wanted to take advantage of her, or maybe they were just hoping she'd make a fool of herself. Either way, being drugged had inevitably contributed to whatever had happened to Izzy the last night of her life. And when I found out who drugged Izzy and—intentionally or unintentionally—set her up to die as a result, there would be hell to pay.

40.

The next morning, I stood outside the Campus Security office, staring at the broken piece of glass in my hand. I still couldn't believe I was going through with this plan, but I'd spent hours trying to find a way to get access to the Campus Security database that didn't involve me talking to Jay or ending up in a rubber room. This strategy was the best option I'd come up with, and to make it work would require a little pain on my part and someone exceedingly stupid not to see right through it.

Luckily, I knew the Campus Security officer for the job. I also happened to know he was still on duty.

I took a deep breath, then knelt down in the damp dirt behind some bushes off the path. I'd put on an old pair of jeans I didn't mind ruining, but now that the time had come to do the deed, I hesitated. Cutting myself seemed kind of extreme, and my hand hovered an inch above my leg as the glass between my fingers shook slightly.

Suck it up. This is for Izzy.

I jerked my hand downward, slashing at the right knee of my jeans with the sharpest edge of the glass. It cut through the thin cloth and bit into my skin, blood welling around the frayed edges of the torn fabric. Two quick slashes and the faded blue of my jeans bloomed bright red with fresh blood. I swallowed hard at the bile in my throat as the metallic copper tang hit my nose. I took the glass and cut a few tiny cuts into the palms of both my hands to complete the picture I was going for. The wounds stung as blood flowed, deep enough to look bad but not so deep I'd need serious medical attention. I smeared the blood so it looked worse than it was, my hands shaking with the effort. Add a little bit of waterworks, and I was ready.

I limped over to the Campus Security office door and pushed it open, dragging the foot with the cut-up knee slightly. Sure enough, Officer Brighton was sitting behind the counter, feet propped up on the desk as he flipped idly through a car magazine. I sniffled loudly, alerting him of my presence.

"Lordy, girl! What did you do to yourself?" He scurried around the desk. I cradled one bloody hand against my chest and moved farther into the office, fat tears rolling down my cheeks.

Aiming for high melodrama, I collapsed onto a chair. "I went for a walk this morning. It's been so pretty out." I gestured helplessly toward the glass door where the rare November sunshine glowed beyond. "I was almost back to campus when this car came out of nowhere and nearly ran me down." I sobbed loudly and was rewarded with sympathetic tut-tut noises from Officer Brighton.

"What kind of car was it, honey?" Officer Brighton busied himself getting the first aid kit, tossing a box of tissues unceremoniously down on the chair next to mine.

I widened my eyes at him, blinking in a way I hoped resembled a scared deer. "A green one?"

He sighed, and I could practically see the sign on his face that read 'useless little girl.' *Exxxxxxcellent.* "Did it have two doors, or four doors? Was it a car or a truck?"

I let out a noisy hiccup as he knelt in front of me, handing me a tissue to me. "Umm, car? I think? I don't remember how many doors." I shook my head as though remembering the number of doors a car possessed was simply beyond my feminine capability. Had my father been present for this feigned vehicular ignorance, he'd have keeled over where he stood. He'd taken me to dozens of car shows, teaching me all the various details until I knew the difference between production years of classic American muscle cars by sight based on headlight shape and whether or not they had a spoiler.

Brighton, thankfully, had no way to know that, and the longer he stared at my wet cheeks and wide eyes, the more obviously convinced he became that my ability to discern differences in vehicles with engines was non-existent. He sighed heavily and pulled up a chair, planting himself on it as he took my hands in his own.

"How did you get these cuts?" The way he was looking at them and frowning, he seemed to suspect there was something wrong with them.

Shoot. Maybe he's smarter than I thought.

I choked up another sob. "I had to dive out of the way. There was some glass. I cut my hands, and…" *insert loud sob here* "…I ruh-huined my favorite jeans." I wailed, blowing my nose noisily into a tissue.

Officer Brighton patted my shoulder. "Don't worry. We'll find you some new jeans." He opened the first aid kit, which I was starting to think of as a permanent Callie accessory, and wiped at the cuts with antiseptic pads. It stung, but it made keeping the waterworks going easier.

"So you don't remember anything about the car? No distinguishing characteristics?" He pursed his lips together. "Do you think you'd recognize it if I gave you a book to look through?" I could tell he was thinking of the car magazine he'd been flipping through when I came in.

"I...I guess I could try." I widened my eyes and batted my lashes again. "I know it had an AC sticker on the back window. Is that important?"

Officer Brighton rubbed his lips together as though he was chewing back words, then forced a smile. "Yes, that's important. It means the car probably belongs to an Astoria student."

"Oh!" I acted as though such a thought would never occur to me. "I got a pretty good look at the driver. Maybe I'll see him again around campus."

I stared wide-eyed at Officer Brighton, hoping he'd take in the blonde hair and dumb stare and go with the stereotype. *Please be as stupid as I think you are.*

Officer Brighton's face turned several shades of red as he gaped at me, clearly mentally revising whatever he wanted to say several times before he spoke. "Do you think you'd recognize him if you saw a picture of him?"

I paused for a long moment as if I was lost in thought, watching the muscle on the side of Officer Brighton's jaw throb with irritation. This was kind of fun. Maybe I'd take a theatre class next semester.

"Yeah," I said finally. "I think so. Do you have pictures I could look at?" *Marilyn Monroe, eat your heart out.*

"Yes, sugar," Officer Brighton said as though I was so stupid my head might explode if I was forced to think too hard. "We take your ID pictures here, remember?"

"Oh! That's right! Do you think I could look through those? Maybe figure out who that jerk was?" I made a pouty face stolen directly from Izzy's playbook, and Officer Brighton bought it hook, line, and sinker.

Who said sexism never worked in a woman's favor? Occasionally being discounted for possessing a single shred of intelligence or common sense paid off.

He nodded and patted my shoulder again. "Let me clean up that knee, then I'll log you into the system." He tottered off to the bathroom to get a clean wet cloth. It was all I could do not to jump around the office, hooting in excitement. I managed to wipe the smile off my face before he came back, but inside I was bursting with self-satisfaction. Now all I had to do was find Will-the-Devil's full name and get out of there before I ran into someone I knew, someone who would never fall for the dumb blonde routine.

It took me two hours, five tearful breakdowns, and three glasses of water to "calm my nerves," but when I left the Campus Security office around noon, I had the name I wanted.

I'd had to sign an injury report, but other than that, I was scot-free. I told Officer Brighton I wasn't sure of the identity of my phantom driver, pointing out several possible candidates, all of whom looked absolutely nothing alike. Then I'd batted big sad eyelashes at him, and he'd believed me. He told me to come back if I figured out who it was, promising they'd punish the guy if I could positively identify him. He'd repeated the *positively* part twice to make sure I understood what he meant. I thanked him profusely for his help and left the office.

I said the name over and over in my head as I walked back to my hall: Nathan William Cordano. Or Will Cordano, as he was known to his friends and dance partners. That's why I couldn't find him online. Astoria College senior, Communications major, lived off-campus.

It was no wonder I'd never seen him. I didn't take Comm classes and I spent almost all my time on campus in my room, in class, or in the library. I remembered from the vision he was immediately familiar to Izzy. Izzy hadn't declared a major yet, but Comm had been on the short list. She'd gone to several department events to suck up to the faculty. She must have run into him there.

Since Will lived off campus, he didn't have a phone number listed with Campus Security, but he had an email address. Everyone at Astoria was required to regularly check their AC email because the faculty used those addresses exclusively for class-related information, including changes to the syllabus or canceling classes. When I got back to my room, I locked the door and I settled myself in front of my laptop.

"Will Cordano," I whispered into the room as I began to type. "You are about to meet your worst nightmare." After a few minutes I sat back and looked at my masterpiece.

```
To: <nwcordano@astoria.edu>
From: <cmccayter@astoria.edu>


I know what you did to Izzy Miller.
Meet me tomorrow, two o'clock, at Astoria
Coffeehouse.
Come Alone.
If you don't show, I'm going directly to the
authorities.
```

Not exactly poetic. I pressed <send>. Sometimes, though, the situation required a blunt instrument.

Make me your instrument, I prayed silently to the universe.

41.

When the day came to meet Will, I took extra care getting dressed. I made sure to put on durable clothing that was light enough to run in. Though the weather had turned cold and wet again, I opted for a light hoodie layered underneath my jean jacket instead of a bulky winter coat. Not the warmest choice, but it did leave me room to move freely if things took an ugly turn and I needed to fight. I wore my steel-toed Doc Martens with a pair of jeans and shoved my keys in my pocket.

After a few minutes of nervous pacing, I pulled a box down from the top of my closet and dug around until I found a small container of pepper spray, still in the plastic packaging. Crystal had insisted Izzy and I have one on our school supply list, even though we were leaving the big bad city for small town college life. "You never know," she'd said as she pressed the small sprayer into my hands. Looking down at it, I had to agree with her. I guess you never did. I took the canister out of its packaging and stuffed it in my other pocket.

I couldn't think of anything else I needed, so I set out towards town. I had over an hour to spare, but I wanted to get there early enough to choose a seat where I could see Will when he came into the coffee shop. One of the few advantages I had was that I knew what he looked like and I felt fairly confident he had no idea who I was. I'd locked down all my online profiles before I'd sent him the email, so unless he already knew me, he wouldn't have a face to go with the name. After all the effort it taken me to locate him, it seemed only fair.

Even though it was Sunday and people were returning from break, the campus was eerily quiet as I walked out to the main road to catch the shuttle down the hill. In town, people bustled around, engrossed in the holiday shopping weekend and saying goodbyes to visiting friends and relatives. I ignored them, but I couldn't avoid a pang of sadness as I passed along a row of shops advertising their Black Friday sales. I remembered standing in line for hours with Izzy, Crystal, and Amelia waiting for stores to open. Thanks to Izzy, it was a sacred family tradition in the Miller household. I wondered if anyone had bothered this year.

Izzy will never cackle with glee over a bargain. I weaved my way through the happy strangers with their collections of pretty bags. *She will never again haggle for a discount over a loose button or perform a parking lot victory dance over a new pair of shoes. This loser is at least partially responsible for that.* I doubled my pace as the sign for Astoria Coffeehouse came into view.

Luckily the coffee shop was empty enough to give me a pick of tables, but busy enough the employees didn't have time to chat. I ordered myself a skinny latte and took it to a small table near the entrance of the glassed-in portion of the shop, which had a roll-down door they kept open when it was sunny. I passed up the black leather booths, my normal preference, for the maneuverability free-standing furniture would give me if Will decided to try to strong arm me right there in the restaurant.

I still wasn't sure what I was expecting; I didn't think Will would jump across the table and try to throttle me. I guess I wanted to be prepared for anything. "Leave the gun; take the cannoli," as Greg would say, patting his nonexistent stomach in his best *Godfather* impression.

I took out my cell phone and flicked to the "notetaking" app I'd downloaded the night before. I hoped it was sensitive enough to pick up our conversation if it was in my breast pocket, which was the other reason I'd opted for the jean jacket. I'd have a hard time getting to the phone if I suddenly needed to call for help, but I could record for hours and not worry about the battery dying. I pressed the record button and closed the top flap of the pocket without buttoning it, leaving the sensitive speaker exposed.

Halfway through my latte, the devil himself walked into the coffee shop. He was a half-hour early. I guess he'd had the same idea I'd had. I studied him, trying to figure out how best to handle my approach when he spotted me and made a beeline for my table. *So much for my supposed anonymity.*

As he stalked toward the table, I had a brief moment to appreciate why Izzy had been attracted to him. He was movie star hot and moved with a strut that said he knew it, which would have pushed every single one of Izzy's buttons. She loved nothing more than a challenge.

Taking a deep breath, I gave him a small nod of acknowledgement.

"What the hell is this?" he spat, tossing a copy of the email I'd sent him on the table.

Calm, I reminded myself. *Keep calm.* "What do you think it is?" I inquired, shooting him a smile sharp enough to cut glass.

"I think it's you accusing me of something I had nothing to do with." He jerked out the chair across from mine and flopped down when he noticed he was attracting attention.

"Which is?" My tone was achingly sweet.

"You think I killed your friend. Roommate. Whatever."

"So you know who I am."

He snorted. "Of course I know who you are. Everyone knows you. You're the crazy girl who keeps having public meltdowns over Izzy's death. And who apparently likes to go around accusing people of things they didn't do."

I gritted my teeth but kept my smile frozen in place. "And you're Will Cordano, Izzy's previously unidentified dance partner. A whole house full of people saw the two of you together at that party. Unfortunately for you, that makes you the last person anyone remembers seeing with my *best friend* while she was still alive."

"So?" Will almost shouted the word, and two older women sitting in a nearby booth gave him a sharp look. Lowering his voice, he leaned across the table toward me. I leaned in close, getting in his face to show him I wasn't afraid. At this distance, the recorder would definitely be able to pick up our conversation. "What does it matter if I danced with her?"

"From what I hear, you were after more than a dance," I countered. "And you went through what must have been a lot of trouble to keep your name out of all this. Lots of people have been trying to figure out who Izzy was dancing with, but if anyone knew who you were, they've been suspiciously tight-lipped about it. All that gossip and investigation and not one person mentioned your name? That makes me think you asked them to keep their mouths shut." Will's silence was palpable, so I pressed on. "You also could have come forward. You didn't. That makes me think you're as guilty as you look right now."

"Of course I tried to stay out of it." He banged his fist on the table, startling the women again. I smiled at them, and the larger of the two shook her head sadly at me as I took another sip of my drink. The scenario reminded me vaguely of ugly scenes with my father and I felt a flood of relief that I'd chosen a public place for our confrontation. I couldn't lose control now. I needed to keep it together for Izzy. I swallowed hard against the rising panicky feeling threatening to choke me.

"Because you did something wrong."

"Because I have a girlfriend! A Very. Serious. Girlfriend." Will buried his face in his hands. "She's studying abroad in Barcelona. I haven't seen her since last spring. I wasn't looking to hook up when I went to that party, but Izzy was there and she came onto me."

"You're lying. You approached *her*. You hit on *her*." Like all the other visions, I could still see him swaggering toward Izzy as though it had happened only moments before.

"Yeah, yeah, okay." He removed his hands from his face, and I was surprised to see nothing in his eyes but sadness and remorse. "You're right. I did hit on her. What can I say? I was lonely and Izzy was hot." He swallowed hard, avoiding my glare. "But she was totally into it! She was all over me. She was even cool when I suggested we go somewhere a little more private and I took her to one of the bedrooms. "

"That's because you drugged her! When she downed that drink before the two of you started dancing, she got more than soda. You drugged her and you raped her. That's why she's dead now, because after everything you did to her she was too out of it to even make it back to school in one piece." I sat back with a flourish, waiting for him to beg for mercy.

Only it didn't come. Will couldn't have looked more surprised if I'd shown him scientific proof of the existence of the Easter Bunny. He opened his mouth and closed it a couple of times, as if unable to figure out where to start first. Finally he began to sputter.

"Raped her? You think I *raped* her?" He shook his head wildly. "We *never* had sex. We made out, yeah, and it got pretty hot and heavy when we were alone. Everything was fine, at first. She seemed really into it. Then she freaked out."

I didn't believe a word he was saying, and it must have shown on my face, because all of a sudden Will stood up, shrugging off his black leather jacket to yank up his sleeve. There was a fading but still visibly vicious bruise in the shape of a bite mark on his right forearm. "Your psycho friend bit me. One minute, she's shoving her tongue down my throat, and the next she starts screaming and sinks her teeth in so deep my arm got infected." He sat back down on the chair so hard to clattered. "As for drugging her, she was trashed when I got there. I didn't have *anything* to do with that."

I felt shaken. This wasn't what I'd expected. The story didn't add up. Confronted with the bite mark, though, I had a sinking feeling he was telling me the truth.

"You certainly didn't hesitate to take advantage, though, did you? You know if you slept with her, if you violated her in *any* way, it will come out eventually. All I have to do is point the authorities in your direction. After all, they did an autopsy. All they need to do is match your DNA."

It was a bluff. I had no idea what the autopsy showed; no one had told me. But I was betting Will didn't know that.

"Go ahead." His lip curled. "I'll take whatever tests you want. I didn't hurt Izzy. She hurt me. After she bit me, I went to the bathroom because I was bleeding everywhere. She took off while I was gone. I never saw her again."

I sat perched in my chair, glaring at Will, who stared back, his face a mashup of terror, loathing, and indignation. As much as I hated to admit it, he was probably telling the truth. I felt like a large balloon with a hole suddenly ripped through it, all my hope for finding Izzy's killer seeping away.

"She was definitely drugged," I said more to myself than to Will. "If you didn't do it, then who did?"

The desolate look on my face must have gotten to him, because when Will answered, he didn't sound half as angry as he had before. "I don't know. I'm really sorry, but my girlfriend cannot know what happened that night. She'll never forgive me."

His downcast eyes and doleful expression got to me. Despite myself, I felt a little sorry for him. I didn't want to feel sad for him. I didn't want to feel sad at all. I wanted to be filled with the strength and purpose of vengeance that kept me going the last two days. Looking across the table at Will, I knew with certainty he wasn't the one who deserved to be on the receiving end of it.

We sat awkwardly together for a few minutes, neither of us knowing what to say.

"I gotta go." He stood up, not waiting for me to respond. "I'm sorry about your friend, really. But I didn't do anything to her."

Will was already walking away before I said, "I believe you." I wasn't sure he heard me, or if it mattered much. I didn't bother trying to stop him. There wasn't really a good way to apologize for wrongly accusing someone of being a rapist.

For a full fifteen minutes, I was like a statue. My body was completely numb and my mind was blank. Once again, all my leads were adding up to a dead end. Eventually I reached into my jacket and took the phone out, turning off the recording function. Then I made my way back to campus, feeling worse than I had since just after Izzy died.

42.

The rest of the day passed in a haze. I sat in my room, waiting for some flash of inspiration, either of my own or from Izzy, but nothing happened. I tried talking to Izzy a few times, but there wasn't any indication she was there. I wished I knew what made her come and go, but that was one more unsolvable mystery in my life at the moment.

I wrote my last response paper for Gender in Popular Literature and Film. It wasn't great, but it was passable. I forced myself to outline my presentation while I was at it. I could wait until Winter Break to crank out my final paper. One class down, three to go.

It was still early evening when I finished, but I was already exhausted. I packed up all my books for class the next morning, put on my pajamas, and crawled into bed. I picked up the phone twice to call Colin, then put it back down. He knew I was trying to reach him. If he wanted to talk to me, he would.

I got out of bed and turned on the mp3 player on my laptop, setting the volume low. I turned all the lights off, but there was still a low bluish glow into the room. I curled up in a ball, gazing at the laptop and waiting for sleep to come. After about twenty minutes, my screensaver kicked in. I hadn't left my laptop open and unattended in months, so when it started rotating through the pictures on my hard drive, it caught me by surprise. I watched as photo after photo of Izzy and me appeared, then dissolved. Izzy and me dressed as fairies for Halloween when we were thirteen. Izzy shoving a handful of birthday cake in my face while our sisters laughed. Izzy and me stretched out on matching towels next to one another, leaning together and grinning at the camera.

Tears flowed down my cheeks at the parade of happy times we'd spent together. If I was brutally honest with myself, I knew I'd trade Colin and Jay both to have Izzy back. I didn't want either one of them as much as my beautiful, smiling, adventurous friend, but that was impossible. Crystal had once told me how happy she was that Izzy and I had each other. "Boys will come and go, Callie, but what y'all have, that's for life," she'd said. "You think you're so different, but sometimes that's what it takes to last a lifetime."

Despite everything I knew now that I wished I didn't, Crystal's words rang true. Boys would come and go. Izzy had been my soulmate.

"I love you, Izzy," I whispered into the dark room as I drifted off to sleep. And even though she couldn't say anything in reply, I knew she heard me, and that she loved me, too.

When I woke up Monday, I was sadder than I'd felt in a long time. It was a strange, hollow kind of sad I'd only known when my mom had died. Inside me it felt like I imagined the floor of the ocean would if all the water evaporated suddenly—lots of emotional wreckage left behind to remind me of what I had lost.

I went through the motions because it was the last week of regular classes. I figured if I put in those last two or three appearances at least my professors would see I was trying. When Colin didn't show up, it took all of my resolve not to make a beeline to his room. If I was the teacher's pet, then Colin was usually a close second. He never missed class. The look on his face as he'd stormed away from Jay's apartment haunted me. Wherever he was, I knew he was skipping to avoid me. As the week dragged on, Jay was also blessedly absent, and every time I made it back to my room and didn't find him waiting for me, I felt a fresh mix of disappointment and relief.

Each day, I forced myself to focus. One more day, one more class while I tried to figure out what to do next about Izzy. By the end of the week, all I had left was a massive paper for Dr. Cliff. Otherwise, the semester was winding down. Despite everything that had happened, it looked like I was going to survive with my GPA more or less intact.

I also had to survive one last meeting with Dr. Yates, a final delicate counseling performance that balanced grief with the appearance of moving on. If I could keep it together for Dr. Yates and make it through the end of the semester without another scene, everyone would leave and forget all about Izzy, about me. By January, I'd be the oldest of news.

But even as I smiled and nodded and handed in assignments, my every secret thought revolved around Izzy. I was convinced that if she pointed me in the direction of Will and the party, I was missing something important in the vision. Since it wasn't Will, it must have been the drugs. Thanks to my super sharp vis-o-memory powers, I made several mental trips back through those moments, trying to see who was close enough to put something in her drink. Izzy had been sure it was the fruit, but no one else had been affected, and I knew she couldn't be the only girl there with a lime in her cup. I wondered if it was possible other people had been drugged, but it had happened after Izzy had blacked out, which is why she didn't notice.

Everyone had said all along it had been an epic party and everyone was more trashed than usual, but I'd previously assumed their perspective was skewed by all of the hubbub surrounding Izzy's death. Now I wondered if there hadn't been a little extra kick in everyone's drink. Shannen and Lauren hadn't said anything about it, but Lauren hadn't been drinking.

I could try going back to Gabe or go straight to Danielle, but I didn't really believe either one would talk to me. I needed to find the last piece of the puzzle: Bethany. I made the trip over to her residence hall to stop by her room a couple of times, but she wasn't ever there. By the end of the week, I was determined to find her, even if it meant getting my hands on her finals schedule and camping outside her exam room.

But in the end, it didn't come to that. Much to my surprise, Bethany finally came to me. I had just made myself a celebratory end of classes dinner of microwaved ramen and was about to swallow my first mouthful of limp, salty noodles when there was a knock at my door. Sighing, I sat the spoon next to the untouched soup, hoping it was Colin, but dreading our inevitable confrontation. I mean, who else would come rap-tap-tapping at my chamber door on a Friday night? But when I opened the door, there was no one there.

Sticking my head out, I caught sight of Bethany's rapidly retreating form. "Beth!"

She scurried faster in response, pretending not to hear me.

"Oh, no you don't," I muttered, hurrying after her.

When I caught her, she was already at the top of the stars. "Bethany, stop!" I reached out to grab her shoulder. It was only then I saw she was sobbing uncontrollably.

"Bethany, what the hell—"

Bethany flung herself into my arms, practically knocking me down in my surprise. I held her awkwardly as her noisy crying echoed down the stairwell. I saw a door crack open as one of my neighbors looked for the source of the commotion. So much for flying under the radar.

"Bethany, it's okay." I patted her hair. "I'm not mad at you, I swear. I just want to talk."

I led her back to my room and deposited her on my bed, but she wouldn't stop crying. Her hair was shorter than I remembered, tightening her natural curl to the point that she looked like she had spiral wiring cascading to the nape of her neck. Her big blue eyes, coupled with the sprinkle of reddish freckles across her round cheeks, made her look like a grown-up Cabbage Patch doll.

Tear-streaked and swollen, Bethany looked young and naïve, ready to serve as someone's sacrificial lamb. It made me feel bad for her, but also suspicious. I wondered who sent her to me, and why.

I dragged the chair over from my desk and sat down across from her. "Bethany, I'm not upset with you. If you can't remember anything about that night, it's okay."

Her full-force sobs ebbed to a quiet hiccupping. "I don't remember anything,"

"That's happens a lot, though, doesn't it?" I knew I was on thin ice here. I didn't want to call her a lush, but it seemed important to point out.

"Not like this," she whispered, her big eyes shining. "I don't remember *anything*. I remember getting there, I remember Gloria giving me a soda, and that's it. The entire night is a complete blank. It's never like that. And then…" Her lower lip began to tremble.

I grabbed a box of tissues from my desk and put them next to her. She blew her nose and continued. "After that night, Gluh-Gluh-Gloria told me I couldn't be friends with them. She said having me around was humiliating, and they were done pretending to like me." Bethany began weeping openly into a wad of tissue.

"Bethany, Gloria can't cut you off from Shannen and Lauren." I patted her knee. "Or me, for that matter. I don't care what she thinks. Shannen and Lauren will have to stand up to her sooner or later."

Bethany smiled weakly at me, but it quickly melted to a frown. "What if she's right, though? What if I do have a drinking problem?" I could see the waterworks starting up again.

"That's okay!" I said desperately. "I mean, it's not okay, but we can get you some help. You know about my dad, right?"

Bethany nodded hesitantly.

Thanks again, Izzy. At least your big mouth is going to speed up this conversation. "I know what I'm talking about. I don't think you have a drinking problem. I think you tend to overdrink at parties, but there are ways to fix that. Do you drink any other time?"

Bethany shook her head vehemently. "No, only at parties."

"There you go." I shot her an approving smile. "Now we need

to work out some strategies for keeping your drinking under control when you go out."

"But I was trying," she wailed, tears flowing again. "Izzy told me about your dad, about how it affected you, and how I needed to stop partying so hard before it became a problem."

"Bethany, what do you mean you were *trying*?" I chewed at the inside of my lip. She'd said something important during all her teeth gnashing but I couldn't quite put my finger on it.

"I had a shot when I got to the party. Well, okay, two shots. But then I switched to soda. I was determined to show Izzy I could do it. I wanted her to be proud of me."

If anyone had idol worship going for Izzy, it was Bethany, who repeated everything Izzy said like it was holy gospel. Not even Amelia idealized her big sister the way Bethany did. Izzy always pretended it annoyed her, but I knew she secretly loved the attention. "Did you put any fruit in your soda?"

Bethany shook her head. "I took mine out."

"So there was fruit in your drink?"

"It was like that when Gloria brought it to me. It smelled weird, though, so I took it out. She'd put lime juice in my drink, so I figured I didn't need it."

"Gloria brought you a drink—a Coke with lime juice and limes floating in it?"

Bethany paled slightly and gave a brief nod.

"It was in a red cup?" Red cups were for alcohol. Clear cups at AC parties were for DDs. It made it easier to keep drinks straight and allowed hosts to pretend they weren't serving to minors in case the party got busted.

Bethany tilted her head like she was struggling to remember, but I could see it all there, in the vision. Bethany's cup was red. So was Izzy's. Gloria had given them both their drinks, and Bethany had the worst blackout of her life, worse than anything she's experienced before. Izzy hadn't paid any attention to the cup because it had come from someone she trusted. Since she hadn't thought about it in the vision, I'd missed it, too.

Gloria.

All this time, I'd been thinking it was some guy trying to get into Izzy's pants. Instead, Izzy had been betrayed by someone who was supposed to be her friend. I had no idea why, but the truth was staring me in the face, horrific but undeniable.

Gloria drugged them both.

"Bethany, what—*exactly*—did Gloria say to you, after that night?" It was everything I could do to hold back my rage. I had to keep it together. I was going to need Bethany. I couldn't scare her.

Bethany flushed with shame and began playing with a crushed tissue. "She said that this should be a lesson to me about what happened to girls who couldn't keep their shit together. She said that what happened to Izzy could easily happen to me, that until I learned not to embarrass myself and all of my friends every time we went out, I couldn't hang out with them anymore."

The forlorn look on her face made me pity her, but I pushed the feeling away. I leaned toward her, lowering my voice. "What would you say if I told you there was evidence Izzy was drugged? And, based on what you've told me, you may have been, too?"

Bethany's eyes were as round as saucers. "Did the police say that?"

"There are sources," I said with quiet confidence. Okay, dead sources no one else would believe, but one problem at a time. "The college may need corroborating testimony if the issue comes to a hearing." I gave her my most solemn look. "Do you think you would be willing to tell the college exactly what you've told me?"

Bethany squirmed. "I don't know, Callie. I don't want to get in trouble…"

I got out of the chair and moved to the bed, sitting beside her. "It would mean so much to me if you would help us catch the people who hurt Izzy." She looked up at me when I said Izzy's name, and I could see, even in death, that Izzy was still Bethany's hero. Maybe more so. "Izzy needs your help. Could you do it to help Izzy?"

It felt like I was overplaying my hand, but her face shone with certainty. She nodded, deep and slow. "Yes. I could do that. For Izzy."

"For Izzy," I repeated, already working on a plan of attack.

43.

Before Bethany left, I swore her to secrecy. "If anyone finds out before the college finishes its investigation, they might never get the people responsible." I gave her my best cop expression, thinking about how much, in this moment, I was my father's daughter. "You cannot tell anyone about this critical piece of evidence. Not even Lauren or Shannen. Do you understand?"

Bethany paled a little, then nodded. I scrutinized her for any sign of weakness, and Bethany never wavered. I was betting a lot on Bethany's devotion to Izzy, but given the circumstances, it was the best I could hope for.

I walked Bethany to the end of the hallway and down the stairs, hugging her and telling her how good she looked, how much I'd missed her. I promised her I'd talk to Lauren and Shannen for her, smooth things over. "I'm sure I can convince Gloria." I smiled, trying to keep the vitriol from my voice. "Just give me a few days to work it out." Bethany seemed thrilled with my promises to fix all her problems.

Normally I'd find my own sycophantic display revolting, but I was beginning to realize that when it came to Izzy, there were a lot of things I was willing to do. Lying to Bethany barely gave me pause.

As soon as the exit door banged closed, I raced down the hallway toward Gloria's room, pushing two surprised firsties out of my way. I swung around the corner and banged hard on the door of the quad.

No one came to the door right away. I pounded on the door again with my fist. It rattled in the frame.

"They're not home," a flat sarcastic voice said behind me.

I whirled around to find Marissa, floor RA and former Colin paramour, glaring at me. "Is there something I can do for you?"

"No." I stretched my fingers wide to avoid balling my hands into fists. If Marissa got the impression I was feeling homicidal, she might try to stop me. "The new episode of *Top Model* is starting. I thought they'd want to watch it with me."

Marissa ran her tongue across her teeth, rolling her eyes to indicate she knew I was lying, but couldn't care less. "Colin didn't want to watch it with you?"

From her sickly-sweet tone, I could tell she was fishing for something meant to hurt or humiliate me, so I forced a laugh. "Colin's not much for *Top Model*."

"Oh! You're still together?"

"Of course."

Marissa faked a look of surprise, then cast her eyes to the ground and bit her lip as if she was hesitant to tell me whatever was coming next. "Then you're probably not going to like this, but—" she glanced around and took a step toward me, dropping her voice to a stage whisper "—the last time I saw him, he was leaving with Gloria. And they looked, you know…" Her expression was heavy with implications. "Friendly."

Bile rose in my throat and tears sprang to my eyes.

Not here. Not in front of her.

"Really? I didn't know they were friends." I struggled to keep my tone polite and unfazed, pretending Marissa had told me we were expecting rain rather than implying my boyfriend was hooking up with the girl who'd drugged Izzy.

Marissa nodded and the look of fake pity she threw at me was Oscar-worthy. "Gloria's been interested in Colin for a long time. I guess they hit it off over the weekend…"

I locked my jaw, willing myself not to shake with hurt and anger. Better to pretend I hadn't picked up on the not-so-subtle innuendo. Instead, I went for my best Bethany impression. "When you see the girls, will you tell them they missed *Top Model*? Unless you want to watch with me?"

Marissa's eyebrow drew together. "Ummm, no."

"Okay then." I grinned wildly. "See you later."

From the stunned look on Marissa's face, I'd nailed clueless. Time to make my exit.

I walked slowly back to my room, forcing myself to keep my head up and not scurry like an insect running from unexpected bright light. I barely made it back to my room and closed the door before I began to hyperventilate.

Colin.

And Gloria.

Colin…and…Gloria?

Marissa had to be lying. Didn't she? I mean, wasn't Colin still my boyfriend? We'd had a fight, but we hadn't actually broken up…had we? I knew I was sort of new to this whole relationship thing, but I'd seen Izzy dump enough people to know there was a "talk" involved. Colin and I had definitely not had that "talk." So

Colin was still my boyfriend, and Marissa had to be lying.

Didn't she?

And even if Colin wasn't my boyfriend, didn't he have better taste than Gloria? She was about as deep as a puddle and twice as mean as Izzy, even at her Queen Bitchiest. How could he hook up with someone as awful as Gloria, not to mention someone who would do something so awful to Izzy?

Ohmigod. *Was…was Colin in on it?*

I fell to my hands and knees and began dry heaving. No. He couldn't be. I would never believe it. He was too upset about Izzy. He missed her. He loved her. He had tried to help her that night. He would never…

But as I fought to regain my composure, Jay's warnings that Colin was a bad guy rang through my head. How much did I really know about Colin? Other than the standard college stuff, very little. Jay had implied something Colin had done or said spooked Izzy. I'd never really believed Jay. I always assumed Izzy told me everything and chalked Jay's dislike up to jealousy. But maybe there was another reason she hadn't told me. After what I'd gone through with my dad, maybe she hadn't wanted to upset me.

Or…what if she'd never gotten the chance?

After a while, I got my breathing under control and sat back against the door, resting my head against the mirror. I closed my eyes, but I couldn't stop the small romantic moments I'd had with Colin from dancing across my eyelids, each one a scene in an epic film highlighting my unintentional betrayal of Izzy. No wonder she was furious.

"I'm sorry," I whispered hoarsely into the room. "I didn't know. I'm sorry."

Izzy didn't respond and, for once, I didn't blame her.

44.

I had a finals study session the next morning and barely made it. Luckily it was for one of the classes I didn't share with Colin. Given how distracted I was, I wasn't sure going would do me much good, but it seemed better than sitting in my room, stewing.

As much as I wanted to hunt down Gloria and Colin—I wasn't honestly sure in which order—I knew that acting rashly out of emotion wouldn't help me or help Izzy. I had to be calm. I had to be calculating. I had to think like Izzy did and make sure that the next step I took was absolutely right. Otherwise I might never be able to corner the responsible person into admitting responsibility for Izzy's death.

Person...or persons. The thought of Colin being involved made me so sick inside. I didn't want to believe anything Marissa had said, but I just couldn't forget about it. Could I really be that blind?

As I walked to the Counseling Center, I pushed the thought out of my mind. Keeping it together meant keeping my temper and my appointment with Dr. Yates. I knew blowing up or skipping out was the fastest way to end up on every professor and administrator's radar again, and now that I had Gloria in my sights, that was the last thing I wanted.

Ms. Bloom wasn't at her desk when I arrived at the Counseling Center, so I took a seat and started flipping through a magazine without really seeing it. It was rare to see the Counseling Center so empty, but at the end of the semester, I guess most people's attention was focused elsewhere. I'd intentionally brought my iPod, keeping my earbuds in but the music off, as I wandered around campus. I wanted to keep my ear to the ground for any mention of Gloria or Colin, hoping the AC phone tree would work in my favor for once. All I'd managed to pick up was people groaning about finals and how ready they were to go home.

I was about to knock on Dr. Yates' door when the office door next to hers opened. The counselor inside hugged a girl with light brown hair hanging to the middle of her back. As the girl turned, I realized it was Shannen.

Shannen noticed me in the same moment, a look of panic passing over her face. Her expression was all I needed to confirm the niggling suspicion that she definitely had information I wanted. If it was about Colin and Gloria—barf, but whatever. I'd come to live with the disappointment. All of that was a distant second to confirming that Gloria had drugged Izzy. Shannen's version of the evening played back in my mind as I scrutinized her. Now that I had the full story, it felt like she'd carefully avoided certain details when I'd cornered her. She'd also been pretty emphatic that Bethany in particular wouldn't be worth talking to. At the time I'd been so touched by her tears I hadn't noticed.

"Hey, Shannen," I tossed the magazine on the table and gave her a sharp smile. "Have a good Thanksgiving?"

Shannen glanced toward the exit, gauging how much she had to say to me before she made her escape. "Yeah, but I'm swamped with finals. First ones ever. I'm scared I won't do well. That's why I'm here." She motioned toward the door. "Anxiety."

"Ah," I said with feigned sympathy. Shannen was a pretty good student; I didn't see her flipping out over a set of exams. "It's great I ran into you. I wanted to see you before you left for break. Maybe get that coffee?" I tried to keep my face open and my tone friendly, but there was an angry current rolling underneath and Shannen caught it immediately.

"Sure." Shannen worked her way past me. "I have to get to a study group now, but maybe this weekend?" She opened the door, tossed a "See you!" in my direction, then scurried away.

I looked at Dr. Yates' door. Still closed. If I wasn't here when it opened, there would be consequences. At the same time, what were the chances I'd get another shot at Shannen alone? I was out the door before I could think too much about it.

Shannen had covered an impressive amount of ground in the half-minute it took me to follow her. I had to jog to catch her, grabbing her arm to stop her from full-out bolting. Shannen spun around, fear plastered all over her face.

"Callie, I really gotta go," she said desperately, but I pulled her closer, tightening my grip.

"You're hurting me!"

"You haven't begun to hurt." Our faces were inches apart, and I forced a smile as I spoke in a low voice, trying not to attract attention. "You're going to be straight with me. I know you didn't tell me everything you know about the night of the party. If you don't come clean, and I mean *right now*, you're going to wish you'd been the one out there on the road instead of Izzy. Start talking."

"About what?" Shannen glanced around, obviously looking for

someone who might come to her rescue, but everyone else was too busy lost in their own pre-finals world to notice us.

"Let's start with the fact that you knew Colin was there that night. He's the guy you said was passed out on the couch. Right?" She nodded. "Why did you lie?"

"Because Gloria told me to," she wailed loudly.

A little *too* loudly, if the heads flicking in our direction were any indicator. If she kept this up, we would definitely attract attention. There was a small courtyard outside the entrance to the Counseling Center that sat empty in the colder months. It had a half wall that left it partially obscured from view. It was closer to the Center than I'd have liked, but it would have to do. I wasn't letting Shannen get away again.

I warped my arm around hers, linking elbows. "Walk with me," I said through a gritted smile. Shannen gave in, allowing me to lead her over one of the small wrought iron tables, then push her into the chair across from me. She didn't look like she'd try to take off again, so I let go of her arm.

"Why did Gloria tell you to lie?"

"Because she didn't want Colin to get in trouble." Shannen rubbed at her arm where I'd grabbed her. "We all saw him get into with Izzy. Gloria thought it might make him a suspect."

That didn't make any sense. "Why would Gloria want to protect Colin?"

Shannen's expression was a mixture of pity and amusement. "Because she's been into Colin for over a year. Gloria threw herself at him every time he showed up, but he never paid any attention to

416

her. Colin was always all about Izzy. When the cops came to talk to us, Gloria did most of the talking. She didn't mention him, so we didn't. Later she told us that if we told anyone he was there, we'd pay for it."

"And they're together now?" Despite telling myself over a hundred times since my run-in with Marissa that I didn't care, I held my breath.

"Where did you hear that?"

"Your RA told me last night."

Shannen snorted. "Then Marissa lied to you. Colin hasn't spoken to Gloria since Izzy died. She tried to talk to him a couple of times, played up the whole let's-be-united-in-our-grief thing, but Colin wasn't having it. He blamed us for leaving Izzy."

A felt a pang of relief, though it wasn't enough to quench my anger. I'd been right. Colin had cared for Izzy; he hadn't hurt her. And he hadn't cheated on me. I was the cheat and the liar. As soon as this was over, I had to find him and apologize. But first, I needed to extract one final thing from Shannen.

"Shannen," I said, my voice low and thick with emotion. She inched away from me in response. "Did you know Gloria was going to drug Izzy and Bethany?"

"How did you…" she whispered, then clapped her hand over her mouth, horrified.

Black spots swam across my vision as I struggled to keep from erupting. Our *friends* did this. They drugged Izzy, they left her, and they let her die. I closed my eyes for a long moment as I tried to calm my swirling emotions, then opened them wide and threatening.

"If you don't come clean immediately, I'll make sure when Gloria goes down, you go right along with her. I'm giving you this one chance to tell me everything, and if you don't, so help me, you won't be able to get into clown college when I'm finished."

"I didn't know, I swear!" Shannen grabbed at my hands, desperate now as tears filled her eyes.

I shook her off, crossing my arms over my chest. "Talk."

She hesitated, and I could see her trying to decide if I had the power to do what I'd promised. For once, I was incredibly happy to have a cultivated reputation as an unstable, potentially violent weirdo. At least all the broken windows and screaming and public sobfests might finally find their use. In the end, it took less than ten seconds for Shannen to realize that Gloria was the lesser of her two evils.

"Gloria was sick of Bethany constantly getting trashed. She said Bethany was damaging our reputation and keeping us from meeting decent guys because we kept getting stuck babysitting her." Shannen picked at her nails as she mumbled her confession. Once she started talking, they seemed to come faster and faster. "She decided to teach Bethany a lesson. Gloria thought if she could make a big enough deal out of the situation that she could strong-arm Bethany into staying away from us without having a fight with you and Izzy."

"So Gloria's solution was to drug her?" I asked incredulously. *And people think I'm insane.*

Shannen nodded. "It was ecstasy. It wasn't GHB or anything. Bethany told us she'd taken it a few times in high school, so Gloria

figured it wasn't anything Bethany wouldn't already do to herself."
Her tone was pleading, as though, if I could see things from her
perspective, I'd understand. I curled my fingers around the cold
metal edges of the chair to keep from slapping her.

"Gloria wasn't planning to drug Izzy?"

"No! At least, not that she told me. She was meeting some
senior at the party to get the X. She's been hooking up with him off
and on all semester and he told her he could get some."

Shannen hesitated, then blushed furiously, and I motioned for
her to continue. "I guess Gloria told him she wanted to try it while
having sex. Apparently, he was more than happy to get her as much
as she wanted after that."

"Gloria asked for drugs for sex to get back at Bethany for over-
drinking and being too flirty?" I shook my head in disgust. "That's
pretty twisted."

Shannen shrugged. "When we got to the party, Gloria
disappeared. When she came back, she had me keep an eye on
Bethany. Bethany had downed two shots by then, so she was already
tipsy, which is probably why Gloria figured she wouldn't notice."
She glanced at me and winced. "I thought, I don't know, that maybe
Gloria was right and Bethany deserved to have a bad night after all
the nights she'd spoiled for us."

"So you helped Gloria drug her." Shannen nodded almost
imperceptibly. "What about Izzy? If she wasn't part of your
teachable moment, how'd she gets dosed?"

"Gloria. It was all Gloria. First, there was the thing with Colin.
Then they got into that fight on the way to the party… I guess Gloria

was tired of being invisible when Izzy was around."

I sucked in a deep breath. I'd never have believed these girls Izzy had taken under her wing could be so cruel. Shannen grabbed at my knee. I didn't even bother shaking her off.

"I didn't even know she'd given Izzy a drink. You have to believe me." Shannen babbled on, eager to explain now that the truth was coming out, how it wasn't really her fault. "I didn't realize anything was wrong until I saw Izzy dancing with that guy. Then she told Gloria off in front of everyone, and Gloria was surprisingly okay with it. That's when I suspected."

"But you didn't tell anyone." My voice sounded flat and far away, like it was coming from somewhere else.

"I waited because I wasn't sure at first," she insisted. "I asked Gloria about it later, and that's when she told me that if I ever told anyone, she'd make me sorry. She said she'd blame it all on me."

"So in order to protect yourself, you hid the fact that Izzy was drugged against her will. You left her at a party to be preyed upon by any guy who wanted her. You let her walk up the hill alone, so out of her mind she got hit by a car and died."

Shannen looked away. I reached over and grabbed her by the chin, forcing her to look me in the eye. "Because you are a pathetic, weak, spineless sheep, you let my best friend die, and you never said anything at all."

Shannen winced as I tightened my grip on her face. But as much as I might want to do Shannen serious harm, I was too close to getting justice for Izzy. I had to keep it together. I had to.

I pulled myself away from her, chair scraping slightly as I

rocked back from the force. "Did Lauren know any of this?"

Shannen shook her head no, and I felt a small ripple of relief. Two people betraying Izzy was two too many, but at least they weren't all complicit. It hurt so much to think that Izzy had been betrayed by these girls whom she'd given so much of her time and energy to. She had trusted them—so much so she'd taken an open drink from one of them without a second thought.

But Izzy was like that—giving, trusting. She could be a Class-A Mean Girl sometimes, but she would never have guessed her friends would violate her trust or actively try to hurt her. After all, Izzy'd had a good life, full of people who loved and protected her.

Me, on the other hand…I'd seen too much of betrayal to be so easily fooled. I shivered, but it wasn't because of the cold. It was because I couldn't believe I hadn't seen Gloria and Shannen for what they were. I felt stupid, naïve for not watching them more closely, for not seeing the signs.

I stood, shaking all over. I wanted to run away, far away from the ugly truth, and from my own blindness to it until it was too late. Shannen's eyes followed me like a terrified animal wondering if it could escape before its distracted predator struck. I leaned over her, bracing myself against the arms of the chair on either side of her. Shannen went white as a sheet as she cowered beneath me.

"You aren't going to tell Gloria anything about this conversation. Do you understand me?" Shannen gave the barest of nods. "You're going to let me find Gloria and deal with her my way. Then you're going to tell the truth to every single person I point in your direction."

Shannen spluttered, beginning to protest. I leaned over closer, so that my lips were almost touching her ear.

"If you don't," I whispered, "I'll make sure you pay, and pay, and pay, Shannen. If you don't do exactly what I tell you to, you're going to look back fondly on the days when Gloria was the worst thing you had to worry about."

I pushed myself away from the chair and walked toward the Counseling Center door. I didn't look back. I was afraid if I did the thin thread of resolve would snap. I'd never wanted to hurt someone so much in my life, but in that moment, I was brimming with an anger I didn't know I could feel.

I remembered clearly the blackout rage in my own father's eyes. Even then I'd known it wasn't all alcohol; it was a dark thing that lived inside him. I was beginning to realize the same darkness lived in me, too. Somewhere, deep down, I had a remarkable capacity for violence. It was a place I never wanted to go. If I did, I wasn't sure I could come back.

Inside the entry way to the Counseling Center, I leaned on my hand against the wall, pausing to catch my breath. I felt like I'd run a marathon. Every part of my body quaked with spent adrenaline and exhaustion, and I had to fight to keep crying. I took one ragged breath after another, telling myself I had to calm down before I saw Dr. Yates. She could not see me so rattled. It would make her suspicious. I needed a few more days. After that, I didn't really care what happened. They could expel me. I'd go down fighting if it was for Izzy. As long as I took anyone who'd hurt her with me, I could live with that. I owed her that much.

Wiping my eyes carefully with my sleeve and pasting a smile across my face, I pushed open the Counseling Center's inner door. Mrs. Bloom, who was back at her desk, glanced at me.

"Sorry I'm late." I dropped my bag next to her desk and pretended to smile. "I got caught up studying for finals and completely forgot my appointment. I ran right down here as soon as I remembered."

"Oh, dear." Mrs. Bloom looked slightly chagrined. "Didn't you get my message? Dr. Yates had an emergency. She asked me to reschedule your appointment for next week."

"In the middle of finals?" I gasped, displaying an exhaustion I didn't have to fake. "I really need to focus."

"She did say that since you've been doing so well, you could meet with her over Winter Break if that was better for you."

"Over break?"

"Your AD Mike told her you'd asked to stay for the break, and Dr. Yates agreed to supervise you since most of the staff will be gone and the Center will be closed."

Great—exactly what I need. Christmas with my therapist. It didn't really matter. For all I knew, I'd be expelled by then.

"That would be perfect." I kept the plastered grin in place. At least it would keep me here long enough to deal with Gloria. At this point, that was all that mattered.

That, and making a really important apology to someone I'd been quick to misjudge, even though he didn't deserve it. If the next week was going to be my last in Astoria, I needed to make things right with Colin before it was too late.

45.

I stood outside Colin's door, shifting my weight from one foot to another. Twice I raised my hand to knock before letting it fall back to my side.

I needed to apologize for so many things I didn't know where to start. I could start with Colin's suspicions about Jay, which weren't off the mark, even if the situation he'd walked in on was innocent. Then there was the matter of the few hours I'd spent convinced Colin was involved in Gloria's plan to drug Izzy. I wasn't sure which one was worse.

Of course, Colin didn't know I'd thought—even for a minute—that he had contributed to Izzy's death. Nonetheless, that was the part I felt the worst about. For the better part of a single night, I'd thought a wonderful, caring, loyal guy who wanted to be my boyfriend was a predator and sadist. It was a testament to how screwed-up I was that I'd completely missed Gloria's potential for disloyalty and meanness, but I hadn't been able to trust the one person who'd never doubted or judged me, no matter what flavor of crazy I brought his way.

Guess that's something I can spend Winter Break discussing with Dr. Yates. If, of course, I don't get thrown out first.

I raised my hand again to knock, promising myself for the thirty-fifth time I would make it up to Colin, whatever it took. Before my hand hit the wood, the door opened.

"Colin," I said, a wave of relief washing over me as I stared into his sparkling blue eyes.

"What do you want?"

"I came to apologize."

Colin picked a large trash bag up off the floor and slung it over his shoulder, pushing past me. "I'm not interested."

"Colin, stop." I trailed after him. "Please. I need to talk to you."

Colin pushed his way out the exit door and walked to the dumpster under the sky bridge. I watched as he lifted the top and lobbed the bag in, the dumpster ringing as the bag thudded against the back. "Please just let me explain—"

Colin wheeled around, his face red and blotchy with anger. "Explain what, Callie? That as much as you like me, you can't seem to help yourself when Jay is around?"

I sucked in a breath at the harshness of his words. It was all the confirmation he needed.

"I am so sick of being the good guy, the nice guy, the patient guy!" He slammed his fist against the dumpster and the lid fell down with an echoing bang. "Maybe I should keep showing up and forcing some girl I want to be with to spend time with me even when she says no. Who cares if she has a boyfriend, right? It obviously works for Jay."

"Colin, please," I pleaded, reaching for him as he pushed past me. "Nothing happened, I swear."

"But you wanted it to." He couldn't even bring himself to look at me, instead keeping his gaze to the ground. "You wanted to be with him, wanted it bad enough to forget about us."

"It wasn't like that."

"It was exactly like that," he yelled. "You know what the worst part is? I mean the terrible, awful part? I trusted you. Despite everything, I thought you and I were going to be together." His voice went soft, quivering. "All I wanted, the entire time I was home, was to get back to you."

I took a step toward him, but he put his hand against my shoulder, holding me back from him. "No, Callie. We can't kiss and make up this time. It won't work."

I hugged my arm to my side, trying not to cry. "Please," I begged. "I'll do anything."

Colin took a deep breath, closing his eyes. "No." He shook his head without opening his eyes, as if he could make me disappear from view if he wished hard enough. "No."

I nodded silently, afraid to open my mouth. I turned away, trying to get away before I had a full-scale breakdown. I couldn't ask him to take care of me after I'd hurt him so badly.

"Callie," he called after me. I froze in place, unable to turn around. "When you see Jay, why don't you ask *him* about the party?"

I heard the words but couldn't process them. Jay…and the party? He wasn't there. At least, I didn't think he was. But the way Colin said it made something inside me tighten into a cold knot.

Unwilling to wait for me to react, Colin planted himself in front of me so he could see my face. "Why don't you ask him why *he* didn't save Izzy, if he's so interested in saving people?" His tone was merciless. "Ask him. Ask him why he didn't walk her back to campus. After all, he was there. He was on duty. It was practically his job to protect her."

"He wasn't—"

"He was." The utter contempt in Colin's voice was thick, hanging on every word. "I talked to some friends over break who were there. I thought maybe they'd remember something I didn't, something that could help Izzy. Jay was there. He broke up the party."

The world seemed to hush to the sound of everything but my own rapid breathing. Panic squeezed my chest, and I fought to keep myself from succumbing to the swell of numbness within.

"That's what I thought." Colin shook his head, and the sad smile on his face was cold and heartbreaking. "You didn't know he was there. All the time you two spent together and he *never* told you." Colin swung the door open so hard it bounced off the side of the building. "You two deserve each other."

46.

I didn't remember how I made it from Calhoun back to Spruce. I wasn't even conscious of where I was until my building came into view. My body brought me home on autopilot like it had in the first days after Izzy died. I'd look up find myself at some other point on campus with absolutely no memory of how I'd gotten there. It reminded me of the blank spaces from my childhood, moments lost in a sea of misery and pain so grim that my body simply skipped over them, trying to protect me from ever knowing the worst.

Shell-shocked. A grim giggle that bordered on hysteria bubbled past my lips. *I'm shell-shocked. One emotional bomb too many, and now I can't feel anything at all.*

I felt around in my pockets for my swipe card without looking at the people passing in and out of the building around me. I was vaguely aware of sounds around me—mumbling voices, the crunch of gravel underfoot, a nearby car door slamming. Nothing penetrated the bubble. I focused on finding my swipe card, only capable of processing one task at a time.

I pulled it from my pocket and raised my head only to find Jay standing in front of me. I was so out of it, I wasn't even sure where he'd come from.

"Where have you been?" He was wearing his Campus Security uniform and for a millisecond I'd seen my father's face superimposed over Jay's, one dark uniform standing in for another, older memory. He reached toward me when I didn't respond.

"Get your hands off me," I snarled, yanking away from him.

"Callie, what is wrong with you?" Startled by my reaction, Jay backpedaled from his own anger as he gazed at me with a bewildered look.

The rational part of me knew having it out with him in public wasn't a great idea, but reasonable Callie seemed to have left the building. "Don't touch me," I choked. "Don't you *ever* touch me again."

"Callie, I—" he began, but I wasn't going to hear any more excuses, not from anyone.

"YOU WERE THERE!" I screamed. Jay shook his head slowly, like he didn't know what I was talking about. "AT THE PARTY! You were there. You saw her. You could have saved her, and you didn't! And you hid it from me!"

Jay looked at me, panic-stricken. "I tried. She wouldn't let me."

I slapped him in the face, as hard as I could. Two girls passing us jumped back in surprise, then scurried toward the door, swiping in as fast as they could.

Jay rubbed his face with his hand. "Are you finished?" His tone was hard and smooth as glass.

"With you? Absolutely."

"I was there." His eyes were readable. "We got a noise complaint from a neighbor, so we went to break up the party. Izzy came out of the house while we were talking to the guys who live there, telling them to shut it down."

"And you two had a nice little chat?"

"I attempted to make contact, yes." His tone was flat and

clinical, just another officer giving his report. "She was extremely intoxicated. I debated whether to call the Astoria P.D. and send her to detox for the night. I tried to calm her down, to convince her to get in the vehicle, but she was in about as good a shape emotionally as you are right now."

My fists tightened, and he glanced down at them and back at my face. "She kept babbling about not remembering things, about needing you and you not being there. She wasn't making any sense. I couldn't calm her down. She ran away from us, down the road."

"And she was so strong you couldn't physically stop her?" I demanded, trying to ignore the part of me that died the moment he told me Izzy had been begging for me while I'd been safe in bed, fast asleep.

"Campus Security officers aren't allowed to physically restrain students," he said simply. "Too many liability issues."

"But letting them get themselves killed doesn't bother anyone?"

Jay kept talking, ignoring the barb. "I confirmed the party was being shut down by the hosts, left my partner there to supervise, then engaged in pursuit of the subject in my vehicle. Unfortunately, she left the road and ran into the woods at the end of the street. I exited the vehicle and continued pursuit on foot. In the dark, I was unable to locate her. I returned to my vehicle and engaged in a search of the area. I was still looking when the call came in. When Astoria Police contacted Campus Security, I was the first to respond. I confirmed the victim in question was Elizabeth Leanne Miller, Astoria College student. As soon as I was relieved at the scene I returned to campus to alert her next-of-kin."

"Meaning me," I retorted. "You came here. You dragged me to the Counseling Center, and you didn't bother to tell me you were one of the last people to see her alive, that she was messed up, that she begged for me!"

"You were in no shape to hear it." He looked me up and down as if to emphasize his point.

I reared back to hit him again. This time Jay saw it coming, catching my arm and pulling me into him so my fist was trapped against his chest beneath his hand. Startled, I dropped my bag. "Do *not* do that again, Callie," he said through gritted teeth. "I don't care how pissed you are. You cannot go around hitting people, especially people bigger and stronger than you, and expect there to be no consequences."

"I guess there's no rule against physically stopping a student from hurting someone else, then." We were close enough I was spitting the words in his face. "Just themselves."

"Of course there is," he hissed, shoving me away from him as he released my arm. "I stopped you because I don't want you to get in trouble. To hell with me."

"You got that right."

"You're already in enough trouble, Callie." He stepped as close to me as he dared, dropping his voice. "I know no one ran you off the road the other morning. I've been looking for you ever since I saw Brighton's report this afternoon. Someone is going to figure out you faked it, and when they do, they're going to know you cut yourself up to do it. What were you thinking?"

"I was thinking that I am the *only* person who cares about finding out what really happened to Izzy."

Jay shook his head. "What are you talking about? You know what happened. She was hit by a car. It's terrible, and eventually we will find the driver, but that's something you need to leave to the professionals."

"I'm not looking for who hit her," I snapped. "I'm looking for the person responsible for putting her out on that road when she was too messed up to take care of herself. I'm after the person who put her in front of the car."

Jay cocked his head to one side. "What—exactly—do you *think* happened?"

Anger got the better of me, and the words were flowing out of me before I could stop them. "Tell me something, Jay, have you *ever* known Izzy to get drunk? Have you ever seen Izzy even a little tipsy?"

"No. But that doesn't change anything."

"Of course it does."

A muscle in his jaw twitched with strained patience. "You weren't there. She was definitely drunk. I saw her."

"You don't know what you saw!" I closed the gap between us, whisper to make sure no one else could hear me. "She was drugged, Jay. Someone drugged her. She could have been raped. Then you let her run off into the night when she didn't even know where she was."

For the first time since I'd met him, Jay was stunned speechless. I watched the horror in his eyes as the meaning of my words clicked into place. "How do you know that?"

He believed me. I could see it all over his face.

"I just do." I took a step back, an angry but triumphant smile playing over my lips. "And pretty soon, I'm going to prove it."

When his eyes narrowed, I realized, belatedly, that I had overplayed my hand. In my anger, I'd said too much. I could tell by the way Jay's eyes flicked over me—my bag, my shoes, my clothes—that he was looking for looking for some indication of how I'd come to know what I did. He wanted to know what I'd been up to the last few days. If I wasn't careful, he would figure out where I'd gotten my information. I had to get away before I gave anything else away.

"I have to go." I grabbed my bag and headed for the door.

Callie, stop." He followed, hot on my heels. "Let me help you. Come on. There's got to be something I can do."

"Do?" I pushed past him, heading for the door. "You can stay out of my damned way."

I was at the top of the stairs when I heard Jay open the door. "Callie!"

I ignored him. I needed to lock myself in my room until he went away. I'd had all I could stand of Jay and his patronizing, holier-than-thou savior complex. Izzy was proof positive that even a guy like Jay, a guy who made it his life's work to rescue kittens from trees and help old ladies cross the street, was no remedy for the dangers of our ugly world. In the end, the only person you could count on to save you was yourself.

I reached the door and fumbled with the lock, Jay hot on my

heels. He'd gotten over being surprised by my revelations and now seemed determined to get information out of me. Hell would freeze over before I let him get to Gloria before I could. The lock finally gave and I yanked the door open, stepping inside.

As the bright overhead lights flickered to life, I saw the reddish brown marks on the wall above Izzy's bed, but my brain refused to register them as words. Blinking in shock, the only thing that shook me out of my stunned state was the feeling of Jay grabbing me as he dragged me out of the room and into the hallway. The room began to spin again and my knees buckled as I finally unscrambled what I was seeing.

"HELP ME, CALLIE," was written on the wall in large letters. And despite Izzy being nothing more than a ghost now, she'd somehow managed to leave me a message written in her own blood.

47.

Jay struggled to hold me up, bracing himself against the hallway wall to keep from falling under my weight. His face was bent over mine so that he looked at me upside down, which was disorienting. I heard him calling my name from far away, the words arriving slightly after his lips formed them, like watching a movie with the sound slightly out of sync.

"I'm here." I tried to stand on my own legs, but they didn't want to support me yet. "I'm here."

"I'm going to put you down, okay?"

I nodded. Jay lowered me to the floor, then stepped around me, striding into the room. I sat in the hallway for a handful of seconds that seemed to pour past me like thick syrup, while I breathed slowly in and out. As soon as I thought I could move, I forced myself to my feet and stumbled back to my door. My body was weird and heavy and my field of vision tilted a little as though rocking with a gentle current, but I didn't think I'd faint.

Jay seemed to be purposefully trying to take up space in the doorway to block my view. "Move, Jay," I demanded, disappointed by how weak and hoarse my voice sounded. "Move," I said again with more force. He stepped a little farther into the room, clearing the way for me.

The message was even more grotesque on closer examination. The words glistened wetly against the wall, bright except for the edges, which seemed to have dried a flakey brownish-red. Each letter was shakily formed, as though they'd been drawn on in haste

435

by blood-coated fingers. If you looked closely, an occasional partial fingerprint graced a smeared stroke here and there.

A huge pool of the brownish-red liquid gleamed from the middle of Izzy's mattress. It looked as though someone had bled out on the bed, the blood left seeping into the otherwise pristine blue-and-silver blanket. I gripped the doorframe with one hand as I clutched at my stomach, doubled over in dry heaves.

Jay turned back to me and put his hands on my shoulders to steady me, and I grabbed onto him. The heaving gave way to uncontrollable sobs bubbling up from somewhere deep inside me. I heard a terrible choking sound, and it took a few minutes to realize it was coming from me. Some small part of me knew that I didn't want Jay, of all people, to hold me, but that part wasn't really in the driver's seat at the moment. I wasn't even sure any part of me was.

I knew things were happening around me, but it was like hearing a television on in another room. I dimly heard a girl's voice cry "Oh my God!" from the hallway. I noticed Jay talking to someone over my head, but it barely touched me. Instead, I floated away from my body as he hugged me tight, unable to stop the onslaught of anguish that continued to crest over me, wave upon wave. It seemed to go on and on.

When I finally got myself together, I found the door closed and Jenna standing in the middle of my room, staring at the letters. When I pushed Jay gently away from me, he frowned, but let me go. I moved toward my bed, taking a seat on the edge as I wiped at my face with my sleeve.

Jay pulled his walkie-talkie out of his belt and began talking to someone. He was speaking so quietly I couldn't make out his words. Jenna moved closer to Izzy's bed. After a moment, she bent to pick up something from the floor. She held it gingerly, between her fingertips, but I couldn't quite make it out.

Jay holstered the walkie-talkie and moved toward Jenna to get a better look at what was in her hand. I wanted to know what they were looking at, but I wasn't sure I could move.

As I stared at the horror show my room had become, it hit me with startling clarity that the jig was up. I couldn't hide Izzy's attempts to communicate with me anymore. I wondered if she wanted it that way, if that was the impetus for such a brutal and obvious message. She knew it wouldn't be easily hidden. She'd been so quiet lately; I hadn't been prepared. I thought she'd been leaving me alone because I was on the right track. Now I wondered if all this hadn't been another revenge scheme I hadn't seen coming.

I'd have to tell them everyone now. *Next stop, mental hospital*, I mused. *But maybe that's what Izzy wants. Maybe that's the price I pay for not being there when she needed me.* If it was, I'd pay it. It was better than I deserved.

Jenna's rising voice shook me out of my reverie. "—can't believe anyone would do this to her," she argued. "I mean, I've overheard people saying things, really mean stuff, and I've talked to them about it, especially my residents, but I never thought... Who would do this? I can't imagine a single student here could be so cruel."

Jay's laugh was like ice. "I can, and Jenna, if you can't, you're even more naïve than I thought." Jenna shrank back from the unexpected insult. "I'll kill whoever did this," he added, almost conversationally. "I'll kill them."

"You can't kill someone who's already dead, Jay."

Jay turned toward me sharply. The rage playing over his features made him seem dark and threatening. *That's the face of war*, I realized suddenly. I wondered if I had one, too.

"What are you talking about, Callie?"

"It's Izzy." I gestured at the wall.

Shut up! They're going to think you're crazy, the voice inside pleaded.

They're probably right.

Jay and Jenna stared at me in horror. "What did you say?" Jenna whispered.

I tried again. "It's Izzy." My tone was tired, matter-of-fact. Now that I'd started talking, I couldn't seem to stop myself. "She's been communicating with me. She needs my help. I guess I wasn't moving fast enough to suit her."

The glances Jay and Jenna exchanged spoke volumes. Sadness, pity, and horror chased each other across Jenna's face in rapid rotation. Jay, on the other hand, looked murderous.

"When you say communicating with you," he said slowly, "you mean this isn't the first time?"

"No." I shook my head carefully. It felt like it was full of sand. "She's tried a couple of different things, though nothing like this." I pointed at the bloody words.

Jenna started to say something, but Jay reached over and grabbed her arm, shaking his head at her sharply.

"When did this start?"

"A few weeks ago," I said, thinking back. The voice in my head continued begging me to stop talking, but I found it surprisingly easy to ignore. "Thursday night. No, Friday morning."

"What happened? Exactly?"

"I heard someone behind me. I turned around and it was Izzy. She was sitting on the bed. She walked over to her dresser—" I gestured toward it "—picked up a tube of lipstick, and wrote 'HELP ME' on the mirror." I smiled slightly at the memory. It seemed so kind, compared to tonight's gory directness. "Then she disappeared. At least I think she did. I passed out cold. When I woke up she was gone. I think she disappeared in front of me, but I'm not positive."

Jay thought for a few minutes. "The morning after I brought you back from the park?"

"Yep."

"Any other times?"

"Any other times I've seen Izzy?" He nodded. "No. I mean, she picked out some clothes for me, but I didn't wear them."

This revelation seemed to jolt Jenna into action. "Izzy picked out your clothes?"

"Well, I didn't *see* her do it," I explained in a tired voice. "But you know Izzy, she's always trying to tell me what to wear. I went out for a while one morning, and when I came back there was an outfit laid out on her bed for me. Right after I found it, Colin called and asked me to the movies. I guess Izzy wanted me to wear it, but I never let her dress me when she was alive and I'm not about to start now. I left it there, but she must have moved it because it was gone when I came back."

I tried to remember what else Izzy had done. "She moved things around the room," I added after a moment. "Oh! The window. She broke the window. I think."

The world had been slowing coming back into focus as they grilled me. Suddenly, I was feeling acutely aware of how batcrap out of my mind I sounded. Cold fear seized me as I took in the Jenna's worried expression. My eyes flicked to Jay's face, but he seemed strangely calm and controlled. Maybe he believed me. Colin had. I refocused my efforts on Jenna.

"I know it sounds insane, Jenna," I said in my most reasonable voice. "My first thought was that I was ready for a rubber room. But the person who hit Izzy was never caught. No one really knows what happened to her that night. And she wants me to figure it out. She needs me to do this so she can finally rest in peace."

"Callie, the window was an accident. And those other things…" Jenna trailed off, trying to lead me to a rational conclusion.

I shook my head, refusing to listen. "No. There is no way it could be someone else. The door was locked every time. I made sure. It's Izzy." My words fell quickly now, urgency taking over. I needed them to believe me. "She's asking me because she knows I am the only one who loves her enough to believe her and help her."

Jenna's eyes were as round as saucers. She seemed, for once, completely at a loss for words. I turned to Jay. "You believe me, don't you? You believe I'm not crazy, that Izzy needs me?"

"I don't think you're crazy at all."

Relief flooded me. "Really?"

Jay held out his hand, something small dangling from the tips of his fingers. It was a tube of oil paint, which had been squeezed mostly empty, its mouth smeared with a drying reddish brown. As I stared at it uncomprehendingly, Jay continued. "I think someone has been torturing you, trying to make you think Izzy is communicating with you."

"No." My fingers curled at my sides, trying to stop my hands from shaking.

Jay took a step forward, the paint tube still in his grip. "Yes, Callie. You're not crazy, but someone has been trying hard to make you crazy." I watched as he pulled a plastic bag from a small container on his belt, then slipped the tube inside. "When I find out who it is, they are going to be very sorry."

48.

The single, solitary good thing about the entire 'bloody wall' debacle was that Jay happened to be the only Campus Security officer on duty at the time because someone else had called in sick. On our tiny, sleepy campus, two officers were usually enough, but no one really counted on my nutso crap keeping everyone busier than usual. Jay called dispatch and asked them to call in after-hours janitorial staff to come clean my room. I heard him arguing with someone, but I didn't pay much attention, lost in a morass of mixed emotions.

It couldn't all be fake. Maybe someone could have broken the window or moved my clothes around, but I didn't believe it. Izzy had done all those things, from decorating the room to writing on the mirror. Whoever had pulled this stunt with the paint wanted to hurt me and had picked a crude, though obvious, method. I suspected Gloria immediately, wondering if Shannen had run straight to her for protection. After learning Gloria had drugged Bethany and Izzy, I certainly wouldn't put it past her.

Gloria might be able to fake a stunt like this, but I had something else, something I'd held back from Jay and Jenna. I knew, in a visceral way I couldn't in words, that the visions Izzy had shared with me were real. I felt it, in the same way I felt my feet on the ground but could not describe the feeling of gravity holding me to it.

The visions had guided me every step of the way. They were one of the few methods Izzy had to help me catch the people responsible, even if it meant showing me things about herself she might have liked to keep private. I hadn't made the visions up. They were real, and so was Izzy. She might not be part of this world anymore, but she was still real.

Given how badly Jay and Jenna reacted to the mere suggestion Izzy was communicating me with, I wasn't about to tell them I'd been having out-of-body experiences where Izzy led me on vision quests for vengeance. They'd both tiptoed around me since I'd declared I was still communicating with Izzy, as though they were afraid to spook me.

Spook me? What a laugh. I watched Jay pretend to examine the gruesome display for the umpteenth time to avoid meeting my gaze. *I'm already spooked.*

Jenna disappeared for a few minutes. When she came back, my AD Mike and the perpetually frowning AD of Colin's complex, Audrey, were right behind her. They took me into the small lounge at the end of the hallway and closed the fire doors for privacy, stationing Jenna at the top of the stairs while they trusted Jay to stop anyone from entering from the hallway.

"What are you doing here?" I asked as I took a seat on one of the worn lounge couches.

"We're here to help you," Mike said gently.

Audrey rolled her eyes. "I'm the AD-on-Duty. I'm here to deal with all of this."

Great. One ally, one skeptic. I guess that was how my whole evening was going to go.

Mike and Audrey made me repeat my story in painstaking detail. No longer drowning in a sea of raw emotion, I chose my words carefully. With the barest of editing, I couched the same facts in a more doubtful hue. With a few nudges around the edges, I managed to sound a lot more like the victim of a horrible prank than a certifiable lunatic. Mike looked increasingly alarmed with every word, but Audrey eyed me with a vague suspicion. I could tell she was wondering if I hadn't painted the wall myself, one more outrageous act from an unstable, attention-seeking student. Luckily, Mike was in complete agreement with Jay. His primary concern was that I hadn't shared my "ongoing harassment" with Jenna or anyone else.

As I finished talking, Jenna poked her head in. "There's someone here to see you." She glanced at Mike for confirmation. He nodded and she opened the door wider, allowing Colin into the room.

I immediately burst into tears when I saw the concerned expression on his face. He walked directly to the couch and sat down next to me, wrapping his arms around me as I cried into his shoulder. Audrey and Mike moved to the door so they could confer quietly with Jenna.

When I stopped blubbering, I looked into his eyes, which were full of sorrow. "What are you doing here?"

"Jenna." Colin pushed my limp hair off my face with a pained expression. "Mike told her to call a support person for you. She called me."

"And you came."

"She told me what happened," he said, studying my face. "Including the part where you slapped Jay in front of half the building."

"Oh God," I breathed, and he chuckled nervously.

"Remind me to never unleash your fury on someone else again," he muttered, giving me a small squeeze. The look on his face told me that while all wasn't quite right with us, he also didn't think anything was going on between Jay and me anymore.

"She also told me about the message." He dropped his voice. "Do you really think Izzy did that?"

I looked at him wonderingly. Despite everything, he'd never stopped believing me. It was more than I deserved.

"No," I whispered quickly. "But I have a couple of ideas."

"Who?"

I gave my head the slightest of shakes as Audrey and Mike approached us, Jenna in tow. "Later." Jenna gave me a knowing look and smiled happily. I had to give her points for convincing Colin to come. Maybe all her fast-talking was productive if aimed in the right direction.

"Colin," Audrey began, her tone authoritative and unyielding, "have you ever seen any of these alleged messages?"

He glanced quickly at me. "I was here when the window broke."

Please don't mention the book whirlwind, I begged silently in my head. Colin must have read my mind, because he paused for a moment, as if deep in thought. "I can't think of anything else."

"You're sure?" Audrey seemed dubious about my entire story.

"Yes," Colin nodded for emphasis.

Audrey shifted her attention to me. "And there isn't anyone

else who can corroborate any of this supposed harassment?"

"No." I swallowed hard. Jay, Jenna, Mike, hell even Colin might all feel bad for me, but I could tell Audrey was not buying anything we were saying.

"Who do you think would do this to Callie?" Colin asked, trying to shift the focus off me. I made a mental note to add "crafty" to the list of adjectives I could apply to my boyfriend.

If he still wants to be my boyfriend. I was afraid to hope for it, but I snaked my arm around his waist, and he squeezed mine in return.

"We were hoping you could tell us." Audrey seemed to know we were holding out on her. I tried to keep my face innocent as I shrugged morosely.

Before she could press us further, we were saved by Mike, who sighed with exasperation. "Audrey, she obviously doesn't know." He flung his hands up at her. "This isn't the time for the Spanish Inquisition. She thought they were messages from…from Izzy."

"If she had any idea, she'd tell us. Wouldn't you, Callie?" Mike said, turning back to me. I nodded adamantly.

He gave Audrey a pointed look, as if to say, *If she's that crazy, you think she has any idea what's actually going on*? Under any other circumstances I might have objected, but right now insane was working for me, so I let it go.

Audrey rubbed her face with her hands, recognizing she wasn't getting anywhere. "Fine, Mike. Your complex, your resident. Call me if you need anything else."

Mike sighed and sat down next to us as the door closed on

Audrey's retreating form.

"I wish you'd come to me with this," Mike said sternly. "I cannot believe things have gotten so out of hand. I'm incredibly discouraged anyone in our community would take advantage of your emotional state this way. I promise that as soon as we find out who is responsible, they will be dealt with accordingly." He patted my knee. "I don't know how long it's going to take to get your room fixed, *again*, but you can be sure we don't expect you to pay for the damage."

I gave him a small smile. "Thank you. Really."

"You're destroying my budget, though, just so you know." Mike rubbed his face as he stood to leave. "Colin, can she stay with you tonight while we clean her room?" His gaze shifted quickly back to me. "If that's okay with you?"

"If she wants to stay with me, she's welcome to," Colin said, looking at me, our questionable relationship status hanging in the air.

My heart leapt. "I'd like that." Whatever problems we were having as a couple, Colin didn't seem to think they were unresolvable anymore. "Can I grab some of my things?"

"Sure, but try not to move too much around," Mike said. "This situation has gotten serious enough I suspect we will have the Astoria P.D. come out and take pictures, pull some prints."

"Umm, wow, okay. I'll be careful."

"Don't look so surprised," he said, a note of warning in his voice. "Izzy's death remains unresolved, and this is the second major instance of property damage directed at you. When we find out who is responsible, staying in school is going to be the least of their

447

problems. So if you know anything—" He let the sentence hang there, unfinished.

"If I knew anything, I'd tell you," I said, lying smoothly. I knew I would eventually have to come clean, but for now, I couldn't give more away. Not when I was so close. I only needed a few more pieces of evidence, and then I'd tell Mike everything.

Colin and I went to get my things. Jay was in my room, standing next to Izzy's bed and staring at the wall with a small notepad in his hand. "I was just finishing up…" Jay flipped the notepad shut and shoved it into his breast pocket. Jay and Colin exchanged nods of acknowledgement. "Are you going to stay with Colin for the night?"

"Umm, yeah." Time to get us out of here before things got weird again. The faster, the better. "Colin, can you get my laptop?"

Colin didn't respond and I glanced at him. He stood in the middle of the room, gaping at the painted message. I walked over and put my hand delicately on his arm.

"It's paint, Colin."

"It looks real."

"It was supposed to." Jay's expression was grim. "I don't think they left that paint tube on purpose," he added, directing the statement to me. "Which was a huge mistake on their part, because while they did a good job of smearing the prints up there—" he jabbed a finger at the wall before holding up the paint tube, encased in a plastic baggie "—this probably has pristine prints."

"We're going to find out who's been doing this to you if we have to question every student who was in your building tonight." It was a tone that brooked no resistance, and I nodded briefly at him. I hoped it wouldn't come to that; it wasn't going to win me popularity points with my classmates.

Colin drew a shaky breath and turned to me. "Let's get you outta here."

Jay started toward the door, then turned back. "Hey, Colin? Take care of her."

"I will," Colin said without looking up.

Jay glanced at me with a kind of sad resolve. Then he left.

"Men," I muttered, shoving clothes into my bag. "I am capable of taking care of myself, you know."

Colin set the laptop bag down on the floor next to me and wrapped his arms around my waist. "Shh. Let me take of you tonight, and tomorrow you can go back to being a leg-sweeping, punch-throwing warrior princess. Deal?" He gave me a lopsided smile.

"Deal."

I followed Colin out of my room, closing the door behind me. As I did, I couldn't help but reflect on the resiliency of the human heart. Sometimes all it took was knowing that someone, even one person, found you lovable to turn everything around, to give you a glimmer of hope in the darkness. Even after a horrific day full of disappointment and betrayal by people I'd thought of as friends, thanks to Colin, I could still find a reason to smile.

49.

My walk with Colin across campus was silent and sweet, but as the minutes ticked by the more it was apparent we needed to clear the air. Preferably, though, in private.

"So…" Colin began as I settled myself onto the loveseat in his room.

"So…" I repeated, nodding in acknowledgement of our awkward situation.

"I wanted to say how sorry—" He began, talking over me as I said, "Colin, you have no idea how sorry I—"

"Me first," he argued.

"No. Me first. Definitely me first." He made a sweeping gesture at me, indicating I had the floor. "Colin, nothing happened between Jay and me." He opened his mouth to talk, but I held up my hand. "All the same, you weren't wrong to be suspicious and I'm sorry for my part in that. My relationship with Jay has always been complicated. I'm not going to deny that."

Panic edged into my voice as his face turned stormy. "The thing you have to understand is that we can never go fifteen minutes without one of us ripping into the other. That might appeal to some girls, but I'm not one of them. I hate fighting. I don't want the drama."

He gave me a doubtful look, but I shook my head. "You're catching me at a strange point in my life. Most of the time, I'm the boring one, especially compared to…"

Colin sighed. "Compared to Izzy?" He got up from his desk

chair and squeezed in next to me on the loveseat. "You've got to stop comparing yourself to her." He reached up, cupping my face in his hand. "I'm the last person you have to convince of your differences, despite the things I've said."

I opened my mouth, but he shook his head. "No. Now it's my turn. I have been a complete jerk. I cannot believe you're speaking to me after the crappy things I said. The fact that you're still willing to even breathe in my direction is a testament to how un-Izzy you are." He tilted his head toward me, our foreheads touching.

"Callie, sometimes I'm afraid of being left behind again. My birth mom. Izzy. But I love you. I really do." His eyes were pleading and sincere, the color of the sky wiped clean after a long rain. "I have been terrible at showing it, but I swear I'll do better."

"I love you, too," I whispered. I placed my hand on his chest, feeling his heart beating beneath it. He pulled me slowly toward him and placed a gentle kiss on my lips. I snaked my hands up behind his head, pulling him closer. He kept his lips on my mouth, kissing me long and deep. I relaxed into him, closing my eyes as I rested my head against the crook of his neck, feeling safe and at peace for the first time in days. My limbs grew heavy, but I didn't pull away, unwilling to let him go. Colin seemed to feel the same. Eventually we fell asleep that way, bodies awkwardly entwined on the tiny couch.

When I woke up, I extracted myself from his arms and snuck across the hall to use the bathroom and brush my teeth. I'd fallen asleep with my contacts in again and spent a full ten minutes peeling them off my eyeballs. Guess I was stuck in my glasses for the day.

When I got back, Colin was at his desk bent over his laptop. He gave me a sleepy smile as I closed the door.

"Hey." I dug around in my bag for a clean shirt while I talked. "Did I wake you?"

"Yeah," he said yawning, "but that's okay."

"Sorry."

I changed my shirt, turning my back slightly to Colin in a half-hearted attempt at modesty. I turned back to find him watching me, and blushed. He smiled broadly in return. "Don't be."

I busied myself getting ready to hide my smile, pulling out my toiletries to keep my hands occupied. As much as I wanted to go back to making out, there was still a lot I needed to do. He moved to the loveseat, and I scooted over to make room for him. "Can I ask you something?"

"Anything."

"You said last night you didn't think Izzy pulled the stunt with the paint."

I shook my head. "It's not Izzy's style."

"But you have someone specific in mind," he eyed me closely, "don't you?"

I dropped my lotion back into my bag and turned my full attention to him, underscoring my seriousness. "I have two, maybe three solid suspects," I admitted, and felt a little pleased at his astonishment.

"Who?"

"If I tell you, you have to promise you're not going to do anything."

"No." He shook his head. "No way." He jumped up, pacing around the room. "You cannot seriously think you can tell me who is screwing with you and expect me to do nothing about it."

"Colin, you have to promise, or I'm not going to tell you."

He heard the warning in my voice and threw his hands up. "Alright," he said, his face tightening.

I narrowed my eyes at him. "Nope, I don't believe you." I turned to reach for my shoes.

"Callie—"

"Callie what, exactly?" I was mildly amused that after everything I'd been through in the last few days, Colin believed he could cow me.

"Nothing." He collapsed back onto the loveseat next to me, flinging an arm over his eyes. "Callie nothing. Callie, I'll-do-whatever-you-want-me-to-because-I-am-totally-in-love-with-you-and-you-know-it-so-stop-torturing-me." He peeked at me from beneath his arm.

I grinned at him as I pulled on one of my Doc Martens but said nothing, enjoying the moment.

"So? Do I get to know, or do I have to promise something besides my whole heart and unwavering devotion?"

I giggled. "That'll do, I suppose."

He waved his hand in a get-on-with-it motion, and my good humor drained away as I organized my thoughts. "My guesses—" I said, bending over to pull on the second boot "—are, in order of least to most likely: Will Cordano, Shannen Pomerantz, or Gloria Capreni."

"You can't be serious. I know both those girls. They aren't capable of anything this morbid."

I gave him a measured look. "They're capable of a whole lot more than you can imagine."

"Wait. Who is Will Cordano?"

"You remember the guy Izzy was dancing with?" I gave him a smug smile.

"You found out who he is?" he looked me up and down, clearly impressed.

"I found out a lot of things in the last week." I began filling him in on my confrontation with Will, my conversations with Bethany and Shannen, and my plan to corner Gloria.

When I was finished, I sat back and watched Colin chew over everything. "It is truly terrifying what you can accomplish in a week," he finally muttered. "Izzy was drugged. That explains her behavior that night." He ran a hand through his hair, and a little bit stuck up in an uncharacteristically messy spike in the back than before. "Now I feel even worse that I wasn't sober enough to help her."

"It's not your fault, "I said gently, rubbing his arm. "If Jay couldn't stop her, I'm not sure anyone could."

"Yeah." His smile was pained. "I think I owe Jay an apology, too."

"I wouldn't worry about it," I said, mentally tallying up the apologies Jay owed Colin. I glanced at the clock. "We're going to be late." I got up to gather my things for class.

"You're sure she didn't sleep with him?" Colin had a faraway look in his eyes I'd never seen before.

"Izzy and Will?" I shook my head. "Absolutely not."

I dug around in the bottom of my bag until I found my painkillers and slipped them in my pocket. My shoulder hurt worse than ever. I made a mental note to stop by the Health Center between classes.

Colin still hadn't moved from the couch, lost in thought. I knelt in front of him, taking his hands in mine. "I saw the bite mark on Will's skin myself. That was a seriously vicious wound. And it confirms what Izzy has shown me. She came to before anything serious happened, and she fought as hard as she could. Her dad would have been proud."

Colin's head bobbed up and down, but I wasn't sure he heard me. I dropped his hands and picked up my bag. His voice was quiet when he spoke again. "I still can't believe she can show you things that happened while she was alive, things you weren't there for."

"I don't get the impression she can always choose what I see," I said as I reflected on the memories. "I think it's partly her, partly whatever I'm thinking about, and something…else." I shrugged. "Either way, I'm sure there is plenty she wishes she could tell me. It just doesn't seem like either of us have much control."

He nodded, but I wasn't sure he was really listening to me. He was lost in memories of his own, probably of Izzy. I couldn't say I blamed him. I knew it would take Colin a little while to digest everything. I was still working on it. At least now we had each other to lean on in the process.

"Now," I said, turning back to him. "Are you planning to go to class with your hair sticking up like Alfalfa from *The Little Rascals*? Because you know, that's a valid fashion choice." Colin scowled and chucked a pillow at me, but he got up and headed across the hall to fix his hair.

50.

Together, we made it through our classes. We went to the cafeteria together, but neither of us felt much like eating. We sat quietly together, picking at pizza for a while before giving up.

"I still can't believe Gloria would do something like this," he said for the third time.

"Then you really underestimate the ways women can be cruel to one another." I peeled a piece of pepperoni off the pizza and popped it in my mouth.

"But over me? I mean, I'll admit that I knew she seemed interested, but I was so into Izzy, it never really made much of an impact." He shoved the pizza away. "She's got my full attention now."

We went over my plan to get even as we walked slowly back to my building, hand-in-hand. I noticed the occasional surprised glance and whisper, but I ignored it. With Colin by my side, I felt like I was right where I was supposed to be.

I could always try going straight to the administration with Shannen and Bethany's stories, but Colin and I both agreed that, given recent events, my credibility was shaky. Neither one of us felt sure anyone would believe me. I thought Shannen and Bethany would both cave if questioned directly, but it wasn't a hundred percent and no one was going to act on my word alone. Mike and Jay might support me, but Audrey's scrutiny over the paint incident had convinced me I needed more to get real attention from the administration. I needed something concrete and irrefutable before I brought the hammer down on Gloria. I was only going to get one shot at it, so I had to get it right.

My plan for Gloria was simple and direct. I was going to confront Gloria, and Shannen if she was present, in their room. If I got into trouble, Colin would be my backup. He wouldn't be with me, but he insisted on being close by while it played out in case I needed him. I had to hope Gloria was as stupid as Will had been. It was a risky move, but it was all I had. That meant it had to come as a surprise, and the longer I waited the less likely that was. Shannen and Bethany already knew I was looking for Gloria. It was only a matter of time before one of them let it slip. With each step we took closer to Alder, my adrenaline crept higher.

"Ready?" Colin asked me as we reached the entrance.

My heart pounded. "As much as I'll ever be."

When we entered the building, Colin parked himself in the lounge, pretending to read a book as I headed for 103. I knocked sharply on the door, and it swung it open immediately.

As soon as Shannen saw my face, she turned the color of paper. "Where's Gloria?" My tone was light and friendly, but Shannen cowered beneath my cold gaze.

"Bathroom," she mumbled, pointing down the hall. It took me less than half a second to decide to use the change of setting to my advantage. In the middle of the day I felt pretty sure no one else would be in there, so I took a chance and headed down the hall, sliding my cell phone into my pocket as I went.

Swinging the door wide, I heard one of the showers running. I quickly confirmed the stalls were empty, then planted myself between the showers and the exit. *Now or never*, I told myself as the water cut off.

Gloria strolled out of the changing area wrapped in a plush white towel, another one wrapped around her head.

"Hey," she said as she wiped steam from the mirror above the sink, as if I accosted her in the bathroom on a routine basis. "Are you looking for me?" She glanced at me in the mirror's reflection, pretending to examine the pores in her nose.

"You know I am."

"Shannen might have mentioned it," she mused, opening a large bag of cosmetics and extracting a bottle of base.

Then Shannen has even less sense than I thought. "Did she tell you why?"

Gloria's reflection gave me a polite smile. "She said something, but you know how it is with Shannen. She can be *so* melodramatic." She shrugged slightly. "It wasn't very nice; I can tell you that much." She exchanged the bottle of base for a compact of powder.

Might as well cut to the chase. "I know you drugged Izzy. And Bethany, for that matter, but it's Izzy I'm concerned with."

"Of course you are." Gloria turned toward me and placing her hands on her hips. "Everyone knows how obsessed you are with your friend's death." She emphasized *friend* like it was synonymous with *prostitute*. Anger rolled through me like thunder, but said nothing, hoping she'd dig her own grave.

"I hear you've even taken to destroying property and assaulting Campus Security officers." She clucked her tongue disapprovingly at me. "That's the sort of thing that can get you kicked out of school, you know." She gave me a solemn look that reeked of faux concern. "It certainly hurts your credibility with, well, anyone that matters."

I wanted to slap the smug look right off her stupid face, but instead I chose my next words carefully. "If these allegations hung on my word alone, I'd probably be worried. Luckily, there are corroborating witnesses."

Gloria rolled her eyes. "Who? Bethany, the drunkatron, and Shannen, the criminally weak-willed? As if they'd *ever* say anything I didn't want them to. And like you, Bethany's reputation precedes her." Gloria smirked at me. "So I don't know what you're talking about. But even if I did—" she shifted her gaze back to her reflection with an air of complete unconcern "—you'd never be able to prove it." She shot me a triumphant look in the mirror as she leaned forward, turning her face from one side to the other as she swept blush on her cheekbones.

I took a menacing step toward her. "Gloria, do you know what a tox screen is?" Gloria's reflection paled slightly underneath her dark make-up. Sensing my opportunity, I pressed on. "They performed one on Izzy as part of her autopsy. Standard procedure."

"And? Izzy was drunk."

"She was a little more than drunk," I replied, taking another step toward her. "Her tox screen came up positive for ecstasy. It's a funny little drug, MDMA. Since it's not regulated, each time it's made it's slightly different."

Gloria froze in place, interest in her make-up forgotten. I smiled wickedly as I inched forward. I needed to be close enough that the note-taking software would pick up her response. "Did you know it shows up for a long time after you've taken it?"

Gloria turned toward me slowly, and I prayed that she knew even less than I had about drug detection and biochemistry two days ago.

"With a single strand of hair," I said slowly, "you can detect it for years after someone's been dosed. And with the use of chromatographic analysis, they can actually tell if two people took E made at the same time by the same manufacturer." This was a complete lie, but as I watched Gloria press her fingernails into her palms so hard I thought she might break the skin, I knew she believed me.

"It's kind of like a fingerprint." I held up a finger in illustration. "Completely unique. I wonder what will happen when they test the drunkatron's hair against the sample they have from Izzy." I paused, letting my words sink in. "You think they'll match?"

"You bitch!" she snarled, closing the space between us. She was as tall as me, but my boots gave me an extra half-inch and I used my slight height advantage to loom over her.

"No, you're the bitch. You drugged your friends. You got one of them killed. And now you're going to get *exactly* what you deserve."

For a moment Gloria stared at me, seething, and I stared in return. *Please let this work*, I prayed slightly as my chest heaved with a mixture of anger, fear, and nervousness. *Please God, if you're out there, let this work.*

For Izzy.

As if the universe heard me, Gloria's eyes widened, and I knew I'd won. She scuttled around me, trying to escape. I grabbed her by the arm almost leisurely, dragging her back.

"What I want to know, Gloria, is why?" I asked, shaking her. "Why did you do it?"

I watched the fear in her eyes harden into something icy and hateful. "Because Izzy was a slut who couldn't keep her hands to herself." Spittle foam flew from her lips as she went on. "Every time I met a guy I liked, Izzy would come along and drag them off to her lair to keep on a leash. She never wanted them. She just didn't want me to have them."

It was so absurd I couldn't help but laugh. "Gloria, you were so far off Izzy's radar, she barely knew you were alive. She never thought of you as a threat. As far as Izzy was concerned, you didn't even play at her level."

"I guess she underestimated me then, didn't she?" Gloria countered, wrenching her arm from my grip. "Let that be a lesson to you. Izzy is dead, and you're about to get kicked out for being violent and unstable. You lose. I win."

I shook my head as I reached into my pocket and removed my cell phone, unable to process how one girl's pettiness and cruelty could destroy an entire life. "You're completely insane," I said as I stopped the recording. "And now I have the recording to prove it." I wiggled the phone at her before shoving it deep in my pocket.

High on my triumph, I didn't register the fear falling across Gloria's face. She lunged for me, clawing at my pocket as she tried to retrieve the phone. The bathroom tile was slick with steam and I felt my boots sliding out from under me as I tumbled backwards under her weight. I flailed for something to grab hold of, but my head slammed against the cubby behind me. Gloria hung on, riding me down so that her weight was on top of me when I hit the floor, my head rebounding off the hard surface as I landed flat on my back.

I reached up, swatting at Gloria to keep her from getting to the phone as she scrambled above me. Grabbing my shoulders, Gloria slammed me down, using her weight for leverage. My head smacked the ground again, and the ringing in my ears sounded like the bells ringing in the tower of the bright yellow church in town. *God's lemonade stand*, I thought dizzily as my head hit the tile a third time, my phone falling from my pocket and clattering across the floor. I reached for it, but I was having a hard time coordinating my thoughts and movements. Gloria scooped it up and skittered toward the door.

The bathroom door swung open suddenly. Someone was trying to come in. The door slammed into Gloria, before bouncing closed again. It was enough to knock Gloria off her balance. She went sprawling to the floor next to me. The impact popped the phone from her grip and I dove for it. Gloria dug into my hands with her nails, breaking one as she drew blood. I wrenched the phone from her and rolled over onto my stomach to protect it from her.

Gloria flung herself on top of me, screeching. "Give it to me!"

I tucked my arms in as she dug at my sides, trying to dislodge the phone. I felt something drip past my nose and discovered the back of my head was bleeding. Gloria pressed down on top of me as she yanked at my arms, her weight making it hard to breathe. I struggled to hang on. If I passed out and she got the phone, she could claim that I had attacked her. Given my reputation, the school would probably believe her over me.

Black sparks danced across my vision. I hoped whoever had tried to open the door had gone to get help. If someone didn't show up soon, I might not make it. I shifted beneath Gloria, trying to roll her off. Gloria seemed to sense I was growing weaker, because she pressed her forearm against the back of my neck, forcing my chin up. Gloria leaned forward, pressing as hard as she could to cut off my air supply.

I'm sorry, Izzy. I writhed helplessly under Gloria, gasping for air, my hands pinned beneath me as I clutched the phone. *I tried.*

There was a loud bang as the door slammed again, then Gloria's weight disappeared off me. Rolling onto my side, I hacked and coughed, sucking in air. As my vision cleared, I couldn't believe my eyes. Gloria was pinned beneath Jenna, who had never looked more surprised and determined in her life. I saw a girl glance into the bathroom, then take off down the hallway. I hoped she was going to call Campus Security. I wanted to, but somehow I couldn't remember the number.

Colin appeared in the doorframe, falling to his knees as he pulled me into his arms.

"You're a little late," I croaked.

"Well who had the bright idea of coming into the bathroom without telling their back-up?" He touched my forehead. "You're bleeding. Are you okay?"

"We got her, Colin." I reached up to touch his face but missed by several inches. "We got her on tape."

Heavy footsteps pounded down the hallway. I tried to turn my head, but my neck was stiff and didn't want to move. The last thing I saw was the horrified look on Mike's face as I drifted away, bells still chiming loudly in my head.

51.

"Stupid, reckless, irresponsible…" I tried not to bristle as the onslaught of adjectives continued unbroken. "Not to mention dangerous! I cannot believe you did something so dangerous."

"But if I hadn't—" I reached up, touching the goose egg at the base of my skull gingerly and wincing in the pain "—you still wouldn't know what happened to Izzy."

"That is beside the point, Ms. McCayter."

"No, that's exactly the point." I looked from Dr. Yates to Mike for support. Neither seemed inclined to give it, so I pressed on.

"You have a psychopathic girl running around this campus. She drugged two students, one who died as a result." I ticked off Gloria's crimes on my fingers. "She destroyed a window, which resulted in the serious injury and brief hospitalization of a third student. She destroyed school property in order to frame that same student as mentally compromised. Then she assaulted the student when she was confronted." I leveled an even look at Dean Segurd. "Quite frankly, you're going to be lucky if you don't get sued."

Dean Segurd blanched. "I don't see why we need to involve lawyers."

"If you don't think Gloria already has a public defender on speed dial, you're crazier than I am."

Dean Segurd frowned at me, then turned to Mike. "What did the EMTs say?"

Mike frowned in my general direction. "They don't think Callie has a concussion, but they said we should keep an eye on her.

They offered to take her to the hospital, but she refused treatment."

Dean Segurd threw her hands up at me. I shrugged, careful not to move my head too much. "I've had worse. I don't need to go to the hospital."

Dean Segurd turned back to Mike. "And her stitches?"

"Despite Gloria's best efforts, the stitches in Callie's shoulder are intact." Mike gave me a once-over and pursed his lips. "She also insisted they stitch up the back of her head here even though they told her she'd probably end up with a scar."

"I'll think of it as a souvenir," I smiled pleasantly at Dean Segurd, who scowled at me.

"What about you?" Dean Segurd turned to Dr. Yates. "Do you think she needs to be hospitalized?"

Here it comes, the moment they Catch-22 me. I think I'm fine, but I also think I've been receiving missives from a dead girl. No matter which way you sliced it, now that Dr. Yates knew everything, I was royally screwed.

Dr. Yates stared at me for a long moment, then turned toward Dean Segurd. "No, I don't think she does," she said with simple finality.

I almost fell out of my chair in shock.

Dean Segurd looked equally surprised by this assessment. "Let me be clear. After all the stress and trauma Ms. McCayter has suffered in the last month, you *don't* think she needs professional psychological treatment?"

"I didn't say that," Dr. Yates replied serenely. "I think Callie has been through an enormous ordeal. Obviously she needs to be seeing someone regularly, perhaps even daily." I shot her a look of intense betrayal, but Dr. Yates ignored me. "I simply don't see why she can't do that while she stays here and completes her semester. After all—" Dr. Yates smiled slightly at me "—it's not as if she was imagining these interactions with Izzy. If Callie believed that Izzy was communicating with her with no tangible evidence, I would be deeply concerned. Unfortunately, the intense feelings of loss and guilt Callie has over Izzy's death were exacerbated by Ms. Capreni's twisted machinations."

Dr. Yates was obviously rehearsing for the inevitable fifteen minutes of fame she planned to extract when my story hit the papers. I wanted to be annoyed, but I was on such thin ice, I'd take support from anyone, regardless of their reasons. Finding no help in either physiological or psychological medicine, Dean Segurd tried one more run at me from an emotional angle.

"Are you sure you wouldn't rather take incompletes, dear?" she asked in a soothing voice. "I'm sure we could arrange something if you want to take some time away from campus."

And go where? I wondered dismally. From the look on Mike's face, it was obvious he knew what I knew: if I left Astoria, there was nowhere else for me to go.

"Thank you, Dean Segurd, for your generous offer, but I'm fine." I pushed myself out the chair carefully, moving slowly because of my injuries. "What I want most is to finish my courses so I can have a break before spring semester begins."

Dean Segurd pressed her lips together, recognizing she was in a losing battle. Nodding curtly, she was on the phone to her assistant before I'd made my exit.

Sitting in the waiting area in two matching high-backed chairs were Colin and Jay, who both greeted me with anxious looks. Colin jumped out of his chair and strode over to me, hugging me fiercely.

"Ow, Colin," I said into his shoulder.

"Sorry." He let go of me with sheepish grin. Jay eased up behind him as Mike walked out of the Dean's office, completing the circle around me.

Jay gave Mike a questioning glance, and I elbowed him lightly. "I can talk for myself, you know." Mike chuckled as Jay rolled his eyes. "I get to stay. I finish finals, I stay in school, and I come back next semester."

Colin whooped in excitement, but Jay scrutinized me. "That's it?"

"I have to see Dr. Yates a lot more often. Daily, actually." Jay coughed to cover a laugh, which made us all laugh together.

"And Gloria?" Colin inquired.

"Toast!" I cackled, turning to Mike for confirmation. "She gets expelled, right?"

Mike rubbed his face before responding. "While I am legally prohibited from commenting with specificity about any particular student's conduct record," he said, sighing, "yes, after a full hearing, she's likely to be expelled."

I held up my hand for a group high five, but Jay shook his head at me. "You're lucky that's not you."

"Luck? You call that luck?" I demanded. "That was all skill, baby." I rubbed my fingernails against my shoulder, resulting in another chorus of groaning laughter.

Colin gave my waist a gentle squeeze. "You really hit your head hard, huh?"

I narrowed my eyes at Mike. "What about the others? They're out, too, right?"

"Well, that depends on who you're talking about. We've already mandated some additional sexual assault and harassment training for the entire athletics department, and their coaches fully support us."

"Bethany is as much as victim as Izzy and it seems clear Lauren didn't know anything. Shannen…" Mike paused for a moment, considering what he could, or should, say. "It could go either way, honestly. I think it depends on whether the local DA's office wants to prosecute Gloria, and how much Shannen is willing to cooperate."

I swallowed, feeling a little let down. Not what I wanted, but I could live with it.

"What about Will Cordano?" Colin asked suddenly. I was surprised he'd remembered Will's name.

Mike frowned, directing his attention to me. "It's likely Will violated the college's sexual misconduct policy from the accounts we've gathered. Izzy was well past the point of intoxication and she obviously couldn't consent to whatever happened between them. The problem is that without Izzy to bring charges, there's no complaining witness. We can't know what happened, exactly. I don't think we can proceed without someone asking us to."

"So he gets away with it?"

"I didn't say that," Mike shuffled his feet a little. "You asked if he was going to have to leave the college. I'm saying I don't think there will be enough evidence to earn him a suspension or expulsion, but the college may choose to follow-up in other ways."

"That's complete B.S." Colin seethed. I watched in amazement as Jay nodded. I was pretty sure it was the first time they'd agreed on anything.

"It's better than nothing," I muttered. "Thank you, Mike, for everything." I leaned toward him to hug him. Mike gave me a gentle squeeze in return.

Colin and I turned to leave together. "Callie?" Mike called after me. "Next time you think there's a psychopath drugging people on campus, please come tell me instead of trying to take them on yourself. I promise I'll believe you."

Colin and I both laughed a little. As we turned to leave, I saw a look of longing pass over Jay's face, but I ignored it. Better to pretend to have never seen it. It was better this way, for both of us.

52.

The next couple of weeks passed in a kind of blur. Despite the lack of sleep and looming finals, the AC rumor mill had kicked into hyperdrive the moment Gloria was dragged from the bathroom barely covered in a towel, weeping and wailing about how it wasn't her fault, that I'd attacked her. Colin actually heard one version of the story with me at the center of an undercover investigation into an international drug smuggling ring backed by Gloria's Italian relatives in New Jersey. As far as Colin and I knew, Gloria didn't come from a family of mobsters or even New Jersey, but it was so funny neither of us contradicted it. We'd been asked not to talk to anyone until Astoria PD finished their investigation, so we kept the details of what had and hadn't actually happened to ourselves.

Colin and I ran into Jay a few times, and he was always politely distant. He seemed to have accepted Colin and me as a couple, and other than catching Jay during a couple of wistful stares, he remained friendly, but distant.

Jenna, on the other hand, seemed to believe her shining moment of wrestling prowess with Gloria meant we were destined to be friends for life. She was pretty nice, once you got past the constant babbling. I hadn't seen any of the girls from the downstairs quad, but we weren't supposed to be talking since we were all witnesses or complainants of one sort or another in the college's conduct system. I wasn't sure what I was going to say to any of them anyway, so I kept my distance.

One theme remained consistent throughout the gossip. I

emerged as the misunderstood heroine of the tale, a one-woman army of subterfuge and interrogation. I lost count of the number of people who congratulated me, intimating they'd known all along I was completely sane and on a mission to find the people who'd hurt Izzy. You would have thought, after spending the better part of the semester as the campus leper, their attention would have made me happy. Instead, I felt lonelier than ever.

Izzy hadn't said a peep since my showdown with Gloria, not even when Colin and I spent one night curled up together in my tiny twin bed. There were no visions, no dreams, no floating objects or cosmetic missives. It made me wonder if she was gone forever, and I couldn't help mourning her loss all over again. I was glad I'd kept my final promise to Izzy, but her death felt real to me now, permanent in a way it hadn't before.

Luckily, Colin was my constant companion. We were together day and night, which I'm sure made Astoria tongues wag, but it was nice. We spent most of our time watching TV and listening to music, anything to distract me from the Izzy-shaped hole in my life. He kept me awake while I finished my final papers and helped me study for finals. All in all, he was a model boyfriend.

I was still planning to stay on campus for Winter Break, but Colin had invited me to his parents' house for the first few days of vacation, and we were leaving on the train the next afternoon. Dr. Yates was surprisingly cool about letting me go with him even though it meant missing a few sessions. After her unexpected show of support in the Dean's office, Dr. Yates had shocked me again by turning out to be a pretty decent therapist. I still wasn't interested in calling her "Dr. Lara," but otherwise we were making progress. I didn't tell her about seeing Izzy or the visions, and she didn't ask. Instead, we focused on my other issues. I had plenty to choose from.

By late Thursday night of finals week, I was finished with everything and ready to start Winter Break. Finals had ended at noon, and Calhoun was almost empty. I stretched out on my stomach across Colin's bed, watching him pack for home.

"Shouldn't you go pack?"

"It's only a few days," I shrugged. "And most of my stuff is here anyway." I smiled up at him. "Why, trying to get rid of me?"

"Of course not." He grinned at me over a pile of laundry. "I'll take as much as I can get. We only have a few days."

"Yeah." I heaved a maudlin sigh. Now that I'd brought up the prospect of our imminent separation, I felt a little sad. We'd spent so much time together over the last week, it seemed impossible to imagine going almost a month without him.

"Hey, hey now. Don't be sad." Colin chided as he placed a perfectly folded shirt on a stack of others. "What do you want to do tonight?"

"You're just trying to distract me."

"Maybe, but you still didn't answer my question."

"Movie?" I suggested, trying to shake my glum mood. "Holiday movie?"

Colin laughed, nodding his assent. "Anything you want."

"Awesome!" I sat up on the bed, feeling a little excited. "I'll go get my videos. Do you like *Miracle on 34th Street*? It's my favorite."

"Really? Don't most people prefer *It's a Wonderful Life*? Or

The Christmas Story?"

I rolled my eyes at him. "I think you will find, Mr. Turner, that I am unlike most people in all sorts of ways." I attempted a suggestive wink, and he burst out laughing.

I folded my arms across my chest. "Ouch. Way to hurt a girl's pride." Colin walked over to me, placing his hands on either side of me on the bed. I stuck out my lower lip and turned my head to the side in protest.

"I bet I can remedy that," he said, a flirtatious hint in his voice.

"Can you?" I raised an eyebrow at him, as he grabbed the front of my shirt. He pulled me toward him, kissing me deeply until I felt a tingle all the way to my toes. After several long minutes, I pulled back with a sigh. "You're right. All better now."

Colin grinned triumphantly and went back to packing. I watched as he pulled a small stack of packages wrapped in holiday paper from a drawer in his desk and placed them in his luggage.

"Oh crap!" I exclaimed, jumping up off the bed. "Presents!"

Colin chuckled. "It's okay if you didn't have time to get me anything, Callie. You've been kind of busy."

I gazed at the pile of presents in his bag. "No. I have your present. It's in my room. But your parents! Your brothers!" I sat down on the bed again, feeling grumpy at myself for being both thoughtless and too broke to really do much about it. "Some first impression I'm going to make. I feel like the little drummer boy." I covered my face with my hands.

"Pah-rump-pah-pum-pum," Colin teased, easing himself onto the bed next to me. I uncovered one eye to glare at him, and he shook a small box at me.

"What is that?" I eyed the box warily.

"Your present."

Oh no, I stared at the small wrapped cube. It was the exact same size as a standard ring box.

"Colin," I said weakly, looking back and forth between his expectant face and the terrifying box in panic. "You know I love you. But isn't this a little sudden?"

He cocked his head to one side, puzzled. I took a deep breath and tried again. "What I'm saying is…I'm not say no, but I'm not saying yes, I'm *definitely* not saying yes, but I…it's so soon, and we are so young, and you're not a sparkly vampire—"

"Callie, why are you babbling like Jenna?"

"Because I am *way* too young to get married!" My jaw closed with an audible click of my teeth as I tried to stop the word torrent from spilling onward.

"Married? Married!?!" Colin's voice shot up about twelve octaves. "What made you think…"

I pointed at the box in his hand, and he burst into riotous laughter. "Open it," he managed to choke out, wiping tears from his eyes.

I took the small package from him with a frown and tore away the bright red wrapping, revealing a small velvet box. I narrowed my eyes at Colin suspiciously. He sighed, then reached over, popping the box open in my hands. Inside was a small silver lapel pin shaped like a group of cherry blossoms. The leaves were painted a shiny pink, and there were tiny rubies at the center of each petal grouping.

"It's beautiful," I breathed, staring down at the delicate pin.

Colin smiled, brushing the hair from my face. "I saw it in a little shop in town."

"My gift sucks compared to this." I held the box reverently as I examined the pin from different angles. It was beautiful but seemed oddly familiar.

Colin laughed and bent to kiss me on the forehead. "I'm glad you like it." Colin walked over to the bathroom to pack up his toiletries. I could hear him whistling to himself from across the hall.

I couldn't take my eyes off the pin. The feeling it should mean something to me was overwhelming. It was like the feeling you get when you see something moving in the corner of your eye, but when you look, it's gone. You just know something was there, even if you can't describe it.

"Try it on," Colin called.

"Okay," I said, mostly to myself. I reached hesitantly toward the pin, my fingertips feeling almost itchy as I pulled it from the box.

It was cold and dark, and I couldn't walk straight. I didn't know where I was. Was school this way? I thought I'd been walking for a long time, but time was weird and slippery. I couldn't keep track of it.

I stumbled a little, trying to keep my feet on the white line edging the pavement. I didn't hear someone coming up behind me until they grabbed my arm. *Maybe it's Jay.* Maybe he's come to take me home.

"What are you doing, Izzy?" I stumbled as the person jerked me backward.

"Colin? Is that you?"

He snorted. "What's wrong? Having trouble keeping your boyfriends straight?"

"What are you talking about?" I rocked on my heels, trying to keep myself balanced.

"I'm talking about you whoring about at parties." He grabbed my arm again, twisting it slightly.

Why is he being mean? I wondered. Sometimes he was nice, but every time he saw me talking to someone else, he'd fly off the handle. That was the reason I'd stopped dating him, but he still wouldn't leave me alone.

"What business is it of yours?" I demanded, trying to pull my arm away. Colin's grip was like steel. I could feel the bruises forming under his fingers, just like the last time he'd gotten mad. He'd said it was an accident, but he kept hurting me.

"Because I care about you too much to watch you giving it away to some random clown in a mask."

"Let go, Colin." I'd meant to be assertive, but my voice came out timid and strained. Colin grabbed my other wrist, laughing as I pulled against him.

"Not until you realize you'll never find someone who loves you like I do."

Colin bent his face toward me, as if to kiss me. I twisted mine away, and he shook me hard. My head lolled with the force it. Fireworks burst in my eyes. He pressed his lips against mine, forcing his tongue into my mouth. He reeked of alcohol and I gagged at the sour smell on his breath.

"What's the matter, Izzy?" he snarled in my ear. "You'll screw some guy you've never met in front of a room full of strangers, but I'm not good enough to kiss?"

"Anyone would be better than you," I said savagely, blinking hard as I fought to keep my balance.

"You're a real tease, you know that?" He twisted my arm again, and I cried out, tears springing to my eyes. "You're lucky I even bother with you."

I had to get away from him. Looking up, I could see the top of the bell tower for the big yellow church in the distance. If I ran toward it, maybe someone would hear me.

"Let me go, Colin!" I screamed directly in his ear.

Colin winced and clapped his hand against his ear, releasing me. I lurched in the opposite direction, running as fast as my heels would allow down the hill toward town. Colin was right behind me, grabbing at me as I rounded the corner.

Suddenly it was bright, too bright. I meant to turn away from the lights, but I was running blind. I heard a sickening thud. Then I was flying backward, my body twisting through the air.

"Callie?" Colin called from the bathroom. "How does it look?"

My hands were shaking so hard I dropped the pin on the floor. I wanted to stomp on it, but I heard Colin coming and bent to quickly retrieve it.

"Are you okay?" He placed his hand on the small of my back to steady me as I stood up.

It was all I could do not puke all over him. Izzy had worn the pin as part of her costume. I remembered now, my memory of seeing it when she hugged me goodbye that night intermingling with Izzy's memory of it swinging into view while she fought Colin. How did he have it now?

"I'm fine," I stammered. "I think I stuck myself." I jammed my thumb in my mouth and bit down, trying to shake off the vision and focus on the reality of the moment. I had to get away from Colin, but I was terrified he'd realize something was wrong.

He chuckled softly as he took the pin from my shaking hand. "Here, let me do it."

"Where did you say you got it again?" I forced myself to smile, my tone light.

"A little shop in town. I bought it a while ago…" He bit the edge of his lip as he fiddled with the clasp. "But I think it's found the person it was intended for."

He turned my shoulders slightly, glancing at my face as he straightened the edge of my shirt. "It looks great." He ran his fingers suggestively along the edge of my collar, and I shuddered involuntarily as he touched my bare skin.

"Thank you," I mumbled.

He gently pulled my hand from my mouth and turned it over in his hand, looking for the imaginary wound. "Looks fine," he said reassuringly, turning back to his bags. "Though we better not let it get around campus that our local undercover CIA operative is afraid of a little pin prick."

"I should go," I suggested suddenly, and he looked up at me, frowning. "Get the movies," I added quickly. "Our holiday movies?"

"Right!" His smile returned. "Do you want me to come with you?"

"No," I said a bit too quickly. "I mean, I kinda need to finish wrapping your gift?" I tried to look embarrassed.

What I felt was sick. I thought about all the nights I'd spent cuddled up next to the guy who'd been secretly abusing my best friend, all the times she must have lied and covered up the bruises he'd given her. Everything I'd been through with my dad, every horrible thing I'd survived, and I hadn't even noticed when someone was doing the same thing to the girl I lived with. Izzy had saved me from my father by telling her parents, but I had missed every sign when it came to her. I could feel the panic rising inside. I had to get away from Colin before I had an episode.

He eyed me suspiciously for a moment, then shrugged. "You don't need to wrap it now," he said, taking a pair of pressed jeans and placing them in his bag. "You can give it to me later. It's no big deal."

My mind scrambled to make the excuse believable. "But you already gave me mine. I'd really like to give you yours now. If that's okay."

Colin looked at me oddly, and I tensed, feeling sure he knew I was onto him. Instead, he reached out to caress my face, trailing his fingers along the edge of my cheek. It took every ounce of my resolve not to flinch away.

"Are you sure you're okay?" He voice was tender. "You seem kind of upset."

"I'm fine," I stuttered. "The holidays are going to be tough this year. Dr. Yates and I have been talking about grief, how it come in waves, sometimes when you least expect it."

I pulled his hand away, giving his fingers a small squeeze. "I'll run back to my room, wrap your gift, grab the movies, and be back before you know it." I mustered a smile. "I promise."

I sidestepped around him, forcing myself to take slow, small steps toward the door. I turned back at the edge of the hallway to make sure he wasn't following me. "I'll be right back."

"I'll miss you," he called after me as I slipped into the hallway.

53.

When I made it to the H/I stairwell, I paused and tried to shove the feeling of panic down. My feelings of revulsion were intermingled with Izzy's terror, and the combination was making it hard to think clearly. Colin had seemed suspicious of me, but had he really been or had I just imagined it because of Izzy's residual fear?

I decided I couldn't risk being caught by him, not before I could tell someone and not when I had no idea what he's do if he suspected anything. I opened the exit door and let it slam shut, pretending to leave the building. The campus was empty, and Colin's building was right next to a wooded ravine that ran through campus. If I went outside and he decided to follow me, it would be easy for him to catch me before I managed to get to another building and find help.

Instead, I turned and hurried up the stairs, heading deeper into Calhoun. I could just as easily get trapped in the empty building's maze-like corridors if Colin followed me up the stairs. It was a risky maneuver, but it was the best option I had. I figured if he was going to follow me, it was better to head in the direction he'd least expect. I was also hoping someone else was staying for Winter Break nearby, someone I could ask for help. It was a long shot, but it seemed better than risking getting dragged into the forest behind the building.

I ran all the way to the top floor and yanked at the door. It wouldn't budge.

"No," I whispered, pulling again. "Come on."

It was no use. The fire doors separating the stairwell from the other floors were closed and locked. It seemed everyone else in the towers had already left.

I weighed my options. I didn't want to risk trying to cross the sky bridge. You could see people inside it for miles, which would give me away if Colin looked. If I tried going back down to the exterior door, Colin was even more likely to realize something was up and follow me. I crouched in the stairwell, pulling my cell phone from my pocket and dialing Jay's number from memory.

"Please pick up, please pick up." His voicemail kicked in, and I bit my lip as I waited for the beep.

"Hi, this is Jay. I'm probably in class or studying. Leave a message and I'll call you back."

"Jay, it's Callie," I said as quietly as I thought I could and still be heard in the message. "Call me as soon as you get this. You were right. Colin is a monster! He was there with Izzy when she died. I—"

I never heard him coming. Colin's cast slammed into my head, landing near the base of my skull. The world spun as my forehead banged against the stair railing, and Colin's arm came down on me again. The phone dropped from my hands, falling through the railing. My heart broke as I heard it smash to pieces against the concrete floor four stories below.

"I'd ask you how you knew, Callie," Colin said dryly, "but I have a funny feeling I already know."

I grabbed at the metal bars in front of me, trying to steady myself. Colin grabbed a handful of my hair, twisting it in his grip as he yanked my head back to look in my eye. "She told you, didn't she? That ungrateful whore found a way to keep messing up my life even after she died." He yanked hard on my hair, and I screamed in pain.

The hair pull triggered some buried memory in me, and my instinctive self-defense kicked in. Pulling slightly forward for leverage, I flung myself backward with all my strength as I slammed my elbow into Colin's face. I heard a satisfying crunch as Colin grunted in pain, blood exploding from his nose.

I scrambled down one flight of stairs as Colin howled above me. I flung myself at the door between the stairwell and the sky bridge, shoving it open as I bolted for the door at the other end. I bounced off one long glass wall, then the other, unable to walk straight, stumbling and punch drunk. I looked down once and almost fell as the dead leaves and dirty ground three stories below buckled and spun beneath me.

"Don't look down," I muttered, pulling myself along the handrails of the sky bridge.

When I reached the far door, I yanked as hard as I could. It was locked. Screaming in fear and frustration, I pulled again and again, but it wouldn't budge. It was getting harder to keep my eyes open. I wasn't sure I'd make it back, but I turned around, knowing it was my only hope of escape.

Colin stood in the open doorway, his good hand gripping the frame above him as he casually blocked my escape. "I don't know what she told you," he said in a nasally sing-song voice, "but it was all a horrible misunderstanding."

He took a step into the glass walkway and spread his hands in front him as if to show he meant no harm. "We got in a fight. I tried to stop her from running off because she was so messed up. She pulled away from me and ran right out in front of that car." He shrugged and gave me a sad smile, wiping his bloody hand on his shirt. "There was nothing I could do."

"You're leaving out the part where you gave her bruises on a regular basis and tried to force your tongue down her throat." I swayed on my feet, clinging to the handrail to keep myself upright.

"It wasn't like that, Callie." His eyes were clear and solemn. I could see he believed everything he was saying, even now. It made my skin crawl. "She loved me. I know she did. In time, she would have realized it, like you did."

"You disgust me," I choked, swallowing back bile.

"Really?" His voice was steel as he took another step toward me. "Because that's not what you said last night."

"Stay away from me," I warned, even as my knees threatened to buckle beneath me.

"Come on, Callie. Don't be like that." He was only a few feet away now. "We can work this out."

I shoved my hands in my pockets, feeling for my keys. I curled my fingers around the worn carabineer, the metal lying across my knuckles. I'd only have one shot to get past him, and I had to let him get closer before I tried.

"We always work it out. That's the great thing about our relationship." His hands were extended toward me as he moved closer, ready to capture me in his embrace. My eyelids fluttered, and he was inches closer, then again. I shook my head, trying to keep my eyes open. I needed to hang on until he was within swinging distance.

Just a few more inches.

"Do you think you can forget all those terrible things that happened in the past?" His voice was strangely gently, eyes shining with a look I'd once mistaken for love. "We can have a future together."

I was trembling from exertion as I tried to stay upright. *What had Colin done when he hit me?* I felt like I could barely control my limbs. I wasn't even sure I could swing my arm, but it was my only hope. I'd have to let him get right on top of me.

I forced myself to nod at him. "Okay," I whispered. "Let's talk."

Colin's face broke into his trademark grin. He closed the distance between us, stepping in to wrap his arms around me.

Now!

I pulled my fist from my pocket, swinging hard for his jaw. Unfortunately, my legs gave out in the same moment. The arch of my fist went wide, catching him the shoulder as I collapsed in a heap on the floor. Tears flowed freely down my face as I choked on sobs.

Colin winced and rubbed his shoulder. "Oh, Callie," he sighed with exasperation, pulling my limp body into his arms. "What am I going to do with you?"

My head lolled against him. I couldn't hold it up. Colin heaved me forward, and his face doubled in my vision, then tripled. The sad, confused expression on his face looked like my father's every time he came out of one of his rages and found me cowering, as if he couldn't imagine what would make me look at him with such hatred and fear.

"I love you," Colin said sadly. "Don't you know how much I love you?"

In my head, I heard my father echo his words with the same tired voice.

Stupid! a hopeless voice in my head chastised as the darkness flooded in. *You were so stupid to think you could escape this. You can't get away.*

You never could.

54.

I woke up lying on Colin's bed. Turning my head slightly, I saw Colin bent over, humming to himself as he packed. He'd changed out of his bloody shirt into a fresh one. His nose was mangled and obviously broken, but he pretended it wasn't, dabbing at it occasionally with tissue. Otherwise, he acted as if nothing had happened.

For a moment I wondered if it had all been some sort of horrific trauma-induced nightmare. Then I tried to sit up, but my body wouldn't cooperate. I couldn't move my legs. I tried to push myself up on my elbows, but my arms gave out, shaking with the effort. I was too weak to move. I began hyperventilating.

Colin rushed over and pulled me into his arms, rocking me. "It's okay, Callie, it's okay," he crooned. "You had a nasty fall down the stairs. You hit your head pretty hard, but you'll be alright in little while." He smiled supportively as I struggled to breathe.

"How long was I out for?" I gasped, playing along because I didn't know what else to do. I had a bad feeling that if he hit me in the head again, I wouldn't wake up.

"Only twenty minutes." He offered me glass of water, then set it down when I shook my head. "You lay here and rest." He shoved a pillow behind me, propping me up. "When you feel better, I'll help you pack."

I watched in mute horror as he continued to pick up his room, putting things neatly away so that everything would be in its proper place when he returned to school the next semester. I couldn't move my legs, but Colin acted like this was another run-of-the-mill day for him.

Part of me wanted to go back to sleep until help came, but I didn't think anyone was coming. For all I knew, Jay was back in Georgia. Almost everyone had left for break, even Audrey, Colin's AD. By now, people were used to Colin and me splitting time between our rooms; if Jenna or anyone else looked in one room and didn't find us, they'd assume we were in the other one.

No one from school was looking for me. I had to figure out a way to call for help, but first I had to get my hands on a phone. Mine was broken, but I could see Colin's sitting on his desk across the room. To get to it, he either had to give it to me or I had to get to it.

I wiggled my toes, struggling to feel them moving inside my boots. It worked, but I still couldn't lift either of my legs. Until I could run, all I could do was bide my time and wait.

Minute after long minute passed. With each one, I grew weaker, until I could barely raise my arm. I stared at the phone as hope fell further and further away.

Guess I'm coming to you this time, Izzy. The spots in my vision grew larger. *You better be waiting for me when I get there.* I closed my eyes, wishing there was someone I could say good-bye to other than the polo-sporting psycho in the corner.

The exterior door to the H/I stairwell banged against the wall, and my eyes flew open.

"Callie?" a frantic voice called. Heavy footsteps pounded down the hallway toward us. Colin closed and locked the door quickly. He sprinted across the room, leaping onto the bed on top of me, clapping his good hand over my mouth and nose as I tried to call out.

"Shhhh," Colin whispered, as I clawed at his arm feebly, fighting to get air. "If we're quiet, he'll go away."

"Callie?" the voice called again, this time from the other side of the door. The door shook as someone banged on it. "Are you there?"

Jay! I fought Colin with renewed vigor. *It's Jay.*

I moaned as loud as I could under Colin's grip, digging my nails into his arm. Hissing, Colin pressed his cast against my throat, strangling me. As he did, the lapel of my shirt bent under his weight, pressing the brooch against the bare skin at my neck.

When the cold metal met my flesh, I was torn between two realities, both of them dire. I flipped back and forth between Colin, choking the life out of me...

...and...

Colin, standing over me, watching with cold disdain as the life flowed out of me.

Someone was peering down at me, his face bright and clear in the headlights. He was an older guy, fortyish, and his wire-framed glasses pressed into the sides of his head where his hair was beginning to go grey at the temples. He was mumbling to himself and pulling at his hair.

"OhGodohJesus, whadamI-goingtodo?"

I tried to tell him my name, but when I opened my mouth I choked on something warm and sticky.

"OhNo-OhNo-OhNo-OhNo," the guy was frantic, glancing around him. Abruptly he stood up, passing out of the headlights. I heard the car door open.

Oh good. He's going to call for help.

Instead I listened listlessly as the engine started. The car pulled away with a screech, speeding into the night.

"Callie!" Jay screamed, pounding at the door. "Callie, answer me!"

The night was dark, but the full moon seemed to shine down on me like a spotlight. I tried to sit up but my legs wouldn't move. It was getting harder to breathe, and I coughed again, choking on the tangy metallic taste. I touched my mouth with my fingers and held them in front of my face. They were covered in a slick liquid that looked black in the moonlight.

Blood, I realized. *My blood.*

"Be quiet, Callie!" Colin mumbled, pressing harder on my throat as I thrashed against him, clawing at his face, trying to reach his eyes with my fingers.

A face entered my field of vision. Colin stood by my head, staring down at me. There was a strange emptiness in his gaze.

Call for help, I pleaded with my eyes. *Please Colin. You said you loved me. Call for help.*

After a moment, he reached down, pulling at something on my coat jacket. As he stood up, I saw it was the brooch he'd given me. He put it into his pocket, then glanced down at me again.

I could hear the door splintering, but it was too late, far too late. I couldn't lift my arms anymore, limply flopping beneath

Colin's grip. The world grew faint and colorless, sounds quieting around me.

Colin nudged me slightly with his shoe, and I twitched involuntarily. He knelt down next to me, whispering in my ear.

"This is what you get, whore, for not loving me like you should have. If I can't have you, no one can."

Then he walked away.

There are a lot of things you might expect to think before you die.

There are a lot of things you might expect to think before you die.

I can't believe I trusted this psychopath.

Taco bar really isn't much of a last meal.

Now I'll never know what happens next on Riverdale.

Wait—are these underwear clean!?!

Get off me, GET OFF ME, GETOFFME!

Goodbye, Mom. Goodbye, Dad. Goodbye Amelia and Eva, and Grandma Adele.

Goodbye, Jay. Thanks for trying.

Goodbye, Callie. I love you. I'm so sorry.

I'm coming, Izzy.

I love you.

I'm so sorry.

55.

Izzy and I were seated a table draped in fine linen cloth. A full set of sterling silver flatware was laid out before us. A small flame flickered in a tiny hurricane lamp at the table's edge. The room was floor-to-ceiling glass walls and perched on the edge of pier, so it seemed like we floated above the water. Outside, an unseen seagull cawed. Rows of small, empty, well-appointed tables crowded around us.

"This place seems nice," I began, picking up the menu in front of me. "I'm surprised there aren't more people here."

Izzy frowned. "We're too early."

Izzy's makeup was impeccable, as always, but surprisingly demur. You could hardly tell she was wearing any, only enough to accent the curving cat shape of her eyes and the pout of her mouth. Her dress was also conservative, a 1950s cap-sleeved number in a rich brown with tiny white polka dots. She wore white lace gloves that gathered at the wrist. A pillbox hat that matched the brown of her dress perched on her head, complete with a tiny mesh veil falling over her eyes.

"Nice outfit," I smirked. "Very *Donna Reed*. You going to a theme party?"

Izzy rolled her eyes. "No, I've had enough of those to last a lifetime." She chuckled grimly, sipping at a tiny espresso cup. "I'm going to a funeral."

"Anyone we know?" I asked, flipping idly through the menu. The gull cried again, closer, and I flinched.

"Yours, actually."

"What?" The menu slipped from my hands and I bent to retrieve it.

"You heard me." She gave me a tight smile as I emerged from beneath the table. "Unless you wake up right now, this is it."

"You're not funny, Iz." Frowning, I looked out at the water. The reflected light glinting off it was bright, too bright. I held my hand over my eyes, shielding them against the glare.

"Callie!" Izzy slammed the espresso cup down on its saucer, cracking it. Dark brown espresso seeped into her lace gloves in patches, turning sections of them the color of her dress.

"You'll ruin your pretty gloves," I murmured.

Izzy ignored me, casting her gaze desperately around the room. Without a word, she shoved her chair backwards and scrambled onto the table in front of me. The tablecloth bunched beneath her, pulled across the table as the hurricane lamp crashed to the floor.

I sprang back, knocking my chair over behind me. "Izzy, what are you doing?"

"Wake up, Callie!" she screamed. She grabbed my shoulders with her espresso-soaked gloves, shaking me hard. "Please," she begged, her eyes wild and desperate. "WAKE UP! WAKE UP! WAKE—"

56.

My entire body hurt. The light was bright, too bright, and everything was so loud. I tried to take a deep breath, but my throat was dry and I choked instead.

"Here, honey, suck on these." Ice chips slid into my mouth. I tried to suck on them, but I accidentally inhaled one and started coughing. A small frame pressed itself firmly to my side, leaning me forward and banging gently on my back as I spat ice chips everywhere.

"Everything okay in here?" another, more authoritative, female voice called from my left.

"She's awake," said the woman rubbing small circles across my shoulders. She smelled like amber and spicy vanilla, a strong warm smell that reminded me of home.

"I'll tell the doctor." The door swished closed as the second voice disappeared.

"It's okay, sweetheart," the woman said in an increasingly familiar voice.

"Crystal?" I choked out.

"Shhh, honey. I'm right here." I burst into tears as she wrapped her arms around me, tucking my head underneath her chin and rocking me gently. When the tears eventually subsided, Crystal released me and eased into a chair next to the bed.

"You look like complete hell, Callie," she said flatly, taking my hand between hers. "And you are, far and away, the most wonderful sight I have ever seen." Her eyes welled up, and she wiped at them.

"What are you doing here?"

"Well, honey, you've been in the hospital for almost a week." She ran her fingers along my hand absently. "Greg and I are still listed as your emergency contacts. They called us when you went into the ICU and we caught the first flight up."

"Oh." I didn't know what to say to that. "I'm sorry." My voice sounded very small.

Crystal sighed. "No, Callie, I'm sorry. Greg and I both are. We have absolutely no excuse for what we did to you these last few weeks, except that we thought it was what you wanted."

"What?"

Her lip trembled. "You were so angry when we came to get Izzy. It seemed like you blamed us for you both being here. We wanted to take you home, but you refused to talk about it. So we left, thinking eventually you'd call us when you were ready. Only you never did." Her voice broke, and a fresh wave of tears rolled down her cheeks. "Then we got this call to come back to this godforsaken hospital, that we needed to hurry because our daughter was in critical condition and might not make it."

She bit her lip, struggling to keep her composure. "I was so sure I was going to lose you, too. It was like I was dying all over again. I knew right then we'd made a huge mistake leaving you here, that I should have dragged you back kicking and screaming if that's what it took. You were always so different from my girls, though, such a tough little thing." She shivered. "I thought, 'If this is what Callie wants, we have to respect that.'" She leveled a fierce look at me. "We will never make that mistake again."

"I thought you didn't want me," I whispered, and watched as the color drained out of Crystal's face. "I thought you blamed me because I didn't protect Izzy, and she was your real daughter. I thought it was my fault, and you didn't want me anymore."

Crystal covered her mouth in horror. I shrugged and looked down at the bed. "I didn't blame you. I wouldn't want me either."

"Caledonia Eden McCayter, if I ever hear you say such nonsense again, I will kick your butt into next week."

A smile broke over my face, and I gestured to the hospital bed. "Really, Crystal? Really?"

Crystal let out a small laugh, and I grinned at her. She grinned back at me, and soon we were both laughing and crying and hugging each other. It felt so good to laugh. It felt good to cry. Every single part of my body hurt, my head was pounding, and I had sandpaper where my throat used to be, but I was alive, and every ache and pain reminded me of it.

I was alive.

Thanks to Izzy.

Who, as it happened, picked that exact moment to appear again, back in her impeccably pristine 1950s ensemble, right there in my hospital room.

57.

The doctor came in shortly after Izzy made her grand entrance. He introduced himself as Dr. Patel, then gave me a thorough going-over, including that test where they run something up the middle of your foot to see if you twitch. I jumped about a mile, and Crystal beamed like a lighthouse when the doctor nodded to her.

"You'll recover eventually," he finally said, flipping through my chart.

"Meaning what, precisely?" Crystal was back in full-on mom mode now that she knew I wanted her to be one.

"She'll be okay, though I advise she take it very slowly. She had a pretty serious concussion, brought on largely by the fact she'd suffered at least one prior significant head contusion."

He gazed at me over his glasses and I nodded awkwardly. *I guess Gloria got me better than I'd thought.*

"You're lucky to be alive, young lady. If the paramedics had been even a few minutes later, I'm not sure we could have saved you, and even if we had, you might not have walked again."

"What happened to my legs?"

"You had what's commonly known as a brain bleed," he said, making a last notation in the chart and flipping it shut. Dr. Patel moved to the foot of the bed to hang it back on the hook. "It put pressure on your spinal column and the part of your brain that allowed you to coordinate your limbs. We had to drill a small hole at the base of your skull to drain the blood and relieve the pressure. Once we did you made a pretty speedy recovery, but you didn't seem to want to wake up."

"You were in a coma," Crystal added softly.

"But I'm going to be fine now?"

The doctor clicked his pen closed and slid it into his breast pocket. "You're going to be fine, *provided* you take it easy."

Dr. Patel gave a curt nod to Crystal, then exited the room. I turned my attention to Crystal.

"You said Greg is here, too?" I asked, trying to forestall the inevitable talk I knew we were going to have about how I'd come to be in a coma. "Can I see him? Does he want to see me?"

"Of course he does!" Crystal exclaimed. "But right now… Well, honey, right now he's meeting with a public defender and a bail bondsman."

"Am I under arrest?" I checked to make sure neither my wrists or ankles were bound to the bed.

Crystal laughed a little. "No, Callie. But your boyfriend is."

"Crystal, Colin is not my boyfriend! He tried to kill me!"

Crystal looked confused. "Honey, I know you're out of it, but I'm pretty sure Jayden saved your life."

"Jay? He's not my boyfriend."

"Are you sure?" Crystal looked even more perplexed.

"Of course I'm sure!" I said in exasperation. "Why does everyone always think he's my boyfriend?"

Then, it hit me.

"Wait—Jay is in jail? Why?" I felt like I had returned to a favorite soap opera after a year of missing it, and no longer understood the relationships or recognized the characters.

Crystal sighed, uncrossing and recrossing her legs. "Get comfortable, honey. This could take a while."

I leaned back against the pillows. Crystal then set about filling me in on everything I'd missed while I'd been unconscious.

58.

It took Crystal over an hour to catch me up on the spectacle that continued to be my life. Izzy remained with us throughout the entire tale, perched on a chair in the corner of my hospital room. She was apparently as interested in what I'd missed as I was. It was strange to see her in the same room as her mother, without her mother being able to so much as sense her presence. It was difficult to keep my eyes off her, but for Crystal's sake, I tried. Izzy's sadness was palpable on the rare occasion she glanced in her mother's direction. For the most part she stayed focused intently on me, and I did my best to pretend I didn't see her. I'd never known Izzy to stay so long, but I was so grateful to see her I didn't care.

It turned out, Jay had gotten my voicemail after all. When he got to Colin's room, Jay heard me despite Colin's best attempts to silence me, permanently. In direct defiance of Mike's "no more kicking in doors" mandate, Jay broke down the door, yanking Colin off me just in time. He also, apparently, beat Colin within an inch of his life before the police and paramedics arrived. Jay called them on his way to Colin's room as a precaution. It turned out to be the decision that saved my life, as well as Colin's.

As it was, Jay was currently being charged with aggravated assault. Colin had also been charged for attempted murder against me. Colin had asked for a lawyer immediately, and hadn't made a single statement about the incident until he was arraigned, at which point he claimed that Jay had come to his room in a fit of jealous rage, attempted to choke me to death, then beaten Colin to a pulp before the police arrived to save the day. Apparently the judge had taken one look at Colin's face and arms, still covered in wounds from where I'd dug my nails in as deep as I could, and remanded him into custody without bail to await trial. Rumor was he was now trying to trade identifying information about the driver who had hit Izzy in exchange for a lighter sentence.

Jay hadn't been able to afford a lawyer, but Greg and Crystal had made plans to get him one rather than see him saddled with an overworked and underpaid public defender. The judge ruled he could be released on bail, but it was so high Jay never could have paid it.

Once again, Greg and Crystal stepped up, offering their house as collateral if the court demanded it. The judge had been so persuaded by their pleas on my behalf that he'd dropped the bail significantly, and Greg was meeting with a bondsman to post it right away. Jay's attorney felt confident they could get the charges against him dismissed outright if I could testify on his behalf. The big question had been when, or if, I'd wake up.

The college hadn't waited for the criminal justice system to make up its mind about who the responsible parties were. Based on the photos of the three of us alone, the College Judicial Board had met and made its decisions, which were unanimous and preemptively approved by the president before Colin was notified to prevent dragging things out with an appeal. While the criminal justice system required proof beyond a reasonable doubt, as a private institution, Astoria College could make up its own rules for its code of conduct and determine its own sanctions.

Colin was expelled immediately, though statements made

through his attorneys to the local press indicated he intended to fight the decision, in court if necessary. Jay was on conditional probation for the rest of the year and lost his job with Campus Security. This was probably the least the college could get away with giving him. He was lucky not to have been expelled, too.

The College Judicial Board had dealt with Gloria and Shannen while they were at it, expelling Gloria and suspending Shannen for the next two semesters. Bethany and Lauren were cleared of any involvement based on the statements and recordings I'd provided, as well as Shannen's testimony. As much as I loathed Shannen for going along with Gloria's plan, I was comforted to know that when push came to shove, she'd done the right thing. Maybe there was hope for her after all. Unfortunately, the local DA had declined to press charges against Gloria based on a lack of physical evidence. I wondered how surprised Gloria had been to discover that most of the forensic information I'd fed her to get a confession was complete nonsense.

Once again, I seemed to be the only person who wasn't going to get into trouble. I'd been in two fights in as many weeks, but in both cases it was obvious I'd been attacked and any damage I'd done was in self-defense. The College Judicial Board formally declined to issue charges against me, a show of support in light of the upcoming criminal proceedings.

A few other things had come to light in the wake of Colin's arrest. Two of his high school girlfriends had come forward with statements about his history of controlling and violent behavior. A sealed juvenile record was also unearthed, revealing Colin had been charged at fourteen with assault when he'd beaten up a guy who started dating a girl he was interested in, but the conviction had been expunged when he'd finished probation. Colin's mother was talking to every news outlet that called her house. She was completely in denial, telling everyone how her "sweet little boy" could never do such a thing.

"You may need to prepare yourself for the possibility that he won't end up in jail, at least not for the rest of his life like he deserves," Crystal said bitterly.

I was itching to make some statements of my own, but Crystal told me that press conferences emphatically did *not* qualify as "taking it easy."

"Besides," Crystal said gently, and I could tell she was trying to prepare me for whatever was coming next. "I'm not sure how many people will believe you. One of Colin's defense strategies is to discredit you. You're Jay's only supporting witness."

"He's been telling everyone that you'd gone crazy, that you didn't know who you were hurting when you attacked him, thinking he was Jay at the time." Crystal frowned deeply. "He said you kept telling him you were talking to Izzy, that Izzy was sending you messages and showing you things. He's got some other people who are willing to testify for him—two girls, Gloria and Marissa, and some guy named Will?"

I sighed and closed my eyes. "Yeah, I know them."

"Callie, honey. Do you...think Izzy talks to you?"

I looked into Crystal's eyes and I could see the sheer terror lurking there—the loss of her oldest daughter, the fear of losing her surrogate daughter after getting her back again—and I did what anyone would do.

I lied.

"No, Crystal," I said flatly. "Someone was messing with me, trying to make me think I was seeing Izzy, getting messages from her."

I gave Crystal the sincerest look I could muster. After a moment's evaluation, Crystal nodded, looking relieved. "You're sure?"

"Absolutely," I said, turning to look Izzy straight in the eye. "I still talk to Izzy sometimes, like I talk to my mom. I know she's is dead, but sometimes she feels like she's right here in the room with me. In some ways," I paused and smile at Crystal, "your daughter seems almost inescapable."

Sitting across the room from her mother in a worn green chair, Izzy threw her head back and laughed silently. I bit my lip, trying not to laugh at the absurdity of the moment with her.

Epilogue

The cemetery was mostly empty when Jay and I got there. We passed an elderly man in a long dark coat and matching hat standing solemnly over a grave in an older section of the cemetery, where all the plots were long grown over with grass. He didn't acknowledge us as we passed.

We trekked slowly up a small rise to the newer section of the cemetery. A little girl, braided pigtails flying behind her, ran past us between two rows of headstones. I stopped to let her pass. Jay marched on, and she swerved to go around him. He glanced back at me, and I hurried to catch up. I didn't really want to be here, but between Greg and Crystal and Jay, they'd all convinced me it was something I had to do. Closure, they called it. As if I could ever close the book on Izzy, on our collective hopes and dreams.

Izzy's grave lay to the east of a small copse of trees with a stone bench beneath it. It had a nice view of a small artificial lake. It was more or less by itself in this part of the cemetery, and grass was beginning to grow up around the edges of the small dark mound. Crystal told me that instead of burying Izzy with family she didn't really know, they'd looked all over and found the prettiest place they could afford with enough space for them to buy at least three plots. They had decided they would rather be buried with Izzy, as a family, than anywhere else. Greg and Crystal seemed so young to have to make those kinds of choices, but when you lost a child, I guess it made all sorts of inevitable things suddenly immediate.

The cemetery was only a few miles from where we grew up,

which meant the Millers could go and visit Izzy regularly, and that when Amelia and Eva got a little older they'd be able to visit her on their own. In a few years, Amelia would be able to bike here, just as Izzy and I had biked past this area on our way to the park or to get ice cream when it was hot in the summer.

In some ways, it was the nicest possible place for Izzy to be. In other ways, it reinforced how little of the world Izzy had managed to see before she died. We grew up here. Now, except for the fifteen months we spent together on the Oregon coast, she'd always be here.

Or maybe not, I thought as Jay and I made it to the top of the rise. I'd tell you that it was completely unsettling to find Izzy perched on top of her own headstone, smiling at me, but it wasn't. She looked beautiful, dressed in a stylish blue green dress that set off the highlights in her hair and eyes, and her killer heels didn't have a single blade of wet grass clinging to them.

"Hey, Izzy," I said, trying to maintain a solemn air. She gave me a little wave, then smirked in Jay's direction.

"I'll give you a minute." Jay squeezed my shoulder and retreating back toward the bench.

The air was sticky hot, and my hair clung to my face and neck even though it was barely ten in the morning. It was amazing how overdressed I felt in short sleeves and a skirt even in December. Izzy looked cool and refreshed by comparison.

"You look beautiful." She arched her eyebrows at me. "No, really. You look like you always did. Perfect." Izzy threw her head back and laughed and I could hear it faintly, as though it was coming from somewhere over the hill out of sight.

"I'm sorry I couldn't do more for you, Iz." She frowned, and I swallowed hard, twisting my hands around the bouquet of freesia and lilies I'd brought. Looking at her skin glowing and eyes sparkling in the bright morning light, the flowers seemed cheap and unworthy by comparison. "I'm sorry I didn't go with you that night. I'm sorry you'll never get to do all the things you wanted. I hope that you're happy now. I hope you know that I'm safe, and you can go on to your next adventure, whatever that is."

Izzy was still frowning at me, her brow wrinkling like she wanted to tell me something, but couldn't.

"You've been around less." Izzy shrugged in reply. "Is it…" I tried to say it, but the words stuck in my throat. *Do not cry.* "Is it time for you to go?"

Izzy looked down at her shoe, swinging her foot back and forth as if she wasn't sure how to answer. Maybe she didn't know herself.

I stepped forward and placed the flowers on the headstone next to her. In all the times I'd seen her, I'd never been so close to her. We were less than a foot apart, and I wanted to reach out and hug her, but I somehow knew I couldn't.

"I love you, Izzy. I'll always love you. And no matter where I go, I know you'll be with me." I thought I saw tears shining in her eyes, too.

"Are you ready?" Jay's voice was soft and strong behind me.

I shrugged. "No."

I gave him a rueful smile, and he wrapped his arms around me, hugging me. Izzy smirked and nodded toward Jay, and I rolled my eyes at her. She grinned wider at me.

"We can stay as long as you want, you know," he said in my ear.

"I know." I sighed. "But I'm ready."

When I started to pull away, Jay grabbed my hand, interlacing his fingers with mine as we walked down the hill together. Part of me wanted to shake him off, but I didn't. I knew I wasn't ready to date anyone after everything that happened with Colin, and Jay hadn't pushed me. At the same time, maybe it was time I finally listened to Izzy and gave him a chance.

Jay had shown up at the Millers' the day after Christmas. Apparently he'd tracked down our contact information and then driven all the way from Savannah to Houston so he could pay Greg back for his bail. When he got there, Greg wouldn't take the money, but he did offer Jay a beer. They'd gone back and forth over it for more than two days, Jay offering to be the bigger man and pay Greg back, and Greg trumping him by refusing, telling Jay to use the money for school. I wasn't sure which one of them was more irritated by their gentlemanly impasse, but it amused Crystal to no end. Crystal and Greg moved my things in with Izzy's while we were at school and turned my old room into a guest room, so Jay stayed there while I was in Izzy's. He was planning to stay through New Year's.

As Jay and I passed, the old man tipped his hat at me, and I nodded in return. I turned back to see Jay giving me a quizzical look.

"Where are your manners?" I teased. "Didn't your momma ever tell you to respect your elders?"

"What are you talking about?" He quirked an eyebrow at me.

"You're a lot of things, but you certainly aren't my elder."

"Did you not see—" I turned to point to the elderly gentleman, but he wasn't there. In fact, there wasn't a single other person in the entire cemetery.

"See what?" Jay's tone was light, but his look was a familiar and calculating one.

Inside I was shaking, but I forced a smile and grabbed his hand again. "Nothing. I'm delirious. Must be the heat."

"Uh-huh," he said, eyeing me suspiciously.

I took a step toward him, so we were standing only a few inches apart, throwing my head back to gaze up at him. "It might just be the nearness of you." I batted my eyelashes, and Jay burst out laughing.

"Yep. You're clearly delirious," he affirmed. Slinging his arm around my shoulder, we started toward the car again.

"At least now the worst is over," he said in a quiet voice. "You can start to put all this behind you a little."

"Yeah," I murmured. I glanced back over my shoulder to find the elderly man watching us with a strange expression of longing. Beyond him, Izzy stood at the top of the hill. The little girl who'd run past us was standing next to her, and they were holding hands and waving. "It's all over."

It wasn't.

Acknowledgements

This book was seven years in the making. It is also the first thing I ever wrote longer than 25 pages. As a result, far more people contributed to it than I will probably ever remember, so I should probably thank the ones that I can.

First, thanks to the amazing staff and faculty of Lewis & Clark College, who taught me many things, but most of all to believe in myself. You are my Hogwarts—teachers, family, mentors, and friends. If home is where the heart is, then mine is forever located at the top of Palatine Hill.

Second, I have to thank all the fine residents of Astoria, Oregon, especially the staff of Coffee Girl, who make hands down the best coffee in the world. I've been a lot of places, but this remains one of my all-time favorites.

I must give all due credit to my intrepid editor, Alicia Thompson. You have my endless gratitude for your feedback. It is a far, far better thing that I write than I have ever written, largely due to you.

Big shout out to Shannon Baker Campbell, Jessica Tristan Foreman, Marti Chandler, Sheri Offenhauser, and Cristina Garcia, the progressive best friends of my childhood: There's a little piece of each of you in this series, just as there will always be a piece of you in me.

Callie and Izzy's love for one another was inspired by my wonderful cohort of beautiful friends:

- Jillian Mackey Simms for your fun-loving nature and amazing baking skills. Izzy has nothing on your style and grace.
- Lillie Mae Stone, who suffered through every decision and revision with grace, humor, and unwarranted enthusiasm.
- Marni Bates, my eternal number one writing champion. I never would have finished without you. You give me hope and inspire me just by showing up.
- Becca Levitte, my real life shero Science Girl, for her vast medical knowledge.
- Ashley Smith, easily the bravest woman I know. Someday I hope to write a heroine half as awesome as you are.
- Leah Kubany Wheeler, my biggest fan. There were days

when I only kept going because of your love for Callie's story.

- I would be remiss if I didn't also thank Amye Scavarda. You saved my life and inspired me in more ways than you intended.
- And of course, last, but far from least, to my very own the Kate Larson. I am grateful to you for literally everything: cross-country road trips, delicious BBQ, frequent rereads, musical outings, late night phone calls, athletic challenges, island adventures. If I tried to list every time you've saved me, no book would ever be long enough.

Respect must be paid to Cara Ponzini, Chris Ling, Evelyn Vasquez, and Denise Thompson, who supported me through the early drafts of this book composed in cubicle hell. Thank you for never ratting me out for my workplace daydreams. Thanks also to Jason Simms, whose casual public revelation of this book's existence spurred me to acknowledge its existence. Andrew Kugler and Margo Dobbertin, thank you for being great Beta readers who never feared to give me strong but necessary feedback.

Special shout out to my FTF family. This book wouldn't have existed without your crazy annual week of antics. See you in September.

I also a debt of gratitude to the lovely people at Acquia. You didn't know this book thing was even happening, but the happiness you've given me helped me get to this point

To my brother, John, because there is nothing in life I ever do that doesn't include you. No matter how far apart we are, you're always a part of my day, my week, my month, my moment. If normal blood is thicker than water, than ours is stronger than concrete.

To Terric, Papaya, Penny, Aldor, Kiren, Ace, and Ellie May: This book would have finished earlier without your snuggly interruptions, but my life would have sucked a lot more.

And to my long-suffering husband, David: I think Death Cab said it best. I will follow you into the dark.

About the Author

Diana Rosengard originally hails from Houston, Texas. Like Callie, Diana studied history and gender studies at a small liberal arts college before attending law school. She currently lives in Saint Helens, Oregon with her partner and their cats and dogs, but sadly, no ghosts. SPOOKED. is her first novel.

Learn more at dianarosengard.com

Listen to her podcast with author Marni Bates at imakewords.com

---

Want to learn more about Callie, Izzy, and the rest of the world of Spooked.?

Visit spookedseries.com for playlists,

social media accounts, books trailers, and more!

Book 2 in the Spooked. series

Burned.

is due out in 2019!

CPSIA information can be obtained
at www.ICGtesting.com
Printed in the USA
FSHW010516061019
62685FS